MAIDEN IN DISTRESS

A scream split the warm, dark night.

A woman's scream, high and desperate, full of fear.

And the voice was, unmistakably, Emily's.

Nigel plunged headlong into the fifth-floor hallway and came to the door with the room number that had been assigned to Emily. He knocked for a second before reaching for the knob. The door sprang open. The room was deserted, but the door in the far corner—the door that presumably led to his own room—stood open. Scarcely pausing to draw breath, Nigel ran through it. And stopped.

The scene within was like a scene out of a fable.

Emily, young and innocent, like the fairy princess in a childhood tale, in her velvet dress, her dark hair spilling down her back, stood by the window struggling with a dark, insubstantial being, seemingly composed of shadow and black cloud.

The creature was twice as large as life and twice as dark. It roared and clawed at her with massive talons. Its mouth ripped into Emily's shoulder, and she screamed and writhed in pain, though her body looked unharmed. Her power, on the other hand, oozed a hazy halo of leaking magic clearly visible to Nigel's mage sense.

The attacker looked like a hyena, but a hyena woven of shadow or darkness. It was as though all the darkest nights of the world had coalesced and taken form. Emily's bright, shining power, which twined her physical form in light, was in a life-and-death struggle.

The beast attacking it hunched and reared and roared, and sought for the throat of Emily's magic. This thing, visible only to Nigel's mage sight, was as much a part of Emily as a heart or a brain. Without it, Emily would not survive. . . .

HEART
of
LIGHT

Sarah A. Hoyt

HEART OF LIGHT
A Bantam Book / March 2008

Published by
Bantam Dell
A Division of Random House, Inc.
New York, New York

This is a work of fiction. Names, characters, places, and incidents
either are the product of the author's imagination or are used
fictitiously. Any resemblance to actual persons, living or dead, events,
or locales is entirely coincidental.

Bantam Books and the rooster colophon are registered trademarks of
Random House, Inc.

ISBN 978-0-553-58966-5

Printed in the United States of America
Published simultaneously in Canada

www.bantamdell.com

OPM 10 9 8 7 6 5 4 3 2 1

To Alicia Lopez, Alyson Lee, Cindy Cannon,
Jennifer Prohaska, Rita Hasenauer, Sofie Skapski—
my e-daughters, aka "the Bennet girls"—
who believed in this book and supported it
when all hope seemed lost

THE WEDDING NIGHT

"What is wrong?" Emily asked.

She sat, naked, on her bridal bed, the waves of her dark hair falling like a dusky veil over her golden shoulders and small breasts. Over it, wrapped around her, she clutched a multicolored flowered shawl, a legacy from her Indian grandmother.

Nigel, her husband of ten hours, stood at the foot of the bed, trying to arrange his blue dressing gown with shaking hands and only managing to twist it, so it hung askew and displayed a portion of his pale, muscular chest.

He had turned away from her, but she could see his face reflected in the full-length mirror. It showed a complexion splotched by sudden high color, pale blond hair on end where sweaty fingers had run through it again and again and gray-blue eyes animated with an odd passion and rimmed by red as if Nigel—Nigel!—were near tears.

Emily pulled her long legs up till her knees came right up to her pointed chin, and clutched her arms around them as she took a deep breath. It wasn't possible that Nigel would cry. Proper gentlemen didn't cry, and Nigel was as cool and collected as a gentleman could be.

"Have I done something?" Emily asked. Her voice wavered and trembled, sounding too childish in this sumptuous suite, all red velvet and heavy mahogany furniture. "Failed to do something?"

Nigel's back remained turned. He didn't seem to hear her. He was tying and untying his dressing gown as if it were the most important task in the world.

Emily wished to shout, to scream, to ask him what had happened and why. But proper young ladies didn't rail at their husbands. Instead, insecurity trembled in her voice as she said, "How did I fail you?"

"Fail?" Nigel's head jerked back at the word. He looked at her, startled, then quickly away.

"Mr. Oldhall," Emily said, making her voice as formal as she dared.

The family name, which she hadn't used since they'd become engaged, made him give her a look of undisguised horror. Emily felt blood rush to her cheeks, though she knew the blush would show only the color of sunset against her golden skin. "Nigel..."

Nigel pulled a packet of tobacco from a dressing gown pocket and a pipe from the other. "Yes?"

"No one ever told me what should happen on our marriage night." She paused. "My stepmother did tell me it was all worth it for the children, but..." Her voice floundered and she shook her head. "I have seen..." A deep breath to gather courage. "I was raised in my father's country house, Nigel. We had dogs and horses and..." desperately, trying to avoid being explicit, she said, "geese. And it seems to me the interaction between men and women cannot be all that different from what happens between...animals. Even horses and cats...and..." Deep breath. "Geese."

She glanced up to see Nigel staring at her, his mouth half-open, his face an odd mix of shock and amusement. Slowly, he turned and drew a long breath that echoed noisily in the room. Turning his back on her, he fumbled. She smelled tobacco and saw him, in the mirror, pushing shreds of it into the bowl of his pipe. He struck the flint to light the wick of his lighter, then lit his pipe and inhaled deeply. The lighter clicked closed and Nigel exhaled, a breath like a tremulous sigh forming a gray, aromatic cloud in the air in front of him. He put the lighter back in his pocket.

"I...I understand your disappointment," he said at last. He pulled a heavy draft from his pipe and expelled it in increasingly neater rings. "Emily, I do understand how in your innocence, you might believe something untoward has happened, or..." He cleared his throat, and a slight flush tinged his pale cheeks. "Or failed to happen, but...Emily, now that you are a wife, you should understand that marriage...isn't always perfect." He cleared his throat again. "There are moments when the body will not...obey the mind."

He smiled suddenly, but his smile vanished just as quickly, and it was only after another puff on the pipe that he managed to shape his mouth to his normal, aloof smile. "Don't let it disturb you, my dear. We're just both tired. The day started devilishly early with the wedding breakfast and...with the parties. You've been trotting too hard, my dear, and no mistake. Let's have a good night and then we'll . . . we'll both feel better in the morning."

He reached over to pat her arm, then strode toward the closed door between their two rooms. He'd no more than set his hand on the polished brass doorknob when the whole room shook.

Emily stopped, holding her breath. It had felt as though, three floors beneath them, the magic carpet that supported the luxury carpetship, cruising above the clouds toward Cairo, had fluttered unsteadily on some air current.

"It's just the magic field we're crossing," Nigel said. "Or the weather. I'm sure the flight magicians . . ."

But the curtains danced again and a rattle echoed through the ship, composed of stemware and crystal mage-light chandeliers colliding in liquid notes, crockery clashing down in the kitchen, and the groaning of wood in framing and floors and furniture. Emily clutched at the bedcovers. She remembered this noise—it bought back memories of her first trip to England. Every little current, every jolt had terrified Emily then. The ship had been all strange and scary. And her mama had been in her room, very ill, leaving no one but a cool English nurse to tell Emily not to be a goose.

But that trip had ended well. The carpetship had not fallen. Yes, Emily's mother had died six months after arriving in England, leaving Emily stranded in the midst of her father's family. But the carpetship had landed safely. She closed her eyes and willed the ship to keep flying.

The carpetship trembled again, harder. Every window frame rattled. Every bed bucked. The support beams mounted on the carpet and holding up kitchens, ballrooms, parlors and passenger rooms twisted and groaned like a dying beast.

Emily opened her eyes and caught a moment of panic in Nigel's expression. He grabbed for the bed to steady himself. The ship rattled again and started a ponderous half-roll, throwing Nigel against a green-velvet sofa. Emily barely managed to hold on to the bed, whispering prayers to a divinity in which she very much wished to believe.

With a groan of stressed lumber, the carpetship started rolling the other way. Nigel held on to the sofa, his panic no longer hidden. His lips were moving, and she supposed he must be saying words, but no sound reached her over the creaks and groans and sharp sounds of breaking glass and pottery.

Horns sounded, magically amplified, alerting everyone on the ship to the danger. This meant they should seek the lifeboats outside, on the deck. It meant the carpetship was falling. Falling through the dark night sky to the cold ocean far below them.

Nigel's hand was on her arm and Emily opened her eyes, without realizing she had ever closed them. Nigel was very pale, holding on to the headboard of the bed with one hand and on to her with the other. His lips moved, but only a word here and there emerged above the shrilling distress of the alarms. "Madam," and "sensible," and, she would swear to it, "decent."

Emily was sensible of her need to be decent; sensible of the fact that she was naked and clutching only a flowered shawl. Her panicked mind told her she

. would die naked, her shamelessly nude body washed ashore in some foreign land.

And then she realized Nigel was dressing her. He had somehow gotten hold of her white dressing gown embroidered with green sprigs and was attempting to pull her hand up from the bed.

Clinging, frightened, one hand clawing at his shoulder, Emily forced her other hand to let go of the bedcovers and to allow Nigel to put it into a sleeve. He was murmuring at her, but she could get no more than a general feel of comfort and an attempt to calm her. She clutched at him and allowed him to slide her other arm into another sleeve. And then he was tying her belt firmly and pulling her up, still talking.

"Must," she heard him say before the words submerged in other sounds. And then "safety."

She rolled from the bed, with Nigel gripping her. Safety meant the lifeboats—mounted on smaller flying rugs tethered to the side of the ship. Each of them would take ten travelers apiece and lead them, unerringly, to the nearest patch of terra firma.

Fumbling, she and Nigel scrambled, holding each other, toward the French doors that opened from Emily's room onto the deck. They held on to furniture in passing, and Emily had a moment of gratitude that every piece was firmly bolted to the floor.

Nigel struggled to open the door, kicked it open and yelled, "Go, go, go," propelling her through the open door to the deck outside.

THE ROYAL
WERE-HUNTERS

Emily stepped out the door and onto the polished ma-
hogany of the deck. "The boats!" Nigel yelled above
the din. "No one has pulled in the lifeboats!"

Emily looked across the deck where bedlam had
been unleashed in the form of half-dressed—or hardly
dressed at all—men and women of all ages. Emily's
dressing gown was positively proper compared to
many of the people who were rushing about in their
underthings; one young, disheveled woman was
clutching a sheet to her otherwise naked body and
shrieking in fear. One of the gentlemen nearby wore
his hat, his gloves, and his underwear and seemed
perfectly composed, until one realized he was strolling
about pointing with his cane and giving orders to
no one.

On the other side of the deck, past the frightened
throng, a glass partition six feet tall and composed of
small glass panes protected passengers and crew from
otherwise deadly flight-breezes and the frigid air at
this altitude. And past that partition, on the other
side, lifeboats knocked against the frame with a noise

like the damned attempting to storm the halls of heaven.

To allow people to board the boats, those would need to be tethered close to the frame, not allowed to blow away from it on the currents. And doors in the glass partition would need to be opened by the crew.

None of this had been done.

Nigel stopped a passing man—an amazingly groomed and properly attired employee in the blue serge uniform and cap of the *Star of Empire* Carpetship Line. "Good man." Nigel yelled to be heard above the confused din of voices around them. "Good man, why haven't the lifeboats been pulled in and made accessible? My wife must be taken to land at once."

The man tried to pull away from Nigel, but Nigel held his arm and wouldn't let go. "The magicians are trying to save the carpetship, milord," the man said, also yelling above the babble, but with every appearance of eager obsequiousness. "They think they can save it, milord. That this will pass."

"Pass how?" Nigel yelled back. "When a carpetship's magic fails—" He stopped as the ship trembled, more violently than before. "What?"

The ship shuddered again, in great spasms like a dying beast. It should have caused a blind panic on deck, but instead everyone fell silent. Nigel looked as startled as Emily felt. And then Emily saw something in the unrelieved black outside the glass partition. Something shimmered there, not quite as bright as the stars. It was more like a bit of shining dust in the wind, like glimmers of flame.

Without knowing quite why, Emily pushed through the crowd, toward the glass barrier. Pressing against its

cool smoothness, she heard something—a sound like
another wind beating within the wind, like the murmur
of a heart composed of the hissing flames . . .

She looked toward the sound—perceived more
with her mage-sense and her mind than with her ears.
And there, by the side of the carpetship, something
deep blue-green seemed to glitter and churn the air
beside the ship. Slowly, it sailed closer, becoming
clearer and revealing itself as a large, reptilian-looking
creature.

Moonlight flickered on a long sinuous neck, bright,
sparkling eyes, an elongated body and a curling tail.
Moonlight struck wings that looked as unreal as an
artist's dream, as if their armature had been carved in
the finest ivory, then covered over with transparent
fabric, upon which myriad fireflies had been caught.

The carpetship trembled like a frightened beast,
but it groaned to altitude again.

*So it was a dragon's magical field that disrupted
the flying spells. A dragon!* Her breath caught at the
word.

She'd read about dragons in history books and stories, but Emily had never seen one. They were were-
creatures, whose other form looked wholly human but
who—in the period of their episodic change—craved
the hunt, the chase, and tore their prey alive with
their impatient fangs.

Watching the dragon, Emily breathed in little puffs
that fogged the window. She wiped impatiently at the
glass with cold, sweaty hands, and peered through the
stripes left by her fingers, not wanting to miss a single
second of the wondrous sight.

If she'd ever imagined dragons, she'd thought

them sinister and frightening. And yet this creature was gossamer and moonlight, living flame and whispering wind. She wished she could engrave this scene upon her memory and relive it later, whenever she needed to refresh her vision from mundane sights.

None of the histories that spoke of the evils of dragons said that the pinpoints upon their wings shone like multicolored fairy lights rivaling the stars. None had mentioned that they transmitted an impression of power and joy. Nor had they admitted that dragons flew so effortlessly and gracefully, like dancing on air.

The only good thing they were ready to admit was that the eye of a dragon was the most powerful scrying instrument on Earth, allowing people to see the future in it and discover hidden treasure.

Looking at the dragon she couldn't fully understand how that could be. Its eyes were just eyes.

From behind Emily came the sound of running feet, and two employees of the *Star of Empire* company came rushing to turn cranks on the side of the glass partition that separated the passengers from the dragon.

"Letting us at the lifeboats, then?" Nigel said in a confused tone.

"No, sir," one of the men said. "Just opening the partition so the Royal Were-Hunters can have at the beast." And turning to Emily, "Miss, you'll have to get out of the way."

Emily turned and saw a whole regiment of Royal Were-Hunters—Gold Coats—wearing gold uniforms with golden braid, about fifteen of them in a line, each pointing a powerstick at the dragon. The powersticks, Emily knew, would be full of were-killing magic.

Like other such creatures that might feast on humans as well as animals—European werewolves and the were-tigers that sailors had brought with them, unawares, from the first voyages to India—dragons were outlawed within the reach and influence of the British sovereign. The Royal Were-Hunters were a regiment specially empowered by the queen to hunt down and exterminate these terrifying beasts.

Emily knew they did good work. Without them, weres would overrun normal mankind and destroy civilization. And yet, she could not move aside and allow them to shoot at the dragon.

"Madam," Nigel corrected, yelling at the Royal Were-Hunters. "She's my wife. Mrs. Nigel Oldhall."

The Were-Hunters in turn were yelling at Emily, but their screams had nothing to do with her marital status. Instead, they were screaming at her to get out of the way so they could shoot. Nigel pulled at Emily frantically, too, fingers scrabbling at her dressing gown sleeve. She heard him as if from a great distance. She could not move. The men in the gold jackets with the powersticks were increasingly frantic, now aiming at her, now away, and begging her to move.

"Please, miss—madam." And, "We must do our duty." And, "It is a dangerous beast."

The dragon probably was a dangerous beast, and more. What she'd heard of dragons said they couldn't control themselves. They ate people. They—

Behind her there was a sound and she turned just in time to see a jet of flame singe along the edge of the carpetship. People screamed and ran, and Nigel grabbed at her arm and tugged her, then pulled her to the ground, covering her with his body in an attempt to protect her from the dragon's flame.

When she managed to look up, there was no fire at all and the dragon had gone. The Royal Were-Hunter captain was standing nearby. "You should have let us shoot it, ma'am. You never know what those creatures are about. We have all sorts, in the isles," he said, offering Nigel his hand to help him rise. "From wolves to foxes. Some of them are harmless enough, and we wink at them. But them dragons, they're desperate creatures that can neither be controlled nor brought down easily." He pulled Nigel up and Nigel pulled Emily up along with himself. "We had a perfect shot."

"She was too scared to move," Nigel said.

And Emily supposed that could be true, but deep inside she didn't think it was. Not scared. More... fascinated, intrigued. She couldn't help turning her head a little toward where the dragon had been, feeling a lurch of dismay that the sparkling, magical being was gone.

She couldn't quite understand why that would leave her feeling empty—as though a yawning abyss of dark, gray nothingness had opened where the wondrous should reside.

Nigel didn't seem to notice. Or if he did, he attributed it to her presumed fright. He said nothing until she was back in her cabin, sitting on her bed in her dressing gown, wrapped in her grandmother's shawl. And then he said, "Dragons are native only to China. It is said their noblemen suffer the hereditary curse of were-dragons and are venerated and given virgins for fodder in the days of their madness. There are many

weres in England, but surely no true Englishman can
be a were-dragon."

He didn't seem to either expect a reply from
Emily or want it. Instead he went through the con-
necting door and into his room.

Emily sat on the bed, hugging her knees. In her
mind's eye was the image of the powerful, elemental
beast. Where had it come from? Where was it going?
And why had she saved its life?

CAIRO FROM ABOVE

Nigel's heart tightened as he looked out from the deck of the carpetship descending toward Cairo. The mission proper was starting. Today he would meet his contact and learn where he was to go and how to complete the mission the queen had given him.

"It's very bright, isn't it?" Emily asked, leaning against him, her open parasol more decorative than practical.

Nigel nodded, looking at the landscape beneath them. It was indeed bright and completely different from the sheep-dotted green fields, the stately country houses, the landscape of Nigel's proper English childhood. It didn't even resemble bustling London, where he had spent the last year. From this far up, all of Egypt looked like a narrow strip of land, squeezed between golden sparkling desert and shining emerald sea, along the green ribbon of the Nile. Where the river met the sea, a green shape formed, resembling a lady's fan. There, the arm of the Nile branched into multiple fingers and along those fingers vegetation grew and white houses nestled, looking—from this far up—like a toy village.

In the desert, away from the city, the fabled pyramids of ancient Egypt rose, golden and eternal, dwarf-ing the impermanent mortals with their majesty.

Nigel wished with all his heart that he was just coming to Egypt on his honeymoon, to see the beau-ties of antiquity and savor the exoticism. That was what Emily believed and it made him wish—madly—that he hadn't lied to her. That he'd never heard of Widefield or the queen's secret mission to Africa.

That mission had caused his older brother, Carew, to vanish. Carew had been the competent older son, forever confident and full of certainty. Nigel, on the other hand, was only the Oldhall's sickly younger boy, kept at home and allowed to attend school only be-cause Carew had attended it also. And only allowed to go to Cambridge on Carew's say so as well.

Nigel was not half the man that Carew had been. The only reason he'd been chosen at all was his blood. Carew's brother, they'd said, must complete his mis-sion—might be the only man who could do it. They never explained why that was, though it seemed to have to do with Nigel's being descended via both his parents from the first man who'd used the compass stone.

Now Nigel could see the squarish houses, without proper roofs but with terraces. And here and there, the protruding, rounded tops of what he presumed were cisterns. It looked like an illustration in a book of Bible stories he'd owned when he was very little. He remembered looking at that picture for hours, fasci-nated by the dark, starry sky above, the alien-looking houses.

He'd wondered what it would be like to be one of the shepherd boys in the picture, away from English society and rules. Now that alien landscape beneath him looked and felt as fantastic as it had when he was little. An exotic land, an imaginary haven—a way to escape his own limited life.

"Did you know it would be this beautiful?" Emily asked. "Is that why you chose it?"

Her warm breath caressed his cheek, more tantalizing and erotic than those experienced and trained ladies of the night to whose boudoirs Carew had introduced Nigel at Cambridge. And yet, he couldn't *have* Emily as he had enjoyed those beauties. And he wondered why. Except . . . except that she depended wholly on him, and she was so innocent. She'd been badly treated and neglected in her life, a waif without a mother and devilishly ignored by her father and his new wife. If he did what he longed to do, it would feel like a betrayal.

And then there was the undeniable fact that he had betrayed her. He had brought her here under false pretenses. How would she react to finding out he'd lied?

He shook his head. "All I knew of Cairo was my teacher of Arabic," he said. "A frightful little man who smelled too much of garlic and always dressed in white suits with a red carnation in his pocket."

He thought he heard Emily giggle amid the noise of the people around them. The deck was crowded with the portion of England that traveled with them—the better-bred portion—pressing about them all around, wearing the best dresses, the best suits, the most exquisite and fashionable attire. And yet he felt as if he were alone with Emily. Alone with the woman he loved, with the woman to whom he was obliged to lie.

Beneath him, the carpetship jolted.

They were close enough now to hear the shouts of workmen and carpetdock workers, a mingling of Arabic and English, both clearly intelligible to Nigel, but in a mixture he'd never before heard nor imagined. Even those who spoke English spoke it with a lilting exotic accent that was fennel and garlic to the ear, evoking hot spices not part of the English cuisine.

When Nigel looked back, Emily was looking at her feet, a faint smile playing on her lips.

He leaned against the glass windbreaker thinking how bright the houses were, how pale the morning-fired sky, how deep blue the ocean beneath them. He'd craved such liveliness through his days in his sickroom, listening to Carew and his friends playing outside.

The ship was descending slowly toward the bright metropolis of Cairo, with its glimmering buildings, its brightly lit feluccas with multicolored sails.

In the carpetport beneath, carpetships clustered. Some were built upon brilliant carpets that showed around the edge of the buildings upon them, and whose fringe—a mix of brilliant gold and red and sky-blue—blew softly in the wind. Other carpetships were smaller, and showed wear and age in tatters and holes around the edges. All of them were woven by descendants of a single Persian family, whose ability was hereditary.

The flags of Spain and France were the most prominent, but at a glance Nigel saw a couple of Union Jacks, a Portuguese flag, two German ones, and others where his geographical knowledge faltered.

At the edges of the carpet, strong navvies threw

down thick ropes, which were caught by natives stripped to their waists and tanned deep brown by the sun. The men's corded muscles strained, and they chanted in Arabic as they pulled the ship down for the final tethering to the strong dock pillars.

A scent rose from the city, along with the increasingly loud babble of voices—a scent of spices and hot cooking oil and heated sand. Many buildings surrounded the carpetport as though the city pressed against it like a child peering through the window of a sweetshop. Up close, the walls looked not white but golden, as if they'd acquired the color and texture of the surrounding desert. Amid the buildings, bright clusters of multicolored tents shone.

Bazaars, Nigel assumed. He had heard much of souks and dim, ancient markets filled with mysterious goods. His teacher of Arabic had spoken of them. Huddled in the cold of a Cambridge garret, he made his living bestowing his knowledge of Arabic language and culture on people such as Nigel. Never quite saving enough money to buy his passage back to the warm sands of his native land, the little man had spoken of bazaars filled with the exotic goods of the East, with the wild spoils of Africa. And of dazzling women who hid their features beneath veils and let only their eyes peer out to tantalize male kind. Women of gold and spice.

Women, Nigel imagined, like his Emily. Emily's hand snaked around Nigel's wrist, and Nigel jumped, drawn back from his daydream. "Does it look like India?" Nigel asked.

She gave him a startled look, her eyes opening wide, like sapphires on a dusky cushion. Then she blushed and turned away. "I don't know," she said. "I was so small. Six. I don't remember."

Nigel nodded, but in his mind this land and India were the same, all part of the empire his mission would save. Yet if Carew could not have accomplished the mission and returned triumphant to the queen of England, the empress of India, how could Nigel do it? What could Nigel add with his poor efforts to Carew's failed, heroic attempt?

Yet something in Nigel seemed to trust itself. Heretically, against all revealed knowledge, something in Nigel believed that he could rescue Carew and return to England in triumph. And then maybe his parents...

But he flinched at the thought.

He'd take this mission step by step, as he'd taken his exercises at school. Nigel had been given precise instructions on how to search for the magic jewel, how to bring it back for the queen. He had to remember he was not in this alone.

First, he would meet the secret emissary of the queen's government in Cairo. This man would give Nigel more exact instructions, including how to activate the compass stone that would show the way to the temple in which the jewel lay hidden.

Nigel leaned forward and scanned the crowd assembled on the disembarking quay.

Lord Widefield, the queen's friend and the overseer of her most secret enterprises, had told Nigel that there would be a tall Englishman waiting there—a Cairo expatriate. He would wear a white linen suit and a panama hat, a bright yellow flower on his lapel. And he would tell Nigel all the specifics of the mission, the particulars that Lord Widefield had been afraid to reveal in London, where he had been sure someone had watched and listened to them. He would tell Nigel where to go, how to proceed with finding the ruby of power that Lord Widefield had called Heart of Light. The ruby that would give the queen firm magical control over Europe and end, once and for all, the blood-soaked republican uprisings.

Maybe the man could even tell Nigel how Carew had failed his mission and where he might be. Or where his remains might be.

But Nigel flinched away from *that* thought. He couldn't bear the idea of taking news of Carew's death to his mother.

Yet no matter how hard he tried to see his contact, no Englishman stood amid the dark faces on the quay and no straw hat was visible amid the turbans and head cloths.

The ship touched down with a jar and passengers called shrilly to their servants, ordered them to retrieve their luggage, then screamed out good-byes to travel-met friends. Nigel had not brought servants, telling Emily that it was their honeymoon and that surely the hotel would have personnel who could assist them with the dressing, the undressing and such necessities. But truth was that Nigel had neither wanted to endanger an old family servitor, nor risk treason if he had been somehow coerced or seduced onto the enemy side. Perhaps that had been the mistake Carew had made. So they needed to trust the ship's personnel to unload the luggage. Or rather Emily was supposed to have seen to it. He turned to Emily, a questioning look in his eyes.

"The trunks?" he said.

Emily, whose father had been so strict that Emily might well think she was supposed to guess Nigel's wishes, nodded.

"The trunks," she muttered. "I'll see to it."

With those words and without even a look of re-crimination or rebellion, she turned and headed downstairs, doubtless to roust the personnel of the carpetship and get them to carry their trunks out. Nigel waited only long enough to see her white hat and her graceful swaying figure disappear amid the crowd filling the deck. Then he thundered down the spiral metal staircase to the bottom deck—struggling against tumultuous traffic of white-aproned maids and dark-attired men servants, against trunk-carrying footmen and shrilling nannies.

They gave him an odd look. The spiral staircase was the sole domain of servants and ship's personnel. But Nigel didn't allow them time to question him— had they dared—as he ran out of the carpetship and down the lower gangway, squeezing past boisterous groups of debarking Englishmen.

Nigel would find his contact and come back up the plank before Emily ever knew he was missing.

All of Nigel's traveling—beyond his few months in London—had taken place in his mind. Thus he had formed a clear picture of himself emerging onto the crowded quay and going about unmolested, as he would have in the best London neighborhoods. He'd thought of himself slipping between groups of people, looking for a man wearing a Panama hat and a white linen suit with a yellow flower on the lapel. He knew he would not be touched by the lower orders in

England. And the upper class would certainly not do anything so rude as to grab at him or attempt to detain him.

But there was more strangeness to Cairo than the white houses with no proper roofs. As soon as Nigel stepped down from the gangway, people surrounded him. Men whose skin ranged from caramel to deeply burnished chestnut babbled at him in Arabic, broken English and doubtful French. So many voices resounded so close together that he could hardly tell what they were saying or what merchandise they were trying to hawk.

Sentences surfaced occasionally from the chatter, shameless pitches for diverse merchandise:

"Elephant hair bracelets, effendi."

"Powerful, ancient statue the likes—"

"Ground mummy. Will make your virile parts—"

"Unicorn horn."

"Perfumes from India—"

"Opium to spice—"

Nigel stopped, surrounded by natives intent on selling him the merchandise of the whole world and took in a deep breath, fearing that someone—an enemy, a secret conspirator—had known of his arrival and had sent this mob to intercept him. But looking at the anxious eyes around him, he realized that these people only wanted money. To them, Nigel was just an Englishman who'd come to Cairo disposed to buy. How many times had Nigel heard stories in his mother's drawing room of people who'd gone to Africa, or India, or even China. *I got this so cheap, my dear, you wouldn't believe it.*

Nigel, though a disbeliever by nature, could believe it once he'd seen the purported treasure: stat-

uettes claimed to be from some ancient tomb but looking no older than a day. Or perhaps silver, so adulter-
ated with nickel that it would break at the slightest
pressure. He pushed through the crowd of vendors.
Some of them tried to grab at his sleeves, others
waved goods before his eyes.

"A fly swat made from an elephant's tail. Very effi-
cacious, effendi."

"A stuffed crocodile." This while something scarcely
larger than a lizard, its tiny jaws pathetically open in
mock ferociousness, was waved in front of his eyes.
"You could tell your lady you shot it yourself."

"The god Toth of the baboon head. From ancient
pharaoh tomb. Robbed at great risk. Sell cheap."
Nigel waved away the crude fakeries and looked
through the crowd for his contact—for a friendly face,
a pale complexion, pale hair, blue eyes, anything that
bespoke England in this sweltering climate. He saw
no one he could call a fellow Englishman.

The same peddlers or their near cousins had followed him, surrounding him again. "Effendi," they
said. "Buy my universal ointment." A greasy clay jar
waved back and forth across his field of vision.

The air itself felt alien, filled with the fragrance of
spices for which Nigel lacked a name.

"Buy this formula for the philosopher's stone." A
greasy paper appeared beside the jar.

The crowd added its own smell to the mixture—
hot human bodies, unwashed hair, and heated cotton
garments that billowed around dark, wiry bodies.

"Buy this true map to lost Pharaohs' treasure."

White and gold and startlingly blue bead necklaces
wiggled in front of Nigel's face. Ivory implements,

brass vases and violently colored, beautiful fabrics danced before his eyes.

"I see you are a discerning man. You'll buy this." An obscene wooden statuette, showing a man with an impossibly large, improbably erect penis.

The breeze that blew from the west brought no relief at all to the stultifying heat. Instead, it felt like the breath from a just-opened baker's oven, hot and dry and stifling.

Nigel looked but couldn't find his contact. A throng of vendors surrounded him at all times, fresh ones rushing in to replace those who'd left to pester new arrivals. In the middle of the crowd, like a man surrounded by a swarm of flies, Nigel pushed and shoved and stood on his tiptoes. He was going to fail in this mission in an abominable way, before he even started. Foiled in Cairo, for lack of a contact and the information he was likely to give him.

Was this a test? Had they withheld the information because they thought Nigel incapable of keeping his mouth shut while still in England? Had they been afraid that he would tell all to his mother or the mistress he didn't have? Were they afraid he would reveal all to Emily's attentive sapphire-blue eyes?

If not that, then what had happened? Had his contact been betrayed?

A fine sheen of sweat covered Nigel's skin and glued his shirt to his back. He thought of Emily on the ship. He should go back to her, get her out of here. Something had gone terribly wrong.

A newspaper seller stood at the edge of the crowd, hawking his Arab-language newspapers, printed in brownish sepia tones upon nasty-looking yellow paper. He stood away from the other sellers, displaying his wares to the locals, with melodious cries of, "Buy the news."

But Nigel read the elegant, twirling characters as easily as he would have read English, and breath arrested on seeing the headline on the first page: "Lord Widefield Dead. British Aristocrat Killed by Anarchists."

A DEATH IN ENGLAND

Pushing aside the men who hemmed him in, Nigel called out, "A paper, here," while tossing a coin toward the vendor.

The newspaper seller, startled and wide-eyed like a man observing a miracle, named a price and forgot to bargain. If what startled him was Nigel's eager hand clutching hungrily for the newspaper or the melodic tones of his native language flowing from a pale English face, the man probably wouldn't be able to tell himself.

Nigel opened the brittle, crackling paper, smearing the low-quality ink with his fingers, then elbowed a clear space in which to stand and read.

Hopeful sellers continued waving merchandise in front of his face.

"Good medicine for every ailment."

"Bracelets for your lady."

"The softest silk."

But as Nigel read it seemed to him as though all the voices around him receded. In his mind, he stood again in Lord Widefield's study. Ruddy and white-haired, the old man smoked his pipe while telling Nigel that the salvation of Europe, the beating back of chaos and the sort of barbaric excesses that had happened since the last century all were in Nigel's hands. Beloved Queen Victoria herself depended on Nigel to keep her throne against anarchists and other ruffians.

Cecil Widefield wore his trademark tattered brown silk dressing gown and, enveloped in wreaths of pipe smoke, looked like a genie swathed in magic while he spoke eloquently of the needs of England and Nigel's usefulness in serving them.

Yet the article before him said that Cecil Widefield—friend and confidant of the queen, beloved personal friend of the late Prince Albert—had been removed from his country estate by mysterious means that failed to disturb his many servants. His captors had carried him off to a distant field, where he was murdered cruelly after prolonged torture.

His murderers must have been anarchists—those extremists who believed all those whose birth had gifted them with high magical power should be murdered, and their power released to settle on the common run of the populace. This redistribution—which any sensible man could tell would leave no man or woman with enough magical power to bid a fireplace light itself—the anarchists held necessary to keep man from preying on man and to keep the powerful from subjugating the helpless. To create the equalitarian society their doctrine advocated.

Still, even for anarchists, the death of Lord Widefield seemed too cruel. It was as though someone had sliced him—a thin sliver at a time—with a very sharp instrument. Or rather with many sharp, small knives. It was as if the giant mouth of an animal with human patience had cut him to ribbons, in such a way that he must have remained alive through most of it.

But what could that mean? And why?

Nigel's head spun. Someone had tried to get Widefield to talk. But what did Widefield know that had any value at all? Only the information about the jewel that the queen must have to stop the mad revolutions around the globe.

What irony for Widefield to die at anarchist hands, when the jewel Nigel was to steal from the heathen temple in the heart of Africa could stop this madness.

Had Widefield spoken? If he had, surely the anarchists would know where Nigel was. He smelled his own fear, a sharp tang in his sweat. His first impulse was to turn back and run to the ship and bundle Emily out of Cairo and back to Europe as soon as possible. Whatever else happened, Emily must be sent home.

But what if Widefield had not spoken? What if Nigel's mission was not compromised?

He remembered Widefield telling him that if the contact didn't meet Nigel, there was a safe house on the outskirts of Cairo. He'd given Nigel directions.

"Nigel?" Emily's voice.

He turned around, forced a smile. Vendors pressed around him on all sides, but he was alone with Emily, alone with his fear. "Quite so," he told Emily's blank face. "You should go to the hotel right away. Have the carpetship personnel call you a carriage, and go to the hotel with our luggage. I'll . . . I'll join you shortly."

Emily looked bewildered. "Alone? You wish me to go to the hotel alone?" She held her parasol so tightly in her hand that her knuckles showed, bone-white through her golden skin. Tears trembled in her eyes, and her small mouth, with the prominent lower lip that gave her the look of a permanent pout, trembled.

"Er . . ." Nigel said. He looked away from her. He could not bear to cause her pain. "I must go . . . out. I have to arrange a surprise for you."

He tore himself away from her gentle touch—from her hand on his shoulder, detaining him—and hurried into the crowd, pursued by peddlers who pushed their wares in his face. He did not dare turn back and see Emily's face, her gaze no doubt tearful and disappointed.

He'd make his peace with Emily. Later.

A PROUD DAUGHTER
OF THE MASAI

Nassira, daughter of Nedera of the Masai, hurried down the narrow metal stairs of the carpetship.

A tall, young woman with skin the reddish-brown of well-polished mahogany, she had features that evoked the statues of ancient Egypt and a proud bearing, in marked contrast to the way she stumbled down the stairs, undignifiedly

The British clothes she wore—a maid's uniform and heavy black shoes that laced up the ankle—made walking difficult, yet she hadn't had time to change, because Nigel Oldhall hadn't waited for his trunks. He'd left his wife behind and hurried out of the carpetship. And Nassira had to follow him.

Running down the stairs against the flow of other servants, Nassira fought maids and trunk-carrying valets. She could read disdain in the too-pale eyes of the doughy-faced women and shabby-suited men who pushed past her, shoving at her with their elbows and shoulders. Nassira swallowed back affronted pride that people such as these, Water People, would think themselves superior to her.

She was a woman of the Masai, the most important

tribe of all, the most favored by God. God, whom the
Masai called Engai, had given the Masai all the cattle
in the world, while the other tribes had received only
the animals of the forest. Over the centuries, some of
the cattle had strayed, some even ending up in the
hands of whites. But the Masai were ever too willing to
recover their stolen property. Their cattle raids had
made them feared, the acknowledged lords of the
region. Even lions feared Masai spears. And now
Nassira had to endure disdain from the white people.
Water People. Long ago one of the Masai holy men had
foretold that white people would come out of the river,
and their innards would be full of lard. Yet Nassira had
long practice in disguising her feelings. She'd lived in
London for six months, and there learned that no one
knew of the Masai, or the offenses of the white people
against the Masai. Instead, they assumed that white
men were the undisputed lords of creation and that
they had brought civilization and peace to the other
continents. And they expected Nassira to be humble,
to give them way. Nassira had done it for six months,
but she had no time to do it now.

She couldn't lose sight of Nigel Oldhall, who was
on the quay and walking fast toward the street, pursued by a group of men hawking goods.

Shoulder forward, Nassira pushed past the multitude of people and leapt over a trunk carried by two
men. Nigel Oldhall would lead her to the jewel and the
instructions for the ritual that would make Africans as
strong as Europeans, capable of casting off the yoke of
European oppression.

Years ago, at the Maniata—the ritual warrior camp
of the Masai in which adolescents learned to hunt lions

and raid cattle—Nassira had learned why Africa was so sorely enslaved by the arrogant Water People. A spell had been wrought by a long-ago European, who had gathered to him the power of all people on the European continent. While that spell had deprived the common Europeans of power, it had given great power to a few Europeans. Power that could not be matched, even by the greatest shamans of Africa.

Burning to avenge the ills done to her people and her land, Nassira had joined an organization called the Hyena Men, which promised to harness the power of Africa as Europe's power had once been harnessed, to put it in righteous hands that would defend justice. But to do it, they needed a jewel of great magical power, the twin of the one the long-ago European king had used.

To find that jewel, called Heart of Light, Nassira had gone to London. Yet once there, she had discovered that an Englishman was being sent to Africa in search of that same jewel. When she'd tried to make mind-contact with members of the Hyena Men in London, all her transmissions had been blocked. When she'd tried to physically find the other agents in London, she found they'd left their addresses and employment with no forwarding notice. It was as though the streets of London had swallowed them.

In the eyes of the white people she questioned, Nassira had read disdain. But Nassira knew better. So she'd resigned her job as a cleaner in Nigel Oldhall's gentleman's club and found employment as a maid aboard the carpetship.

She elbowed and pushed people aside, yet she fell steadily behind the tall blond man. He had a longer stride, and he presumably knew where he was going. As he disappeared into the crowd, she struggled against people who would not let her pass, not give her the right of way because her skin was darker than theirs. Water People, not fully human.

She wished she could go back home, to her mother's comfortable house—its smoky interior and the kraal with the hundred cows, each of which she knew by name. Once she'd made a poem for them and sung it in the kraal.

Impatient, thinking of her home and frustrated by the people around her, Nassira finally managed to push out of the carpetship and found herself in the crowded quay. The Arabs starting toward her backed away as they realized she was not an Englishwoman.

They smelled funny, just as the Englishmen did. Englishmen smelled of soap and artificial fragrances; these other people smelled of soap and spices. None of it was right. There were too many people, all around, just like in London, all crowded together. Nassira longed for pasture and savanna, for the cloud-wreathed peaks of her rift-valley home. But she kept her gaze on the blond head quickly getting lost amid the vendors in the quay.

"Miss. Ma'am—" A hand reached out and grabbed Nassira's arm.

The confusion of names addressed to her made her stop. In front of her stood the wife of Nigel Oldhall.

Not that the woman looked English. Unlike the pasty-skinned women that Nassira had grown accustomed to seeing in London, this woman had skin of a rich golden brown, like the color of the sun shining on summer-dry grass. But she was English and married to Nigel Oldhall, whom Nassira had followed all the way to Africa.

"I need..." the Englishwoman said, and hesitated. She wore a white lacy dress and looked as at ease in it as Nassira felt in her stiff, dark maid's outfit. She clutched a parasol convulsively in her dainty hand. Her gaze turned toward where the blond man had disappeared. She swallowed, then continued with renewed force. "I must have a carriage for myself and my luggage. To take me to the Luxor Hotel."

Her voice was reedy and seemed to tremble on the verge of tears. Her man was nowhere around. Had he told her to go to the hotel alone? Nassira raised her eyebrows. Even she knew that Englishmen didn't treat their women with such carelessness. What could be wrong? And where had he gone?

The Englishwoman stepped in front of Nassira. "You must call me a cab." Tears filling her blue eyes, the woman said again, "You must."

Eyes downcast, Nassira ducked her head and murmured something in purposely broken English, something about not knowing what to do. But the Englishwoman grabbed her arm again. Her hand felt too cold. "Please," she said. "Please, you must help me."

Nassira nodded. Something in the woman's need—in her fear—demanded Nassira's help. Nassira, too, had been a stranger in a land she could not understand. She had wandered the streets of London, lost. And Nassira was not a frail Englishwoman but a Masai who, as the single daughter—the single child—of a powerful man with three wives had been trained to herd the cows. Her father had even, despite disapproval from the tribal elders, allowed her to use his cattle stick. Nassira had faced the savanna and found herself quite strong enough to defend her cattle against the wild beasts.

But Englishwomen were frail creatures who could die of a breath, and who, in Nassira's experience, were quite capable of losing consciousness at any moment because of a shock. And Nassira, strong woman of the Masai, had once had a brother. When she was ten, her mother had given birth to a baby boy. Though small and frail, he had nonetheless been welcomed by everyone. But one night, during a long dry spell, he'd died in his sleep, next to Nassira. Though Nassira knew it was not her fault, to this day she still thought she should have been able to save him. And for the sake of his memory, she could not abandon anyone truly helpless, not even a Water Person.

"I need my luggage put in a carriage, and I need a seat for myself in the carriage. My husband and I . . ." The woman's hand trembled. "My husband and I have reservations at the Luxor." A small hesitation and tears trembled on thick, dark lashes. "My husband was called away on some business."

A look at the distant glimmering of blond hair, and Nassira thought that the Englishman would come back for his wife. Surely, he would not abandon her. Even among the Water People, such things were not done. The woman's family and people would punish him if he did.

Nassira could find the Hyena Men and tell them to find the Oldhalls at the Luxor. So she smiled at the Englishwoman and said, "I'll call the carriage."

Striding past the press of debarking passengers, Nassira reached the road that circled the carpetport and that was filled with a great press of carts, carriages, and other vehicles, all so close together that it was a wonder anyone ever moved at all.

Holding her shoulders square and herself as upright and proud as she could, she approached one of those carriages. Looking up at the man who sat in the driver's seat—a most disreputable personage, wearing a dirty caftan and head cloth, but then all of the drivers looked disreputable, even in London—she commanded, "Take the English lady over there to the Luxor Hotel with all her bags. Fast."

The man looked bewildered for a moment, perhaps marveling at the impeccable English issuing from the dark woman.

"Now," Nassira said. "The English lady to the Luxor Hotel. And get her bags."

He jumped from the driver's seat and hurried toward Mrs. Oldhall. He picked up her bags and salaamed, saying he would take good care of her. Nassira smiled at the Englishwoman, who smiled back tearfully.

"Thank you," Mrs. Oldhall said. "Thank you so much."

Nassira nodded, embarrassed, and turning her back on the Englishwoman, she walked toward the carpetship. She must try to find the Hyena Men. She knew they were in Cairo.

Her cabin in the servant's quarters was very small and narrow and the walls seemed to her too smooth and straight. Sometimes she would wake in the middle of the night and not be able to believe where she was, in this place of straight walls and floors one on top of the other, in this strange ship that flew atop a magical carpet, on the currents of air.

The Masai had no carpetships, nor did their magic allow them to make anything fly. But over time, she'd become comfortable here, with the small bed covered in its dark blanket and her trunk where she kept all her belongings.

Slowly, she got out of her uniform, folded it, set it in the trunk. From the trunk, she removed a loose caftan she had fashioned in London for this purpose, which would allow her to blend in better in Cairo. In her heart, she longed for the wrap of her people, but it was not to be, at least not yet.

She must find the Hyena Men. Then, having done her part, she would be allowed to go home. She would tell them where Mrs. Oldhall stayed, and that if they kept a close watch on her, her husband was bound to come back. And then someone else could follow the Englishman to the jewel.

It wasn't that Nassira believed less in Africa's cause than she did when she'd first decided to leave tribe and family to struggle for her land's freedom. But she thought she had done her part, and perhaps now others should carry it forth.

How to find the Hyena Men, though? She couldn't look by any normal means, as she didn't know where they hid. And if she just wandered about aimlessly, it wouldn't do much good. Asking strangers would not help, either. She knew three tribal languages and English, but most people in Cairo spoke either French or some Arabic dialect. So she must contact them with magic. Magic was dangerous, of course. Others could track your transmission, hold it and through it overtake your magical power ... into their control. But it was the only resource left to her.

Both her parents were high holders of magic power. From them, she had inherited a level of magical power comparable to that of the best shamans. Her father's oldest wife, whom Nassira called Lamb— after the gift the woman had given Nassira at birth— was a shaman's daughter and she had taught Nassira to use that magic, revealing to Nassira much ancient lore of powerful Masai in the process. It was that magic that had allowed Nassira to discover Nigel Oldhall's mission. When Nigel stayed in his club in London, ostensibly to be near his fiancée, he always received correspondence, and always burned it in his ashtray.

Curious about this, Nassira had taken the ashes and performed a spell on them. The letters that had been on the burnt paper had then formed in midair like ghosts and allowed her to find out Nigel Oldhall's travel plans.

But calling upon the Hyena Men was not as simple as reconstituting words upon paper. Not only did Nassira have to ensure that she was safe, she had to attempt to contact people she did not know, who resided she knew not where, except that they were somewhere in Cairo.

A summoning spell would serve better than a communication spell, as it would find its recipient on its own. From her trunk, she withdrew a branch of a tree from her native land, the desiccated tail of a lion her father had killed when he was a young warrior, and a dozen stones picked from the ground around her mother's house. Touching these, Nassira felt the magic of her land flow through her, awakening her power. She set the pebbles and stones in a circle around herself on the floor of the cabin. Holding the branch in one hand, the lion tail in the other, she felt as though she sat in the center of her homeland's power. Calling to her magic, as if to a wellspring within herself, she visualized the hyena that was the symbol of the Hyena Men organization.

The hyena had been chosen because it worked against the more visible lion, and often won its victories in silence.

Thinking of the hyena and the jewel of power that belonged to Africa, Nassira felt a tug that pulled her outside her own body, to float free above it. From above she saw herself, like a beautiful ebony sculpture wearing a red caftan.

She floated farther, through the roof of her cabin and up till she could see the entire city settled into a midafternoon glow. The sun had declined from its noonday brightness and shone mellow and golden over the white buildings.

The city was too big and too crowded. She felt the pressure of too many humans, too close. Yet she seemed to fly over it, and felt a tug pull her in a southerly direction.

Nassira tried to focus on the point from which the pull came, and felt it grab at her mind like fresh pasture calling to starved cattle. She saw the picture of a townhouse emerge. It had narrow windows and a turquoise painted door. But before she could touch the place, she heard a sound. Not a real sound as ears would pick up, but a sense of giant flapping wings, moving closer.

The thought-entity that was Nassira—just a small point of consciousness floating above Cairo—ducked and turned and, with magic vision, saw a gigantic dragon—or the spirit essence of a dragon—mouth wide open, teeth glistening, bearing down on her.

She screamed and plunged, down toward the carpetport, sending an obfuscation spell toward the thing. The sound of wings stopped.

Nassira's spirit stopped also, just short of the top deck of the carpetship, where the last, straggling passengers said protracted good-byes to each other and the ship.

She remembered the dragon that had flown beside the ship and almost made them crash at the beginning of their voyage. But that dragon, having been brazen enough to appear in public and disrupt the commerce of the white men, had doubtlessly been killed by the British army or the carpetship company. Was she now seeing this spirit presence as a dragon only because her subconscious retained her fear of that beast that had almost made them fall from the sky?

Yet what beast had attacked her? Perhaps it was a misguided vendetta and nothing to do with her. Or perhaps a strange magic in this strange city. She floated up again, tentatively, away from the pale passengers and the polished mahogany decks of the carpetship.

She must locate the Hyena Men. She held the image of the hyena in her mind again, and she felt a pull and a call.

What are you doing? A loud voice with a strange accent yelled in Nassira's mind-sense. *Why are you calling attention to us?*

With her mind-sense, Nassira saw a young man's face, the owner of the mind-voice. Darker than her, he had more elongated features, ending in a strong, square jaw. Something about his accent—in English—or his bearing told Nassira the man was a Zulu. Three years ago, when she'd joined the Hyena Men, she hadn't even known what a Zulu was. But the Hyena Men came from all over Africa and comprised all nationalities.

She had found the Zulus disturbing. Large and fierce, they were altogether too inclined to have a good opinion of themselves and their collective accomplishments. Perhaps this put annoyance in her mind-voice now, a note of irritation as she said, *Who are you to question me?*

I am Kitwana, he said, and looked as though he'd declared himself lord and master of the universe. *And I work with the ones you seek.*

The Hyena Men? Nassira asked, and projected an image of a hyena, spotted and ferocious, looming over Cairo.

A flap of wings echoed in her mind-sense and the young man did something that looked like he cast a veil over the hyena.

Do not proclaim that name. There is something . . . an enemy we can't find, killing us in great numbers.

I need to speak to you. How can I do that, if not in mind-voice?

You know who we are and you know where. Come find us.

I do not know where you are. Not exactly, Nassira said, and with her mind felt for the location she'd sensed before, trying to identify it more exactly.

No, Kitwana shouted. *Do not do it again. Use your memory.*

My memory is poor. Why can't I see it again?

The enemy. It will follow you.

What is he, this enemy? Colonial authorities?

Kitwana's mind-image shook his head. *I will talk to you when I see you,* he said. *After you identify yourself.*

And with that he vanished, leaving Nassira wide awake and sitting on the floor of her cabin, within a circle of rocks from her distant homeland, and holding in one hand a branch and in the other the dried-up lion's tail.

She felt drained. And annoyed at the overbearing Zulu.

It was quiet in the carpetship. The servants must be debarking now, leaving the ship empty to be prepared for another trip. The regular personnel would have lodgings in Cairo for a few nights, probably in a building owned by the carpetship company. People like Nassira, who'd signed on for only one trip, must also leave their lodgings, but she had nowhere to go in Cairo. Nowhere, except to the Hyena Men.

DEATH BY FIRE

Nigel set out across Cairo with almost no directions at all and nothing but a determination to find the safe house Widefield had told him about. He was supposed to go there if his contact failed.

He kept telling himself all would be well. Perhaps an un-British lack of punctuality had crept into the habits of these Cairo expatriates and they thought that they need not meet the ship exactly when it arrived, that a few hours later would do as well.

Nigel found himself in a neighborhood of broad streets paved with brick and faced on either side by grand mansions that looked as if they belonged in the better suburbs of Paris or London. The sidewalk was a mosaic of black and white pebbles, forming the sort of ingenious abstract designs with which the Muslims—forbidden by their religion from representing any creature in creation—artfully decorated their living space.

Nigel vaguely remembered that his Arabic teacher had told him about a governor of Cairo, a khedive, who for some great event had wished that Cairo looked like the great European cities. He had invited the dignitaries of the world to come to a great exhibition and he had paved the streets they were likely to walk and gave people great incentives to build mansions in the European fashion.

Nigel remembered Widefield's voice giving him directions, in the unlikely case they were needed, Widefield had said. *And if your contact doesn't show, young man, you are to go down the broad street facing the carpetship until you come to your first shrine to a Muslim saint. You will know it because it has a minaret and a wild profusion of people will cluster around it, praying and touching the thing. The Arabs build these things everywhere and believe that great virtue devolves on those who visit them. As bad as papists, what? They believe . . . but never mind. They are but heathens. Find that shrine, and then turn left down a narrower street and proceed down that street till you come to what looks like a church with one of those onion tops, like the ones the orthodox people build. There you will turn right . . .*

Widefield's voice echoed in Nigel's mind as he walked past the broad white mansion in whose gardens palm trees crowded shoulder to shoulder with rosebushes. Past that he found himself very far afield, indeed. He was in an older neighborhood, far from the European-looking mansions and from any vestiges of Western civilization.

The streets could more properly be called alleys. This neighborhood branched into a maze of narrow streets that turned and twisted with no seeming direction. Facing the street, the facades of houses were white-golden, seemingly corroded by sun and sand and ages uncountable. The only windows were narrow slits far up the featureless walls. The ground underfoot squelched like mud and smelled like a midden. Nigel looked and felt as out of place in these streets as his dark, small tutor doubtless felt in Cambridge.

The women who walked past wore long flowing dresses and covered their faces with veils from behind which they looked with intent, dark certainty at the passerby. And the men, huddled in groups at the street corners, all wore ankle-length tunics and head-dresses tied with cord. None of them stood much taller than Nigel's shoulder, making Nigel feel like a giant amid dwarves.

Nigel wondered briefly if he'd look less conspicuous had he worn native attire himself, but of course not. His face and his hands would still show. Pale and pinkish, they would betray his origins as easily as his suit did now.

Following Lord Widefield's instructions, Nigel turned down an alley scarcely wide enough to allow him to walk without touching either of the buildings on each side. The buildings went up five stories, to obscure the pearly-blue sky above. Here, in the alley, a permanent twilight reigned, and the smell of urine and old grease overlaid the spicy undertones that permeated all of Cairo.

A goat ran toward Nigel, bleating madly, pursued at a distance by a half-naked youth. Nigel squeezed himself against the wall as goat and boy went by him without so much as a sideways glance.

He passed a mausoleum—an opulent Muslim funerary monument dating from the Middle Ages—and squeezed between two unremarkable buildings facing a dreary, muddy alley. None of which kept it from being crowded and thronged with bowing and praying pilgrims. In the half-light, gold-etched tiles in front of the monument proclaimed this to be the tomb of someone who had been a direct descendant of the Prophet. Three houses after this would be the safe house. Nigel quickened his step, only to stop short of the house.

Like every other building on this alley, it was tall—perhaps five or six stories—and narrow, its upper levels indistinct in the permanent twilight of the alley. Its front had once been fully tiled, but many of the tiles had fallen off over what must have been centuries. The remaining tiles were white, engraved with blue arabesques. The stucco left behind by the fallen tiles was a dark yellow turning to brown. It looked like a toothless mouth, grinning wantonly at Nigel.

The windows, quite unlike those narrow, tall holes cut high up into the walls of most houses in newer and more prosperous parts of town, were fanciful, counter-curved shapes, resembling mysterious keyholes or voluptuous women's forms. Nothing like the proper and prim windows of England.

Nigel recoiled like a nervous horse rearing from the smell of an abattoir. For the deep-set, stone-encased doorway looked black and burnt.

A wooden door hung from crooked hinges and looked charred through. It seemed that a violent conflagration had torn the place apart from the outside, blasting the door outward and burning it whole in the same moment. Around the stone doorway, curious black marks showed, consistent with the shadows of the tongues of flame sweeping out of the doorway and imprinting themselves in black soot and darkened film of smoke upon the aged, golden stone. Looking up,

Nigel could dimly discern the same marks around the stone parapets of the windows on the first floor. Yet the houses on either side looked untouched by the conflagration.

He felt his hair stand on end, and he grasped the walking stick in his hand with desperation.

Some of the houses in the poor districts of London used gaslight instead of the safer, but much more expensive, magelight. Sometimes, Nigel had heard, one of those houses would fill with gas from a leaking socket, till the whole exploded inside. But Cairo had no gaslights. Or at least, Nigel had never heard of it. Like most countries in the poorer continents, where magic had never been made the prerogative of the upper classes, Egypt kept its magic widespread enough that almost every peasant could command enough power to create light. Oh, nothing like the bright, civilized magelight of English magicians, but enough to guide one's way to bed, or to light one's way down the stairs. And it never occurred to the natives to want more. To read by magelight or to conduct one's social life on, into the darkened hours of the night, would never cross an African's mind.

So it was unlikely the explosion had been caused by gas. Besides, the houses on either side had remained untouched by any trace of smoke or blaze of fire. Gas, more often than not, took the whole block, even in those parts of London where houses stood farther apart than this.

Nigel stepped carefully toward the doorway. And stopped again, directly underneath the stone arch. His hair felt as though it were pulling on his scalp, attempting to uproot itself. And his mouth tasted acrid, as though he'd been sucking on a mouthful of ashes. His mage-sense tingled.

This was no natural fire. Magic out of control had ignited this. Out of control or—worse—controlled and directed to attack.

Poor Lord Widefield, killed. And now the safe house in Cairo was destroyed, burned by a great power. But what power? What army? What great mage?

Nigel forced himself to step into the house, his once immaculate shoes crackling over unidentifiable burnt bits on the floor. The smell stung his nose and the feeling of magic tingled so strongly that he could barely breathe.

The front room showed signs of a sudden conflagration. The wallpaper looked largely intact—an innocuous design of pink roses tied with blue ribbons climbing coyly up the walls of this alien building proclaiming it as clearly as if a sign had hung on it, the abode of a British expatriate.

Only here and there, marks of soot and darkened stains showed that fire—or magic—had passed by in great, hurtling force.

The furniture around the room also looked largely unscathed—still polished, still varnished, its pulls shining brass. A vase of marigolds upon a carved wooden table stood fresh and intact. In the center of the room, where a round table must once have occupied pride of place, destruction reigned. The table retained its rough shape, but was hollowed out and burned as black as the door. And around it . . . six skeletons sat at the table. Or at least they were mostly skeletons, but in the way of magic fires this one had burned unevenly. Here half a face remained intact,

showing a wide-open, surprised blue eye, a pale lip
drawn back from pearly white teeth, a thatch of blond
hair above it all. There a hand, manicured and clean,
rested upon the black hull of the table, its tapered finger displaying the signet ring of a noble house of
England.

Nigel recognized all the men sitting at the table, could
name them all—Jones, Tarfoil, Castairs, Michaels,
Knighton and Brightly. All of them belonging to the magical secret service. All of them come to Africa on the
same mission, to support first Carew and then Nigel in
finding the ruby for the queen of England.

A cold chill shot up Nigel's spine and he became
aware that sweat soaked his shirt.

When Carew had disappeared, these men had
been ordered to help the younger son of the Earl of
Oldhall upon the same mission that had consumed the
older and better brother. And now these men were
dead. A piece of charred ceiling fell just in front of
Nigel. It crashed against the table, sending dust and
fragments into Nigel's hair and face.

Nigel was in Africa but he had no help, no support,
no aid, no direction. His mouth felt dry. His hands
shook.

Nigel's quest could change the shape of the world
and set power firmly in the hands of Queen Victoria.
It could stop all anarchists, the massing forces of
destruction and chaos. For hundreds, thousands, of
years, it could freeze them in their tracks. If only
Nigel could accomplish his mission.

He was the man his sovereign had chosen, so Nigel
would stay in Africa. He would find the ruby for the
queen. He would find Carew for his parents.

But Emily had no business in a game that had just turned deadly. She must go back to England and bide her time at her father's house, till news of Nigel's death released her to make a more suitable marriage. Or till Nigel returned, in triumph, to claim her.

A LADY ALONE

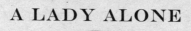

Emily looked perfect—except for the shimmering wetness in her blue eyes and the way her lips insisted on quivering. She bit her lower lip to punish it for showing her weakness, and told herself how much of a fool she was being.

What juicy stories the expatriates in this hotel must be cooking up, even now, while they sat around the marble-topped tables and reclined upon the velvet settees in the palm-dotted reception area. She was a married woman, arriving alone . . .

Emily bit her lip harder, till the marks of her teeth stood white upon it. She wished she knew how to explain her strange marriage. Perhaps Nigel didn't want to touch her because she was not properly English. Or perhaps her stepmother had been right and English men and women embraced only when they meant to have children.

But no man in the world left his bride alone for her honeymoon. Or did he? Alone in an alien city where he could have no other business? Had his marriage to Emily been only a blind, an excuse to come to Cairo? Did he have a paramour waiting here? It made a certain sense. Too much sense. It explained his lack of ardor.

But it did not explain his insistence that they both pack sturdy clothes. And it did not explain why Nigel would need such an elaborate subterfuge. So many men—most men—had mistresses in the open. Besides, why had Nigel not taken his clothes with him now if he meant to leave? Surely the deserted wife would need only return to England. What need would she have of extra clothing?

And how could Emily's father, in his investigation of Nigel, have missed a paramour of such importance in Nigel's life? None of it could be true.

The hotel was the best in Egypt, and perhaps the best in the world. At least, that was what the gentleman at Cook's had told Nigel. It managed a combination of the best features of an English hotel with the exoticism that tourists necessarily expected in the place to which they traveled—particularly a place resounding with ancient lore. Thus, the hotel was built in a square, each of the walls bordering streets of Cairo, but opening to them no more than three doors—well guarded by porters—and a series of narrow windows, high up on the walls of each of the three floors. The third door, on the inner side, faced a vast garden, at the bottom of which was a tall, locked gate. Each of the rooms had a wide balcony overlooking the street and another facing the lush, verdant inner garden of the hotel, well away from the dust, noise and excessive strangeness of the Egyptian street.

Outside the rooms, a long, broad hallway followed the external walls of the building, and staircases at each end connected the floors. The walls were white, and a permanent twilight, lit by windows high up on the walls near the ceiling, gave the space a restful feeling. The staircases and railings were dark, polished mahogany. The effect was a feeling of being in both England and abroad.

To add to it, one was as likely to meet with Arabs as with well-dressed British gentlemen and gentlewoman in this shaded, protected atmosphere. Men in caftans and men in suits, women in fashionable dress and women in a profusion of veils all passed by Emily, going in both directions.

Emily ignored the stares of the other guests and adopted the expression she had often worn when meeting new girls at the boarding school, or when new staff was hired at her father's home. This helped control the trembling inside and the feeling that at any minute she would burst into tears.

Where was Nigel? And when would he return?

The dining room, at the lowest level of the hotel, was a vast, square room, outfitted with a row of English-style windows facing the courtyard garden. Mahogany partitions and frosted glass protected the privacy of white-draped tables, turning each into a little, sheltered niche. Potted palms throughout added to the illusion that this was a civilized and partitioned jungle. An attendant led Emily to a table by the window, where she could look out at the garden.

At the nearest table, a tall, dark-haired man was being served. He appeared be holding his head up with as much forced pride as Emily's own. From the back, she saw a slender neck emerging from an ice-white shirt collar. His hair was dark and tumbled, as though he'd combed himself carelessly. He wore an immaculate white linen suit.

"Will you be waiting for Mr. Oldhall?" the server asked Emily.

She shook her head and was given a list of the available foods, from which she selected a suitable succession of courses, starting with some crudités and ending with cheese—the bouillabaisse and the roast lamb and curry being served in between.

The server departed, but the tall, dark man who'd had his back to Emily pushed his chair away from the table and stood. When he turned, his face looked so extraordinarily handsome that her breath caught in her throat and for just a moment her thoughts stopped. He called to Emily's mind the Greek and Roman statues she'd glimpsed in her trips to London museums.

Dark, deep-set eyes lit his chiseled features, surmounted by just slightly unruly black curls, all of it set above the broad shoulders of an athlete, narrowing to a waist almost as small as Emily's own, though the man stood a good two heads taller than her. His creamy coat and pants highlighted a long-legged, muscular build.

His gaze met hers and Emily realized that she'd looked him in the eyes. Then his craggily handsome features opened in a dazzling smile.

Averting her eyes, Emily fixed her attention upon unfolding her napkin and laying it across her lap. As she did, she was aware that the man approached her in decisive strides, arriving at her table so close that he almost touched the tablecloth. Emily continued to look down in embarrassed confusion, a painful heat burning in her cheeks.

He could not be thinking of accosting her. It was most improper. They had never been introduced.

Emily had heard that in outposts of the empire and in far-flung lands, when Englishmen met they often dispensed with the customary courtesies observed as a matter of course in the motherland. Perhaps the man thought she was single.

Emily twisted her linen napkin in her lap, refusing to look up, lest she encourage the man to do the unfathomable. But he cleared his throat and when she glanced up, involuntarily, she found herself staring into the darkest pair of green eyes she'd ever seen. They were so dark that at a distance she'd assumed they were black, save for the glistening currents of color that moved within like a vast, frozen, unlit ocean.

His eyes reflected increasing amusement, and Emily realized she'd been staring again. Before she could look away, the man assumed a military posture, clicking his heels together—not so much on purpose but as though long years in the army had formed his manner of standing and being in the world.

"Mrs. Oldhall," he said, and bowed, polite and respectful like any gentleman in any receiving room.

Emily looked up, puzzled. How would he—? Of course, the waiter had said her name, but how did he dare use it, as though they'd been introduced?

She lowered her eyebrows and pursed her lips just as her stepmother did when she wished to freeze someone out. But his lips stretched in a slow, ironic smile, and—within his eyes—the glacial currents of a primeval ocean swirled and spun, betraying amusement and something else—something she couldn't even imagine, much less put into words.

"You'll forgive my introducing myself in this way," he said, polite and composed. He spoke with a high-bred accent, a lot like Nigel's. "You'll forgive me if I trample upon those rules of courtesy that I normally would strive to observe." He again straightened himself and appeared to stand at attention. "It is just that I heard the servant mention your name, and I used to know the Oldhalls passingly well. I wondered if you were Mrs. Carew Oldhall or . . ." He hesitated and looked away from her. She was aware of it, though she did not look directly at him, but ostensibly at her hands gathered on her napkin. He cleared his throat. "Or perhaps Mrs. Nigel Oldhall?"

Surprised at the names, Emily looked up. Because she was fairly sure there was no other Oldhall family with two such an names amid its offspring. She met the man's gaze and saw that he was embarrassed, though he seemed to hide it under a faint veneer of amusement. A high color tinged his prominent cheekbones and he looked away from her, even as his lips tried to form a smile.

"I am Mrs. Nigel Oldhall," she said, emboldened by his shyness. This man—with his athletic build—was doubtlessly one of Carew's friends. Carew was, after all, the athletic one who excelled at all games, or so Nigel had told her.

But the man smiled wide at the name. "Excellent. If you'll forgive me, my name is Peter Farewell, and I am one of Nigel's school fellows. Indeed . . ." His grin stretched, amused and gregarious, transforming his handsome face into the picture of friendliness. "Indeed, I would own that I was Nigel's best friend in our boarding school days. We were like brothers, he and I. Companions in a dozen escapades and mad breaking of the rules." He clasped the back of the chair across from hers.

He had dark fingers, almost as golden as Emily's own and, like Emily's, slender and tapered. A single gold signet ring with a massive black stone at the top ornamented the ring finger of his right hand.

A wealthy family, Emily thought. A well-born man. And Nigel's friend.

"Indeed," Farewell said as the devilish smile split his features and made him look irresistibly handsome again. "I can't imagine anything more interesting or more unlikely than meeting Nigel's beautiful wife, by happenstance, in Cairo." He bowed slightly to her. "I am delighted." His gaze ran over her features and paused, as though to take in her dark blue eyes, her pouting lips.

She blushed and looked away, but he didn't seem embarrassed.

"I must say that Nigel is very fortunate indeed."

Embarrassment and heat rose in twin waves through Emily. "Sir—" she started.

The man cleared his throat and seemed for a moment at a loss. "Er," he said, "you are Nigel's wife, not his widow, I trust?"

"Oh, no," Emily said, looking up. "Not his widow. His wife, this last week. We were married just last week, at Oldhall."

"You'll pardon me," Peter Farewell said. "But since you were alone—" He stopped and frowned, his dark, well-delineated eyebrows gathering over his dark eyes. "This week? And Nigel has left you alone on your honeymoon? How? Why? Is there something wrong?"

Emily felt the color flee her cheeks. How dared this stranger echo the questions in Emily's own heart? "Oh, no. Nothing wrong. It's just that he . . . He had some business to attend to in Cairo. He'll be back presently."

"Is that so? Then if you'd allow me to sit with you, perhaps we can talk for a while. I know it's not altogether proper, but . . ."

Emily was thinking that even a stranger would be a protection against the looks of other strangers amazed at her being alone, a young woman with no chaperone in this busy restaurant in this strange land. And besides, Mr. Farewell was obviously not a stranger. Or not totally. He knew the family. And he came from a wealthy background. She waved him toward the chair, and he sat down.

The server showed up then and regarded the situation with raised eyebrows. "I realized the lady is an old family friend," Peter Farewell said. "If you'd bring my food here . . ."

"Certainly, sir," the server said, and gestured wildly at what turned out to be a company of underlings, each carrying little portable, foldable tables and trays. Emily smelled the distinctive odor of curry, beloved to her from childhood and well known because among the staff her parents had brought to England was an Indian chef, an old servant—some said a relative—of her mother's.

A glimpse of the trays showed her lamb and rice, chicken dishes and stewed fruit. The server used a silver ladle to dispense a variety of dainties onto each of their plates, and filled their cups with wine. Then leaving the serving tables set up near them, the trays covered with great silver domes, he retreated into the shadows of the restaurant, doubtless to attend to other diners.

Peter unfolded his napkin upon his lap and plied his silverware with the easy, effortless grace of the ton. "So, tell me, how is Nigel faring? What holds his interest these days?" Peter said, his lips curving in an expansive, craggy smile.

"Ah...Nigel administers his father's lands," Emily said, between bites of savory morsels. She avoided looking at Peter Farewell, and tried to hide from him how little she truly knew of Nigel's business, his daily occupations. Their courtship had consisted of him visiting her home, of his talking to her. Not about estates and children, money and real life, but about poems and stories, delicate constructions of words, the foreign languages he loved. And asking her about India. Asking her so much about India that presently Emily feared he loved her only because part of her came from India.

But she didn't want Peter Farewell to know any of this. He was a stranger and, at that, the most handsome stranger she'd ever met. Even if he had indeed been Nigel's friend in school, surely it would be improper for him to discern too much of his school fellow's marital felicity—or lack of it.

Her eyes averted, color burning in her cheeks, Emily spoke softly. "Or rather, he helps Lord Oldhall administer them. I imagine he's a great comfort to his father. And he performs those magic feats that are necessary—healing animal illnesses and looking after the magical needs of his servants and renters. He provides them with needed light and healing for their children, and such." Indeed, she did no more than repeat what her father had told her when he had investigated Nigel's background before giving his consent to their marriage. It was all she truly knew of the man.

Farewell's eyebrows rose. For a moment he looked grave and somber, a man consumed with vast and weighty cares. "Yes," he said, "I imagine he would be. Old Nigel was always very punctilious. The headmaster's pet and the example to us all."

Was that bitterness in his voice? Before Emily could decide, Farewell smiled. "And he was a caring boy, even then. If I had sixpence for every lame dog, every wretched cat that Nigel adopted and nursed, in direct contravention of the school's policy . . . He just couldn't bear to see any living thing killed or in pain." And here it appeared as though Farewell's gaze skittered sideways away from something. It wasn't a physical movement, but a reflection of some internal change, as though he flinched from a thought triggered by the words he'd pronounced.

He ate a mouthful of food, took his crystal goblet to his lips and frowned—not a true frown but a gathering of his dark eyebrows. Looking intently at Emily, he said, "There is only one thing I do not understand. Where did Carew go? Because he is the oldest son. Shouldn't he be—"

"Carew disappeared some years back," Emily said.

"Disappeared?" Farewell raised his eyebrows. Voice and expression, together, mirrored shock.

Emily blushed. "As I said. He disappeared during an . . . exploration trip in Africa."

"An exploration—?" Farewell's eyebrows rose

even more, in shocked surprise. "Carew was exploring Africa? I always thought him a man of his comforts—a drawing room emperor, ready to lord it over everyone and everything, but not very adventurous."

Emily had met one or two women, in the course of her engagement, who'd told her she was unfortunate in marrying the much less desirable of the two brothers, and how much better off she would have been with Carew. They spoke of Carew as a handsome man, virile and full of strength. Emily thought that Carew would have been exactly the sort of man who went to Africa on a voyage of exploration and somehow got lost in the fever-inducing swamps or fell victim to a foul attack by ambushing natives.

"I didn't know him. I didn't know Carew. I've known Mr. Nigel Oldhall for one year only, the space of his courting me."

"I beg your pardon," Farewell said. He looked away from her. His lips, which were broad and sensuous-looking in a way not often found in an Englishman, formed words that he never actually pronounced. "I beg your pardon," he repeated at last. "It is not in my scope, nor within my rights, to question your family or your associations with them. It is just that we knew Carew too well, Nigel and I. He was the kind of man that takes delight in . . . matches where he knows he'll win. A man who wouldn't risk his own precious skin, his own precious comfort on anything short of a done deal." He looked at her, and for a moment his dark green eyes were unguarded and it seemed to Emily that she was glimpsing a time when both he and Nigel had been wide-eyed, trusting children, afraid of an older brother.

Had Carew been a bully, then? Or had Nigel and Peter, in the way of younger children everywhere, resented the older youth's ruling over them to such an extent as his age entitled him?

"Oh, it means nothing," Peter Farewell said. "It is only, I suppose, that Nigel and I were five years younger and it was obvious that Carew was Lord Oldhall's favorite. Perhaps Nigel resented his brother and perhaps I, his best friend, simply caught this resentment."

Peter gestured for his glass to be refilled, and Emily noticed a high webbing between his long, tapered fingers. It wasn't high enough to make his hands look deformed, but it was longer than that between the fingers of most people, and as such an eccentric characteristic. The first less-than-perfect detail she had noticed about him.

He drank, though his plate remained mostly full. He'd pushed the food around with his silver fork, drawing unknown patterns and shapes upon the glossy surface adorned with concentric golden rings.

"It's just that no one can imagine one of their older acquaintances becoming an intrepid explorer in Africa. Which organization did he favor? The National Geographic Society, perhaps? For you cannot tell me that he meant to work for one of the missionary associations."

Emily drew breath to speak, but she could not. Because indeed she knew nothing about who had sponsored Carew, much less of Carew's religious opinions or interests.

"Emily," a voice rang out, too loud, in the dining room. Several people looked over the partitions that separated their tables, to watch what promised to be rich melodrama. For there stood Nigel—pale, shocked, outraged and disheveled. Quite unlike his normal unruffled, mirror-smooth, polished self.

His suit was dusty, stained with dark greasy smears that might have been smoke or ash. His blond hair, too short and neatly cut to be in great disarray, still managed to look unbalanced, combed all up one side and down the other. And his face was pale, his gray-blue eyes surrounded by dark circles, his expression scared.

He stared with wide disbelief at the table, where his wife of less than a week had obviously been entertaining a gentleman friend.

SHOULD OLD ACQUAINTANCE BE FORGOTTEN

*Later on, Nigel would tell himself that he never sus-*pected Emily of being unfaithful. Not for a second—though his breath had caught in his throat and his heartbeat had seemed to skip like a startled wild thing. And yet he had to own he'd felt the sudden pain of betrayal and loss, and that suspicions ran riot through his mind, though never finding words to express themselves.

He'd thought that he'd failed Emily to such an extent that she'd already found a more virile replacement. He'd thought that Emily had always had another lover and that she'd only accepted his proposal so that he'd bring her to Cairo, where she could meet this other man. He'd thought half a dozen other improbable schemes, all of which would have meant that Emily had never loved him and that Nigel remained as he'd always thought of himself, unlovable and despised—the sickly younger son and brother whom no one could care for.

Then the man at the table turned his handsome, chiseled features toward Nigel, whose mouth dropped open in surprise, a sound of recognition and joy escaping through his lips.

It was a face Nigel could never forget. Peter Farewell—Nigel's best and often only friend. When school had ended, imagining for himself no more than a dull life of studying languages, Nigel had begged Peter to write to him. To write often. Nigel had thought that his only respite from boring solitude would be Peter's letters, which would echo of foreign lands and spicy, exotic women. But somehow, the letters had stopped after a few months.

Now the force of childhood friendship and idolatry-like admiration of Peter hit him like a physical blow and relief swept over Nigel like a chill, cooling the sweat of fear upon his skin. He was not alone. He might have found the British Magical Secret Service house burned out, and every man he expected to call an ally dead. But Peter was here. Nigel would not be braving danger on his own.

The relief of the thought was such that Nigel's legs went suddenly weak, as if only fear and desperation had been steadying him.

Peter stood up and smiled at Nigel. "Hello, old man."

He gestured eloquently to the black-suited servants who hurried up to the table, carrying an extra chair. While Nigel sat, they arranged a place setting in front of him and dispensed food and drink noiselessly.

As Nigel unfolded his napkin upon his dark pants, Peter said, "You'll forgive my having introduced myself to your wife, Nigel. I heard her name, and I couldn't help seeing if by any chance she knew you."

"No problem at all," Nigel said, and felt more than

saw Emily relax. What had she thought, that he'd berate her for talking to a man to whom she'd not been introduced? "But what are you doing in Africa, Peter? What brings you to Cairo?"

Peter sighed and opened his hands, a show of charming artlessness. "I am here at my leisure, as you see." He smiled, but his expression looked bitter. "I am a man of leisure."

"Leisure?" Nigel said. He raised his eyebrows. "I always thought you'd go into law or the army, or..." The Farewells had an old and prestigious title, but hardly any money at all. The family house, to which Nigel had been invited often enough for holidays, was a large, ramshackle building. It had been the seat of Peter's family since the Norman invasion, and of the Farewells' once vast domains all it retained was a small park and a couple of ill-treated farms attached to it. All the rest had been sold or lost at the gaming tables or in exotic pleasures at specialized brothels, by Peter's grandfather, whose debauch had since become legendary.

Peter's father in turn had married a woman from a family of dubious ancestry, with little magic but much money. However, her dowry had been too little, too late, and failed to stop the drainage of Farewell's funds. They held on to those farms, but no one knew quite how they managed.

Peter colored a bright red and looked past Nigel's shoulder, at the middistance. "Ah...I tried law and army both, but neither would suit."

Nigel was not sure what that meant. How could Peter survive in the absence of gainful employment?

But he realized he'd trespassed upon Peter's feelings and private shame.

Emily said, in a small voice, "You know, the pyramids look fascinating—"

Peter cast Emily a grateful look, but said to Nigel, as though Emily hadn't spoken, "It doesn't signify. I am, as you see, on my own and unencumbered by any of those cares of the world that make beggars of us all. I've traveled to Greece and Rome, studied the world and history. And until I saw Mrs. Oldhall's face, I had never come across any reason to regret not having married or burdened myself with family."

The look that Peter gave Emily was so full of earnest admiration that, for the first time Nigel felt as though he were the victor in the unspoken competition. He grinned, feeling absurdly happy—forgetting that his marriage remained unconsummated and that the mission that had brought him to Cairo had just suffered unexpected tribulations.

"But I should let you be," Peter said. "I am not, after all, such a bad sport that I would interrupt another fellow's honeymoon." He smiled disarmingly at both Nigel and Emily, and rose. "If you'll excuse me."

"No, stay," Nigel said, at the same time that Emily began, "But, Mr. Farewell—"

Nigel added, "Stay. We had time together alone on our carpetship cruise here. And we'll have time alone again soon. We plan to see the pyramids. So, sit down, man, sit down."

Peter sat down, with rather more willingness than he'd shown toward leaving. "You came in aboard *Victoria's Invicta*?"

"How did you know?"

"I heard it had just left from London. And you appear newly arrived." He looked at Emily and bowed slightly. "I do not think it is possible for me to have been in a hotel with the lovely Mrs. Oldhall for more than a day without being aware of her presence."

The comment disturbed Nigel, because Peter had never been a rake, never been obsessed with women. Yet his compliments to Emily seemed heavy indeed.

Nigel raised an eyebrow to his old friend, in silent inquiry that Peter pretended not to understand. "I hear that each of the rooms in that ship cost upward of a hundred thousand pounds to outfit."

"Yes, it's very fine stuff," Nigel said. "The best furniture and silk carpets and draperies." He chuckled. "Better than at home."

And for the next few minutes, they discussed the carpetships and the general flourishing of the flight trade between Britain and its colonies.

"A good thing for everyone," Nigel said, "this far-flung trade. It makes the lot of the common man much easier."

"Yes," Peter said, but his eyes narrowed, as though he'd meant to say no. "Although it costs so much to that same common man."

"Costs?" Nigel asked, quite at a loss for Peter's meaning.

"And, Mr. Farewell?" Emily asked at last. "You came to Africa aboard what ship?"

The question seemed to confuse Peter. He stopped, with his dark face and those eyes that had always seemed to Nigel as inscrutable as the mysterious center of any savage continent, turned toward Emily. His expression became suddenly opaque, as though a shutter had been closed across Peter's features. It did not cover his face, but it made his emotions and behavior inscrutable to any mere mortal. Nigel knew that expression all too well.

Throughout most of their career in school, Peter had been the teachers' blue-eyed wonder child who knew everything, could answer every question and whose mind, coupled with his dauntless courage, reflected the hope of the brightest of futures. Yet, now and then, there were teachers who, for some reason or other, took a dislike to Peter. Perhaps they were intimidated by his brilliant mind. Or perhaps they feared his status as a member of one of the oldest, most respected and magically powerful of the titled families in Britain. But when a teacher disliked him, Peter would affect as blank and empty a stare when answering their questions as he now turned toward Emily Oldhall.

"Pardon?" he asked Emily. "Ship?"

"Oh, you said you were here before us," Emily said, and colored like a child who has unwittingly committed social solecism. "I wondered by what means you traveled here."

Peter smiled. "I flew," he said.

Then he turned to Nigel and his face showed the same false smile no more open than a painted front. "Have you heard from Borne-Watkins? I heard he went into politics and had hopes of climbing very high indeed. There were rumors..."

Borne-Watkins had been a weasel-faced boy and the class snitch, ever ready to run to a teacher or monitor with a story about someone else's misdeeds.

As Peter slid smoothly into rumors and insinuations on the nature of Borne-Watkins's political career and what he might or might not have done to deserve it, Nigel listened in amazement that such a creature, so flawed in character, could climb so high. Their school—Four Towers Academy for the Education of Boys—had prided itself on instilling character, and yet here one of their gladuates was still without a character, prospering. It was almost interesting enough to make Nigel forget Peter's momentary blank look, his obvious confusion at Emily's question and his smooth refusal to answer it. Almost, but not quite.

Because Nigel had lived long enough in the world, and had known Peter at that innocent age when disguise is ineffective and all emotions are painted upon the face like colors on a blank canvas. He knew very well what Peter's reaction to the question about his means of travel meant.

Peter's conveyance between Britain and Africa was far less distinguished than the hundred-thousand-pounds-apiece price for the rooms aboard *Victoria's Invicta*. In fact, from the way Peter spoke, Nigel would not be surprised to learn that Peter had worked his way to Africa, manning the magical engines of some cargo ship. Which would explain Peter's financial survival. But it also tainted him with the dreaded hand of commerce—something none of his class would admit.

How could Peter have fallen so low?

No matter how poor his family might be, Peter's old, hallowed name, his being descended in a direct line from Charlemagne himself, made him capable of being as good as the best. What governmental department would not want to add Peter's name to its rolls? What regiment would not take pride in having him for an officer? Particularly when someone like Borne-Watkins, of lower birth and with far less intelligence, prospered so greatly.

It was none of Nigel's business. And yet, as a portent of the world's being turned upside down, it interested Nigel very much indeed.

A FOOL'S ERRAND

"Who are you?" the young man who opened the door asked Nassira.

She could easily have asked the same, but she remembered him from their mind message. Perhaps he hadn't seen her image, she thought. Perhaps he'd only heard her.

She straightened her back and glared at him. "I am Nassira, daughter of Nedera. Of the Masai."

He smiled as if he found this funny, and his hand closed the door some more—his foot doubtlessly behind it, to prevent her pushing past him. His voice mocked her as he replied, "And what do you wish of me, Nassira, daughter of Nedera of the Masai?"

Nassira almost turned and went away. In her heart, she longed to ignore the Hyena Men and their machinations, but she couldn't allow this man to scare her away that easily. He was arrogant and in dire need of a lesson. If they'd been still in Masai land, her father would thrash him for speaking to her so disrespectfully. A wealthy man, with only one daughter and no sons, Nassira's father wanted everyone to treat his daughter as the marvel she was to him.

The door the rude young man had opened was a

nondescript one for this part of Cairo: red inset in a tile-covered facade. Though this part of town—at least judging from the people that Nassira had seen during her walk here, and from the faces that peered from windows and looked out of half-closed doors— was inhabited mostly by people from deeper in the African continent, yet it was—like the rest of Cairo— a Muslim town. That meant that the facades were composed of tiles inscribed with indecipherable arabesques in blue and gold, or red and gold.

The man who'd opened the door to Nassira looked like his mind image, and yet different. He was as black as everyone else she'd seen around here. Blacker than Nassira, in fact, a black as dark as a starless night over the savanna. He stood very tall, too— taller than all the Englishmen that Nassira had met in England. Tall enough, she judged, to be a Masai. But *that* he wasn't. His features lacked the clear-cut Masai traits, their prominent cheekbones, the straight, high-bridged nose. In their place was a face more long than broad, and features that belonged to no tribe, no people that Nassira had ever known. He didn't even look that much like a Zulu in person. His eyes were too large, his chin too square.

She straightened her shoulders and faced him, standing as straight and proud as she knew how. "I owe no explanation to anyone," she said. "Certainly not to you." She glared at him. "In your mind message, you called yourself Kitwana. Is that your real name?"

The man smiled spontaneously, without seeming to think of how it projected. She might have thought he was laughing at her and be offended, but it was clear this was not so. He was smiling at himself.

"I am Kitwana," he said. "It means Pledged to Live."

Just that. No people, no village, no parents' name attached to that singular name. He seemed to think that *Kitwana* alone meant everything. Good thing he was pledged to live, since, doubtlessly, many people had probably often felt like killing him.

She frowned at him. With an air of confidence he wore an Englishman's suit, well cut, well fitted.

"You answered my summons," she said. "My mind summons."

He nodded. His hair was cut so short you could almost see his scalp beneath. A fine-looking man, if one could see him in his natural element, without the trappings of the white man about him. She wondered what he looked like in the native dress of his people, and what that would be.

Even among the Masai, dress standards differed. The clothing of the Il-Purco left most of their bodies uncovered and used cloth and beads strictly as ornamentation. The Il-Sungo, the Masai subgroup to which Nassira belonged, found this scandalous. They covered up in shoulder-to-knee wraps and accused the Il-Purco of going around naked, like cows.

What attire would Kitwana favor, and how much of his broad-shouldered, long-legged body would it leave uncovered? Nassira banished the thought forcefully. She was not here to allow herself to be seduced by a non-Masai, an arrogant son of people to whom Engai had refused cattle.

"I am a member of those who work in the night

and stalk the mighty," she said, using the Hyena Men's description of themselves.

He raised his eyebrows and said nothing in return. For a moment, she wondered whether he understood her, or if she'd somehow come to the wrong place altogether. Then Kitwana narrowed his eyes. "Like calls to like," he said. "Water to water, blood to blood."

As he spoke, he unfastened the white cuff of his shirt, beneath his suit coat. Then he pulled it up just a little. At the point at his wrist where the vein divided into a delta of life, a small half-moon-shaped scar marred his flawless skin.

Nassira understood.

She lifted her own wrist, displaying the twin of his scar—a scar so small and unremarkable that it would pass unnoticed to the uninitiated.

When close to one another, both scars glowed momentarily with a bright brilliance, like a pinprick of sunlight beneath their skins.

"Lion to lion, and hyena to hyena," Kitwana said, and threw the door open.

The scars were the magical remainders and marks of their initiations into the Hyena Men, and linked to one another by the collective magical power of the group.

Though Kitwana spoke as good English as Nassira did herself, it seemed to her that she detected in his pronunciation a hint of an accent. A man she'd met early on in the Hyena Men had spoken with a similar tinge in his voice. And that accent sounded Zulu, but Kitwana's features were like no other Zulu Nassira had met. Yet what did she know about the Zulus? They lived many months away, in the western end of

Africa. As for his giving her neither name of parents nor of tribe, that, too, would fit in with the Zulus, the proudest—some said the maddest—people in Africa. Not so long ago, they had terrorized the British with their strength, their warlike ways.

They still erupted into sudden violence now and then and remained an empire within an empire, a confederacy within the greater confederacy. There were several of them in the Hyena Men, and looking at this tall, dark man with his expressive dark eyes and his broad shoulders, Nassira wondered if perhaps he wasn't the power behind the Hyena Men. He looked strong enough to carry the organization. Besides, the magical power she felt in him—strong, shapeless and immense—had an unexpected quality that was like an unknown taste on the tongue, a name she couldn't quite recall.

But no matter how powerful he might be, she was Masai and would not be intimidated.

He let her into a small, shabby living room, furnished in nondescript British furniture.

"Forgive my suspicions," he said, unexpectedly polite. He closed the door behind her and refastened his sleeve. "But we're under attack and we don't know by whom. That force that disturbed our mind communications has disturbed all other mind links with our brethren throughout Africa. It sometimes seems to shut them down altogether. And many of our men have been found dead—stabbed many times through the heart, or consumed in a great magical fire."

"I tried to contact the Hyena Men from London," she said, and set her face in the stern disapproval that had been known to send young Masai children running for cover. "And no one answered me. My messages were blocked."

The young man sighed. "As I said." He walked up to the fireplace and leaned on the mantel, like a warrior of the Masai might lean against a tree. It was an incongruous sight in this place that might have been the living room of the head servant at the club.

There was a shabby carpet on the floor, and upon it a dining room set, its varnish coat blistered and peeling. Probably bought second- or thirdhand from some European expatriate about to return home. A sofa took up the corner, and tattered red velvet showed around the corners of a colorful shawl draped over it.

The fireplace was swept, and from the lingering smell of char and old grease around it, one could tell it had been used for cooking. On the mantel rested a strange melange of curios, laying on their sides, none of them all that decorative. A powerstick, Martini-Henry brand—polished mahogany—favored by English hunters; the power mace of a Xhosa chieftain, a Zulu assegai.

All of this appeared only dimly in the pervading twilight within the room. The only light came from windows placed high up on the walls, and cut in narrow slits as was normal in Egypt. Magelights and an oil lamp rested upon the scarred table, but Kitwana made no move to turn any of them on. Nor did he invite Nassira to sit. Instead, as she stepped forward, he moved away from the fireplace and walked backwards in front of her, barring her way to the narrow little stairway that presumably led into the bowels of the house. Despite his English suit, his posture was so warriorlike that Nassira could practically see the muscles on his broad chest as he threw back his head and looked down at her. "These are dangerous things to talk of in the street."

Nassira sighed. She'd joined the Hyena Men at fifteen, while staying at the Maniata—the warrior camp—of the warriors of her generation. For the next three years, she'd served the Hyenna Men by helping recruit members among her peers. Though there were many other girls there, the lovers and companions of the warriors, Nassira had found that most of her friends were the warriors themselves. And not only friends in the sexual way, though she'd enjoyed her trysts and liaisons. But she could also talk with these virile warriors and hold her own in their conversations.

Through these male friends, she'd become intimately acquainted with the male predilection for rules and codes, or secret passwords and hidden gestures. Though she understood that the Hyena Men were a secret society, and that the Europeans would crush them if they could, she'd always wondered if most of the games around it weren't just a reflection of that male love for secrecy and rules.

Right then she had no patience for it. "It is indeed dangerous to broadcast our affiliation," she said. "But it is more dangerous, and far more stupid, to block transmissions from the member you sent to London to spy on the Englishmen. I have important news to tell you. And I couldn't get it to you in time, because the transmissions were blocked. Not just interfered with by this enemy you speak of. Blocked. At this end."

She crossed her arms on her chest and threw her shoulders back. "No doubt a measure of security instituted by one of you."

Kitwana had lost his warlike stance and stared at her with a puzzled expression. He put his hand on his forehead, fingers splayed, as though she'd made his head hurt. "You're saying that you were sent to London? By the Hyena Men?" He gave her a suspicious look. "I didn't know we had Masai women among our members."

Nassira shrugged. If he were the leader of the Hyena Men, this man was very ill informed. "I am the only one I know personally. The Hyena Men emissaries came to our Maniata—our warrior camp—and they talked to us of Africa's cause. I enlisted. The man I helped for years to recruit other members, Adili, came back last year and said I was to go to London and gather information about the great magic that was said to have made the Europeans so much more powerful than us. They didn't know what I might discover, or what I might not, but they told me they had other men and women in London, gathering intelligence. And then I came across a great piece of information. I tried to talk to the men here, through the mind link that I'd been given, but found the transmission blocked."

"It shouldn't have been blocked," Kitwana said. "Perhaps you were incompetent in your mind-send."

Nassira withered the crazy man with a look, then turned to leave.

"No, wait," he said, as her hand touched the doorknob. "If you're going to leave, tell me first, what did you find?"

Nassira turned. "Why should I tell you anything, you who have no understanding of anything and no respect for anything I've done? In my land, the men hunt the lion and the women do not tell them how to do it. The women look after the children and the goats and men do not instruct them."

Strangely, the young man appeared to be amused by this. His lips curved upward, almost imperceptibly, and he muttered something she didn't understand, in a language she didn't know. Then he looked serious. "This is true," he said. "And I was arrogant." He rubbed his forehead again, with his square-tipped fingers. "But there are other things happening, people dying..." He shook his head. "Please, Nassira, daughter of Nedera, tell me what you've discovered. It will greatly help our cause and make you a heroine of all dark-skinned people."

Nassira wasn't sure she believed his sudden repentance, but she also didn't know what else to do but report to him. He was the only one of the Hyena Men she'd been able to trace in the wilds of this Cairo that, though African, remained as alien to her as London. And though she longed to return to her homeland, to the craters and lakes, the volcanic mountains of her childhood—though she longed to see again her mother and her two stepmothers and revel in the homey feel of her father's kraal—Nassira had left that well-beloved home for a reason. The reason was to help Africa. To rid Africa of the white, bloodless people who would pillage it. How could she return home without having accomplished her aim?

So, standing tall and proud, she turned to Kitwana. "You know the stories we heard, of how there is a sacred temple in the heart of Africa to which all of mankind's magic is bound, and with it all the worlds without end?"

Kitwana stiffened, his shoulders becoming more square, his eyes narrowing. "It is a legend," he said. "Nothing more."

Nassira sighed. This man quite obviously suffered from the illusion that he knew everything and could not be proven wrong. "No. No, it is not a legend. We thought it was, but we were wrong, and by ignoring the truth of this, we have condemned our continent to slavery."

She half expected him to protest. But, surprisingly, he didn't. Instead, his eyes went very wide and he stared at her expectantly.

"There is a temple in a well-defended village. In this temple, there were once two jewels," she continued. "Into these jewels, which were set as the eyes of a statue meant to represent the mother of all mankind, wise ancient ones poured spells that bind the magic of humanity to this world. That stopped the splintering of primeval worlds, and made our world the center of the possible universe."

Kitwana nodded. She could tell from his bored, complacent expression that he had heard this many times.

"After that comes what I know that is new," she said. "You know how the whites are different from us. Their magic is not small magic, dispersed over every family and every man; instead, only gathered where, by chance or design, a father with great magic married a woman who was also similarly endowed."

Kitwana waved his hand, a look of impatience in his

eyes. "This is known. Only a few families of whites have the magic, but those have it powerful enough that they can charm magic sticks and make carpets fly—a feat even our greatest magicians couldn't manage."

She smiled. He really did think he knew everything. "Exactly," she said. "But that magic is not natural to the race. They were like us, too, not so long ago. Forty generations back, a king of the Water People bid one of his servants steal the eyes of the goddess. With these he meant to bind to himself and his descendants all the magical power in the world, so they alone would rule forever."

"He failed," Kitwana said, then looked annoyed, as though he'd not meant to speak.

Nassira smiled. "Partly. His envoy, armed with the compass stone that was supposed to guide him to the ancestral temple and the ancestral jewels, got caught at his theft, or failed in some other way. His account to his king said that he had stolen both jewels, but the guardians of the jewels—some ancient village— caught up with him and after fierce battle took one of the jewels back. Perhaps this is so. Or perhaps he only got the one."

Kitwana nodded. Nassira enjoyed making the self-centered man abide in silence and listen to her. She had known many like him—warriors and elders of her tribe who would not learn anything new. They were usually the ones who objected to the fact that her father had let his only daughter use his cattle stick and look after his cows. Men's work. They had told him he let Nassira run wild too much and speak her mind too loudly, that her freedom and confidence was more than most boys were granted and that he should take a stick to her back and make her humble.

"But that ruby," Nassira continued, "called Soul of Fire, was enough for the king to bind to himself and those related to him all the magical power in Europe. So he started the time of great monarchies in Europe. But we all know kings have many wives and mistresses, and each of those kings sired many bastards. The descendants of those bastards, without title or fortune, are now numerous and powerful enough that two or three of them together can do things such as run a magic carpet on an overseas trip or make huge trains move under magical power alone."

"Or run the mills that flood our continent with cheap cloth," Kitwana said, and narrowed his eyes with impatience.

She smiled a tight, superior smile. "And so there are revolutions against the royal houses, and now the queen of Britain, the empress of white men, has decided it is time to take the magical power from all those petty users and concentrate it again on a royal blood line. Her own."

Now Kitwana's eyes widened.

"In the club where I worked as a maid," Nassira said, "I used my magic to listen to two men speak of this in one of the private rooms. One of them was Widefield, the queen's friend, the other a white man known as Nigel Oldhall, of no great knowledge, no particular distinction, and without particularly great magic for one of his station in life. They said that years ago the queen had sent Oldhall's brother to Africa to find the other ruby, Heart of Light. And that because he'd failed, she had decided to send this young man and his wife on the same mission. He's been given the compass stone and granted transport to Africa."

"You are sure of this?"

"He has disembarked in Cairo today," she said. "I tried to warn you mentally, and my transmission was blocked. So I left my post and took the same flying carpet to Cairo. As soon as we got here, the man vanished. But I know where his wife is staying, and I'm sure he'll come back to her. What are we going to do about this, Kitwana?"

She crossed her arms and waited, having given him the power, but also the unavoidable duty, to reply.

But he looked bewildered and sighed, and ducked his head. "I must go," he said. "I must go ask someone."

"Someone?"

He shrugged. "I will return shortly."

Leaving her in the narrow little room with its British trappings, he made his way through the hallway to the back of the house, where she could dimly see, in the gloom, a spiral staircase climbing upward.

"Do not follow me," Kitwana said. "We must keep levels of secrecy amid the Hyena Men, so that if one is caught the whole organization doesn't tumble into disarray."

She nodded and frowned, because she'd never had any intention of following him.

Instead, she stood in the living room and imagined her father's house, her mother's face. She imagined how her mother would look, happy and relieved to have Nassira back when she returned.

Afraid of what the colonial authorities might do to her family, Nassira had just disappeared, without telling anyone where she was going or giving them no-

tice once she'd gone. She wondered how her father
had taken her disappearance. With a pang, she remembered that her father counted on her to marry
and give him a son by marriage who might then pronounce the proper rites at his death.

Nassira had long passed marrying age. And what
Masai man would offer for a woman who'd lived almost a year in London?

From outside the house, the sounds of Cairo disturbed her thoughts. A thin chant, calling the faithful
to prayer, intruded on her recollection of her mother's
soft, welcoming voice. A noise of footsteps, a woman's
voice calling a stray child, interrupted her thoughts of
home.

Then loud voices echoed from upstairs, men's
voices yelling at each other. They sounded angry, yet
at a distance and separated by a floor, she could not
tell what language they spoke, much less what they
said. All she knew was that two men were arguing and
she would wager one of the men was Kitwana. His
rumbling tones came through, irate, full of certainty.

Something crashed, like a piece of furniture
pushed down, and then both voices started up again,
loudly.

Afraid they would kill each other and leave her not
knowing where to go or to whom to take her hard-
earned intelligence, she started toward the stairs. But
before she reached the first step, a door slammed upstairs, and fast steps echoed, descending.

Looking up, Nassira saw Kitwana. He was frowning like someone who was being forced to take bitter
medicine. Footsteps upstairs reassured Nassira that
no murder had occurred. And then Kitwana came

face-to-face with her. "Where are you going?" he asked.

"It sounded like you needed help up there." She gestured with her head toward the upper floor.

He composed himself. "I was only discussing... er... what to do."

"I've done what I was sent to do," she said. "I want to go home."

"You cannot leave. Oh, you've fulfilled what we first asked of you, but times have changed. Our numbers have been reduced. We need everyone."

"If it's the compass stone you want, I can steal it before I go. I've seen the trunks Oldhall keeps locked with magical seals. I could break into them." Warming to her subject, she continued eagerly. "And then you could find the ruby yourselves. No fight, as the Englishmen would still be fumbling in the dark looking for the compass stone. And you could concentrate the power of all of Africa onto the Hyena Men. Then you could rebuild the continent, present a credible opposing force to the invaders. I could be free. Now."

Kitwana looked at her and frowned, not as if he were angry but as if he couldn't quite understand her words.

"No," he said. "There are... uh... we've made other plans. Different plans." He pointed upward. "He says we must keep the British group intact and follow them, without their ever being sure where we are. He says if we interfere with them, chances are the British will crack down on us and that would be disastrous, weakened as we are. We'd lose and Africa would lose. All hope would be gone."

"What plans?"

He looked cowed, like a beaten dog. Or like a man with an unbearable headache, which would explain the way his fingers kept massaging his forehead. "Plans that he's outlined. My superior in the organization," he said. And then, defensively, "Hyena Men have been killed by a strange force both here and in London. We don't know the force, but we think it's the work of the white men who are afraid of us, as the lion who wins by day is afraid of the hyena that moves in the night." He looked up at her and, despite the force of his words, his almond-shaped eyes looked apologetic, as if he knew he spoke nonsense. "I've been told I cannot tell you the whole of the plan. There is a traitor in our midst and we don't know who."

Nassira drew herself up. "I am no traitor."

"I tried to tell—" Kitwana started, then sighed. "I don't think you are, else why bring us this intelligence? But there are others who do not believe as I do. For now your orders are to keep watch on the white man and his wife, and come back here tonight. We'll let you know more later."

"I should go home," Nassira said, half in pique, half in earnest. "None of you have the authority to stop me. I must go home. My father has a hundred cows and I used to know them all by name. Now I do not know which have died and which new ones have been born since I've been away."

Something like overwhelming sadness crossed the man's eyes. It was as though a large, dark bird had taken flight between his eyes and his mind. And what he felt made his voice tremble as he said, "I'd like to go home, too. But we neither of us can go home until we free Africa. As we speak, our brothers are being killed in Congo, massacred throughout this land that once was ours. And all so that the Europeans can find new places to grow their cotton and their coffee—to plant their luxuries and improve their commerce. We owe it to our brothers to free them. We who can."

He swallowed hard and Nassira would swear he was fighting not to cry.

As she walked to the door, she wondered what homeland in his memory called forth such emotion and longing.

HOMESICKNESS

Kitwana shook his head as he closed the door.

I am Nassira, daughter of Nedera, of the Masai, she'd said. He smiled at the memory, then flinched, as he thought that he could never introduce himself that way. Oh, he could give his father's name and the name of his village. But what would people think if he said, "I am Kitwana, son of the priest-chief Wamungunda, of no people, from the village with no name"?

Ever since he'd left at thirteen to live with his mother's brother, amid his mother's people, the Zulu, Kitwana had doubted what he had learned as a child—that his native village stood at the center of the universe, or that his father was the great priest of an ancient god.

For one, he didn't remember discerning any great aura of power around his aged father's head. He didn't remember his father performing any miracles or using magic in any great way. He lit the fire, yes, and he called the rain, and sometimes he healed cows or helped them to a speedy birth. But sometimes the cows still died and sometimes so did people, despite his father's ministrations.

The village was a poor assemblage of fifty houses—

built of stone, granted, but more comfortless inside and colder than the Masai constructions of cow dung and branches. They'd colonized a plateau atop a tall mountain and there they resided with their cows and tended their fields.

His people had survived untold centuries, sure—long enough to have a language not related to any of the other languages in Africa. But it was not, as Kitwana's father claimed, because some great power had protected them. They survived, Kitwana knew now, because only one road provided access to the village, and it was narrow enough to be blocked with a giant boulder. And because there were both pasturing fields and freshwater springs atop the plateau.

Invaders usually didn't even attempt to climb to the village, reading the situation as impossible. In the consolidation wars of the Zulus—and the Zulus' fights with English and Boer—over the last generation, refugees had been swept up to the village's doorstep. But no one had ever attacked the village. Not successfully.

Kitwana thought the village survived only because it was well protected by geography and it didn't fight or take sides in wars. They only subsisted by being cowards and not fighting. Kitwana had chosen to fight.

"Kitwana," Shenta called from the stairs. His ponderous steps sounded on the way down.

Shenta was an older man—thirty or so to Kitwana's twenty-two. Though he remained strong-looking, with broad shoulders and a look of authority, his age showed in the weight around his middle, his sagging cheeks, his sunken eyes. It made him look like the bulldogs that white men kept and that Kitwana had seen in his travels through England. And, like a bulldog, Shenta could bite down and never let go—of an idea, a concept or a plan.

"Is she gone?" he asked.

Kitwana nodded and Shenta came all the way down the stairs and into full view. He wore an old shirt, a pair of ragged green shorts, and a pair of cheap loafers—doubtless the discard of some European functionary—cut down into slippers.

"What did you tell her?" He had the sort of low, raspy voice that held a menacing tone in everything he said, even the most casual of his pronouncements.

Kitwana shrugged. "I told her to go back and follow the white man and his woman, and make sure they are at the hotel. Then to return here tonight for a great magic ritual."

"Good," Shenta said. "Good."

Shenta was an enigma to Kitwana. Like Kitwana's father, he didn't seem to have as much magical power as it would take to rule over such a complex organization. Yet Shenta was the highest Hyena Man that anyone knew.

"I don't know what you plan to do, either," Kitwana said. "She offered to steal the compass stone and I thought this was good, because—"

"Nonsense," Shenta interrupted. "I told you that if we stole the compass stone, then the Englishmen would know that we're after the ruby. Then they could ambush us and use our supposed theft to come after all the Hyena Men till they eradicate us." He glared at Kitwana. "You keep forgetting, pup, that we're hyenas and not lions. The strength of armies and an organized force is not with us. The greater strength is the enemy's, and they're the ones that rule by day, the ones that fight openly and in full light. We're the small ones, the cunning ones, who fight by night and stealthily.

"We'll not steal the stone," Shenta continued. "Instead, we'll do something so secret that though they know it's been done, they'll never be able to trace us. The only way the Europeans would then be able to bring justice on us would be if they admitted their mission and laid out their secret ambition for all to see." He paused as if for effect and stared at Kitwana with something like pride in his gaze. "We'll set a magical bind onto the Europeans. And then we'll be able to follow them without their knowing we're following."

"A bind?" Kitwana asked. His headache was worse, pounding in thick pulses, almost visible like a smoking fire beneath his vision. He must have heard wrong.

Magical binds were dark magic, illegal in most of the civilized and, for that matter, the uncivilized world. A magical bind was an invasion of someone else's mind, stripping it of its natural defenses, a layer of what made them individuals. While it allowed the setter to follow the recipient everywhere, it also allowed him to enter that mind, to take it over, to erase it, to make it his. It made the victim little more than a walking corpse with little awareness of himself. Someone under a magical bind would eventually become the helpless slave of the person or group who'd set it.

Among the Zulus, the setting of magical binds was punishable by death. And even in Kitwana's village, it was the only death sentence that Kitwana ever remembered his father supporting. Kitwana's father had disdained the use of force to punish theft, or murder, or even genocide, and had been known to offer refuge on his mountain to deposed tyrants and infamous killers. Yet he had turned away a witch doctor accused of mind-binding his wife. And he'd told Kitwana such people deserved to die because what they did to their victims was worse than death and it reduced the victim to something nonhuman.

Kitwana's father said that the binds were dangerous to those who set them, too. They made the setter feel superior and forget the common ties that bound all humanity. Besides, if someone set a bind and the enemy somehow had been forewarned, the attack could be reversed, and the bind-setter could find himself the victim. And the Englishmen were cunning enough they might somehow have anticipated this move. Or something might. Something was going around killing Hyena Men. Something was stronger than they were.

"Binds are illegal," Kitwana said weakly.

Shenta laughed. "It is also illegal, or it should be, to murder our people and enslave our children, but they have done it. Don't be a fool, Kitwana. We do not have enough Hyena Men—even if we called our members from the whole world—to follow these Englishmen unnoticed. But we do have enough power to set a bind on them, and then half a dozen of us can follow them."

Kitwana shook his head, but didn't voice an objection. He couldn't think of an objection or anything else through his headache. And his father's face, in his

mind, looked sorrowful and filled with gentle reproach.

"Now what? You disapprove of my plan, Kitwana?"
Shenta squared his shoulders, looking every bit like a
warrior facing a challenge.

Kitwana sighed. "No," he said. "Yes, but— No. I
have a headache. I can't think clearly."

Shenta grinned, displaying eerily even teeth.
"You're not meant to think, only do the will of the
Hyena Men. Now mind-summon all our members in
Cairo. We'll need full strength to place this bind. And
watch for the enemy."

Kitwana started to open his mouth to say something, he didn't know what. But Shenta had already
turned his back and headed up the stairs.

Kitwana sighed. If the Hyena Men did manage to
secure the ruby, if they did manage to use it to bind
power to someone in Africa, would it be, as Nassira
had said, to all the Hyena Men? Or would the power
be bound to someone like Shenta and all his descendants in perpetuity?

Kitwana fetched the ceremonial candle from the
kitchen cupboard where it had been stored, and lit it
with a small zap of magic. Carrying the candle to the
table in the front parlor, he tried to shape his mind to
the summons he must send out. But he was no longer
as sure that what he did was the best for all of Africa.

He missed his father's village and the certainty
he'd had when he was a child that he lived in a village
at the heart of the universe, and that his father was
the priest of an infallible god.

HIS HEART'S SECRET

Emily was cross. Nigel had sent her to bed. Sent *her* to bed, as though he'd been her father, and she a child. She banged the bedroom door closed.

Oh, she knew she was his wife, his to command. But to send her to bed like that on their first night in Cairo, with no reprieve. As though Emily must retire before the real conversation, the truly interesting things could happen.

Which Emily felt was true, as she came into the hushed atmosphere of her bedroom.

The pink velvet spread on the bed and large pillows with broad printed roses that seemed to choke the life out of the room with their untamed vitality. Lace on the window, woven tightly and small, doubtless served as much to keep flies out as to provide decoration.

Emily frowned at the large mirror mounted atop the elaborately draped vanity. But for her knowing she was married... She tore off her elaborate hat and her lace gloves and tossed them on the bed. He mustered more enthusiasm for his old school fellow than for his newlywed wife.

And at this, a thought of Peter's starkly planed

face, of his aquiline nose, his vivid green eyes made
Emily draw breath in hastily, before removing every
thought of him from her mind.

Curse Peter Farewell. She'd thought to find an ally
in him. Though never confessing it—not in such
terms—she had toyed, in the very back of her mind,
with asking Peter if he knew of any impediment to her
union with Nigel. Did he know of some school sweet-
heart, some woman without dowry and disapproved
of by the Oldhalls, who languished in a home far away
and left Nigel forever with a broken heart?

She looked toward Nigel's door.

Memories of every plot of every novel that, unknown to her father, she had read in the privacy of her
room came to haunt her. She should know what secrets hid in Nigel's heart.

He was downstairs, somewhere, with Peter Farewell,
having their port and their cigars and discussing those
things both of them deemed too arcane and strange for
what they imagined to be her childlike, female mind.

Let them, because while they were there, Nigel's
trunks were in his room, alone and unprotected.

From her vast experience of the male soul—
gleaned wholly from such novels as she managed to
sneak here and there—Emily knew it for a sure fact
that no man was ever without a token of his love: a
picture of his beloved, a betraying lock of hair, a piece
of jewelry, letters or some other fetish.

She took a deep breath then opened his door.

His room felt cold—not physically, which might
well be impossible in Cairo, but a spiderweb touch
upon the senses, like an uninhabited place. As well it
should, since Nigel had not so much as looked at it yet.

His bed was covered in heavy brown velvet, which also covered his window in thick folds. Someone, presumably a maid, had lit the magelights by the bedside. They burned white and pale behind the jutting hurricane glass. By their cold light, Nigel's travel trunks loomed huge and intimidating—brown leather, strapped down, each half as large as his bed, each with a vast rounded top like a fat belly—heavy, portentous and daunting.

Emily opened the trunk straps and pulled the trunk lid up. Within were mounds of clothes, carefully laid. Too carefully laid—shirts and cravats and coats lay precisely disposed. These had surely not been set into the trunk by Nigel's hand. The way these clothes were laid, carefully folded in exact, symmetrical lines, spoke of a professional hand. Nigel's valet.

The idea of Nigel's having entrusted his heart's token to a valet made Emily smile as she stepped over to the next trunk. It was also too carefully packed.

The next trunk, Nigel's last, was guarded with magical spells. Emily could see the energy of them, running in little sparks along the straps. It tingled on her fingers when she approached.

She'd heard once, long ago, that nonmagicians or those of very small magic couldn't see magical locks. But they could feel them, much more so than magicians. There would be a burning upon the skin, a scream in the soul. Although Emily only felt a tingle, she was not so foolish as to imagine that meant she was immune to them. On the contrary, she knew that if she continued and opened the trunk lid despite the wards on it, the magic would attack her, and if not kill her, at least injure her mind and soul, leaving them blank and damaged.

On the other hand . . .

She ran her hand over the wards from above, feeling the magic as one might taste a sweet—for flavor and strength and efficacy. It was strong magic, designed by Nigel. But it was not long ago that Nigel, in a transport of passion while courting, had handed her the key to his magic, letting her sense the shape of his magical power and from it know and determine how to open every lock he set, how to enter every room he warded.

With trembling hands, Emily wove the spells in the air and unlocked each of the spells that Nigel had so carefully lain upon this trunk.

Why protect the contents this well, unless there was that token of his love that he couldn't leave behind? She flung the lid wide. And there, inside, was a style of packing that looked more like Nigel's hand. Still smooth and still well folded, but no professional touch about it, and also a hint of irrational exuberance—shirts overlying pants, overlying coats, then shirts again. Beneath a layer of clothing lay objects diverse and strange. A Martini-Henry powerstick; a sturdy rounded sun hat, quite unlike the more civilized panama, as though Nigel planned to go hiking through the jungle and a large, round stone, wrapped in the finest silk.

Emily stared at this last item, puzzling as she ran her hands over it, feeling within a great power of crouched magic. She pulled back a corner of the silk, smoother and better woven than her own finest silk dress. A stone about the size of her small closed fist looked brutishly common, a piece of granite with nothing to distinguish it from any plain rock picked up from any street. Yet power tingled in it and magic ran around its veins like blood in a human heart.

Was this, then, a token given to Nigel by his true lady love? Of course it would be. An object so common that it could not be suspected. Perhaps, under the right magical stimulus, it spun dreams of his love into his sleep. Or perhaps it sang to him in her voice. In novels, magical love tokens did all of these things and more.

Emily cringed at the thought. Until she held the thing in her hand, she had only suspected that Nigel was unfaithful to her in his heart. But now she could not doubt, for what else could this be?

She felt a great anger at her husband's unknown paramour. How dared she give such a token to a married man? Emily would know the secret of this stone and drain it of its magic. Then, deprived of the memento of the other woman, Nigel would have no choice but to turn his attentions and his love to Emily.

And surely her actions, though perhaps reprehensible, had at their heart a most proper aim. She picked up the magic stone and stood holding it in the palm of her hand.

The room was dark and still and too hot. Or perhaps the heat came from her shamefaced certainty that she should not do this, that she was debasing herself and Nigel, also. But how could she debase them further than Nigel's unfaithfulness that had made a mockery of their sacred vows of marriage? Still, she tore the velvet drape wide. Beneath was a lace curtain like her own and, beneath that, a window with many small glass panes framed in wood. She opened the window, turning the knob and throwing the panes wide. As she stepped back, wind furled the curtain, bringing fresh air into the room.

There. That was better.

Emily picked up the stone again and brought it to her chest. It glowed softly. Her mind sensed the pattern print of its magic, looking for the key that would unlock it. And bring to her the secrets of Nigel's love.

GENTLEMEN'S TALK

Nigel and Peter smoked thin, Turkish cigarettes, which Peter extracted from a battered silver cigarette case in his pocket and offered to Nigel, who didn't want to offend him by refusing. They sat on white wicker chairs beyond the great windows of the dining room.

Within, the dinner hour wound down. Outside, the night surrounded them—warm and deep and dark. Palm trees stretched into the distance, and bushes for which Nigel lacked names blanketed the reddish soil. From somewhere deep within the garden came a strange shrieking sound that might be a bird or an insect, but sounded like a lost soul begging for release. Occasionally fireflies flickered in the night. Here and there, something golden glimmered at brush level—probably animal eyes.

The Turkish cigarettes smelled minty and sweet, like tobacco crossed with an exotic confection. They left a honeyed, sickly taste in the mouth, similar to what followed a great fever or debilitating illness.

Smoke drifted in clouds around the two men, making Peter appear to Nigel as an illusion—magic-called. Nigel closed his eyes partly and wondered from where the ethereal feel came. Peter did not look immaterial in the least, with his British, rugged good looks, his curling black hair. He had grown up just as Nigel expected—a dark Englishman, broad shouldered and blunt featured, a credit to the empire, a notable example of British youth.

So what was Peter doing here, alone and unattached to any governmental outfit, any outreaching arm of the queen's might? Not a man given to profound studies of character, still Nigel felt that men like Peter were dangerous when their passions were not attached to a safe cause.

Nigel filled his mouth with aromatic smoke and exhaled forcefully, blowing more clouds of blue smoke into the air.

The breeze whispered through the leaves and the wicker chairs creaked beneath the Englishmen's weight. The fragrance of plants and wild growth mingled with the scents of curry and cooking from within the restaurant. And though Nigel knew there was no jungle close to Cairo, he knew he was in Africa and imagined the jungle like a green animal, stretching over the continent.

They were alone in the smoke-wreathed calm outside. The tourists and the locals within the restaurant could not hear them. The exotic city of Cairo beyond the hotel's garden might as well have been in a different world. Alone with Peter, Nigel was conscious of the uneasiness between them, as palpable as the dry heat that surrounded them.

Once they'd had no secrets from each other. Of course, they'd been boys and innocent, their secrets few and mostly pertaining to illegal pets and filched biscuits. Now they might still be friends but a barrier had fallen between them. Peter was not living the life he should be living.

"I thought you'd be in the army by now, old chap," Nigel said. "The army or the diplomatic corps. Why didn't either suit you?"

Peter slanted his eyes and looked sideways, like a lizard spying his way out of a tight corner. His eyes seemed to flicker, yellow-green, as if he'd blinked an invisible inner eyelid.

Nigel could not define in words the exact shading of evasion in Peter's face. But he knew that something about Peter's career bothered him, or hurt him, like an old wound still raw to the touch. Something more than Nigel's expectations had been disappointed.

Peter scuffed at the ground with thick armylike boots, quite out of keeping with the refined lines of his suit. He stretched his legs, an obvious attempt to look relaxed and casual. "Oh," he drawled, his voice forcing itself to a slow and contemplative cadence, "you know, old bean, I was never one to fit the mold. I was no Carew."

It was Nigel's turn to narrow his eyes in suspicion. Perhaps not. Perhaps Peter had never fit in, which was why they'd become friends. So that the two, outcasts in different ways, had made a pact against the blustering flange of unruly English schoolboys.

And yet, for all his strange ways, Peter had the ability to not do exactly what he'd been asked and yet achieve what the masters desired all the same. He'd been the owner of his own destiny, only conforming enough to be left in peace. But this should not have stopped now that he was an adult. He *should* have charmed his way to success and riches.

Peter shifted in his chair. "Listen, Nigel," he said. "I couldn't really join the army. Or that other army of paper-pushers that's the civil service." He looked over his shoulder at the lighted windows of the hotel, as though he feared someone within might be eavesdropping on them. But inside, all remained as it had been—ladies and gentlemen, attired in the best English fashion, laughed and gossiped, quite unaware of the two men outside.

"Why not?" Nigel said. "You'd be an officer, you know. It would require no more discipline than our days at Four Towers did, surely?"

Peter's gaze fell pityingly on Nigel for a moment. It was the glance of an adult looking down on childhood follies. "Nigel, do you think it's quite right what we're doing? What Britain is doing?" Peter sucked at his cigarette like a dying man, then expelled the smoke noisily, as though it were his last breath. The great cloud that enveloped him felt like a visible exclamation mark aimed at Nigel's thickheadedness.

Peter had often looked like that back in their Four Towers days, when he'd tried to persuade Nigel of some theory they'd not yet learned, or to show him math beyond what the masters had expounded. "I mean, the empire on which the sun never sets and all that rot?" Peter coaxed, his voice on the thin edge of exasperation. "Don't you find it funny that an insular race would storm out of their tiny island and feel no qualms over laying down the law and ruling strange peoples whose history is much older than ours?

"Doesn't it worry you, at times, how the empire

works? What we're doing in all these foreign lands, telling natives how to live a life that surely they knew how to live before we arrived here? I mean India..."

Nigel's eyes widened. He'd never thought about the empire much, other than to ascertain that it existed and that it seemed to have a right to exist. He tried to articulate such a thought. "Well, we've done a lot of good, haven't we?" But the words seemed leaden and nonexpressive. He tried to name some good the empire might have wrought. "I mean, we stopped tribal warfare and... and human sacrifice, and mad, power-hungry tribal chiefs, and all—er—haven't we?"

Peter watched him with an ironic smile that was more in the expression in his eyes than in the curve of his lips. He flicked ash from his cigarette with a quick, tapping finger. "Have we? Or have we simply taken the place of the tribal chiefs and bathed our hands red in as much blood as any local despot ever did—only more so, because we don't have the need? It's not our survival at stake. Just our hunger for power, our need to prove we're stronger than other nations."

"Er..." Nigel said. He cleared his throat and looked down at his hands holding the slim-looking cigarette that leaked a curl of bluish smoke into the air. "I suppose we had to crack a few heads to get the natives to listen, what? I suppose we were sometimes a little brutal. The Highland regiments..." But he remembered in time that Peter's mother hailed from Scotland, and stilled his tongue. "Overall, we have made these parts more civilized and brought the rule of law to a people who never before had it."

"Nigel, if you're talking of Cairo, they've had law in one form or another since the Code of Hammurabi."

"Oh, I know," Nigel said peevishly, because he had absolutely no idea who or what Hammurabi might have been, or since when this code had existed. He really didn't care for history or law, or the history of law among backward men in distant lands. "But their law is not like ours," he said. "And our law and our magical science have improved these people's lives. Even if that required some blood to be shed. Surely we did the right thing. You know, white man's burden and all that . . ." He searched his memory of newspaper reports on the disturbances in the far reaches of the empire.

Peter whispered something under his breath. It sounded to Nigel's ears as "We taught them to wear pants . . ."

But Nigel didn't challenge it nor ask for an explanation. He was not about to discuss the ancient roots or inherent merits of native attire, about which Peter doubtless knew a crushingly great deal. Instead, Nigel forged headlong into *his* explanation. "At any rate, there's no great insurrection in the empire now, is there? Pax Britannica and all that. The last great battle was that Zulu uprising put down at Isandhlwana a generation ago. You can't tell me the region isn't better off without Zulu imperialism."

"The region can only take one form of imperialism at a time," Peter said, and showed his teeth in what clearly wasn't a smile. "And yet, we keep troops all over the empire," he said.

"Plum assignments, and you know it," Nigel said. "Almost a vacation for the troops."

"Plum assignments, indeed. A vacation, Nigel?" He stubbed his cigarette upon the wicker arm of his chair and rose in one fluid movement and turned. "Let us not argue, Nigel. You're my friend and I—"

A scream split the warm, dark night.

A woman's scream, high and desperate, full of fear.

It came from above, in the hotel, and the voice was unmistakably Emily's.

MAIDEN IN DISTRESS

"Emily!" Nigel exclaimed.

Peter started through the door behind them and into the restaurant, running headlong between the tables. Nigel threw himself upright and surged after Peter, bounding between the white cloth-draped tables, seeing but not thinking of the shocked expressions of the remaining diners.

He avoided a waiter who appeared in front of him by jumping sideways, and felt his hip nudge the corner of a table. A woman exclaimed in outrage, and crockery broke. He did not turn back, nor did he offer excuses. Instead, he ran with the nimbleness that had eluded him on the sports fields. Following the feel of Emily's distress, he overtook Peter, and ran past him onto the staircase that led to the upper floors.

A floor beneath Emily's, her magical call and her scream both stopped abruptly, a candle snuffed.

Nigel plunged headlong into the fifth-floor hallway where'd he'd reserved rooms months ago, ran madly down the hallway, came to the door with the room number that had been assigned to Emily. He knocked for a second before reaching for the knob, trying it. The door sprang open. The room was deserted, but the door in the far corner, which presumably led to his own room, stood open. Scarcely pausing to draw breath, Nigel ran through it. And stopped.

The scene within was like something out of a fable.

Emily—young and innocent, like the fairy princess in a childhood tale, in her velvet dress, her dark hair spilling down her back—stood by the window struggling with a huge ethereal being, seemingly composed of shadow and black cloud.

The creature was twice as large as life and twice as dark as the blackest coal. It roared and clawed at her with massive talons. Its mouth ripped into Emily's shoulder and she screamed and writhed in pain, though her body looked unharmed. Her power, on the other hand, oozed a hazy halo of leaking magic, clearly visible to Nigel's mage sense.

Nigel blinked, realizing he'd stopped dead in the doorway as Peter, coming up behind, collided with him, then checked his advance with a sudden gasp.

The attacker looked like a hyena, but a hyena woven of shadow or darkness. It was as though all the darkest nights of the world had coalesced and taken form. Emily's bright, shining power, which twined her physical form in light, was in a life-and-death struggle.

The beast hunched and reared and roared, and sought the throat of Emily's magic. This thing, visible only to Nigel's mage-sight, was as much a part of Emily as a heart or a brain. Without it, Emily would not survive.

Nigel heard himself scream in denial as he surged forward. He grabbed Emily's shoulders and pulled her backward, trying to wrench her away from the creature. But it was as though her feet were stuck fast to the floor. She could not move without her power, and her power was held captive.

Nigel took a deep breath. Carried on a tide of crazed bravery—Emily's name upon his lips like a prayer—he forced himself between Emily and the thing. The touch of the shadow creature was like a burn. Nigel knew he would die as the men at the safe house had died, consumed by a magical flame.

Yet better he die than Emily, and he reached for the thing. "Deal with me, you monster!" he yelled through teeth clenched against a scream of pain. His voice came out high and agonized. "With me!"

"Nigel, no!" Peter said. "It's too late. You can't—"

The creature turned toward Nigel and its spectral teeth touched Nigel's face. They were icy cold and dark.

Nigel put his hands up to push the thing off, but he couldn't feel his hands nor his fingers.

Ice and darkness closed in on him from all sides.

He was lost, and Emily with him.

THE MARK OF THE HYENA

Emily woke with something cool and soft bathing her wrists and forehead.

She had dreamed that she was small again and recovering from a fever in her room in her parents' mansion in India. The smell that surrounded her, reminiscent of feverish sweat and burnt paper or fabric, harkened back to her early years and the incense her nanny used to burn when Emily battled some childhood illness.

The longing for that warmth and love she'd known in childhood—but never since—caused her to open her eyes and say, "Ayah."

The word died upon her lips. As her eyelids fluttered open, she saw not her nanny, but a male face, craggily handsome, with wavy dark hair and wide, startling green eyes that appeared to swirl with currents like those in a deep ocean. He smelled of tobacco and some indefinably masculine cologne.

The man sat back on his heels, looking concernedly at her as she lay on the floor. Peter Farewell. Her husband's school friend whom she had met so briefly over dinner, and whose haughty manner in dismissing her had helped anger her enough to lead her to rummaging through Nigel's trunks. What would this stranger be doing in her room? But this was not her room. Nigel's trunks still lay by her, half-open. She'd been caught trespassing upon her husband's privacy. Caught by a stranger.

Worse than that, she was now alone in a room with a strange man

As she thought this, she realized to her horror that her dress was unbuttoned at the neck and down to just above the top of her rounded breasts, exposing silky golden skin that no one but her husband should ever have seen. Heat climbed her cheeks. This man had touched her. He had unbuttoned her, as if she were a common woman of the streets. She grabbed both halves of her collar and held it closed as heat flared upon her face.

"Nigel," she said, using her husband's name as a shield—an attempt to convince herself *and* this intruder that she was truly a virtuous married woman who loved her husband. A woman who had strayed out of nothing but excessive devotion.

Peter's eyes veiled. His gaze lost all expression and he stood up, gesturing with his head toward Emily's other side.

She looked. On the floor lay Nigel.

"Nigel." Emily managed to pull herself up to her knees. Part of her felt a great relief. She hadn't been alone with Farewell after all. To the outside world it would appear that she'd been chaperoned by her husband. But Nigel was pale and still and cold. Was he unconscious? Why?

She crept to him. Nigel had always looked to her like an ivory statue, but never as much as he did now.

His skin and hair, all pale, seemed to merge into a sameness, and his closed eyes, his still face, devoid of expression, gave credence to the illusion that he was a doll, a mannequin. Nothing human.

"Nigel," she said. Her fingers hunted for Nigel's pulse on the smooth, cool skin. But even when she found it, beating steadily beneath her fingertips, it seemed like a distant beat. An echo of life rather than life itself.

"What happened to my husband?" she said in a ragged voice. "What have you done to him?"

"I? Done to him?" Farewell looked shocked. He gave Nigel a glance that expressed all brotherly concern and serious fear. "Tell me, rather, Mrs. Farewell, what you did to him. Nigel found you being attacked and he interposed his body between yourself and danger. Whatever was meant for you took him also. And I have some idea what it might be, but nothing that should have been here. What did you do, Mrs. Oldhall? I must know."

"I?" She shook her head. Nothing she'd done could have caused this. She stood. Standing, she was still smaller than Farewell, but not small enough to feel like a child. She drew herself to her height while her fingers buttoned her collar by touch.

"How did you and Nigel get into this room?" she asked, her voice trying to sound as haughty, as cold, as aggrieved as his had. "I was alone. You were downstairs."

Peter Farewell nodded. "I'm sorry, may I?" He waved a slim cigarette case midair.

Never looking away from her, he reached in his pocket and took out a slim silver lighter, with which he lit a thin cigarette scented of mint and spice. The oddly sweet smell enveloped her.

"You were indeed alone," he said. "And no doubt you thought yourself private enough. Until you screamed, both voice and mind. And then, hearing you scream, both Nigel and I rushed headlong to your rescue." He took a long puff on his cigarette. "Though we did not guess the nature of the threat. Even when he saw it, I don't think Nigel comprehended it. His experience is limited." His expression seemed suddenly that of a much younger person, and sad. "Then, before I could stop him, Nigel interposed his body between you and your . . . attacker. To save you."

Peter drew another long drag from his cigarette. The dark stone of his signet ring glinted by the light of the magelamps. "What were you doing in Nigel's room, Mrs. Oldhall? What magical object did you touch that brought on this attack?"

She shook her head, cheeks flaming. How could she tell this . . . stranger that she'd been looking through her husband's private possessions? And how could she tell him why without dying of mortification?

He raised his eyebrows. "You touched something magical. Some object that excited interest in a dangerous quarter."

A dangerous quarter? Nigel's old lover? Who had Nigel been involved with?

She looked at her husband, still stretched on the floor and looking somehow less than real. She'd married a stranger, and not realized it till the deed was done. He wouldn't tell her anything, even if he'd been awake and aware.

"Well, Mrs. Oldhall, I assure you I know something else is going on beneath this honeymoon, if that's what stops you from telling me more." Peter Farewell graced her with a cool, evaluating gaze.

Emily blushed. Had Nigel told Farewell what had transpired, or not, on their honeymoon? Had he so forgotten himself?

The thought that Peter Farewell—mocking, ironic Peter Farewell, practically a stranger—might have been treated to Emily's rambling about the lives of farm animals made Emily not only speechless, but unable to think of words.

Peter looked imploring. "Only I must know what you touched or did. Else you'll be risking Nigel's strength, his sanity, perhaps his very life. I know you performed some magic. I'd dearly love to know what."

"What I touched," she said, feeling the flame of embarrassment burning on her cheeks, "was only a love token. Nothing more."

"A love token?" A dark eyebrow rose quizzically up the straight forehead. "Nigel's love token to you?"

Emily sighed. This was not going to be easy to explain. "No. I thought . . . I judged from a certain reserve I noticed in my husband's character that his affections might have been otherwise engaged before he swore his love to me. I thought that perhaps there had been another woman of whom he was fond and from whom his parents judged it best to separate him."

She looked up at Peter Farewell. He nodded to her. "And on this suspicion you presumed to search your husband's room? And you presumed to interfere with some magic or some spell of his that he kept among his private things?"

Emily felt the harshness of his unspoken judgment,

but struggled on. "The truth is," she said, "that in novels, such unhappy love affairs often leave behind them love tokens, or poems or letters, or such things by which a woman in doubt can discern if her suspicions are correct."

"Novels?" Peter Farewell echoed in disbelief, his eyebrows arched and lifted.

"I found a rough stone, a common field stone, wrapped in fine silk, and I thought this was the sure proof of all my suspicions." She looked up at Farewell to see the extent to which her revelations shocked him. But instead of shock or disgust, his classically handsome features showed...hunger. It was as though his whole face had sharpened and strained toward her words, intensely interested, eager, almost starving for revelation. An animal look.

"What did you do then?" he asked. "What did you do with that stone?"

"Nothing. I did nothing with it."

"You must have done something," Farewell looked toward Nigel. "Such attacks as the one you suffered are not brought about by nothing."

"I unwrapped it," Emily said. "I held it. It felt warm and alive to the touch, as such bespelled objects often do."

The intentness in Farewell's look intensified. "So you unlocked the spell," he said. "What did you use to unlock it?"

"In novels," she said, her voice sounding small and childish to her own ears, "such love tokens are activated by being touched. I did nothing else. I did not know how to do anything else."

Peter Farewell frowned. Then his look of sharp curiosity returned. "And where is it?" he asked. "This love token you claim to have found?"

Emily shook her head. "I don't believe it was a love token, really. Not any longer. It—"

"Where is it?" Farewell asked. He looked as if at any moment he might lose his temper.

"I had it in my hands," she said. "And then . . . the thing . . ." She swallowed hard, against the remembered touch of the unholy spirit creature, the remembered stench of rotting flesh in her nostrils. She shook her head. "And then I don't know." Bewildered, she looked about her, half expecting it to be at her feet, or somehow caught in her clothing. "Perhaps it vanished. Some spells do when they activate. But why would Nigel keep such a foul thing in his luggage? Was it a defense, you think? A—"

Farewell growled, a sound that came deep from within his throat and didn't sound quite human. Alarmed, Emily stepped back and away from him. But she could not step away quite fast enough. His arm brushed her skirt as he dove past her and toward the foot of the bed. There she saw something glowing bright red, like an ill-extinguished fire amid the fringes of the velvet bedspread.

Farewell grabbed at the glow and straightened with another growl. In his hands was the same round rock that Emily had found in Nigel's trunk. It had stopped glowing.

"The compass stone," Farewell said, his voice still echoing his annoyance. "The compass stone. And you activated it, attuned it to yourself."

"I beg your pardon?" Emily asked.

He held the stone in front of her face, waving it

within inches of her bewildered eyes. "This, madam, if you truly don't know it, is a compass stone. It shows the way to something: some secret treasure, some secret hideout... Something that doubtless you and your husband know far more about than I. By touching it and by being... of whatever bend of mind it was attuned to select for, you bonded it to your magical power. It will show *you* the way to what you're searching for."

"But I am searching no—"

"And only you." Farewell dropped the stone and Emily instinctively had to grab at it to prevent it from crushing her toes.

As her hands closed around it, the sense of a small being clinging to her for dear life engulfed her again, and something else, a sense of belonging and being loved, such as she hadn't felt since her mother's death. Was this why, then, she had dreamed of her childhood in India?

The red glow formed again upon the stone, though it remained quite cool to the touch—a red glow filled with mists of belonging and acceptance. And then it coalesced into the glow of an arrow pointing west and south.

"And whatever you're searching for lies southwest from us," Peter Farewell said. "As does most of the African continent, of course."

"But I'm not searching for anything." Emily protested again, just as she realized that perhaps Nigel was. But what could he be seeking?

As Emily held the stone, she became conscious of a burning feeling on her arm, just at her wrist. It increased steadily. "You may stop that," she told Peter, annoyed, thinking only that he was punishing her for meddling in Nigel's affairs.

"Stop what?"

"The burning upon my wrist. And besides, even if this were a compass stone leading to the finding of great treasures, how could it have caused the dark creature to—" The burning had become unbearable. Emily set the stone down on a small table and held on to her wrist. "Please, stop."

"It was not the compass stone that caused the hyena creature to appear. But if I'm right it was your activating of the stone that caused the creature to home in on you. Oh, it might have found you—or Nigel—in time, but it would never have fastened so tightly had you not been using a powerful magical object."

Closing the distance between them in three decisive steps, Peter grabbed at Emily's hand before she could pull it away.

"Sir, what—" But he followed outrage with injury, tearing at her sleeve, roughly exposing her arm from wrist to elbow.

Emily yelped and struggled to get away from the madman who had obviously acquired a taste for undressing her. And then stopped. Upon the white skin of her wrist, a dark, hyena-shaped mark glowed. Like the spirit creature that had attacked her.

A shiver went down Emily's spine, and she shook her head as air seemed to rush out of her lungs. "What is that?" she asked. "What does it mean?"

"That," Farewell said, frowing distastefully at her arm, "is the mark of the Hyena Men. They have put a magical bind on you!"

A GENTLEMAN'S DUTY

Nigel became aware of his body, lying flat on the thick rug of his hotel room in Cairo. He knew where he was from the residual smell of spices in the air, and the feel of the air on his skin—moist and too warm, like a lustful kiss. His shoulder hurt where he'd fallen, and the memory returned. He'd interposed himself between Emily and the thing attacking her.

Urgent concern for his wife's safety forced Nigel to claw his way up, step by step, toward consciousness. Pushing himself to control his limbs and possess his senses, he became aware of voices in the room. Familiar voices. Emily and Peter. For a moment the voices were audible but the words weren't. It was like listening to a conversation late at night on a public thoroughfare. You passed by in your carriage and you heard your name, but were never quite sure what it meant or even if it referred to you or just someone of the same name. A small, insistent sound joined the words. A sniffing and whimpering.

"Good God, madam," Peter said. "You cannot be crying. You must have known the danger you were in."

"Oh, but I have undertaken nothing but my honeymoon," Emily said, her voice small and brittle, like silver bells superimposed on the roar of a stormy night. "Nothing at all."

Sobs followed.

"Nigel didn't tell you?" Peter sounded shocked

"Nigel? What . . . What should he have told me?"

"Why, what you are searching for. And the dangers attending it."

Nigel tried to move, but it felt as though a great weight sat upon his chest, holding him still. And no matter how he tried, his body would not move. Yet the sound of Emily's sobs, and Peter's voice, rallied him to himself, and he drew his will up through his body, forcing himself up, forcing himself to wake. And as suddenly as he'd fallen senseless, he was awake, sitting up. The whole room seemed to gyrate dizzily about him and his stomach clenched in nausea, but he fought through it to speak.

"Here," he said. "What nonsense is this? Leave off, Peter. She knows nothing."

Emily and Peter both jumped and turned and stared at Nigel. Nigel closed his eyes, but he still felt the room spin. He opened his eyes again and flinched and glared. Both intensified his discomfort and the way in which the room appeared to spin around him.

Emily's eyes were red, and she clutched a little lacy square of handkerchief in her hand. Peter looked pale, waxy, like a man in the grip of a great fear. He came toward Nigel, his voice anxious, his movements abrupt. "Good God, Nigel. Good God." Forced laughter. "You gave me quite a turn. I thought you dead."

Nigel shook his head. He did not stretch his hands to meet the hands that Peter extended to help him up.

"You were asking Emily some nonsense about

Hyena Men? Some damned African cult?" Nigel spoke gruffly, all too aware that the cult's involvement in this must be related to his secret mission. Peter had tried to get Emily to confess what their mission truly was, but she didn't know.

Fresh guilt stabbed Nigel's conscience at the thought that he had brought Emily to Africa as innocent and unaware as a lamb to the slaughter.

"Oh," Peter said. He straightened. He paced away from Nigel, then back again. "The creature she was fighting was a spirit hyena, obviously sent by the Hyena Men. A...a secret African organization. And she has taken their brand. They attacked her when she activated the compass stone from your luggage."

"The compass stone?" Nigel repeated, sure he sounded like an idiot, just repeating everything Peter said. "She activated the compass stone?"

He stared at his sobbing wife with open-mouth wonder. Even the operatives of the magical secret service, trained in magic, great in power, did not know how to activate such a thing. They'd given it to Nigel with the vague hope that between his contacts in Cairo, his training and Emily's strong magical power they might manage something. Carew had known how to do it, but he was lost. They hoped something in the blood knew how to activate it. When Lord Widefield's men had recovered it—through what means, Nigel had never been deemed worthy of knowing—it had been back to its dormant state.

"How, Emily?" he asked. She looked away from him. "And why?" He made his voice very gentle, but at the same time sought to speak more formally. He did not wish to have a marital argument in front of Peter.

Emily blinked. She looked very red—the sort of blush that was like a fever, with great pallor lurking just beneath. She shrugged. "I don't know," she said. A few tears dripped from her eyes, but she seemed quite unaware of them. "I thought it was a love token. From some great love from your past."

And here was wonder that passed all wonders. Where did Emily expect him to have found such a love? In his cloistered childhood in his parents' home, or in his days in Cambridge, in almost exclusively masculine company? "But . . ." he said, confused. He opened his hands, as if to show that he held no weapons. "I never loved anyone but you."

At this, she, too, seemed confused, and stared at him with a surprised look that cut him to the heart.

"Very nice," Peter said. "But the truth remains that between the two of you, you've managed to attract the attention of the Hyena Men. You need not tell me why, now that you are awake, but you should know the extent of the predicament in which you find yourselves."

Peter stepped toward Emily, then seemed to think better of it, as she whimpered and recoiled. "Mrs. Oldhall has been stained with the spirit mark of the Hyena Men upon her wrist. That means they've placed a bind upon her. They'll always know where she is. And if you seek to obfuscate them, they can reach for her power. If they access her power three times, she will be mind-blanked—their mindless slave to do with as they please."

"Slave? Emily," Nigel heard the tender reproach in his own voice, and thought himself a fool.

Emily answered sullenly. "I didn't know. How could I know? What is the stone? To what does it show the way?"

She crossed her arms on her chest and seemed to grow two feet taller. She suddenly looked very different— an Emily Nigel had never known: a reserved, remote matron. Her eyes were still red, her skin still pale. She looked lovely though in no way soft or intimidated. Instead, she seemed as full of righteous authority as Nigel's own mother. "Why are we in Africa, Mr. Oldhall? What is this charade? It is obvious there is more to this trip than simply our honeymoon."

Nigel looked from Emily's demanding expression to Peter's inquisitive one.

Peter stubbed his cigarette hard upon the ashtray. "I think you'd better fess up, old man," Peter said, and again extended his hand to Nigel.

Nigel stretched his own hand to meet it, to help himself up, and in doing it, as his sleeve slid up, he noticed upon his wrist a dark mark in the shape of a hyena. He knew enough of dark magic—academically if not in practice—to know this was a spirit mark, like the one Peter said Emily had received.

Shocked, he stared at his wrist in disbelief.

Peter pulled him up, jarring him from his reverie, and Nigel stood, seemingly through no effort of his own.

"The mark," he said, and held on to his wrist with his other hand, disbelieving. His wrist felt normal, nothing strange about it. But the dark patch remained there, visible between the pale, elongated fingers of his other hand. "They put a mark upon me, also? Will they also make me their mind-slave?"

"Undoubtedly," Peter said. "If they have occasion to reach for your mind three more times. Nigel, I'm not asking what your business is in Africa. I know what it is. I know it's not...a long-lost love of some sort. However, I have to warn you that you are in grave danger, from which nothing can save you except maybe leaving Africa right now. I'd return to London and look up a good enchanter of the kind that can treat ills of the spirit and the magical power. And I'd pray that my path never crosses that of the Hyena Men again."

Nigel backed up under the gaze of his observers, toward an armchair, into which he fell like an ill-filled sandbag. Sweat beaded his forehead, dripped into his eyes. But Emily had recovered and turned to Peter.

"How do you know of this organization, Mr. Farewell?" she asked, her newfound poise lending her authority. "You ask what we're doing in Africa—but what are *you* doing here? How do you know about these men?"

Peter looked at Emily and smiled in wry amusement. "I've been here and there," he drawled. "Done this and that. The Hyena Men are a secret society in the sense that, though the governments of the world know very well they exist, they don't know all their workings nor where any of their members are at any moment. Though it's not a subject that would come out in an English drawing room, one hears about them...when one is experienced and travels the world enough."

Nigel chewed his lower lip as he thought of possible

solutions for the enigma his old friend had become. Peter was exaggerating the ease of acquiring the knowledge he possessed, Nigel knew that. Unlike Emily, Nigel's life hadn't been completely sheltered, nor his experience circumscribed to the safe realm of the drawing room. Oh, he'd not traveled that much, but he'd talked to people who had. In Cambridge he'd met fellows who had lived abroad. Yet none of them had been well versed in secret African organizations, nor in the mechanics of empire. Nor even in the dark magic like the mark now blotting Nigel's wrist. He himself only knew about such things because Lord Widefield had briefed him on them.

Nigel reached for a kerchief from his jacket pocket and patted at his face. The whole added up to an alarming picture. Peter was undoubtedly in the secret service. Her Majesty's secret service.

And he'd been sent here to test Nigel. Nothing else explained his probing comments about the British right to be in Africa or his knowledge of secret organizations and dark magic. He'd desired to know for sure where Nigel's loyalty lay.

But why would the organization test Nigel?

Well...why not? Obviously, Nigel was an unknown quantity, chosen primarily because he had been Carew's younger brother. Of the same blood, they'd said. As likely to impress the compass stone as Carew, they'd said. And then there had been treason done; the burned-out safe house was an eloquent enough proof of that betrayal.

Who else should the secret service suspect of treason but Nigel, the stranger in their midst?

Peter had probably been elsewhere in Africa on some mission and been called here suddenly when the safe house had been lost. That explained why Peter had been so evasive about his means of travel. He'd been here all along.

Yes, it all made perfect sense. It was the only way to explain Peter's oddness. Had he suspected Nigel of the attack on the safe house? Or of having betrayed its location? For a moment Nigel was stung by the thought that his old friend—smoking impassively a few steps away—had suspected him of murder.

But now the question remained—should Nigel trust Peter?

Lord Widefield had told Nigel not to trust anyone but himself and the men in the safe house, but all those people were now dead. Nigel was alone, his mission already compromised, perhaps beyond repair.

He must seek help. Or else surrender entirely, here and now.

"Mr. Oldhall," Emily said, her voice imperative. "Why should any secret African organization be interested in us?"

Nigel looked at Peter, who said nothing, only raised his eyebrows.

"Peter," Nigel said, "you know what we are about."

It was an appeal. He wanted Peter to explain to Emily that Nigel had not lied to her. That he hadn't brought her, blithely and blindly, into harm's way. That Nigel was no more than a pawn serving the might and the needs of the empire.

Peter raised his eyebrows again. He flicked ash from his cigarette onto a conveniently placed ashtray. "Somewhat," he said. "You could say I've been . . . briefed."

It was, from the tone in which he said it, a confirmation that Nigel had deduced his motives correctly.

Peter had been sent in to judge the trouble in the organization and— And what? To help Nigel? Then why had Peter said that Nigel should leave? Was he testing him again?

Nigel wiped his forehead with his sodden handkerchief. "Well, you know I was sent . . . by Lord Widefield. He said Emily and I should . . . You see . . . I was Carew's only full-blood relative, and both our mother and our father are descended from Charlemagne's servant who first impressed the compass stone. We're the only ones they could trace with such blood. That we were ideal for—"

"Searching out the Heart of Light, yes," Peter said.

Emily stared at Nigel with disbelieving eyes, obviously having understood what his words meant. He'd come here for reasons beyond the honeymoon.

"Emily. They . . . Lord Widefield approached me after our engagement was announced. He said with your great power you could help me in this mission. This is the mission my brother disappeared on." He looked at her, searching for a sign of understanding, a sign of empathy. "Remember the legend that centuries ago an emissary of the great Charlemagne found a jewel in Africa that he used in a ritual binding to the great king the magical power of everyone in Europe?"

"Soul of Fire. It was in my primary reader, but expert taumathurgs think it never existed. That it is no more than a mythological explanation for why, in Europe, the magical power follows a single familial line more strictly than it does anywhere else in the world."

"It's not a myth. There is a temple in the heart of Africa and in that temple there lies the remaining jewel, Heart of Light, onto whose physical form the strength of mankind at its beginning was bespelled."

"You mean..." Emily started. Peter stood by quietly, looking at both of them attentively.

"My brother, Carew, worked for the secret service...as...as I think Peter..."

Peter nodded and Nigel went on. "In the present day, the power in Europe has become so diffuse and fallen into the hands of all the rabble that there are revolutions and insurrection all over and violent attacks on the rightful rulers of various lands. So the queen, having discovered among her late husband's effects the compass stone and an account of the discovery of the Soul of Fire, has ordered that some of her friends, secret service leaders, contrive a scheme to acquire the remaining jewel from the heart of Africa, and with it bind magic again to our royal line, to put power in the hands of our most worthy sovereign."

Emily went pale, and her eyes glistened with tears, but she was taking all the revelations like a true British wife, her features hardened into an expression of stoic courage. She nodded once.

"Carew disappeared," Nigel said. "And apparently no one else had the necessary power. Or the necessary type of power, which no one quite knows what it might be. They tried to activate the compass stone, but it didn't work, so they sent me and...and you...Because, you see, to reach this shrine where the jewel resides, we need to use the compass stone and have it activated. Carew had a large enough power to do it. And...and so do you..."

Emily swallowed. "I cannot use most of my power. I told you that. Long before we became engaged." She looked distraught. "It is locked within me and I cannot reach it."

Nigel nodded. "Lord Widefield thought you . . . He thought it would be different after we married." He blushed a dark red, thinking of Widefield's actual words and that Nigel had not actually done what Widefield had said would free Emily's power. "He thought that you'd be able to activate the stone, with the help of some people at a safe house here. That's where I went when I left the carpetship. There was no one to receive me in the quay and there should have been a man. I thought perhaps they'd misunderstood the details of the rendezvous." He swallowed frantically, remembering the dead men around the table, the smell of charred flesh. Their families wouldn't know yet. In their comfortable drawing rooms they'd speak of their boys in the foreign service, quite as if they were still alive. They'd expect them to return home any day. Nigel thought of his mother, surrounded by portraits of Carew, daily awaiting a letter, a message or her favorite son, himself, to come riding back home. "They were dead," he said, refusing to tell his wife the details of the carnage he'd encountered. "And there was nothing I could do . . ." He nodded. "But you have activated the compass stone anyway. Even without their help."

"And got attacked by the Hyena Men," Peter added.

Emily said nothing. She swallowed several times and a couple of tears escaped her eyes. When she finally spoke, her voice wavered a little. "So you brought me to Africa, on this mission, without telling me? Shouldn't you have told me, Mr. Oldhall? Shouldn't you have told me what you meant? You brought me on an enterprise that could cause my death, and you didn't think me worthy of knowing why and how and of judging my danger on my own, the way you judged your own danger? With your eyes open and your mind alert? Consciously weighing duty and risk?"

"You are my wife," he said, confused and lost. "Under my protection. I am supposed to be your guardian and make decisions for you as I would for my child."

Emily opened her mouth, then closed it.

Nigel had always believed that Emily had a better mind than his own, had always doubted what men like Emily's father believed—that women were children. He couldn't believe what he'd just said. Panic at her anger had fueled his words.

Emily looked pale as a woman who'd suffered a mortal injury but her expression seemed to say that men thought like this and—no matter how inane—she'd been trained to obey them.

"So will you take her to England now, the safest place for her, as it would be for your child if you had one?" Peter asked. He raised his eyebrow and his lips twisted in something more mockery than smile.

Nigel, his mind intent on his wife, had forgotten Peter's presence and now looked at him. "Should I?" he said. "Go back to England?"

Peter shrugged. "It would get you out of reach of the Hyena Men. It would ensure you'll live." He stubbed his cigarette out and lit a fresh one.

"And abandon my mission?" Nigel asked.

"Is there anyone else who can imprint the stone to himself?" Emily asked. "Anyone with a strong enough power?"

"Power has nothing to do with it," Peter said. "You've bonded to the stone. While you live, no one else can command it."

"It doesn't signify," Nigel said. He seized now at this opportunity to show Emily that he loved her above even his mission and his duty. "I will take you back to England. I will come back on my own, and without the stone try to find my way to the shrine, and I—"

"No," Emily said. "If the cause is so important that my life must be risked without my knowing, we'll go on." She swallowed again, but now her voice trembled not at all. "I have, through my own decision, on my own head, against the manner and education of a British lady, looked through my husband's trunks, and that way I have imprinted the compass stone to me. As such..." She swallowed. "As such, I think I should follow through. I should help my husband and master," she said, without irony, "and I should prove his worthiness to our queen and help him make the world a safer place."

"Emily, are you sure that we—"

"Quite sure," she said. "We will go on."

"We will?" Nigel asked. He looked at Peter. "I was supposed, you see, to have support on this mission, only all at the safe house were dead. You know that." He took a deep breath. "I don't suppose... I mean?"

Peter hesitated. He looked from one to the other of them. "It was not what I was sent to do," he said, at last. "But . . . if you're asking for my support, for my help in this mission . . ."

"I am," Nigel said, embarrassed.

"Well, then . . . it would certainly make everything easier."

Nigel realized Peter had meant to shadow them anyway. He nodded toward Emily. She tightened her lips and looked severe, then nodded, like a woman taking bitter medicine. She looked at Peter and Nigel with the same cold, distant look, as if both of them had wronged her. "You gentlemen may work out the details of our progress and how we can travel without being followed by the Hyena Men. I will be in my room."

Turning, Emily walked out of the room. As she passed Nigel, he smelled her scent of rosewater and another undefinable fragrance—lilac, perhaps. And he saw that her face was tense, as if she was using all her strength and willpower to keep from crying, like a wounded child who refused to show her pain in front of her tormentors.

"Emily," Nigel said. But Emily had already closed the door between their rooms. Nigel took a step toward it and heard her slide the bolt home. In front of Peter, he could not pound on the door and beg to be let in and retain any sense of honor and dignity. Instead, Nigel turned to Peter, resigned to working out with his old friend—his minder?—the details of how to continue with the mission that he wished he'd never undertaken.

A CONSCIENCE OF GUILT

Kitwana came out of his trance with his hands clenched into such tight fists that his nails bit into his palms and drew blood. Before he was fully awake, sensations came at him—confused sensations like those received in a dream. Or a nightmare. He was in a room full of people, and even half-conscious, he knew what that room was. The tiny, too-English front parlor of that home in Cairo that the Hyena Men had commandeered. Before the ceremony to set the bind on the Englishmen, many Hyena Men, complexions ranging from mocha to midnight black, had trickled into that house, silent and determined. For the ceremony they'd sat all over the room.

Kitwana smelled too many human bodies pressed close. He could feel all the Hyena Men in the room, breathing as people in a trance—or just coming out of one. And he could still sense their minds, so recently joined with his own to form the collective mind and power of the Hyena Men.

They had succeeded in setting the bind, though the actions of the spirit hyena seemed foggy and clouded in his mind. Like a dream, or an episode of drunkenness, or even a memory of a story or a song.

Still, he remembered touching the woman's mind, and the man's, and . . .

He felt as if a cold finger drew slowly down his neck. There had been another power there, another . . . thing with the Englishmen.

Not a man—or at least Kitwana dreaded calling the creature such. Oh, it was human, or at least it once had been, but it was also something else—a mass of fractured scars and cold, shifting power, deep like a bottomless ocean and just as mutable and unpredictable. Something that seemed to meld human and alien in shifting amounts.

Just thinking about it sent the chill creeping down Kitwana's back.

Around him, the other Hyena Men stirred, looking bewildered, like children awakened from a dream. Kitwana wondered if the others had felt it also, that immense power near the man and woman whom the Hyena Men had marked. Strange as it was, it had not been physically linked to them, so it had escaped the power seal. And perhaps that was a good thing.

Kitwana was not sure that the Hyena Men together could have controlled it.

He blinked. There was a woman standing in front of him. He blinked again and recognized Nassira, of the Masai.

"It was him," Nassira said. "The creature."

"What?" Kitwana said.

"The creature in that room, with the Englishmen." Nassira spoke in a whisper, though surely one or two of the nearer Hyena Men could hear her. "It was the same as in our mind talk. The dragon thing."

She was right. The presence he'd sensed in the

room with the Englishmen was the same he'd felt in his talk with Nassira. The same dark, nameless thing had killed several Hyena Men already.

He felt the shiver return, clamping cold fangs onto his back like a hungry jackal. The problem was that if you tried to set a bind onto a creature—or a person— with a stronger power than your own, then you could find your mind emptied into the other's control. You could find *yourself* becoming a mind-slave. And the Hyena Men had almost touched the thing. This had been a foolish idea from the first.

Kitwana stood on legs that felt like water and turned to Nassira, whose mind must be very quick to have followed the same path Kitwana's had taken. She looked as frightened as Kitwana felt.

"Whose idea was it?" she asked. She was still whispering, but her indignation seemed to make the words boom and crackle in Kitwana's ears. "Who was so foolish as to try this magic while yet our enemy is at large?"

Without speaking, Kitwana looked up, tilting his head imperceptibly toward the floor above, where Shenta had sat throughout the whole proceeding, directing the attack without ever allowing any of the men below—the subordinates and the new recruits— to learn his identity.

Did Shenta know what he was doing? If it all went wrong, would Kitwana be held responsible?

Kitwana thought of his father's village with a near physical craving. So what if it wasn't the center of the world? Kitwana knew it would still be his home if he returned, and he imagined climbing the ramp up the mountain slope, and walking past the boys who guarded the boulder that could be rolled to block the passage of armed enemies or sneaking malefactors. His father would come out to meet him, and his mother would cook him his favorite meal.

"Oh, Father," he said in his native language, knowing no one would understand him here. He looked at the Masai woman. "You stay here," he said. "You keep them here. I must . . ." He looked up.

He half expected her to argue with him. She seemed the kind to argue about everything. Typical, in fact, of Hyena Men, even a female member of the breed. But she nodded once, restrained and quiet. He pushed past her, past the other men. Most of them wore native dress—beads and shells and leather aprons and wraps and everything in between.

Kitwana felt very strange in his English clothes. Confined. The fantasy of wearing his native loincloth as he made his way up the verdant slope toward his village was so strong in his mind that he could almost taste his mother's cooking, almost smell the coal fires in the village hearths. He could almost hear his father's voice blessing him, and kneeling for that blessing and asking pardon for the harsh words he'd pronounced at their parting. Yet he knew it would not be *that* simple. His father had *expelled* him from the village for just cause. He'd angered his father as it shouldn't have been possible to anger peaceful Wamungunda.

There was as good a chance that Kitwana would be turned away yet again. Perhaps a better one. Particularly if his father ever found out about these mind-binds.

He pushed between men still dazed by the mind-work they'd done. And up the stairs, trying to go unnoticed.

"Where are you going?" a strange man asked, his hair tightly braided in myriad braids intertwined with colorful twine and beads. "Are you running away?"

Kitwana shook. The man reached for his arm.

They were probably the same size and age and evenly matched for muscle and strength. In the back of Kitwana's mind, not quite consciously, came the idea that he could punch this stranger. But if he punched this anonymous Hyena Man, what would it do? To the men in the room, Kitwana was the leader of the Hyena Men, the only leader they knew. Would they turn as ardently against the organization as they were now for it?

They all knew there had been attacks against them and that an enemy walked abroad, uncaptured and unpunished. They were all afraid. And no one gave them an explanation or an answer. Who could blame them for being suspicious?

Kitwana looked around the room and saw narrowed eyes, doubting looks.

"I have to go upstairs," he said. "My head hurts. I feel I have overstrained my magic. Upstairs, I have some fetishes from my native land. I will go up and restore my power. And then I'll return."

"How do we know?" the man asked. "How do we know you won't be gone for good, gone to use the keys of our power, which you must have obtained in this ritual? How do we know you won't enslave all of us and make yourself our king?"

Kitwana sighed. He couldn't blame the man. All of these things had been done throughout the ages, in Africa and elsewhere.

"I wouldn't be king if you made me one," Kitwana

said tiredly. "Slaves have more freedom than great kings in their palaces."

Still he read only suspicion in the man's eyes.

"He'll come back," Nassira said. She was the only woman in the room. Her gender and youth and straight-backed grace made her stand out.

Males around the room widened their eyes in shock that a woman would have the courage to speak before them.

And the woman, who had not known him for more than a day, the woman who Kitwana was sure didn't like him, stepped up, regal and straight as only a Masai could hold herself. She stood at the foot of the stairs, between Kitwana and the man.

"He'll come back. I'll stay as surety for him. I swear to the truth of what he says."

His head did hurt and he did want to use his native fetishes. He also wanted to talk to Shenta. To ask him to stop this madness. The *enemy* was with the Englishmen. The enemy might, indeed, be an Englishman, linked to this mission by his white empress. If they tried magic again, of the type they'd used last night, it would backfire and they might very well die. Or worse.

He nodded to the woman again, an insufficient thank-you for her intervention, but it was all he could afford in front of all these others. And then he ran. Up the stairs, down the dark hallway and to the door at the end. He opened the door without knocking, because knocking would have told these other men that there was someone else up here. It would have violated the secret of the Hyena Men.

Shenta looked up, startled, as Kitwana entered. He sat at a round table, still wearing only the dingy shorts and old shirt he'd worn earlier in the day. His hand rested on the table and held a glass. Beyond the glass was a big bottle filled with amber liquid. His other hand rested on a small dark wooden box. Probably a box of fetishes from Shenta's homeland, designed to increase his magical strength.

Shenta looked rumpled and creased, as though his skin had been worn too long and not tightly pressed.

He was drunk, Kitwana thought, as his headache overwhelmed him. Shenta was drinking alcohol. The worst thing you could do after collective mind-work, while your shields were still frail, your mind still confused. Most people used fetishes or magic to cleanse their mind. Shenta used fetishes and alcohol—together. It was ridiculous, scary. Yet it made Kitwana think better of the man. If he resented this dark magic he'd ordered them to perform so much that it caused him to drink to erase the memory, then he could not be a bad man. He could not be totally devoid of a conscience. Only a wounded conscience could demand appeasement in the coin of forgetfulness and blurring.

Kitwana closed the door carefully behind himself and spoke in a voice just slightly above a whisper. "Shenta, the enemy was there. In the room with the Englishmen. Did you feel it?"

Shenta nodded, lifting his glass of amber liquid and draining it at one go. He wiped his mouth on the back of his hand.

"We must stop now, Shenta," Kitwana said. He kept his words gentle. The last thing he wanted to do was make Shenta lose control of his powers of telekinesis—as he did when annoyed. Too much smashing of things up here, and people would come

running and all would be over. They'd know about
Shenta, sure, but they'd also know there was dissen-
sion in the upper echelons of the Hyena Men. The
whole organization would collapse.

Something Kitwana had learned, in his brief time
climbing the structure of the secret society, was that
those at the bottom should never know about doubt at
the top.

"This must stop," he said as kindly as he could. "It
has gone too far. If that thing had touched us, we could
all be dead."

Shenta shook his head. "Not all. We'd have over-
powered him in the end."

Had that been the plan? Kitwana stared at
Shenta. Perhaps that was why the man was drinking.
To forget the deaths he'd almost caused.

"I didn't know," he said in response to Kitwana's
horrified, wide-eyed look. "Didn't know it was there.
And I'm glad it didn't touch us."

"Right," Kitwana said. "But it stops now, you see.
We disband before more deaths occur. I'll go back
to my village tomorrow." His skin itched to shed
Western clothes. If only his father would let him back
home. And even if he did not, Kitwana would never
use dark magic again. "To stay together will only invite greater attacks. The thing will find the current of
our power and take us one by one, like a man spearing
fish by the stream."

Shenta looked at him with dull eyes that appeared
scratched and worn, like a much-handled spear or
a pebble tossed by a great river. "But then the
Englishmen will win," he said. "If they take this last
jewel, they will have all the power. They already took

it from us once, and now they'll take it again. And this time it is possible that they'll suck out not only the power of Europe, but of Africa, too. That it will all be gone. Then the king of the whites will be our king forever. Our forests, our lands, our cattle and our beasts, our sons and our daughters, all will be theirs." He raised his eyebrows. "Can you allow that to happen, Kitwana? And sleep at night?" Slowly Shenta stood and removed his shirt.

"There is a vine in my land. The Europeans crave the sap, which they call rubber. They came into my land and demanded that every able-bodied man go out and collect this. When we tried to resist, they took our women and our children. They . . . tortured them . . . Killed them, till we obeyed. They . . ." He turned his back on Kitwana and showed a network of pale-pink scars covering the space between his shoulders. "Those of us who brought in what they deemed too little rubber were whipped with a rhinoceros-hide whip. Many died. I was one of the lucky ones. Or not.

"I escaped. I organized a group to harass the whites. I hoped they would give up on torturing us, give up on the rubber. We burned a few rubber-collection stations. They . . ." Shenta's lips trembled and tears rolled down his face. "They found out who we were. They went to our villages."

He stumbled to the table, opened the box upon it, then carried it to Kitwana with the reverence of a man transporting sacred relics.

Inside, to his horror, Kitwana saw three mummified hands—an adult's and two small ones.

"My wife," Shenta said. "And my daughter and baby son. The children died of the infection after the whites cut off their hands, my wife in the famine because every man was out hunting for the ever-scarcer vine. No one hunted for food. No one grew food."

Shenta caressed each of the hands with a gentle forefinger, then closed the box softly. He put it back upon the table and sat down. "Should we quit now, Kitwana?" he asked. His eyes welled with tears. "What can this creature, a . . . dragon do to us that the whites won't? And is it not the duty of every warrior to stand between death and his loved ones, even if he dies for it?"

The shiver was back, creeping down Kitwana's back. How could he compare his longing for home to this man's desire to protect others from that evil that had befallen his family? How could he preach his father's avoidance of violence to a man upon whom violence had been visited in such a horrible form? He'd joined the Hyena Men so that Africa could be free.

He took a deep breath. "But we can't do more magic," he said. He'd thought it was a reasonable statement, but it came out sounding something between a groan and a whimper, a protest of the soul, not just the mind. "Not until we know the creature won't touch us."

"We don't need to do magic," Shenta said. He brightened somewhat, as if a new idea had only just occurred to him. "You know the bind will tell us where they are. We'll follow them from a distance for now. Sooner or later, they'll want to hire guides and carriers to go into the jungle. The woman says they brought many trunks. Surely you don't think they'll carry all of those themselves? They'll want to hire natives. We'll just make sure we're those natives. And then we'll be with them. Right there. We won't need to use magic."

"But," Kitwana said, "that was what this magic should have prevented—the need to be with them. The need, and the risk to us."

Shenta inclined his head to one side. "Yes, but it won't be possible after all. We must do as we can do, Kitwana. The other choice is to let the ruby go, and all the power and freedom of Africa with it, into white hands. Forever."

Kitwana groaned. Shenta watched him, head tilted slightly to one side, like a bird spying an insect. "I have spoken," he said. "And it must be."

It sounded like ritual, and for just a moment Kitwana wondered if Shenta had been a tribal chief as well as a medicine man before he joined the Hyena Men. And if he intended to be the same again. Or more. To be the king of all Africa.

"Just tell all of them to be back here tomorrow," Shenta said. "We'll pick a group to follow the whites. And then, when they get ready to hire carriers, we'll be ready."

From downstairs came the noise of too many men in uneasy confinement, asking too many questions. He heard Nassira's voice giving a curt answer.

He didn't like what they were doing, but he had no choice.

What else could he do to keep the ruby in Africa? And keep at bay the horrors of Shenta's story? Horrors too familiar wherever the might of European magic so outstripped African magic that it left the sons of Africa defenseless.

LADY IN DISTRESS

In the cold light of morning, Emily Oldhall looked at both men in her room. She wondered whom to trust, or, indeed, why she should trust either of them.

She wondered if Peter was truly just another barrier between them. A barrier her husband used to separate them. Yet she couldn't imagine why he wanted to stay away from her.

Nigel looked bedraggled and tired, his eyes circled in dark, his skin too pale. A restless, sleepless night showed in his slow movements and in the way his shoulders slumped. He had entered her room almost stealthily, and stood by the door as if afraid of coming any farther. He hadn't even looked Emily in the eye yet. She would have felt sorry for him, except that Nigel had told her he'd been ordered to bring her to this dangerous place on a honeymoon. And he'd obeyed. What kind of man would obey such an order? What kind of man would lie to the woman he loved? Unless, of course, he didn't love her.

Farewell, on the other hand, had knocked perfunctorily upon her door and upon being told to come in, had sauntered in confidently. He now stood in the middle of the room, holding a lit cigarette between his long fingers.

"So, Mrs. Oldhall," he said. "Are you ready to consult the compass stone?"

Emily understood from what had passed the night before that Peter Farewell had been sent to Africa as their guardian angel, or their shadow.

He should look rested and contented in pursuit of his business. He was also the only balm to Emily's abraded feelings. Knowing that Nigel didn't have the full confidence of his superiors made Emily feel somewhat less slighted—but more scared. For if no one was trusted and no one was fully in control of this mission, then who was responsible for it? And who could reliably save them from disaster?

"Will there not be a danger in consulting the stone?" Emily asked. Her hand touched the spot on her arm that showed the mark of the Hyena Men. "You told us that if we performed magic—"

"All of this will bring danger," Farewell said. "But I think they will not expect us to do magic again so shortly after what happened."

"What are you saying?" Nigel asked, impatient and jumpy. "That we are trusting our daring to protect us?"

Peter smiled at Nigel. "Sometimes daring is the only thing that can protect anyone."

"But Emily—" Nigel said. Farewell gave Nigel an amused look, then shrugged.

Emily still felt enough loyalty toward her husband to interrupt. "I do not know how to consult the stone."

She didn't know what Nigel had been about to say nor how thoroughly Farewell might mock him. But what good was it for Nigel to speak as though he was afraid for Emily's safety, when he'd brought her into this without consulting her?

"I know I held it before and that it showed an arrow indicating we should go south and west," she said. "Is that all I have to do now?"

Farewell tilted his head as though considering her question.

"You could do that," he said at last. "However, then we'll have to consult the stone frequently, to make sure our route hasn't deviated. I think there is a better way. You must understand that I am by no means sure about how to operate this particular compass stone. It was activated at the same time that the rubies were made sacred, and that was a long time ago. Magic has shifted and changed and practices of incantation have improved, or at least varied. But I've read in accounts of adventures using a compass stone that if you have a map and concentrate on allowing the compass stone into your mind, it will indicate a more clear direction upon your map. At least you'll be able to see it upon the map and often know ahead of time the journey for the next two or three days."

"I've read the same," Nigel said, stepping forward.

"Will it not show the path all the way to the objective?" Emily asked.

"It might," Farewell said. He stubbed out his cigarette and lit a new one, cupping his hands protectively around the flame. "If it was only a couple hundred miles away, it assuredly would. It might even show us a thousand-mile path. But I doubt we'll be that lucky to have our prize so close. If it was that near civilization, surely someone would already have stumbled upon it by accident."

Emily looked toward the window. Outside, a stripe of red cut across the sky in the east. Voices sounded, calling the faithful to prayer. A routine day was beginning for the inhabitants of Cairo.

"If we're going to do it," she said, "we should do it now. Have you a map?"

"I do," Nigel said, and hurried out of the room to his own, returning moments later with a map that he spread on the table. Emily got the compass stone, which she'd kept under her pillow throughout the night. She unwrapped it and set it atop the map.

"Just open your mind to the stone," Peter said.

Emily tried. She felt the spell greeting her, like a child reaching for his mother. Then images enveloped her—a rush of them. Canals and white villages isolated amid a seemingly endless desert. Palm trees swaying in the wind and overarching a narrow canal. Then a large city—as large as Cairo.

At its center, she saw a vast palace, upon which flew a foreign flag and the Union Jack. And the entrance to the palace was guarded by an Englishman and a native guard.

Then the images vanished, leaving her exhausted and confused.

"Where are we to go, Mrs. Oldhall?" Peter Farewell asked.

She thought she didn't know, but even as she thought it, her hand shot forward and landed on a point on the map.

"Khartoum," Farewell said.

Emily looked at the point on the map, separated

from Egypt by an immense desert. Visions of arduous, slow progress, of camel caravans moving from oasis to oasis rose before her. "How are we to get there?" she asked.

Farewell bent over the map. "We could take the train to Port Said, and the Suez Canal to Suakin. But then we'd still have to make our way inland to Khartoum via train or flying carpet. I'm not informed of any such convenience linking the two cities, nor am I sure there is a railroad between those two—"

"Emily," Nigel cut in.

It didn't surprise her. Without looking at her husband, she'd been sensing his mounting anxiety. "Emily, I beg you to reconsider."

"Reconsider?" she asked, as if the word were unknown to her.

"We . . . uh . . ." Nigel took a deep breath. "Er, look here, Emily, can we not convince you to go back to England? It is not safe for you here. I'll come back to you when, er, when all is done."

Outside, the cries of fish and fruit vendors formed a weird harmony of voices.

Emily looked up at her husband's anguished expression. Now he worried about her safety? After he dragged her to Africa and exposed her to danger? After she'd been touched by the Hyena Men and branded by them?

"If I went back to England," Emily said, "what would I go back as? Where would I live?"

"What do you mean what would you go back as?" Nigel asked. He looked agitated, and a high color climbed like a tide from his collarbone to his cheeks.

"You'd go back as my wife, of course! And you'll stay with my parents till I return."

Emily could not understand why Nigel was acting so obtuse. In their long conversations during their courting, she'd never suspected him of being either slow or stupid. "And how will you ever accomplish your aim, Mr. Oldhall? The stone is spelled to me."

"I'm hoping that... Perhaps the ruby is in Khartoum," Nigel said.

"That's not very likely," Emily said at the same time as Farewell scoffed.

As Nigel turned a betrayed look toward him, Farewell said, "Pshaw, Nigel. You know better than that. Something of that magical magnitude hidden in an area that has been under British control for some time? Why do you think that could happen? Would not Chinese Gordon, not a mean magician himself, have sensed its presence?"

Nigel looked uncomfortable. "Perhaps," he said. "And perhaps not. Such a thing must perforce be very well disguised, wherever it is."

"Well, then," Emily said, even as she felt for the shield with her mage-sense and found it there, reassuring and deadening, like a blanket. "Well, then, Mr. Oldhall, it must be very well disguised. How do you expect to ever find the jewel when the compass stone is attuned to me? How will you find it if you have no maps, no compass? How will you return to me when you are also branded by the Hyena Men and you have no hope of reaching your objective? And what happens to me if you do not return? I will be in your parents' home, an unwanted daughter-in-law, all sympathy for me fading as the hopes that I might be carrying your child die. Your parents will be left alone, without either of their sons, and with me to burden them. And, since I'll not be able to tell them why I've returned, they'll think I committed some great crime, some enormous offense against propriety that caused you to discard me during our honeymoon, and caused you to go into Africa to forget your grief."

"Well . . ." Nigel said. "I'll write a letter to my parents, explaining that I've gone in search of Carew. They cannot blame you for that in any way. Please, Emily, consider it. I don't wish you to risk your life this way."

"It is too late now to think of that, Mr. Oldhall," Emily said. She turned toward Farewell, who smoked his cigarette as he studied the map.

"Now, you were saying the sea route might not be the best?"

Farewell nodded without looking up. He frowned at the map. "I believe it would be best, from my experience and reasoning, if we took the train from Cairo to Port Said. I believe it runs daily. But the choice is yours. I believe the sea route more perilous. However, if we go on river boats, the trip will be quicker and there's a good chance we can, by happenstance, get a flying carpet headed inland. "I hear that missionaries often take that route in their efforts. Perhaps we can convince them to give us a lift. Carpets usually have some sort of sleeping accommodations." He looked up at Emily, visibly worried. "If, on the other hand, you choose the train, you should be aware that there are no sleeping compartments and I'm not sure there are berths of any sort. I believe we'd have to sleep in our seats. And the locals call it the Shake and Rattle, so it's not the smoothest of rides. It is, however, the shortest, most direct route to Port Said, and from there the canal boat will take us to Khartoum."

"Peter," Nigel said. "I'm still not sure about the wisdom of taking Emily on a public train. I'm sure neither her parents nor mine would approve of her being tossed together with strangers."

Emily frowned. Why was Nigel talking to Farewell and not to her? If he worried about her reputation, why discuss it with Farewell, who was neither her relative, her husband nor her guardian?

"I do not think my parents or yours would approve of my being put into harm's way, either," Emily said, surprising herself with her sharp words, her bitter voice. "But it cannot be helped."

Peter Farewell looked up at her as she spoke. She did not know if his gaze showed admiration or shock. Whatever it was, it caught him with his mouth half-open, about to speak.

When he recovered, he closed his mouth and coughed discreetly. "Mrs. Oldhall has a point, Nigel," he said.

"And besides," Emily put in, "it is the very unlikelihood of taking a lady on a train that makes such a mode of travel safe from the scrutiny of the Hyena Men."

"But . . ." Nigel looked at Emily and his gaze conveyed greater distress than Emily had ever seen other than on their wedding night. "Emily, please. Would you not consider returning to England? Are you sure you wish to risk your life in this way?"

"Quite sure. I would not doom our mission and yourself to failure in such a way. I hope I'm a better wife than that."

Although she wasn't even sure if she wanted to be a good wife anymore. Her softer feelings for Nigel had been replaced with frustration and anger. Did she still love him? She did not know. Had she ever loved this man who would not consummate their marriage, this man who had dragged her to Africa to complete his brother's mission?

"Mr. Farewell, notify me of the train schedule as soon as may be. And now, gentlemen, if you'd leave me to myself?"

SHAKE AND RATTLE

Nigel had to admit he was excited. The admission surprised him, because had the experience been described to him back home, he would have presumed it would be dismal or squalid. Certainly not something he'd like. But here he was, on a cheap night train surrounded by working-class men from Cairo, rumpled-looking Europeans of unknown provenance and even tribesmen, some in loincloths, some in what looked like colorful tunics, holding spears and staring around with faint disapproval. And instead of feeling scared or humiliated, Nigel felt exhilarated by the unfamiliar surroundings.

They'd traveled through the night and through the day, then through both again, crossing a landscape that seemed nothing but blighted desert and sun-blazed sands. They'd slept a little in their seats and gotten up now and then to walk around. They were walking around now, or at least standing in a clear space at the end of the carriage.

His only concern, through the days and nights, was Emily's view of him and her comfort. His constant attention to her throughout the trip seemed to be softening Emily's perception of him—to such a point that

Nigel dared approach her occasionally and invite her for a walk to the open space in the center of the carriage: a spot devoid of seats, where people could stand and stretch their legs. He rather liked those walks.

The train rocked beneath his feet, reminding him of crossing the Channel in stormy weather. But even in this space, the windows were shut tight against the outside. The air was too confined and smelled of sweat and dirty clothes. Men and women jostled together under the uncertain, vacillating magelight above.

Emily looked pale. But then, she wouldn't have the same reaction of thrilled excitement he had. Emily had been gently brought up, and for her this must be a strange conveyance, and uncomfortable, indeed.

She stood next to him, sometimes stretching a gloved hand toward his arm to balance herself. She clutched her parasol tightly in her other hand. Why she was holding a parasol in the dark of night was something that Nigel could neither fathom nor ask about. He supposed it was one of those things women did, like embroidering cushions: activities that must satisfy some profound need for ritual, but which left men—and all those not initiated in the feminine rites—baffled.

She wore a dark dress of some sturdy fabric that should make her look governessy and unremarkable. Instead it highlighted her exotic beauty. Nigel asked himself how Peter could possibly think she'd go unnoticed, here or anywhere else. Hers was the type of beauty that men must stare at and remember.

"Emily," Nigel started, whispering in her ear,

breathing in her scent, feeling more in love with her than ever. "Emily, I meant to tell you—"

"Nigel?" she asked, turning her dark blue eyes toward him. It was the first time she called him by his given name since she'd found the true purpose of their travel.

She'd pulled her hair back severely from her face, but all that did was reveal her delicately sculpted features and make her sapphire eyes all the more startling. And the dark dress and hat she'd chosen for this arduous travel made her skin appear all the more golden, her unlined face all the younger. Nigel stood by her, interposing his body between hers and the bodies of those pressed all around.

"Emily, I meant to tell you . . ." He reached for her hands and she let him hold them, warm and soft, between his. "I regret not telling you about . . ." He looked around, making sure no one else was near enough to hear him.

There were a few natives, but not too close. Indeed, the only one close enough to them was Peter, who had walked after them, doubtless moved by a wish to guard the woman he referred to as *the lovely Mrs. Oldhall.*

"Only loyalty to country and queen," Nigel went on, "kept me from telling you what our true mission was. And yet I think it was an error, and I beg your pardon."

Emily looked at him, and for a moment her eyes seemed full of wonder. "I believe you, Nigel," she said.

Nigel's heart swelled. He wished he could take Emily in his arms, right here and now, and reassure

ier of his regard, but he didn't know what to do. So he
ust smiled at her, and she at him, and then they both
urned away. Emily looked down, and Nigel looked
around, slightly embarrassed for letting his affection
show in public in such a way.

He stared at Peter, not knowing where else to look.
Besides, Peter was acting oddly. He seemed to glance
about with an anxious expression that Nigel didn't
think would either endear them to their cabin mates
nor help keep their presence here secret. And he had
coughed once or twice, and looked distinctly unwell,
as though his stomach hurt him. Nigel hoped that
Peter was not about to fall ill now.

"This is not as bad as I expected," Nigel said, and
smiled at Emily, who blushed and looked away again.
"I had thought the trip would be more uncomfortable.
But it's jolly good fun, really. All these people . . ." He
spoke in a half whisper, looking around, though he was
sure that no more than one person in ten in this conveyance would understand even the rudiments of
English. "Do you wonder where they're going, Emily?
What they're doing?"

As he spoke, he looked curiously at the man nearest him, a tribesman wearing what appeared to be a
toga made entirely of some spotted pelt. Leopard?
Had the man hunted the beast? Nigel tried to imagine
hunting a beast and making clothing from it, but he
could not. Oh, sure, he'd participated in fox hunts,
but those were orchestrated, polite affairs. And no
Englishman in living memory had torn the bloody pelt
off the poor beast and draped it, gory and barbarous,
about himself. At least no Englishman that Nigel
would acknowledge.

Even Nigel's infrequent trips to the more run-down parts of Cambridge had not prepared him for a life this different from his own. He wondered what it would be like to be the tribesman with his sharp spear and his pelt. Nigel could never imagine going up against a wild beast, hand against claw, anger against tooth. Unless, of course—he cast a look at Emily, standing beside him, lovely and sweet—unless Emily were in any way threatened

He emerged from devout contemplation of his wife to find Peter staring past him, glowering with visible distaste at something at the back of the carriage.

Worried that somehow the enemy would find them, afraid of looking back and seeing a contingent of men in hyena skins, Nigel followed his gaze. At the back, pressed in a tight group that looked somehow defensive, were ten or fifteen English soldiers in distinctive red coats. Carrying their rifles, they huddled together and looked around with just the same kind of hostile glance that Peter was giving them. Two of the young men wore white bandages, one around his head, the other around his arm. The bandages looked grimy, and were dark with bloodstains.

Looking back at Peter, he realized that Peter's glare was not so much hatred or hostility as a confused mixture of annoyance and pity.

He looked away from Peter and toward Emily again. "It is not so bad, my dear, is it? Not so bad as you expected?"

She tilted her head slightly, as though considering. Then she smiled a little. "Not so bad," she said. "Probably not so bad as it will be once we arrive, and

have to brave the jungle with beaters and carriers."
She shivered.

"But it is exciting, too," Nigel said. He held on to
her arm, reassured that she'd smiled at him. "It will
just be an adventure. Something to tell our grandchil-
dren about."

The train rocked and rattled. People held on,
steadying themselves by holding on to straps affixed
to the ceiling. Their bodies swayed with the train, as
though they'd been long accustomed to this mode of
transportation. Their conversations mingled many
languages, a mélange of nationalities.

"Look at that group of soldiers in the corner,"
Nigel said. "How young they are! Probably no more
than seventeen, eighteen. And here they are, in a
strange land, doing their duty for the empire."

Emily turned to look and Nigel looked toward
where Peter had been standing, but he was not there
anymore, having been swallowed by the mass of bodies pressing close. With his black hair, he was not
as immediately obvious in this crowd as a blond
Englishman might have been. Yet Nigel would have
thought that Peter was tall enough to stand above all
others. Of course, the space was lit only by a couple of
cheap, vacillating magelights, which must have been
cast off by some more upscale enterprise. They projected a faint, waxy glow that left lots of dark corners
and secret places.

He looked toward their seats, across the carriage,
but they remained empty. Seats were by number only
and conductors walked along the train at intervals,
ready to tear from his seat anyone who had one of the

cheaper standing tickets and who should be so foolish
as to occupy another's place.

Nigel squinted against the shadows, but he still
could not discern Peter. He turned back to Emily.
"And look, those Arabs there," he pointed to some
men in caftans, near the front of the carriage. "I believe that one is a conductor, a ticket inspector, one of
the company men. See that badge on his tunic? Probably every three days he does this route, back and
forth. Does he have a wife in Cairo or Port Said? Or
one in each place?"

Emily giggled and Nigel relaxed. This reminded
him of their courting days, when he'd walked with
Emily and talked to her of everything and anything,
including what he imagined and what he thought.
Things he'd never told anyone else.

"How would it be to be him?" Nigel asked. "How
would it be to traverse these great distances every day,
and to live in two countries, two cultures? What a distance there must be between Khartoum and Cairo, in
mode of living, not just land."

Suddenly the train lurched, like an animal leaping.

The door to the carriage—a sliding door opposite
them on the other side—flew open. Women screamed,
men cursed. As the carriage lurched upon the narrow
track, everyone seemed about to slide out the door,
but someone—one of the stout Arabs from the front—
launched himself at it, pushing over and around and
through groups of people. He reached for the door and
brought it closed.

"Nothing to worry about," he said in Arabic, obviously disregarding the fact that not everyone on the
train spoke that language. "The latch gives some

times." The noise level in the carriage increased, but it was reassuring noise, as those who understood Arabic translated the conductor's words to those who didn't.

"He says the latch gives sometimes," Nigel told Emily.

Emily smiled. "Very exciting, Nigel, but—"

The carriage rocked under them again, as the spells faltered. A woman screamed. A baby, until now invisible in the crowd and the gloom, let loose with a piercing wail.

The carriage trembled, then the train stopped and rocked in place, first to one side, and then to the other, then started to tilt dangerously toward its left side.

"The moving spell," Nigel said, while at the back of his mind he tried to calculate his chance of fixing it by the power of his magic alone till they were safe. Until Emily was safe.

Only, of course, a train required far more magical power than Nigel had. To move the vast machinery of gears and iron parts, it required half a dozen magicians all united in mind and spirit. Emily might have enough power, but Emily couldn't use it. And then there was Peter. Nigel looked for Peter and couldn't see him.

Something beneath the carriage groaned. The carriage's wooden walls rattled and trembled, as if it would fall apart. It continued to tilt on its side, slowly. People crushed against each other. The magicians must be holding the train upright, yet it still tilted.

Emily threw her arms around Nigel. She was breathing quickly, shallowly. "Nigel," she said. "Nigel, we're going to die."

"Nonsense," he said, but his own heart sped up.

The carriage rolled till they were all pressed against the right side, and then it started rolling to the left.

The Arab conductors shouted excitedly, all at the same time, so loudly and so enthusiastically that Nigel could not understand what they said.

"Kiss me," Emily said, her voice breathless, her breath hot against his face. "We're going to die. Kiss me!"

This time, Nigel feared Emily was right. The carriage had stopped moving forward and was falling inexorably on its side. He could almost feel the effort of the magicians to hold it upright, causing it to lurch up now and then. But in the end, it would fall, and as full as it was . . . well . . . they might not die, but they would all be wounded, here in the middle of Africa, with no one to rescue them.

Nigel and Emily slid toward the back, as did all their fellow passengers, crushed together against the broad bench that ran across the side of the carriage, where the soldiers had sat, their red coats vivid in the gloom.

The baby cried more shrilly. And in this situation, for the first time since his marriage, Nigel felt the stirring of unabashed desire for his wife. Now that he could no longer protect her, now that he couldn't even feel guilty for lying to her, he could enjoy her.

He dug his hands into her shoulders, pulling her about, so that they faced each other. Their lips joined, and her lips were hot and sweet. He kissed her and hoped to die kissing her, as the train surged and bumped beneath them.

A stray thought told him they were giving an indecent spectacle, but his saner self did not care. He smelled Emily's perfume—lilac and rose. He pressed her close and felt her heart beat against his, her breasts pressed against his chest.

What a fool he'd been. All this was his and he'd not taken it. Fear for his mission and guilt about bringing her to Africa under deception had combined to make his body not function. Now excitement surged through him and desire for Emily burned like molten gold through his veins. He craved her touch and her feel, the silk of her skin, the cinnamon of her breath. His tongue felt hers, sparring against it. Her hair brushed his face.

What a way to die, in the middle of the night, in the middle a mysterious continent, kissing the most beautiful and exotic woman he'd ever met. His wife.

The train groaned then trembled and, slowly, creakingly, righted itself.

People picked themselves up. Stranger muttered apologies to stranger, in a language the other might not understand. The tribesman in a pelt bowed and muttered something that sounded apologetic to an Arab in a sturdy caftan. Yet the screaming hadn't stopped but changed tone, and now indignant voices mingled with it, in Arabic and some in English, demanding to know what the train line was going to do about this and that—a ruined hat, a spoiled basket of food. The people speaking other languages were probably also complaining, but Nigel could not understand them.

He pulled back from Emily, breaking their kiss. She clung to him, her arms around his shoulders. He took deep breaths. They weren't to die after all. He would have time to show her how much he desired her, how much he loved her.

He gulped the stale air of the train carriage. It stank of sweat and vomit and urine and the irrational fear of a scared mass of humanity penned in the dark.

Someone opened the door on the far side, and a strain of warm night air, perfumed with vegetation, rushed in. Somewhere nearby, water ran.

Nigel adjusted his cravat. "I should go see what's happening," he said. "I should go see where we stopped and why."

It seemed to him that Emily looked at him with a disappointed expression.

"I'm a magician," he said. "I might be able to help."

They were stopped somewhere between Cairo and Port Said, in the land of Kush. They might be in the middle of the desert, but Nigel could hear water running. More likely they were in one of the oases that, like hopeful flags of life in a desolate landscape, broke the parched despair with some semblance of habitation.

If the train couldn't be made to go any farther, would the company send rescuers for them—perhaps a fresh train? With such a scrape-by operation, it was hard to tell. For all Nigel knew, they didn't own another train, and would be forced to come on foot looking for the stranded passengers. But surely some of the people—he eyed the man in the leopard toga—would know how to survive in the wilderness. It was all a matter of someone's taking charge. Peter surely had some idea how to do it. But where had he gone?

Nigel pulled away from Emily's reaching arms.

"I'll go see what's happening," he said. "I'll be right back."

He pressed through the door with a massed group of many men, all speaking different languages, but all seemingly addressing each other, full of shared purpose and determination.

They were, as he'd expected, in the middle of a verdant oasis, so thick with vegetation as to be called a jungle. Except that most of the trees seemed to be palms, and the ground vegetation was some sort of high, thin grass.

"Look out," the conductor yelled in Arabic, and reaching out pulled back three men, Nigel included, so they were more or less hidden in the gloom cast by the vehicle.

"Look out why?" Nigel asked in Arabic.

The man turned and gave Nigel a casual look that, on seeing Nigel's pale hair and skin, turned to a slow inquiry. He removed his large hand with its hairy knuckles from Nigel's middle.

"The dragon," he said, as though it were self-explanatory.

"Dragon?" Nigel asked.

Both the other men started babbling. One of them spoke a dialect of Arabic from which Nigel could only understand the stray word: *went* and *look* and *blood* and *eat*. The other one was even less helpful. He was a tribesman from deeper into Africa, with dark skin and kinky hair clipped close to his oval-domed head. He spoke just as fast and animatedly as the Arab, moving his long-fingered hands for emphasis, but in a language that Nigel could not begin to fathom. And he punctuated his jabbering with pointing toward the edge of the woods with his short lance.

"Bloody hell," Nigel said, and immediately repented of the cursing, looking over his shoulder to ensure no women or children had heard it.

Thankfully, another stout Arab behaving with the authority of a railway employee was at the open door to the carriage, forcibly holding the passengers inside and haranguing them in Arabic and broken English.

Nigel looked at the other two men cowering in the darkness outside the carriage, clinging to its shadow for cover. Dragon? There were no dragons in Africa, though there might be beasts that looked like them.

He thought of the dragon that had disrupted their flight over the coast of Spain. Problems with the moving spell on the train. Problems with the spell on the carpetship. Was a dragon following them? But surely, any dragon that had dared fly so blatantly close to a carpetship and its passengers, disrupting commercial flights, would have been hunted down by now.

And if it had escaped, it had surely sought refuge in northern Europe or Asia, where the natives retained enough respect for the beasts to never turn one of their number in.

Why would it have come into Africa, where no dragons had ever lived? And besides, what need had he of a dragon to explain the failure of the Shake and Rattle's moving spells? It was an old thing, working with patched magic. Was it possible that these ignorant, credulous natives had crashed the train and put everyone in this impossible situation because they fancied they saw a threatening beast in the bushes? Oh, he had it. Suddenly he smiled. He was sure they'd read of the dragon disrupting the flight of the carpetship and in their naive innocence had so been expecting a dragon field to interrupt their travel that they'd done something stupid to the moving spells for the train. *That* would be it, for sure.

Nigel had heard from other Englishmen who'd been abroad that natives often behaved in irrational ways. Perhaps they had been right.

The night air felt close and hot. The train tracks stood in a little clearing that must have been hard won from the verdant oasis by railroad workers with sharp blades and shovels. Even then, their respite from encroaching vegetation had been short-lived. Already the vegetation was creeping back, growing nearer and nearer to the train tracks, shooting exuberant green trunks and twining vines close enough that, from where Nigel stood, he could touch them with an extended arm.

Of course, the problem with vegetation growing that close was that it cast shadows and darkness near the railroad as well, so that any movement, anything out of the ordinary, would be magnified in the minds of the conductor and the other railroad men, obviously not very aware of the reality of the world beyond their tribe or squalid huts.

Try as he might, Nigel could see nothing moving in the shadows of the high-canopied trees or even beneath them. He saw no eyes peeking from between the blades of vegetation, nothing threatening.

"There can be no dragon," he said in Arabic. He tried to take a step toward the jungle and found the railroad man's hand again on his middle, stopping him. Nigel was strong enough to overpower the man, of course, but it wouldn't do to be seen brawling by the side of the train. And even if there was no one to see him, Nigel remembered his father's oft-repeated injunction that wherever a well-born Englishman went, there was England.

"Dragons are an oriental beast," he said. "A thing of China or India, which you no doubt read about in newspapers and mythical accounts. But they do not occur in Africa. Dracus Horriblis is a creature of—"

"Mister. We know what we saw," the railroad man said. He spoke in heavily accented English and exhaled an odor of cloves and garlic in Nigel's direction. "There was a dragon. He swept close in front of the train. And the first passenger who ran out of the train—an Englishman like you, sir—was eaten by the beast. I saw it with these very eyes." And his expression, the way he had insisted on speaking English, all showed disdain for Nigel and his opinion.

But the other Arab shook his head. "We don't know he ate him. Only that the dragon was chasing someone or something."

The other Arab argued, "No simple man could resist a dragon!"

"You saw a man, but I say it was only an antelope."

Nigel strode forward, freeing himself from three pairs of arms which struggled to hold him back. The railroad man said something in Arabic that seemed to imply that Allah would punish Nigel for his impudence.

Right then, Nigel would like to see anyone try. As far as he could see, his trip had been interrupted and he—and, worse, Emily—had been exposed to great inconvenience and danger because one of these natives had read or heard a terrifying news story about a dragon.

He tucked his walking stick beneath his arm and made for the shadows of the forest with renewed enthusiasm. There would be nothing there. He'd show these poor natives that there was nothing to fear. If there had been a dragon, if it had eaten a passenger, surely there would be something left at the edge of the forest: blood or guts, spoor or discarded, torn clothes. But there was nothing. Not even any feeling of a strange illusion spell. And the only other Englishmen on the train were the militia men. He was sure none of those had been eaten, or his comrades would be raising a fuss. As Nigel beat at the ground with his stick and pulled up blades of grass and straggling, trailing pieces of ivy, he knew he was doing it more to gratify his annoyance with the natives than to find traces of something he was sure could not be there.

Presently he heard other men edging hesitantly behind him, but it could not make him feel better. Not even when, from the voice, he realized one of them was the Arab railroad man who had detained him before.

Looking over his shoulder, he realized that another man had taken over guarding the door and his old acquaintance was now following him around.

"I don't know what happened," the man said, speaking Arabic again. "But there was a dragon, save as I'm here and breathing—"

Nigel shot him a glare. He looked toward the front of the train, where the insufficient light of the magelights affixed there gave the train the impression of a felled beast with baleful, yellow eyes. In that light, it would be easy to mistake a squirrel for a tiger, a lizard for a dragon.

"We must get back under way again," Nigel said forcefully. "I have a schedule to keep." Peter had spoken of maybe gaining a day on the Hyena Men. That wasn't very long at all. But it was their own, scant margin of safety.

But the corpulent Arab cast Nigel a dispirited look. "Under way, effendi?" he said, in English again. "We can't. The moving spell has been destroyed. We told you we'll have to wait till a crew comes to repair the spell. Next week, the week after, if we're lucky."

Nigel patted his jacket, pulled his pipe from his pocket and filled it with tobacco, while thinking that at any rate the spell had broken. But then, it didn't mean there had been a supernatural agency or a magical agent, much less a dragon at work. And it didn't even mean that it had been done recently. It could have been some malicious spell—the work of miscreants a day or more before, after the last train had passed and before this one arrived. Yet—he lit his pipe and inhaled deeply the aromatic smoke— whether it had been a dragon or not, recent or not, the moving spell remained wrecked. And the train remained stopped. For a week, maybe two.

And the Hyena Men would at best be just a day behind.

ALL THE DRAGONS IN
THE WORLD

As soon as Nigel left the carriage, Emily tried to fol-
low him. Oh, it might be disgraceful for a lady to leave
the carriage and follow her husband into the dark
night on her own. But then, honestly, wouldn't it be
more disgraceful for the same well-bred, well-born
lady to stay in a carriage filled with strangers, close to
each other, and most of them men?

She started toward the door, where she was met by
an Arab who gesticulated frantically at her while
spewing forth a barrage of Arabic—amid which, now
and then, a single English word emerged.

"Dragon," the man said. And then a stream of
Arabic, and then, "Dragon," again.

"Nigel!" she called out. But as she said it, she
spied Nigel, standing and obviously well, at the edge
of the forest and a few carriages down. Even half in
shadow, she recognized his very pale hair, his broad
shoulders, the manner in which he stood and swung
his stick. And recognizing him, she felt that she could
not possibly be angry at him for long. Even if he didn't
love her enough to disobey the queen for her sake,
and refuse to bring Emily to Africa, she'd convince

him to truly love her. And his kiss seemed to bespeak a great love, indeed—or at least great desire. Surely she could use that to tie his heart to hers.

"Nigel," she called out, this time louder. "Mr. Oldhall."

Nigel walked farther away without turning. It was clear that he had not heard her.

A group of other men stood around him, and they seemed to be in a great conversation, though the mind boggled at what language they used to communicate.

"Nigel," Emily called again.

She tried to push past the Arab who guarded the door, but he only unleashed another barrage of alien language at her. Nigel flailed at the forest with his stick, oblivious to Emily's words. Had he forgotten she was in the carriage? And where was Peter Farewell? She looked for him, but could not find him. "I must join my husband," she told the Arab, speaking very slowly and distinctly, as though by doing so she could force the man to understand English. She felt a sting of guilt for behaving as she'd often seen her father behave, treating non-English speakers as though they suffered from some deficiency of either intelligence or hearing, but she did not know what else to do. "That is my husband, there." She pointed a Nigel with a trembling finger. "I must join him."

The Arab looked blank. Emily made to push past him and he gibbered at her, moving his hands rapidly near her face, without touching her. Emily backed up, shook her head, and using her parasol to hold the man at bay, she attempted to step down from the carriage.

She took one step down, onto the first of two rickety wooden steps that led down to the ground. She felt hands on her shoulders, from behind.

"Wait there," said a voice with a strong working-class British accent. "Wait."

Emily turned to see that the hands belonged to two soldiers who stood behind her, one on either side of her. She was struck at once by how young they looked, and the fact that they both seemed to be leering at her. And they were touching her. *Touching* her. She'd never before been touched by strangers, much less strange males.

Just then, each of the soldiers laid another hand on her, grasping her shoulders painfully and attempting to pull her back into the carriage by force.

Emily was so stunned at their violence that she sought in vain for voice. "Unhand me," she said at last, her voice strangled with outrage. "Unhand me! How dare you?"

The younger of the men, who stood on her right, leered at her ever more atrociously. "Oh, a *lady* like you should not go out there alone."

"No, it would be a waste," the other one said, and chortled.

She turned and saw that the rest of the detachment, a mass of Red Coats, pressed behind her, a few more stretching hands toward her. They closed in on her as she'd once seen dogs close in on an injured fox.

"My *husband* is out there," she said. "I simply want to join him. I will *not* be alone. This is very improper."

But the soldiers only grinned wider. "Ah, you know he's not your husband," said one of the blond ones, with a bandage across his head. "You know you're a fun-loving wench, do you not? Where are you from, now? India? I was in India. By Jove, your kind are a fiery breed." As he spoke, he reached for her.

Emily attempted to pull away but she could not do it without pressing against another soldier.

The man traced her cheekbone with his thick, sweat-slick fingers. She shrieked and started laying about her with her parasol. Why did Nigel not hear her? Why did Nigel not turn? Why did Nigel not come? Why did he ignore her?

"Mr. Oldhall!" she yelled with all her might.

And now Nigel seemed to hear. He turned hesitantly and faced her. He was five carriages away, and she could not see his face.

But she saw him start to run toward her, some of the other men with him following.

Through the mess she saw a tall black man with almost classical features reach for her also. Strangely, from the look in his eyes, she felt he was reaching to rescue her. He pulled back at one of the soldiers, but the soldier only pushed forward, toward Emily again.

"Hey there, what are you doing?" Peter Farewell asked. He stood on the step below Emily and addressed the soldiers. Perfectly coiffed, his suit still looking impeccable, he brought his hands to his hips and managed to look at once both full of bonhomie and quite capable of fury. He hoisted himself up to stand beside Emily.

"What did you think you were doing?" Farewell asked, and his green eyes flashed with such menace that even Emily herself tried to step away from him. But he gripped her wrist and pulled her behind him—

self, interposing his body between her and the soldiers.

The black man had fallen back to the deeper shadows of the carriage, but Emily was sure he was still watching them with interest. She wondered if he could understand anything they said, and why he'd sought to rescue her—as she was sure he'd been trying to—while her own compatriots had tried to attack her.

Farewell glanced at Emily, his features grave. "Are you well, Mrs. Oldhall?"

Emily composed the disarray of her clothing by touch, as though her fingertips could erase the feeling of the soldiers' intrusion on her person.

"I am . . ." she said. "Or I will be."

"Come on," the blond, leering soldier said. "She ain't ever no Mrs. She is a fancy bit, dragged about by you two *gentlemen* for your comfort."

Emily felt her cheeks flame.

"I say, you gentlemen should share and share alike," another soldier said.

"Yeah, we're the defenders of the empire."

"We deserve some home comforts," another soldier said, and laughed.

While they spoke, Peter moved slowly so that he was now entirely between Emily and the soldiers.

Just then Nigel arrived at the door of the carriage, breathing hard. He pushed through the ring of Arabs and locals who pressed all around outside, without interfering. "Emily," he said. His warm hand touched her shoulder. "Emily, for heaven's sake, are you well? What did these men do?"

"We just wanted a little company," the soldier said.

"Did you pick her up in India, mister? How much did she cost you?"

"Why you—" Nigel said. Color flooded upward through his cheeks, and he clenched his hands tightly into fists.

"What are you going to do, Nigel?" Peter said. He spoke calmly and set his hand on Nigel's shoulder. "Call them out? They're not gentlemen."

"They're savages," Nigel said, his voice harsh with anger. "Our own men, soldiers of the empire. Savages!"

"Used to facing savagery and hostility, yes," Peter said. He turned to the soldiers, speaking calmly and earnestly. "I still feel you fellows owe the lady an apology." He lifted his hand, forestalling speech from a couple of men who'd opened their mouths. "You must believe she is a lady, and a young and respectable bride."

"Respectable bride taking the Shake and Rattle?" one of the soldiers said. "Pull the other one. It's got bells on."

"Not at all." Peter smiled. He managed to radiate easygoing amusement, as though he were in a party of his own friends, and all were comfortable and just as it should be. "You see," his voice descended to confidential tones. "My friend here is a poor but honest man, who went to school with me thanks to a scholarship. And he met and fell in love with a teacher's daughter. Of course, her parents would not give consent for her to marry a carpenter's son."

He reached for his pack of cigarettes and lit one with his silver lighter. He looked strong and fully awake, rested like no one around him. The cough Emily had noticed before seemed to be gone.

She leaned back against Nigel and let Peter say what he wished. "So my friend, being truly in love, eloped with the lady, and they're here in Africa, avoiding the pursuit of her relatives. Which is why we are in the Shake and Rattle, because they'll never look for her here."

There was a silence that extended for a few seconds, and then one of the soldiers said, "So, a carpenter, uh? My father is a carpenter."

And another soldier said, "I bet she brought a great dowry."

And another, "I wish I could catch me a lady with a dowry."

But the mood had changed.

Nigel tried to speak once, to defend his wife and himself against the charge of having eloped. "But we did not—"

"Oh, own up," Peter said. He took cigarettes from his pocket and passed them around. Then he passed his lighter around also. "We're among friends here."

And indeed, these soldiers were now behaving like Peter Farewell's old friends. They talked together, and Emily, weak with relief and confusion, sagged against Nigel and let the words wash over her.

She woke from her reverie when she heard Peter say, "So, do you know any places around here where the lady might lodge? Because we're stranded. The natives won't go any farther; they claim they saw some beast or other."

"Ah, sir," the soldier with the bandage said. "The bloody natives are always getting excited. I tell you, the only good savage is a dead savage."

The words shocked Emily, but Peter only nodded

understandingly. "Anywhere around here a lady can stay in peace?"

The men looked at each other.

"There's a farm in this oasis," one of them said. "The Great House. It's a farm, really, and the people are none too good a quality, but they keep a boarding-house of sorts for Europeans. And they trade with caravans. A good sort."

It seemed to Emily that her senses blurred and time sped by her sluggish mind. It seemed like no time at all before they were walking through the oasis—which the soldiers said was five miles long and two miles deep—toward the house at the opposite end. The soldiers formed an escort ahead and behind them. She walked with Nigel, holding on to his arm. He was very quiet and she thought she still sensed, in his silence, an anger he'd not express. She wondered if he was only angry at the soldiers, or if he thought that she'd done something to bring about their attack. She did not dare ask.

The soldiers behind them carried Emily's and Nigel's five trunks. Peter walked with the soldiers in front, who slashed at the forest with rifles and knives.

"The dragon," Emily asked Nigel. "What was it about a dragon?"

"Tommyrot," Nigel said. "Pure tommyrot. A dragon in Africa? Imagine." He swung his walking stick out at either side of the path.

"I thought—" Emily said.

"Oh, it's true we saw a dragon. Over the south of Spain," Nigel said. "And, having exposed himself, the beast was probably hunted down and killed by the Gold Coats by now." He shrugged.

"Stupid imagination of stupid, backward natives. These fellows probably read news about the sighting of the dragon from the carpetship. And, because of that, we'll be stranded in the middle of the oasis at the mercy of the . . . of them."

He glared toward the Red Coats.

Emily did not dare mention the dragon again. She feared that Nigel might well blame her Indian imagination.

"Oh," she said. "But, perhaps with our being lost, our pursuers will find it harder to find us."

"Perhaps," Nigel said. "But it's damn bothersome."

Emily thought it best not to speak again. Instead, she watched Peter Farewell walking ahead of them. In the dark, she could see his broad shoulders and his swinging arm, his gesturing hand, in which a cigarette glistened. She heard his voice speaking in a continuous, reassuring patter. And she wondered at his stamina. For even she, who would call herself a good walker, felt tired, her legs aching, her stomach growling with hunger. The food supplies they'd brought were in the trunks and she didn't dare ask Nigel if they might stop and eat. But Farewell walked as if he'd had a good rest and a good meal.

She wondered if Peter would listen to her, should she ever decide to talk to him about the dragon.

Emily was sure, at any rate, that he would not tell her it was only her fevered imagination.

OASIS

They walked through the luxuriant oasis growth for a long time—the soil too soft underneath, the noises of animals in the green canopy above unlike any animal noises Nigel had ever heard in England. Shrieks and hissing and something like deranged laughter, which Nigel imagined was a hyena's cackling, gave him a feeling of being lost in enemy territory.

Feeling his own strength flag, Nigel could only wonder at Peter's strength, as his friend walked ahead with the soldiers, who seemed likewise unflagging.

When they got to the large house, Nigel did not at first realize that they had reached their destination. From far off, he thought they had arrived at some great encampment or bazaar. Huge white tents, some of them lit from within and resembling white lanterns, were set up in no apparent order. All of them were surrounded by milling camels, flocks of goats and greater flocks of brown-skinned children in various states of undress.

Great fires were lit amid it all, and around the fires sat groups of men in long tunics and loincloths, and women scantily clad and carefully veiled so only their dark eyes peered out. And all of this great, unorganized multitude turned to stare at the Europeans who made their way gingerly through the encampment.

It was not till Nigel and his companions had passed the glare of fires and the crowds of people that Nigel saw the house they sought. It was tall and blocky, and built of pale stone. It looked neither English nor French, Spanish nor Arab, nor indeed like any other nationality, though it resembled a bit of all of those. Yet the windows weren't properly squared and the whole thing gave the impression of having been built over a weekend by unskilled laborers.

Peter and the soldiers stopped at the door, and by the time Nigel came up to it, Peter was pounding upon the rickety wooden door so forcefully that it might come down at any moment. The few flakes of red paint remaining on the splintered wood flew in all directions at Peter's pounding.

"Likely he's drunk," one of the soldiers said. "The gentleman within is a good man, but he drinks." He reached in his back pocket and withdrew a flask, from which he took a long swig.

At that moment the door opened, to reveal a man, half-submerged in darkness, holding an old, battered oil lantern. By its yellowish light, he looked, like the house, of no particular nationality or breed. Just an older man, fifty or so, with dark hair and a hirsute face. He cast a half-amused, half-despairing glance at the soldiers around the door.

"Ah, no," he said. "Did the Bedouins, the Berbers or some other native do something to offend Her Majesty the queen again? I heard no rumors of it, and no big party afterwards, so there could be nothing to it. Maybe they pilfered from some caravan, but what does it signify? And now you'll stay in my house and tomorrow they'll all be angry at me, and . . ." His accent sounded like a composite of the whole empire, a snapshot of all the hot spots of India and China, of Africa and Britain itself. It was, Nigel reflected, an accent on which the sun never set.

All the soldiers took off their caps and held them in their hands. They looked uncommonly like schoolboys being chastised by a stern schoolmarm.

"Well, sor," the one nearest the door said. "We were on our way to Port Said. But the train was attacked, or broke down, or something. Maybe some of the Moran, in their warrior camp, cast a spell to interfere with the train's moving spell. We don't know. But the train almost derailed and it will be days before it can progress. And there are these gentlemen and this lady stranded here." He gestured toward Peter, Nigel and Emily. "They need a place to lay their heads and a caravan amid which to make their way to Khartoum, Mr. Martin, and if you'd be so kind . . ."

The presumed Mr. Martin lifted his lantern, and revealed even more of a confused ancestry than Nigel had already suspected from the man's nondescript features, his strange accent. The yellowish oil light shone on his sharp nose, which might be French; his pale blue, bulging eyes, which might well be British; his straight, thin lips, possibly German; and his thinning, black curling hair, which might be Italian or Greek. His skin was a light golden brown, too light for Mediterranean and far too dark for Anglo-Saxon.

He stared at Nigel and Emily, then Peter, who looked—Nigel reasoned—surely the most respectable of the three. Emily was red-faced and clearly rumpled, her dress dust-stained, her hair undone by her trials at the train. Nigel was aware of the dust and creases on his clothes and that his pale blond hair looked disheveled and unwashed after three days of travel. But Peter somehow managed to look impeccable, just as if he'd stepped out of his dressing room and the care of his valet a moment before.

Mr. Martin nodded to Peter. "A railway accident, is it? Does this mean we'll have a never-ending stream of injured and confused people needing Mrs. Martin's tending?"

"No," Peter said. "It wasn't so much an accident. Just a problem with the moving spell. I don't think anyone was actually injured. Oh, some more of them might come seeking shelter here, but they won't need any medical help."

Mr. Martin harrumphed, but stepped within and held the lantern aloft, illuminating a narrow front hall, the walls as rough stone as the outside. "Well, I have three bedrooms and I can put the three of you up. Anyone who shows up later, we'll put in the downstairs rooms. And you scapegraces—" he cast a skeptical look at the soldiers, "may camp out in the kitchen and harass the cooks, as you're bound to do anyway."

Nigel opened his mouth, about to say that they did not need three rooms but only two, as he'd be happy to share his room with his wife. But his tiredness betrayed him. He could not speak fast enough, and already Emily had stepped forward, bobbing a curtsy to the host and walking past Nigel into the rough hallway.

He followed. He slipped on the wicker rug on the floor, recovered, rushed to offer Emily his arm. But

Emily had already started up the stairs, her hand on the banister that had been hewn roughly from a twisting branch like a writhing snake, affixed to the wall, and provided the only means of support for anyone foolhardy enough to climb a staircase that looked as though it had been built from pebbles, randomly assembled and stuck together with barely dried mud.

Nigel tried to hurry immediately behind her, but the host had taken his place beside Emily and slightly behind her, holding his lantern aloft.

"There are two sets of bedrooms, miss, one at the far end of the house and the other two near my wife's and my room. Those used to be our sons' rooms, but they're now in England, at school. The room at the end of the hall is the most comfortable, and I think it should be yours, miss, if you have no objection, while the gentlemen can have our family's rooms."

Emily nodded her assent and followed the host to the end of the hallway, where Mr. Martin threw a narrow door open.

Quite unlike what Nigel had expected, the room within was spacious, even opulent by European standards. Though the walls were just subtly out of plumb, and the two windows on the far wall sat ever so slightly crookedly, the huge bed that sat solidly in the middle of the room. The vanity at the far end and the chair next to it were all made of mahogany and heavily wrought. The mirror behind the vanity was huge, too, though it showed one or two dark spots upon its reflective surface. And the plain white ceramic basin was supported by a fancy iron stand.

"Is it to your satisfaction?" Mr. Martin asked, as he stepped back, allowing them into the room.

"Very much so," Emily said. "I could never expect to be so comfortable after our travel plans were so overturned."

Behind him, Nigel heard Peter direct the soldiers as to which trunks to place in the room.

"We can't provide a maid," Mr. Martin said. "It is just me and my wife and a half-dozen natives, only one of them qualified and trained to work as lady's maid, and she too old and deserving our respect too much to be awakened in the middle of the night."

Emily again assured him that she would be quite all right and nothing lost. She could take care of herself and it put her to no inconvenience, and indeed, she was grateful to find such lodgings in the middle of Africa.

Presently, when Mr. Martin either tired of apologizing and bowing, or could think of nothing else to apologize for, the soldiers deposited Emily's heavy trunks at the foot of the bed, bowed and left. Then Peter, too, took his leave. It seemed to Nigel that Peter kissed Emily's hand too long and smiled at her with a little too much understanding. Yet he fought back his unworthy suspicions of his best friend and his wife. No. They wouldn't do anything so dishonorable.

"I will be back," Nigel said, speaking softly because Peter and Mr. Martin had retreated a few steps away and were whispering to each other—from the sound of it, talk of tribal troubles and African politics. "I will be back, later, for a . . . few moments with you."

Emily frowned a little, and seemed to regard him from a long distance off, as though he were an intriguing feature in the landscape that she couldn't quite make out.

"I am very tired," she said at last, her voice trembling. "And I'll probably be asleep before my head ever touches the pillow."

"I understand," Nigel said, though indeed he didn't. How could she claim to be too tired for his visit? "I just want your company for a few moments. And you are my wife."

Something flickered in Emily's blue eyes, something Nigel couldn't quite understand. She bowed to him, the briefest of bows, and then arched her eyebrows high as she smiled. "Indeed," she said. "I am your lawfully wedded wife."

Reassured she understood and consented, Nigel smiled at Emily and bowed over her hand, kissing it briefly but with an intensity he hoped would convey his true feelings. Then Nigel walked out of the room, following Peter and Mr. Martin, sure that he was understood and that Emily waited for him with as much longing, body and soul, as he had to get back to her. To claim her, finally, as his own, forever.

His mind and heart were equally divided between elation, anticipation and a fear that his body would betray him once more. But no. The worst had happened—the Hyena Men and their brand, and the train wreck. And yet they remained alive. Even here, in the middle of the desert, they'd found adequate, civilized shelter. Nigel was starting to believe that a providential spirit hovered over them, easing their way through every trouble. He was starting to believe it would all turn out well after all. And Emily now knew what they were about. And he'd somehow manage to screw his courage to the sticking point and to behave as a man should to her, no matter how much it might shock her. She was his wife, he told himself. Making love to her could not hurt her. And tonight he would let no unworthy fear stand in the way of his passion. Of his love.

In this frame of mind he allowed himself to be shown to a room at the other end of the corridor and across from the room assigned to Peter.

These rooms were smaller than Emily's, and now Nigel understood why Mr. Martin had assigned the farthest one to Emily—it was his gallantry and his way of assuring that the most fragile member of the expedition was allowed the greatest comfort.

The rooms the men got were also homier, with a narrow bed apiece, each bed plain and without ornamentation, looking as though headboard and footboard both were carved of raw wood. Upon each bed was a coverlet in a strange print that might have been local homespun. On the wall of Nigel's room, a native mask grinned down at him.

He could feel the magic from it, a protective charm that seemed to radiate golden warmth.

"It belongs to my son Jonas," Mr. Martin said. "He was friends with the Masai down in Kenya, where we used to live. He became close to a few of their young men the same age. Still is, for all I know. In early childhood, one of the Masai holy men had this made to protect Jonas from evil influences and were-creatures, they said. He couldn't take it to school in England, of course—he would get an awful ribbing. So he left it behind for when he returns. And he will return. Loves Africa, that one, more than his brother ever will."

And with that, the proud father cast an approving

glance at the grinning mask and turned to leave the room. Peter followed him.

Alone after the door closed, Nigel noticed that his trunks had been brought to this room and placed at the end of the bed, just like Emily's. The one containing the compass stone remained sealed and, from the light shining around the seals, inviolate. Nigel knew he probably should check it, but right then he had more urgent business. He tore into the trunk that contained his clothing, opening its fastening with eager hands. He must change into his dressing gown, and he must make himself presentable for Emily. The stand at the far end of the room contained a plain ceramic basin, which held a bit of clear water, with more water in a porcelain jar beside the stand.

This, with a bit of soap from his luggage, and his razor, Nigel used to make himself as clean and civilized-looking as he could under the circumstances. Though their marriage might be consummated in wild Africa, he still wanted Emily to think of him as that tender, gentle man she had married in England.

His hands trembling with fear of shocking her—of hurting her—he undressed and put on his sleeping shirt and his dressing gown. Then he started down the hallway.

It was dark and he did not bring his magelight with him. He assumed that Mr. Martin was none too sure what Nigel's relationship with Emily was, and he was hardly in the mood to have to explain that no impropriety was being committed.

But the hallway was straight, and though filled with shadows and smelling strangely of the smoke, cooking and camel dung from the surrounding encampment—

as well as an unknown, sweet animal smell that Nigel couldn't quite place—it was not hard at all to find one's way across it.

From downstairs came the sound of the soldiers' voices, raised in a wild song. They joined other voices, male and female, and Nigel wondered if all the other passengers from the train had found their way here.

As he approached Emily's door, his heart beat so hard that he could not believe it didn't awaken everyone around. No light escaped under the door. Nigel wondered if this was a good or bad sign and settled for thinking that, as shy and inexperienced as Emily was, she obviously felt more comfortable in the dark.

Shaking, he knocked on the door.

No sound, not even a rustle of a body upon the mattress, answered his knock. He knocked again. Again no sound.

"Emily," he whispered at the door. "Emily. It is I. Please, open the door."

There was no answer.

Nigel stood there a long while, staring at the door. Could she have fallen asleep and not heard him? It seemed unlikely. He had, after all, warned her of his intentions. How could she not be awake and waiting? Did she not desire him as he desired her? Did she not love him?

He stood there a long time before it dawned on him that perhaps Emily was taking revenge for his own seeming indifference the previous week. But would Emily do that? Wasn't she the kindest and sweetest of women? And yet he remembered how furious she'd been, knowing he had lied about the purpose of their trip to Africa. Perhaps she viewed this as his just deserts for his behavior so far.

Walking back to his room, in the dark, he patted the pocket of his dressing gown for his pouch of tobacco, but he'd neglected to put it in. What he longed for was some stronger relaxant anyway—wine, or port, or brandy. But he had none about him, having assumed he'd be on his honeymoon and not wanting to shock Emily.

At the end of the hallway, listening to the soldiers downstairs now joined by a high female laughter of unknown provenance, Nigel knew he would not be able to sleep without something to help him.

He hesitated for a moment before deciding to knock on Peter's door. He'd never discussed brandy with Peter—their association in school had taken place before either of them was old enough to drink. However, Peter looked to Nigel as someone who would carry brandy upon his person.

Turning, Nigel knocked halfheartedly on Peter's door. He thought he heard a rustle within, but not any answer. Tonight was his night for being ignored, it seemed. He knocked again, hard. The door—insufficiently held by its latch—gave under his knock and revealed Peter's room. Empty.

Nigel stepped into the room, stupefied, unable to think of what this meant. Peter was gone. Where could he be? The room was almost exactly like Nigel's own—barely able to contain a bed and a washstand and a very small trunk, which seemed to be all of Peter's luggage. A fire burned in the fireplace, and the water in the basin looked dingy and gray. Peter's clothes lay, neatly folded, at the bottom of the bed. But then, what was Peter wearing?

Nigel heard the laughter from the soldiers downstairs. No chance that Peter was down there with them, talking and laughing and socializing with whatever woman might have come straggling in from the train. Peter would not go out in his dressing gown. But then . . .

Mute and still, Nigel stood in the middle of Peter's room and felt as though the building was collapsing around him. He thought of Emily's closed door, of her lack of response. His fists closed and tightened, just as a pressure tightened around his heart. No. Emily wouldn't do it. Nor would Peter. They were honorable English people, not savages who gave in to every impulse.

Rage, like a red flood, seemed to build behind his eyes. It couldn't be. Emily loved him. She would not betray him. And yet Nigel had not consummated their marriage. Nigel had rebuffed her more than once.

Peter's window was open, Nigel noticed, and it looked over an immense space of treetops and dark, starry sky. Strange screams and hisses echoed from the oasis and Nigel wished he, too, could scream and hiss and howl. But he could not. He was a civilized man.

Turning on his heel, he left Peter's room behind and went to his own, where he took off his dressing gown and lay upon the narrow and, it turned out, very hard mattress and tried not to think about his dilemma. Sometime during the night he slept, worn down by his misery, only to wake with his window opening, forcibly.

He blinked and saw, stretched through the window,

a long sinuous neck and, at the end of it, a wedge-shaped head with immense teeth, a mouth shaped to rend and tear. Halfway between sleep and a scream of terror, Nigel caught the impression of an immense winged body outside the window, of narrow, yellow-green eyes glimmering, a smell of fire and scorch, a feeling of being watched. Then the Masai fetish upon the wall threw out a beam of golden light and the huge head pulled back and was gone.

Nigel blinked at the dark room. His window was open and the white, flimsy curtain blew in the wind.

He took a deep breath. Another dragon. He'd seen a dragon. But it must have been a dream. The crazed natives with their talk of fantastic beasts had gotten in Nigel's head. As for the rest . . . Nigel would wish this entire night to be an evil dream.

He extended his hand and wished his magelight lit and spent the rest of the night awake in the humid warmth of Africa, staring at the stuccoed ceiling and longing for England.

THE SECRETS OF HIS
HEART—UNFATHOMABLE

There was a tension in the air that Emily could not understand.

She, Nigel and Peter sat around the table in Mr. Martin's plain but comfortable dining room with its massive, carved mahogany furniture and its chairs that appeared to have been fashioned each from a single block of wood. Two black-skinned maids, attired in black dresses with white lace at the cuffs and collar, served them from a buffet as sumptuous as any Emily had ever seen, consisting of braised kidneys, fried fish, beef and—exotic in England, but perfectly appropriate here—couscous.

The soldiers, whom Emily had dreaded encountering again, were nowhere in sight. Just Nigel, herself and Peter Farewell, sitting around a huge table that could well have accommodated thirty.

Even without the soldiers present, tension was palpable, hanging in the air like an uninvited guest.

Nigel's skin had that dingy gray tone that very pale people acquired when unwell. His eyes looked washed out, too, surrounded by dark, bruised circles. He held himself too straight, too controlled, and kept darting Emily pained, wounded looks, as if she'd done something to hurt him.

"There is a caravan leaving for Khartoum tomorrow," Farewell said brightly. "The unflappable Mr. Martin says we'll be safe." He tore a small piece from a large roll of bread and buttered the piece vigorously. He looked as though he was in a great hurry to do something and it didn't matter what. In fact, he looked the exact opposite of Nigel's spirits—bright, awake, healthy. His eyes sparkled and a smile crossed his lips at every moment, seemingly without reason. He now grinned at Nigel, his smile slowly enlarging, a black eyebrow slowly rising, in a look of Mephistophelian irony. "Nigel, old man, did you hear a single word I said?"

"Word?" Nigel said. "Of course. Caravan. To Khartoum." Nigel lifted his teacup, took a sip and gave Emily another wounded glare. Then he looked back at Farewell and frowned. "But why do we need a caravan? Khartoum is within a few days' journey, is it not?"

Farewell sighed and hesitated. "Not on foot," he said. "No."

"But..." Nigel set the cup down forcefully, lifted his hands in a show of confusion. "Why can't we borrow or lease camels?"

"Good question," Farewell said. He motioned to the maid to serve him more braised kidneys, then smiled. "Mr. Martin implied that it's not safe to travel without an escort."

"Mahdists?" Nigel asked. He looked like he was asking something quite different and more personal, his voice full of anger. "But I thought they were all defeated."

"Ah, Nigel." Peter grinned. "You are too good and,

being good, imagine that everyone is the same—a reflection of yourself. Mahdists were defeated, sure, but there are many other religious groups, just as hostile, on the ground. In this region, each tribe is a sect, and each man has his hand against everyone else. We'll never defeat them all, Nigel."

He ate the kidneys with the appetite of a starving man, then set his knife down and looked up at his friend. His eyes appeared to twinkle with a secret amusement. "Have you ever heard the expression: *me and my cousin against my neighbor, me and my brother against my cousin, me against my brother*?"

Nigel looked annoyed. "Of course, I heard it from my teacher, long ago." He fiddled with a piece of toast on his plate, then slowly spread it thickly with jam. "I'm not a child, Peter, nor the fool you apparently take me for."

Farewell lifted his hands up and out, in a gesture of helplessness and innocence. "I never said you were a fool, Nigel. I don't make friends with fools. And you, Mrs. Oldhall, you have hardly eaten. Are you well?"

Emily nodded, unwilling to speak. Something was happening that she couldn't fully understand.

Nigel sipped his tea slowly, all the while gazing at Peter, as if considering the next move in an intricate game of chess. He'd left the toast quite abandoned on his plate. "Wouldn't it be easier, and safer, to find out if the train will be repaired soon? Would we really gain any time by going in a caravan?" He looked at Emily. "Mrs. Oldhall has never ridden a camel. A caravan, by Jove, like something out of *The Arabian Nights*."

Peter raised his eyebrows. "My dear Nigel." He

looked around and saw that the maids were safely at the other end of the room, then he spoke in a voice that didn't carry. "It would be safer, surely, if both you and Mrs. Oldhall weren't branded by the enemy. But as it is, should they get curious, they will reach for you, and we haven't gone so far that it would be hard for them to track you down."

Emily wondered why Nigel had referred to her as Mrs. Oldhall and not Emily. Oh, it was proper etiquette, of course, and nothing she could protest, but it seemed to her as though Nigel used the honorific to punish her for crimes she was not aware of having committed. Had he taken her rejection the night before that seriously? She'd heard him knocking, of course, but after his nights and days of coldness, to want to visit her bed on that night of all nights, with drunken soldiers downstairs, had seemed improper and presumptuous. She felt a pinprick of anger that Nigel thought he could claim her, body and heart, at any time, in any way he wanted to.

Her father would have said Nigel was in the right. She was his wife and therefore his property. But Emily was starting to really think about marriage and her condition as a woman. She had been lied to, dragged to Africa on a dangerous mission of which she'd not been forewarned. Her consent had not been asked for any of it. So now she wanted Nigel to ask her consent to consummate her marriage. Her wedding vows, though willingly given, seemed to have been given so long ago and had been so little respected— indeed, so little reciprocated—that she could hardly consider it *consent* now. Certainly not informed consent, as she'd never imagined that Nigel intended to drag her to Africa in search of a mythical lost jewel. Had she known, would she have accepted him?

She couldn't tell. Though it was only a few days ago, the woman she had then been might as well be dead. Emily could only dimly remember what she'd thought and why.

She took a small spoon and ate the egg from within the shell in tiny bites.

"Mrs. Oldhall," Peter said. "What do you think we should do? Should we wait here, till the railroad is done?"

"Or should we risk ourselves upon the jungle," Nigel said, "with natives who might not speak the language, nor be respectful of you as they should be? Should we go with a party of natives into unknown territory, where they might easily enough kill us all?"

"Oh, come now," Peter said. "We are not the first safari party, nor the last, to come through Khartoum and hire carriers. The very fact that there is a plaza where we can easily hire workers means there is a continued trade. What merchant cuts his client's throat? Wouldn't that destroy the business?"

Nigel looked at Peter, then at Emily. He was eating a slice of toast, well buttered.

In the center of the table lay a banquet of eggs and fried steak, different breads and fruit compote. It occurred to Emily what a great waste it was that the three of them were eating so little. But she rather suspected the soldiers would be eating after them.

"Mrs. Oldhall," Nigel said, and smiled a little, as if the address were somehow ironic. "How do you choose? For it is clear the choice is yours."

So, *now* she was being given a choice? She felt

another wave of annoyance at Nigel. "How long do you think it would take to get the train repaired?" she asked.

"Well," Peter said, wiping his fingers vigorously onto the linen napkin provided, and tossing it aside to get another morsel of bread, "I believe it will take one or two weeks, at least according to what the railmen were doing early this morning."

Nigel gave Peter a dark look. "You were up very early," he said, as if it was an accusation.

Peter chuckled. "Yes. The bed is awfully hard, is it not?"

"Mine was perfect," Emily said, then blushed, remembering she had denied Nigel a place there.

"Your bed is wholly different," Nigel said, glaring. "So the hard bed kept you awake?"

Inexplicably, Peter seemed embarrassed. "I often have trouble sleeping. And often find beds too hard or too soft. So, yes, I was up early."

Emily wished she could tell Nigel they would wait for the train to be repaired. She knew that was what he wanted, and besides, she now slept in a room appointed with such European comforts as she could not hope to find anywhere else in Africa. But she knew this house was not safe. Not with the Hyena Men hot on their heels, and with Hyena Men brands on their flesh. They must proceed as soon as possible. Find the Heart of Light and return to safe England, where— she looked at Nigel from beneath lowered eyelids— where maybe she and Nigel could become a truly married couple.

"We'll take the caravan," she said, after long, careful deliberation.

"See?" Peter said. "What did I tell you, Nigel? Mrs. Oldhall agrees with me, and since she's the most frail member of our expedition, this must mean it is the right route to take."

All color drained from Nigel's face, leaving him waxy yellow. Getting up from the table, he flung down his napkin as though it were a glove. "Perhaps Mrs. Oldhall heard you thinking aloud," he said, glaring at Farewell. "Last night. When you were absent from your room."

Farewell in turn blanched milk-white and gaped, then recovered with visible effort. "I do not have the pleasure of understanding you, Oldhall," he said, his accents careful and exact and painfully correct. "The only time I left my room was in search of bathing facilities."

Nigel opened his mouth, then closed it. "Oh," he said. And it was patent from his expression that he'd never thought of that.

Emily understood what he meant all of a sudden. She realized that she hadn't answered her door, and that Peter Farewell had been absent from his room. A raging blush burned at her cheeks as she looked from one to the other of the men. Nigel could not for a second have contemplated . . .

She felt a mortified shame, a horrible anger. She bit her lips to avoid any words escaping her control.

"Mrs. Oldhall?" Farewell asked. "Is anything wrong?"

Everything was wrong. And Peter Farewell was the last person in the world whom Emily could tell about it.

KHARTOUM

Emily rode for hours upon the baked, dun emptiness
of the desert. Nothing but sand as far as the eye could
see, and her mind turned upon the words Nigel had
pronounced. Could Nigel think that Peter Farewell
had been absent because he'd been visiting Emily's
room? Could Nigel think Emily so lost to propriety?

Or had he another meaning? She thought of the
way Peter Farewell had blanched. Could Nigel have
another reason to question Peter's whereabouts on
that night?

Lost between offense and guilt, Emily rode the
camel through the parched landscape, and it seemed
to her that the desert mirrored her own heart, where
no hope of life or good could take hold for long. She
would not—she could not—ever forgive Nigel for such
a thought. And now she understood that whether he
had another secret love or not, he could never have
loved her. Not truly.

The camel gave off an evil stench and swayed back
and forth like a rowboat on a stormy sea. But all that
wouldn't matter if she could have been easy in her
mind. Most of the time, Nigel and Farewell rode their
own camels beside her and slightly ahead. Each of the

men carried a powerstick of the best quality—polished English walnut gleaming under the desert sun—on a scabbard at his back, and wore light-colored suits and domed hats. From behind, they looked very much alike, though Farewell was perhaps more thickly built and, of course, dark-haired. Emily couldn't hear what they talked of, nor if they did.

In this numb grief, it seemed to her that the journey took no time at all, or else an eternity. They slept in encampments and rode through unremarkable days. She didn't think of what would happen when they reached the city, she didn't think at all and just lived, in the eternity of the desert, the swaying of the camel, the stench.

As they neared the outskirts of Khartoum, the sight of green, looking cool and impossible amid the desert, brought her back from her musings.

They rode into a wide avenue that ran beside a river, shaded by trees, for a distance of more than two miles. Beyond the trees were private houses, secluded within verdant gardens. Though the vegetation was very different—palms and a riot of large-leafed bushes—Emily felt as though she was walking into a European city. "All of this was built in the last few years," a voice next to Emily said, startling her.

Peter Farewell looked guarded and anxious, as though he feared she was hurt. Indeed, Emily was. But why would he feel this was any of his responsibility?

"So new?" she asked, more to appease the anxiety in his eyes than because she truly wanted to know. She looked ahead to where Nigel rode, seemingly indifferent to how Emily might have taken his words.

She turned back to the city around her, feigning interest. It looked new and clean, but Emily had heard of Khartoum well before ten years ago.

"Well," he said, "perhaps not all of it. The city existed here until the Mahdi rebellion. They destroyed all of the houses and, with strong magic, forced the inhabitants to move to Omdurman, the capital." He gestured expansively at the neat houses in their luxuriant gardens. "It wasn't until the English regained control of this region that they encouraged the rebuilding of the city—first by making it once more the administrative capital of the region, but also by planning the city around new and clean-cut lines."

"Oh," Emily said. Truth be told, she had no interest in city planning, one way or the other.

"We'll go to a hotel nearby," Farewell said, changing subject. "Mr. Martin gave us a recommendation. He says it's in Khedive Square at the center of town, where in the morning it will be possible to hire carriers and guides with whom to proceed into the jungle."

"Should we need them," Nigel said from Emily's right side, startling her.

She'd been paying so much attention to Farewell on her left that she'd not noticed Nigel's falling back to her side. She now looked and found her husband staring at her with such intent eagerness that she almost smiled back at him. But then she noted his mouth, severely closed, and his features, expressionless. And her anger flared again at the memory of what he'd thought of her, the memory of how he didn't understand her.

She looked away, toward the side of the road, where a house under construction was being worked

on by Arab men and strong, tall African women, most
of them wearing no more than a blue sheet wrapped
around their sweating bodies.

The sight of women doing such violent work in
such a public setting was unimaginable in England,
and it made Emily wonder what it would be like to be
one of these women, working with their own hands
and for their own sustenance. Emily had been pam-
pered and protected her whole life, but how much had
this cost her in freedom and the ability to live a life un-
restricted by the yoke of a man?

"If you'd consent to consult the . . . instrument for
us," Nigel said.

Emily nodded without looking at him.

"If it's needed," Nigel said, with seeming great enthusiasm, "then I'm sure that Mr. Martin's directions
on how to find carriers will see us right. Indeed, Mr.
Martin offered us such hospitality as I never thought
to find in an African desert."

"Indeed," Peter said from Emily's other side, his
voice full of irony. "And very easy it is for him to do
that, as he lives in that oasis, in all ease, collecting fees
from all the caravans that must stop and get water for
their animals and food for themselves. Very obliging of
the British army to have got that oasis for his use."

"The British army?" Emily asked, disbelieving.
And was met with a nod from Farewell.

"I heard about the incident myself this morning,"
Nigel said. "I believe it was part of the campaign
against the Mahdi."

"And yet," Farewell said, his voice distant, "the result was the same."

"But," Nigel said, "as long as there is magic, that will always be true."

"As long as there's magic," Farewell said with finality.

This was an irrefutable opinion, and it seemed to Emily that it did not interest either of the men nearly as much as it seemed to. She thought that they were arguing something else altogether.

Unable to know for sure what it all meant, Emily felt shut out, alone. So she welcomed their arrival at a surprisingly well-appointed hotel. It gave her a respite from the veiled hostility between her two companions.

THE DUTIES OF A
STRONG WOMAN

"Out, now. Out everyone," Kitwana said. "Out. They're coming."

One by one, twenty Hyena Men—Nassira the only female member present—filed silently from where they'd been lurking, in the shadow between two tall, white buildings. They'd not wanted to call attention to themselves, in case any other Europeans appeared to hire African carriers to go into the bush.

No Europeans had arrived yet in this lukewarm morning fast turning to sweltering midday. However, the large number of natives of as disparate origin and mode of dress as the Hyena Men themselves spoke to the fact that Europeans often came here to traipse into the bush. To explore or meet new cultures, or to spread their religion. To hunt, or in hopes of finding great riches.

It seemed like a strange thing to Nassira that the Europeans should come with such intents. No African—or at least not enough to note—had ever gone to Europe to experience the different climate, catalog its mountains and valleys, rename its cities or bother its natives with theology or philosophy. But it

was all a part of Europeans' considering Africa their
own. And, in thinking that, she felt her resolve firm.
She'd only come because Kitwana had pressed her to.
Now this large assembly of Africans ready to sell their
services to Europeans who wanted to penetrate
deeper into the continent they believed they owned
made Nassira's blood boil.

She stepped forward, after Kitwana, into the
plaza. He had dressed in European attire today, unlike the African dress he'd worn on the train from
Cairo or on their way here by camel and boat. It
seemed to Nassira a bad idea. Shouldn't they look as
African as possible, since what they were selling was
their expertise of Africa? She'd asked Kitwana, but
he'd only laughed and said Englishmen tended to
trust best those who looked the most like themselves.

The English party entered the plaza, coming out of
the tall gates of the garden that surrounded their hotel. Nassira wondered if they'd be going into Kenya.
She pictured herself walking over the life-rich slopes
of her homeland.

To distract herself, she stared critically at the
English party. A dark-haired man had joined Mr.
Oldhall and his wife. His skin was almost as pale
as Oldhall's. He wore a pale linen suit, well cut and
quite expensive. He wore it as though he was used to
expensive things, too, striding into the plaza as though
he'd just purchased it at a good rate and was only
waiting for them to wrap it up.

Behind him came Mr. Oldhall. He looked deflated.
Nassira had last seen him aboard the carpetship
where he'd seemed worried and scared, but also excited, filled with the certainty that he was doing some-

thing of great importance. And before that, in London, he'd looked happy, excited and very much like a man in love. Now he looked as if twenty years had passed over him in the last few days.

As they walked closer, Nassira looked toward Mrs. Oldhall to see if perhaps her husband's mood had to do with strife in their marriage. Granted, Emily Oldhall appeared less fearful than she had been in the carpetship dock. Here she was near her husband, protected by males as Englishwomen were used to being. She would look more confident. Though she also looked puzzled and out of place in a dress that, though less adorned than the one she'd worn before, yet showed enough lace at cuff and skirt to attire most maids in England. She clutched, over her head, a little white lace parasol, which seemed strange in one certainly dark-skinned enough to withstand the sun of Africa without help.

The dark-haired man led the other two around, and moved—darted—here and there, curiously, full of energy. He seemed to speak several African languages, and to engage each of the various groups in its own dialect.

But while his dark friend was talking to a group some steps away, Oldhall broke away and made straight toward Nassira's group and Kitwana.

He looked them over approvingly, then addressed Kitwana. "These your men?" he asked very loudly, pointing to the group and then to Kitwana, as Englishmen usually did when speaking with those they thought understood no English.

Kitwana smiled, an ingratiating expression that Nassira had never seen on his face before. "Yes, sir," he said, speaking in his excellent English, but infusing his voice with great humility. "Yes, sir, they are."

Oldhall looked Kitwana up and down with a faintly approving look. "Good man." He peered over the rag-tag group, most of them dressed in cheap, secondhand European suits, wholly unsuited to carrying burdens through the jungle. "Do all your men speak English?"

"Only a few," Kitwana said.

"You speak very well."

Kitwana nodded but didn't say anything. Oldhall looked at Nassira, and for a moment, their eyes met. She'd never looked him in the eye before—her position in England required that she look down when she met with a gentleman. But now she looked at Oldhall's eyes, and caught her breath. They didn't look human. She'd never seen such pale blue eyes before, even among the blue eyes of the Englishmen. And yet, as she looked at them, she realized that for all their paleness, they looked very familiar.

She could not remember exactly of whom Oldhall's eyes reminded her, not when they were set amid that face so pale that its owner might well have lived, lifelong, under a rock. And yet something in their forlorn sadness, their look of being lost in a world they couldn't quite take in nor understand, called to Nassira.

Oldhall looked away first, then back at Kitwana. "Your wife?" he asked, gesturing with his chin toward Nassira.

Kitwana shook his head. "No. Just a worker in our group. She's a good cook."

Oh, was she? Nassira had trouble not giggling at this information, which would have been very surprising in-

deed to her mother, her stepmothers and her father—
who were justly proud of all her achievements and
accomplishments, but never counted cooking among
them.

Oldhall looked both of them over again. "Well," he
said. "We'll need a cook, I suppose. Very well. I'll hire
you. We want to go some distance into southwest
Africa for— To look for ancient artifacts." He'd raised
his voice when saying it, and there was in it, Nassira
judged, the defiant tone of a little boy doing that which
he knows is wrong.

The dark-haired man had been some distance
away, talking to a tribesman who wore a loincloth and
a profusion of multicolored bead necklaces. And the
English lady had been halfway between the two, as
though sensing a rift between the men and neither
knowing what to do about it nor to whom she should
pledge her allegiance.

Both of them turned to stare at Oldhall as he spoke,
and the lady walked in the mincing fashion of the
English gentry to stand a step behind her husband. As
for the other man, at first he looked shocked, then angered. He ran across the short distance between them
and stopped short, one hand raised toward Oldhall.
"Nigel, old man, you can't just hire someone. Not without questioning him. What does this man know about
the jungle? What experience does he have living off the
land? What parties has he led? Anyone we know? Any
references?"

Oldhall looked confused and lost for a moment,
like a child caught in error. Nassira could see his lips
trying to shape an apology and she was sure he was
about to say something to excuse himself.

But before his lips opened, his features hardened. "What? Are you going to write to England to confirm those references, Peter? Anyone can tell us he led Lord so-and-so and Lord what-not, it doesn't mean anything." He looked at Kitwana, then hard again at his companion. "I like this man and his group. I have a good feeling about them."

The dark-haired one's face closed, like a stormy day. Nassira could practically see the clouds gathering in the swirling green eyes. He opened his mouth.

"I agree with Nigel," the lady said. "I like this group. This man here," she gestured toward Kitwana, "tried to rescue me in the train. A much more gentlemanly behavior than that granted me by the members of Her Majesty's militia."

Oldhall looked down at his wife and some of the tension seemed to flee his features. "It is decided, then," he said. "You will lead us into the jungle and southwest into Africa."

"Where, precisely?" Kitwana asked. "Where precisely southwest?"

"We don't know," Nigel said. "We're looking for some old ruins, an old city. When we find it, we'll know. Till then, we'll follow any clues we find."

Kitwana frowned at first, as though thinking, then nodded. "Fair enough," he said.

"Right," Nigel said. "We'll leave tomorrow morning, then. We're staying at the Gordon Hotel. Please be there, ready to depart."

"What wages will you pay?" the dark-haired man asked, his withering scorn audible in his voice.

"Oh, customary wages," Oldhall said, and looked

hesitatingly toward Kitwana with an expression that said he had no idea what those might be.

Nassira wondered who had let this poor innocent come exploring in Africa with his wife, when it was patently obvious that he should not be allowed to cross the street on his own.

"Customary wages will be fine, sir," Kitwana said, managing not to betray the slightest bit of irony.

The dark-haired man rolled his eyes. And Nassira looked at Nigel and realized of whom his eyes reminded her. Her first lover. When Nassira had first gone to the Masai adolescent camp, the Maniata, she'd fallen in love with Kume ole Lumbwa, a tall, muscular, straight-backed warrior, the oldest son of the left- hand wife of a rich man. It had taken her only a month, though, to realize that her lover, smart and kind and handsome though he was, lacked a belief in his own qualities.

In Nigel's eyes she saw the same mixture of confusion, fear and attempted self-sufficiency, and a wave of sympathy for this enemy of her people swept over her. She had to fight hard to remember that these were intruders in Africa; that these people were destroying her land, her birthright, and planning to steal the magic of the world for their queen.

She might be lying to this helpless man, but she was doing it for Africa.

She summoned her anger, but she couldn't help still feeling protective and maternal toward the tall, pale alien walking away with his wife's hand upon his arm.

DAWN IN THE JUNGLE: NATIVES AND OTHERS

After days in the jungle, Emily woke to the roar of a lion. It was a soft roar, like distant thunder, and yet threatening. They'd been hearing it for three days now—never getting nearer the expedition, but never going away—lending a permanent aura of menace to the terrain they traversed, which was itself strange and menacing.

This was a land of valleys and sudden peaks, of scarps and jagged ravines, all of it punctuated with craters, some of which harbored deep blue lakes. Dotted here and there were the beehive huts of the Masai and their herds, which, like the lion, they'd not yet seen but had heard and smelled from a distance.

All sorts of wildlife lived in this area, too—a profusion such, Emily thought, as must have been in Eden. She felt as if they were in deepest Africa already and wondered how long till they reached their objective. Surely it couldn't be far now. They'd walked for days and days. Emily must consult the compass stone soon, much as she wished she could avoid it.

Nigel had been postponing it, too. He also feared that her touch upon the stone would call the attention of the Hyena Men again. Peter Farewell disagreed. He said activating the stone had been powerful enough to call the Hyena Men, but now that it was bound to Emily, it would require but the smallest of magic, not enough to awaken vigilant enemies. And most of all, the men seemed to be fighting over her without even admitting it. Nigel seemed at every step to accuse Farewell and Emily of improper and improbable behavior. Emily could neither resent Farewell's anger at this, nor in truth master her own. How could Nigel think that of either of them?

She sat up in bed in her tent. That she had a tent all to herself was another of the puzzles of this expedition. It would have made sense for her to share a tent with Nigel, since she was his wife, but such a thing had never been mentioned. The day they'd left their hotel in Khartoum, Nigel and Peter had struck a deal for three tents with the amiable hotel manager, who seemed to have a great supply of such accoutrements laid by, just against such an eventuality. Three tents, and Emily had not dared protest it. For all she knew, it was customary for people going into the wilds of Africa to sleep one to a tent.

One thing that puzzled her and that she did ask was what the carriers should sleep in.

The manager had laughed at her, good-naturedly, as though she'd been a simple child.

"Sleep in, my lady? Why, they sleep wherever they chance. Very natural people these blacks, and no more needful of civilized comforts than an antelope. They lie down on a dirt mound just as happily as they would lie down on a lace bed. And more comfortably, since that's all they've known from birth."

Yet Emily doubted this assertion. She knew enough—from listening to people's guesses on the life and motives of Indians—to know that Europeans seemed to attribute to every other breed of man a simplicity that was not human. Still, she could hardly invite the carriers into her tent, nor did she want to shock her husband by insisting the carriers be given tents, which would have greatly added to their loads. So she slept in solitary splendor in a little chamber made of white canvas.

Opening her eyes now, she looked at the peaked roof of cloth above her and realized she was truly in Africa. Yet it all seemed like a dream, till the lion roared again. And then she rose, shaking herself, and looked for her clothes, which she'd set at the foot of the bed. She slept in a long nightgown that she now removed and folded into its trunk, to be transported. Strange to live out of a trunk this way. She put her dress on—one of the many sturdy dresses she'd packed for what she'd thought would be a few honeymoon adventures.

Her feet had been much the worse for the wear in the beginning of this trip, the skin blistering from contact with the sensible, hard-leather boots she'd chosen for her honeymoon expeditions to mosques and pyramids. On the third day, she'd been quite miserable. But then the woman Nassira—who reminded Emily of the maid at the carpetdock—except, of course, she could not be the same woman, because what would an employee of the carpetship line be doing this far into Africa?—had anointed Emily's feet with a salve that smelled vile. Emily hadn't dared ask what the salve contained, preferring to think that it must be nothing but a paste of many plants. Still, the salve had worked, and now, days later, her feet were quite hardened to this effort.

When she returned to England—if she returned—she would be able to impress her stepmother and stepsisters by being a most serious walker, able to continue with any excursion long after all other ladies and most men had given up.

The boots, too, that she now slipped onto her feet and laced carefully—because a carefully laced boot reduced her chances of twisting her ankle—had accommodated to her feet, getting, in the process, unshapely and quite unsightly. But much more comfortable.

Fully dressed, in a plain serge dress with hardly any frills, and with her boots on, Emily tied up her long hair and pinned it up, then pinned a broad straw hat on top of it all. She'd found that though she didn't blister or burn to the painful pink that Nigel had displayed for days now, she had been out of the sun too long to take it comfortably, and she was quite glad for the protection afforded by her broad-brimmed hat.

Fully attired, she stepped out of her tent. And again heard the roar of the lion in the distance.

"Don't worry, lady," the chief carrier, Kitwana, said. He still looked too tall, too broad-shouldered, too intimidatingly strong. He'd traded his English-style suit for shorts and a short-sleeved shirt, both of a dun color, which only seemed to make him look somehow larger. That he stood just outside Emily's tent startled her. Had he been spying on her? Then she noticed that he had in his hand the leather bucket that they used to gather water from lakes or streams, when near enough to their encampment. Though not too near, because, Kitwana said—and Peter agreed—if they parked near a water hole, they would be visited by all types of creatures.

He set the leather bucket near the single basin, which they had set upon a rock. "I thought you'd be waking soon and wanting to wash," he said, and smiled.

"Why, thank you," Emily said, and felt confused. Whatever she'd expected of native carriers, Kitwana did not behave like one. Instead, he acted like a prince in disguise, or perhaps a learned sorcerer of great power, consenting to associate with commoners and play their servant. He was unfailingly courteous and humble, but such behavior only seemed to emphasize his condescension.

From his straight bearing and the way he explained it, bringing the water somehow acquired the status of a royal favor, granted by a great personage, and Emily felt as though she should bob him a curtsy and apologize for putting him to the trouble.

And he carried trunks and guided, though more often he protected, and hunted for their supper—all with that same aplomb, as if he were doing them all a great favor.

If he were an Englishman in society, he would be insufferable, Emily thought, so full of himself and his own importance as to be impossible to get along with. Or perhaps he would be a person of some consequence. A duke or a prince, in whom such behavior was expected. She cast a furtive look at his profile and had to admit it had great nobility.

She washed her face and hands. The greater washing was done at nighttime, with water warmed over the fire. She rearranged her hat in front of the small round mirror that one of the men—she didn't know which—had the foresight to bring with him, and that both men shaved in front of.

Kitwana stood by. "As I said, I shouldn't worry about the lion. It's more likely to be a danger to the cattle hereabouts, but some Masai tribesman will dispatch it."

Emily looked up. "Do they have powersticks?"

Kitwana chuckled and shook his head. "No, they confront lions armed only with a wooden spear."

"But that is madness!"

Again he chuckled, this time more heartily. "You're not the first, nor the only one, to accuse the Masai of that. But the Masai use the lion's own weight against the beast, waiting for the creature to spring and positioning themselves so that it impales itself upon their lances. Nassira has seen it, no doubt." He indicated the woman carrier, who squatted by the fire, presumably cooking something since a great cloud of black smoke could be seen rising from it. "She is a Masai."

Emily sighed, less concerned with Nassira's tribal status than with the cloud of smoke that heralded a very charred breakfast.

"You hunted this morning," she said.

Kitwana nodded once, a way he had of agreeing with something, which seemed to be as spare and self-contained as the man himself. The only exception to Kitwana's proud silence was when he thought he could impart fresh knowledge of Africa to Emily. He seemed to have memorized all the facts of all the lands they passed through—plants and birds and men—and to love nothing so much as to regale her with them.

Why, she did not know. And he said the most star-tlingly inappropriate things. Just yesterday he'd told her that the Zulu, which apparently was a tribe with whom he had some connection, were *the blue sky people. That's what their name means.* And then with an oddly self-conscious look, *From the color of your eyes, it's as if you've captured a bit of their spirit.*

Even he had looked puzzled at those words as they came out of his lips. But she had long observed that *every* man loved lecturing any woman fool enough to stand still for it. And this strange African was no different than every other man she knew.

The only difference was that she need neither follow the laws of polite society nor engage him as a potential suitor, and she could walk away from his elaborate explanations. So even as he said, "We found an antelope upon a thicket and we—" She was walking toward the fire, where Nassira was busy in burning slices of antelope, roughly speared through a much too thick branch.

"I believe you're holding them too close to the fire," Emily said. "The bottom part will get quite charred and the top will remain raw."

Nassira gave Emily a dirty look that seemed to say that was exactly the effect she'd been hoping to achieve, but as she turned the branch to expose the other part to the flame, she lifted it a little ways from the fire.

She wore another colorful caftan, from what seemed to be an endless collection, and she squatted barefoot upon the earth. It looked very comfortable and Emily wished she could follow her example.

Of course, the woman was a dreadful cook, and if they'd been in England, Emily would have long since given her notice. But she had the same kind of regal posture that Kitwana possessed, and between the two of them they made Emily feel thoroughly common and inferior.

She wondered where they slept, very much doubting that either of these people was happy to lay him- or herself upon a mound of dirt.

She also wondered *what* Nassira was. She'd denied being Kitwana's wife, and she didn't seem to be attached to any of the other men. It was Emily's understanding that in every civilization upon earth, the woman was to some extent subjugated to a man and did not exist freely without her partner. Yet the men here seemed to take Nassira as an equal. Emily had often watched Nassira intervene in disputes by giving her opinion or by standing between potential combatants and informing both sides of their lack of sense. What must it be like to be a woman like that? Lost in her thoughts, Emily accepted a tin plate with a very dubious slice of roast antelope upon it, and started eating it as best she could with the aid of a fork but no knife. Nassira, meanwhile, helped herself to another slice, and Kitwana to another. They did not observe the etiquette of waiting until their employers had eaten before they started, nor did Emily see why they should, since Nigel and Farewell were still in bed.

Kitwana told Nassira something in a fast-flowing language, and Nassira gave him the same sort of look she'd given Emily, as though she was considering roasting him over the fire. But he only chuckled and turned away, directing the other carriers to break down Emily's tent and stow it away so they could leave before the day got much hotter.

Nigel came out of his tent, fully dressed, and examined his pale blond stubble before the mirror. Apparently deciding that he didn't need to shave, he turned to Emily and the fire.

"I'll make tea," he said.

This was a concession, and given as if he were being imposed upon by a group of hell-bent savages. But Nigel had found early on that left to her own devices, Nassira could and would find a way of burning boiling water. As for Emily, the voluminous cut of her skirt prohibited her getting near enough the campfire to perform such a rite. So Nigel did it, with the serene look of a martyr contemplating death upon the stake.

Emily finished her meat and accepted a tin cup of tea from Nigel. At that moment, Peter came out of the tent and nodded to her, his stubble looking like it needed a good deal more immediate attention than Nigel's. He shaved, employing his straight razor with a will, and while he did it, Emily took her cup of tea and walked about, prowling the corners of the encampment.

They were in a clearing, with scrub brush growing all around. In the middistance, some acacia trees grew—their shape like an open umbrella—providing sparse shade for a herd of antelopes and some creatures that looked like the ugliest buffalo on Earth.

From somewhere came the sound of singing in a language Emily did not understand. She noticed that Nassira looked up. But the landscape was so broken by a series of peaks and sudden valleys that often no person was visible. Until someone stood, suddenly, close by. A youth had appeared in this fashion. He was as tall as Kitwana, though more slender. Not that Kitwana could ever be considered fat, but this boy had that reed-thinness of the adolescent just on the verge of becoming a man—perhaps having entered the process but not yet having come to his full strength. He wore a tunic that Emily noted was draped much as the toga on a Roman statue. Only, this toga was a bright zigzag pattern of black upon yellow.

His hair was pulled back and pasted in place with an ocher mixture that made him look quite red from the neck up. He wore a profusion of bead necklaces around his neck, and a huge beaded earring distended and deformed his earlobe. He'd been singing something under his breath—a strangely moving melody—but he stopped and stared at Emily as though she'd come from an alien world.

Nigel was eating and Peter was shaving. There was no one nearby to defend Emily. She did not feel threatened, however, because this young man seemed so shocked by her.

Kitwana appeared, speaking rapidly to the young man, behind whom, now, two cows appeared, walking slowly like tame dogs.

"This is a Masai Moran," Kitwana said, in his clean British accent. "A warrior of the Masai."

Emily looked behind the youth. "With cows?"

"Cows are central to the Masai life. Warriors still look after their fathers' cattle. And they steal cattle for their fathers, too."

"Steal?" Emily asked, looking at the young man's

open face, his guileless smile. "You're telling me they're cattle robbers?"

"Not the way they see it," Kitwana spoke softly, but just as though he were describing an oddity of nature, a plant or an animal. "You see, they believe God gave them all of the cattle on Earth. If any other people have some, it means that they must have stolen them from the Masai, and thus the Moran do nothing but get them back."

"I'm glad you find the beliefs of my people so amusing," a cold voice said behind them.

Emily turned around and was surprised to find that Nassira had spoken. She'd never before heard Nassira speak in such perfect English, with no accent. But she had no time to ask Nassira any questions, as the woman—Masai?—swept past Emily to speak to the youth.

The youth looked at Nassira with an expression that seemed to Emily to echo wounded disdain. He spoke in tripping sounds that poured from his tongue, bringing with it a strong expression of disgust or reproach. Emily thought they knew each other, that there was some history between them, though doubtless Nassira was much older than he was.

Again her thoughts were interrupted, this time by Nigel's approach. "Kitwana, see to the packing. Make sure it is all stowed properly and the men are ready to go in fifteen minutes."

"Of course," Kitwana said like a king granting a favor. He slid off to oversee the packaging.

Nassira left the youth standing on the path and stomped off behind them, to deal roughly with the tin plates and the pots and pans and the other few cooking implements they'd brought.

Emily stayed where she was. She could feel Nigel behind her, standing still, quiet, wrapped in some dignified hurt that she couldn't understand. She didn't even know if he was hurt by her or Farewell, but she knew that Nigel included her in his long, resentful silences. She could feel his presence like a coldness at her shoulder, quietly disapproving. And she *personally* resented his suspicions

The silence lengthened, till it seemed as though any moment it would burst. But Emily didn't know what it would burst into, and she turned around and faced Nigel.

He looked coldly disapproving, pale, quiet. His glacial blue eyes stared at her and his expression was exactly the same expression her father had regarded Emily with so often, when he did not understand what Emily had said or done.

Emily stared at Nigel questioningly, as she'd never done to her father. Nigel didn't speak. He turned and was gone, leaving Emily alone on the path, looking out on the verdant expanse of Masai land. The herder-warrior had vanished, and the only sign of life, other than their own party, was the sound of the lion in the distance.

HIS SILENCE AND PAIN

It was the end of the day, which came abruptly in this region, the sun setting over this broken land of chasms and peaks with the suddenness of a blown-out candle.

The carriers had set up with quiet efficiency.

In this, at least, Nigel was happy. He'd made the right choice. After all the horror stories he'd heard about rebellious carriers and incompetent guides, he relished Kitwana's well-bred efficiency and his laconic, almost British mode of address.

This was Nigel's only consolation, though, as he watched night cover the savannah, making every thornbush, every acacia tree into a looming monster. Behind him, the tents—lit with magelights inside—swelled like immense lanterns. If Nigel turned, he would see Emily's silhouette against the light. "Nigel," Peter called from behind him.

Nigel turned. He saw, over his friend's shoulder, Emily's shadow inside the tent. She stood by the small portable table. Nigel knew that the compass stone would rest on that table, but from the outside, it wasn't clear what Emily was doing with it, or if she was done. All for the best, as Nigel did not think the carriers should be informed of the magical import of this quest. "Your wife wishes you to be inside with her," Peter said.

Nigel raised his eyebrows at his friend in a mute question.

Peter nodded. "I'll stay outside and attempt to shield both of you from magical interference should ... our enemies trace you."

Peter was so serious. Vanished was his playful attitude, his mocking manner. Their interaction had become strained, weighted down by things unsaid, bent out of shape by Nigel's suspicions of Peter and Emily. But if Peter had only been taking a bath at the oasis, then why had he blanched when Nigel interrogated him? And yet, how could Nigel suspect his wife and his best friend of such gross betrayal? His wife was so in name only, and he had not seen Peter for many years. People changed.

"You must see that I'm more qualified to keep shield, as I'm not marked by the enemy." Peter slanted his eyes toward the carriers, a little ways off.

So Nigel walked into Emily's tent. It was the same size as his, and like his, it contained a camp bed and a table that served as table and desk and vanity. Right now, it had been swept clean and the compass stone sat atop it. Emily stood in front of the stone. She looked up at Nigel as he came in. She wore a dark blue dress of some sturdy material, entirely devoid of ornamentation, which brought out the blue in her eyes.

It seemed to Nigel that the tent was warmer than the outside and that the air itself was suffused by Emily's scent of roses. He took his place across from her at the table.

If something went wrong with Emily's scrying, it would be up to Nigel to help her first. He did not know what he could do. He'd tried to keep her safe from the Hyena Men before and he'd failed. Yet he was willing to try again.

While she bent her head over the stone, Nigel prayed silently that they'd be close to the ruby. He wanted this expedition to be over. He wanted to be safely at home with Emily, where he could make her his wife—truly his wife—and resume the thread of his life that the queen's summons had interrupted. And keep her away from Peter and protect her as he'd meant to.

He watched as Emily's fingertips grazed the stone, and hoped it would just glow with a single red dot. Or point backward. But the glowing red arrow formed on the gray surface. And it pointed, still, southwest.

Nigel almost groaned, but stopped himself just in time.

Emily had opened her eyes and they looked vacant, unfocused. She looked at Nigel as if he were not there at all, then she tottered, as though ready to fall.

Nigel rushed toward her, hands outstretched, to stop her from falling. "Emily," he called. "For heaven's sake, Emily."

But she swatted his hands away. "Mr. Farewell," she said. And then louder. "Mr. Farewell." Her eyes gaining focus, she looked anxiously around. "Mr. Farewell?" She hurried to the tent entrance. "Mr. Farewell?"

Peter turned around and ducked into the tent. "Mrs. Oldhall?"

"I had a vision," Emily said. She focused wholly on Peter and her expression lit up in eagerness. "It came to me from the compass stone and showed me stone walls. Circular houses. Great walls."

"Stone?" Peter blinked. "There is no stone house around here. It is all dirt and branches and cow dung. He frowned. "Are you sure you saw stone? That sounds almost Mediterranean."

Emily sighed, looking impatient. "No. The arrow pointed yet farther south and west."

Peter shrugged, exasperated. "I can ask the carriers if any of them know."

"Please do." Peter strode out.

"You didn't ask me," Nigel said. He hadn't meant to speak, but the words flew out. "You asked Peter, but not me."

Emily looked at him, surprised. "Do you know where such houses are?" she asked. "Tall, round stone houses? In Africa?"

He shook his head. "I've never heard of those," he said. And added, with peevish annoyance, "Neither has Peter."

"But," Emily frowned, "he might have."

Nigel shook his head. "You speak to everyone," he said. "Ask questions of everyone but me. Peter and even the carriers. But not of your husband."

"My husband has shown little interest in my company," she said. "He even sleeps in his own tent."

Nigel hushed her frantically. "Your husband knows that these tents are almost transparent and certainly not soundproof," he said, in a low, vicious whisper. "And the last time I was with you within a sturdy house, you'd not unlock your door."

Emily glared at him. "I had reason enough not to."

Nigel felt color climb, flaming to his cheeks. She

had reasons. He thought of Peter's deserted room, his abandoned clothes. "I do not want to know your reasons," he said. "You could have no honorable reasons."

Emily glared back, shaking slightly. Even her lips were pale and trembled, as if longing to say something.

Nigel could not bear it. He turned his back and stormed out.

LAIRY AT THE BRIDGE

A week later, walking ahead of the expedition through the broken terrain of Masai land, Nigel stopped. Right at his feet, without warning, the earth cleaved into a deep, jagged chasm that extended a good hundred yards across before the more-or-less even terrain resumed. Further, the chasm extended for what looked like miles in each direction.

Emily peered over Nigel's shoulder at the bottom of the ravine, dry as a bone, and filled with a crisscross of jagged rocks, like a open mouth revealing cruel teeth.

"It is wholly impassible," Emily said, stepping up beside him.

"The Masai say that in the beginning, when they first came onto this land, a chasm such as this divided their people and fractured their tribes," Kitwana said, from Nigel's other side.

Nigel looked up and met with Peter's amused gaze. He stood just beyond Emily and had pulled one of his cigarettes out of his pocket. He was shielding the flame with a conched hand while he struck his lighter. And he seemed to view Emily and Kitwana—and perhaps even Nigel, who stood dismayed and still at the edge of the abyss—as a study in nonsense.

"We will have to walk around it," Peter said.

Nigel looked both ways to see if there were any signs of the chasm ending. In the distance, he could barely discern a flimsy, ropelike bridge "We could take the bridge," he said.

Peter shook his head, squinting into the distance. "Looks too frail for us to take the carriers across it."

"Locals take them all the time," Kitwana said. "With herds."

Peter looked puzzled but threw his cigarette down, stepped on it and nodded. "Fine," he said. "We'll walk to it."

Nigel noted that though the idea was his, Peter acted as though he, not Nigel, was the leader of the expedition, making the final decision on how to proceed.

They walked about an hour to the bridge.

The thing was a construction of ropes of unknown origins, some still showing green grass amid their weavings. The bottom of the bridge looked like the work of basketry made by a weaver at the edge of insanity. There were ropes and twigs and sticks and pieces of unidentifiable grayish material, probably decomposing grass. All of it was held together somehow, interwoven, intertwined with other pieces of the bridge, and Nigel was quite sure that it would all give way the first time someone put a foot on it.

But he would not show his fear. Stinging from Peter's easy assumption of command, he refused to show weakness now.

Peter grinned at Nigel with the type of expression that Nigel hadn't seen in many years. It was the grin of a schoolboy challenging another schoolboy to a daring feat. Possibly a dangerous one. Not since the old days had Nigel seen Peter smile like that. He'd seen Carew do it. And many more in Carew's circle. But not Peter.

Now he looked at Peter and arched his eyebrows and managed to sound—he hoped—defiant as he said, "Damn it, Peter. You can't expect Mrs. Oldhall to cross that thing."

"Natives cross it all the time," Kitwana said quietly from the back. "That type of bridge is not uncommon and it often lasts for generations."

Nigel looked over his shoulder at the black man, who stared back at him impassively, giving no impression at all of being aware of any social breach in speaking to his betters that way. In fact, Kitwana seemed to be under the impression that there was no difference between him and English gentlemen—as though his upbringing, his thoughts, his reading, could have infused him with that wisdom of the ages that came to England from as far back as Greece and Rome.

Nigel was no man to judge another solely on his birth station or the color of his skin. In fact, that had often been a point of contention between Nigel and Carew and their parents. Not that Nigel spoke about it, but he often thought that their parents' belief in *old and magical blood* was a bunch of rot—and not very good rot, at that. But he knew from his contact with his language masters and other people belonging to less civilized races that a man's upbringing surely formed the man. And one such as Kitwana—come from who knew what tribe in the deepest Africa—couldn't possibly compete in knowledge and breeding with the Englishmen.

He glared at Kitwana, who impassively stepped behind Emily and said, "It really is quite safe, Mrs. Oldhall."

And there is was, the other thing slowly driving Nigel to distraction. Two months married and he'd yet to consummate his union.

Yet in this long trek through the jungle, there had been scant opportunity to pursue Emily and make her aware of his longing, his desire. The tents were scarcely private, and Nigel didn't wish for their intimate conversation to be heard by all the carriers, or by Kitwana, who spoke such good English.

Meanwhile, Peter and even Kitwana himself— seemingly unaware of their transgression—made love to Emily with their eyes and pursued her with suggestions and questions.

Nigel was so occupied in trying to stare down Kitwana—who looked, oblivious, past Nigel's shoulder and at Emily—that he jumped, startled, when he heard Emily speak.

"I wouldn't want to be the first on the bridge," she said. She eyed the dubious basketry with the same sort of look that Nigel had given it.

Nigel laughed, relieved. "No. Nor would I."

"Nassira tells me that it's a good three days' walk down the road before we come to a place where the chasm is narrow enough to attempt to jump," Kitwana said. "Even then, that is more dangerous. We could breach it with our own ropes, granted, but this bridge has survived the test of time."

Nigel thought to order Kitwana onto the bridge, then bit his tongue. In Roman and Greek histories— which he had read at boarding school—he'd always despised those generals who, having power over their men, ordered them to march forth into dangerous situations. Nigel himself would not do that. Yet neither did he want to go onto the bridge on his own.

Peter chuckled. He tossed another of his interminable cigarettes down and stomped on it with the sole of his sturdy boot. "Come," he said, "is everyone here such a child? I'll take the bridge first. Will you come after me, Mrs. Oldhall?"

In Emily's face, Nigel read her startled surprise at being thus challenged to follow after the first crosser, then he read pleased approbation.

Feeling acid bile climb his throat, Nigel said, "I'll go instead of Emily."

But Emily looked at him and shook her head. "No, Mr. Oldhall, I crave the honor."

"Then I'll go behind you, Emily. I'll protect you."

Though how he could save her if she fell, he had no idea. He imagined himself hanging from the remains of a bridge by one hand, holding Emily with another, and climbing the frayed ropes by the force of his manly arm. But he was not so deluded as to think he could carry off such a feat. He'd done well at games in school, but not as ridiculously well as other boys, Carew among them.

Emily was already striding toward the shaky bridge, following Peter, and looked over her shoulder with a baffled expression at Nigel's words. He scowled and stepped forward, hard on her heels, calling to the carriers, "Follow us as soon as we reach the other side. Come two at a time."

When he turned back, Peter was walking nonchalantly backward on the bridge, with his eyes on Emily.

Emily turned deathly pale as she first set foot on the rickety structure. She handed Peter her umbrella, and he took it without remark as she set her golden, long-fingered—ungloved—hands on two ropes that ran, like guides, to either side of the bridge.

"Come on, Mrs. Oldhall," Peter said, and danced backward with an acrobat's grace. "There's nothing to fear. Quite sturdy bridge, after all, as you see." And he did a little dance, tapping his feet upon the unsteady weave at the bridge's bottom.

He backed up, and Emily followed.

Nigel tried not to look down at the gaping abyss, following Emily as though she was light and love and all that was good in the world. Because she was. Emily was all that mattered to Nigel at the moment as she walked across the bridge, doggedly following Peter.

Nigel closed the gap between himself and his wife's graceful figure, and stepping very close behind her, put his hand over hers on the guiding ropes. "I'm here, Emily. You have nothing to fear."

"I'm not afraid," Emily said. "Only, looking down makes me quite dizzy." She shook his hand away. "Let me do this, Nigel. Do not interfere." And she crossed the rest of the bridge very rapidly, following a fast-retreating Peter.

Nigel walked on, his heart clenched in darkness and filled with ice, cursing himself for not being able to imitate Peter's grace. For not being able to capture Emily's fancy. For being as he was, mute and dumb, forever the second son, hidden in shadow and never stepping forth into the light of glorious deeds.

When he reached the other side of the bridge, Peter

had given Emily back her umbrella and grinned at her. "You are now a confirmed African explorer, Mrs. Oldhall. Crossing that bridge without even a shiver was a feat that would scare most well-brought-up misses."

They both looked away from Nigel as he walked up to them, and lowered their eyes as though they'd been caught in a guilty moment. Nigel wanted to do something crazy: to call Peter out. But then, his marriage was no marriage, and who should court Emily but a gentleman worthy of her? Nigel's own honor told him to step aside. And yet how could he give up on Emily so easily?

THE DUES OF MEMORY

Nassira had lain awake a long time. She was no longer used to walking all day. Her days in London had softened her. And pretending to be a cook was exasperating. No matter what she did, the meat burned. And then, since returning to her homeland, she kept longing for her mother's hut, her stepmother's cooking. Days ago, she'd heard a herd boy sing in Maa. Her tongue and heart craved the familiar syllables that no one around her now understood.

She tossed and turned on the bed she'd contrived from grass and a sheet of fabric from her luggage. She slept on one side of the fire, the men on the other. Not that they were all asleep—they never were. Kitwana demanded they keep sentinels, *to ward off dangerous animals, particularly the ones that went on two feet,* he said. He always assigned shifts of two men to stay awake through the night. And, perhaps with misguided gallantry, he always exempted Nassira from this.

She could hear two men whispering from the other side of the blazing fire. They fed the flames now and then, sending a spray of ash and glowing embers up through the dark night, toward the distant stars. But knowing those men were awake, hearing their talk through the night, could not distract Nassira from her thoughts. They were too far away for her to hear their words. From a few stray sounds carried in the wind, she suspected they spoke a language she could not understand.

Besides, Nassira could not have shared her doubts and her longing with anyone. Well, maybe with Kitwana. But certainly not with these men, anonymous comrades in arms in the liberation of Africa.

She turned again on her uncomfortable bed. Walking the paths of her homeland again revived memories she thought almost forgotten. And all of it was made worse by the fact that the more she knew Kitwana, the more she liked him, whether or not she wished to. He was kind and attentive. And, in time, when she'd seen him in his native clothes, very handsome. But he was also not a Masai and didn't show the slightest interest in Nassira. In fact, he seemed to spend much of his time looking at the Englishwoman— for all the good that might do him. Nassira wondered if he was even aware of how often his gaze strayed to Emily Oldhall.

Ah, Nassira and her unfortunate liaisons.

When she'd been in the Maniata, the warrior camp—where adolescent Masai women were free to choose whomever they wanted and to have as many lovers as they pleased—Nassira had picked first Kume ole Lumbwa, a tall, straight-limbed young warrior with sparkling dark eyes. Nassira had felt an immediate closeness to Kume and loved him as much as she could love someone. In her mind, when she thought of the future mate in her life, she'd thought of

Kume. In fact, she'd had the half-formed intent of marrying Kume when she returned to her home. Traditionally Masai women married men from an older age group, but Nassira knew her father was not likely to deny the fancy of his only daughter. And her father needed an adoptive son more than he needed an ally, and Kume would serve as both.

Turning, she opened her eyes and saw a man bending over her, and sat up quickly with a stifled scream. The man—Kitwana—reached down and covered her mouth with his hand. For a moment, Nassira had the strange idea that Kitwana craved a tryst.

During the last few days, she'd learned to appreciate Kitwana's compassionate leadership, the calm way in which he dealt with even the Englishmen. She no longer thought him arrogant or too proud of his Zulu heritage. But she'd sensed no attraction from him.

She started to open her mouth, to explain she'd only screamed because he'd startled her, but Kitwana dropped to a squatting position by her bed and bent his head toward her, whispering, "The Englishman is gone."

"The Englishman?" Nassira asked, forming the words almost soundlessly against Kitwana's palm.

Kitwana removed his hand and nodded. "Mr. Oldhall. He's taken off from the camp. I want you to find him."

"What?" Nassira asked, louder than she'd intended.

Kitwana flapped his hand up and down frantically, motioning for her to keep quiet. He gestured with his head toward the other side of the fire. "I want you to go because you know the terrain and this is Masai territory. I judge you'll be safer than any of us, walking around this countryside. Any of the men might run across one of your deranged Masai Moran raiding parties and get killed before he can explain he means no harm."

Nassira opened her mouth to protest the term *deranged,* but closed it again. Having been in a few raiding parties, she wouldn't call the brave warriors of the Masai insane, but she knew their behavior as a group was often akin to what Englishmen called *berserker,* a state in which fear was impossible, rational barriers were ignored and bravery became all.

She slid upward in her bed and sat up. She was wearing a tight body wrap, the company not being suitable for a woman to sleep naked. "Why not take a party in search of this man?" she asked. "And why should we care if he went into the jungle? Perhaps he just went to satisfy a call of nature?"

Kitwana frowned, wrinkling his forehead, as though his head hurt. "No," he said. "I saw him leave, and I think he has some foolishness in mind."

"Foolishness?" Like going forth in search of the ruby and leaving them all behind? "How can you tell anything from watching him leave camp?"

Kitwana might have read her thought. He shook his head gently. "You know there's been some tension between the Europeans. The two men and Em—the woman..." He shrugged. "Have you noticed the dark one? Mr. Farewell?"

Nassira felt a surge of impatience. What was she supposed to have noticed about the man? "I've seen him. And listened to him. He likes the sound of his own voice. Why?"

"Well, he might, but... The beasts don't, you

know? No animal comes near him. If he walks away from the encampment, birds fly in front of him and impala flee."

"So . . . he smells bad?" Nassira asked, confused.

"I don't know," Kitwana said. "When we . . . when the binds were set, there was another power in that room. A dark power. It is said that supernatural creatures scare the wildlife."

"And what does this have to do with the other Englishman going into the forest, and your waking me?" Nassira asked impatiently.

"I don't know," Kitwana said. He sounded miserable and confused. "I've asked my superior in the Hyena Men what should be done. He hasn't told me yet. And now the other Englishman has gone into the jungle. I don't know what to do."

"Why are you even worried?"

"Something is going on there, though from the man's expression . . . He looks like one of the deposed chieftains my father used to give asylum to," Kitwana said. "Like a man who's lost his kingdom, his honor and everything he had to live for."

One of the deposed chieftains Kitwana's father gave asylum to? What a strange thing to say. *Where* did Kitwana come from? In her mind Nassira pictured a land populated by deposed despots. "What do you mean?"

"I mean," Kitwana said, "he looked like a man about to commit suicide. A lot of deposed chieftains did, you know. Even after they were safe."

Nassira jumped out of the bed and ran out of the encampment. Before she could think too much about it, before she could fully visualize the pale Englishman with the scared eyes dying in the jungle, she ran to his rescue, picking up the spear of one of the carriers that lay beside the pile of trunks and boxes. He reminded her too much of Kume for her to allow him to die like that.

She found her feet regaining their old ways as she ran over the hillocks. She smelled the familiar scent of the grasslands, heard the roar of the lion in the distance and the faint lowing of cows farther off. Without thinking, she would have been able to tell where all the villages of the Masai were, even those that had moved or been founded since she had been away. She would know it by the smell and the sounds in the night, and the way the grass was trampled in paths by boys who pastured their fathers' cattle.

Following the Englishman was easy. Nassira could see where his big feet had trampled the grass. Nassira set her spear down and looked around, her eyes getting used to the dark and showing her where the Englishman had ripped his heavy canvas pants on a thorn tree, leaving the pale fabric flapping there like a distress flag.

Picking up the spear, she resumed her walk over the familiar terrain, following him, tracing every one of his steps marked on the earth, on broken branches and trampled grass. He was walking foolishly, with the arrogance of all Europeans, trampling ground they didn't know and that didn't belong to them, unaware and without caring, trampling it as though it didn't matter—as if it were, like everything else, including the cultures and souls of occupied peoples, their own to despoil or preserve.

She followed his track, growing closer until she

could follow him by the sounds of scurrying and running creatures scared by his passage.

Her feet hurt where thorns had pricked through her sandals. She'd once walked this country barefoot and at ease, but that was past. The magnitude of what she'd lost in going to England, to fight for the honor of her land, for her land's freedom, came to her like the bitter reflux of indigestion.

She'd once been able to walk on thorns barefoot and not notice. She'd once known her father's cows, each by name.

And Kume...

She remembered how much she had been attracted to Kume at first sight, how much she had admired him. And then, on the first raid—when she had followed the warriors out of curiosity—she'd seen how Kume behaved.

It wasn't that Kume was a coward. He went with the warriors to the thick of things, he tried to ride at the palisade of the other tribe's cow enclosure. He did his best. And it wasn't that Kume was clumsy. There was nothing wrong with the way he leapt forward, the way he brandished his spear, the sure way he ran over the uneven ground.

Had he been alone, dependent only on his own movements, there would be nothing to fault him. But there seemed to be a curse on poor Kume, who always charged in such a way that he caused another warrior to bump into him, or ran in such a way he tripped one of his fellows, or jumped over the palisade in such a way that blocked the onslaught of the other Masai.

After that first raid, Nassira should have stopped loving him. She was conscious most other Masai

women would have. After all, most women wanted
the perfect warrior, who could protect them and raid
for a large quantity of cattle. Nassira, too.

She wanted a life companion to whom she felt at
least equal, if not inferior. But Kume of the velvety
eyes, the noble features, the muscular body, had
another claim on Nassira's affections. He needed
her help to survive. And because he needed her,
she would stay with him.

And because Nigel reminded her of Kume, she
could never ignore him while he needed her help. She
glared at the moonlit high grass, the low thornbushes,
the acacia trees. She listened for the distant roar of a
lion, the near snigger of hyenas, the sound of scurrying
paws. The Englishman shouldn't be out here in Africa.
Had he never heard of the dangers of the bush at
night? Did he not care?

Of course he did not care; they thought themselves
superior to everything.

She continued on painful feet, growing increasingly unaware of her surroundings as her rage at the
Englishmen grew. And then she tripped. Righting herself, she noticed a boot in the path at her feet. It had
caught on some low-growing thorns and sat impaled
by them on three sides. The Englishman had ripped
his foot from it and stepped forward, barefoot, onto
the thorns, on which he left his blood and skin, and little scraps of his sock.

Nassira bent down and pulled the shoe from the
thorns. Carrying it, she hurried forward. Her spine
tingled. A proud man who thought he owned the earth
didn't leave his shoe and willingly step forward like

that. Only a man who didn't care about his own life
would do it. Only a man looking for death.

Kitwana had been right.

What would she find ahead? How could she explain to Kitwana that the man sent to look for the
ruby of power was dead, that the mission was at an
end? Because the other Englishman and the woman
might or might not continue in search of this stone
that would give power back to Africa. She could see
the frail Englishwoman turning back to find her family, her protectors in England. As for the dark-haired
man, if he chose to stay or return for the jewel, he'd
never keep the same carriers. And *he* lacked the
Hyena Men's brand. They could lose track of him entirely.

She hurried forward and, like one who's been
asleep, she was suddenly aware of the stopping of every
sound in the background except for the roar. The roar of
the lion sounded awfully close. Nassira had never killed
a lion. Her father had, and it was the crowning glory of
his life, the story he repeated at every chance.

She ran forward, brandishing a spear in one hand
and the Englishman's shoe in the other. And found
him standing with his arms dangling loosely, looking
not so much like a human being as like a doll, inarticulate, inanimate.

Closer, Nassira could hear his breath, fast and
raspy and catching on the high notes into something
not quite a sob. It was a sound of utter shock and fear.
But what could scare a man who wanted to die?

Nassira peered into the dark velvety night ahead
of the Englishman and could see, amid the tall grass, a

vast shape, larger than a man. A lion. Nassira felt the skin at the back of her neck tightening.

This was the lion they'd heard for days. A lion who followed a human party, neglecting the more abundant cattle that he could eat, was a man eater. Some lions were. The Masai often killed such lions when they threatened their villages and their children. But a lion-killing party usually consisted of several warriors, each expert in handling the spear, many accustomed to the sight of enraged lions.

Nassira had never faced a lion. She'd never seen a lion live and up close. She'd only seen the carcass, when the warriors cut it up for prizes. Somehow, the huge creature crouching just steps away was quite different from those carcasses.

She took a deep breath and tried to think. She could not pull the Englishman away. If she stepped forward, the lion would leap. She could not shout at the Englishman to run. The lion would either lunge at her or run after him.

Nassira looked at the shadow and saw his hindquarters wag, his front quarters lower. In a breath, he would attack.

Her spear shook, in a hand suddenly slick with sweat. She'd often heard young warriors brag of their lion-killing exploits, describing and showing how they brought the mighty beasts down. The idea was to wait for the lion to jump, and when it jumped, to hold the spear upright, to tilt it just so, so when the lion fell on the downward arc of its leap, it would impale itself on the spear, and with its great weight bring about its own death.

Then it was up to the warrior to jump out of the

way of the falling carcass, so that she didn't end up crushed under the lion. Nassira swallowed, and the sweat-slick spear rattled in her hand. Fear filled her completely. She felt like the worst of cowards.

Then she remembered when she was very small and a group of boys from a nearby village had surrounded her, threatened to thrash her for her presumption in speaking to them as an equal though she was only a girl. There were six boys, half naked and furious, incoherent in their perceived superiority. They were all bigger than her, and two of them carried sticks. They'd surrounded her, striking out at her with feet and hands and weapons.

Her parents had been away—Nassira didn't even remember why. There was no one who would rescue her if she screamed, no adult within the reach of her terrified voice. Then, as now, she'd felt totally helpless, completely unable to defend herself. But when it looked as if she had nowhere to turn, she'd found a crazy bravery somewhere inside her. She'd jumped at the attackers, teeth and nails striking at unprotected faces and extended hands.

Her attack had sent them fleeing and they'd never bothered her again. But the lion was not snot-nosed little boys. She doubted the lion would fear her teeth and nails.

She could creep away. The lion, focused on the Englishman, would not even notice. The Hyena Men could maybe still manage to follow Farewell and Mrs. Oldhall. After all, the Englishwoman was the one who had bonded the compass stone to her. Perhaps all would be well without this pale man so obviously unsuited to the rigors of exploring in Africa. He wasn't needed.

It was a gamble, but at least Nassira would have a chance. Where she stood now, in the moonlit night with the stench of the Englishman's fear and the smell of the lion sharp in her nostrils, she could see only two ways out of this.

She could try to save Nigel Oldhall, and then she would certainly die with him. Or she could let him die and hope for the best. If she ran away now, she would live. And no one, Masai or English, would hold it against her that she'd turned away. No one, not even the Masai, expected a young woman to stand up to an enraged lion. Much less for her to do it in defense of someone so completely unconnected to her.

Nassira's heart beat too fast in her chest. She licked her lips—they felt too dry and about to crack. She could turn her back on Oldhall and live. But could she live with herself knowing she could have saved this human being and hadn't? She held on to the spear to steady herself, and the feel of the spear in her hand revived her.

She'd have to kill the lion. Nassira leapt forward, taking a deep breath filled with the scents of her homeland. She exhaled, freeing her fear and rage into the warm night air. She slid in front of Nigel, who let only something like a loud breath escape him.

The lion, enticed by the movement, leapt.

Nassira tilted her spear. She smelled the lion musk and all blood fled her heart. Her breath ached, rattling through her throat. Her arms felt heavy and cold.

The lion leapt like a bird slowly rising to flight, seeking currents of air to soar upon.

She surged forward a few steps. The lion was over her, seemingly suspended in fear-lengthened time. With a growl, it started falling.

Nassira held her spear straight up and moved one step to the side as the lion fell. The spear found the lion's heart. Nassira scrambled back some more. A shower of blood burst from the lion's great heart and sprinkled her face and arms. The lion fell, just at her feet, clawing toward her legs. She pulled the Englishman back.

The lion writhed and screamed and then was still.

Little by little, Nassira became aware that her heart was still beating. The lion had died and she had survived.

She looked toward the Englishman. He was paler than ever, his strange blue eyes wide open as they turned toward her.

In those eyes, Nassira read surprise, shock, gratitude, and something very much like worship.

GENTLEMAN'S DISTRESS, LADY'S DUTY

"What did you think you were doing?" the coppery-skinned woman asked Nigel. She was busily cutting the ears and tail off the fallen animal.

He knew who she was, of course. The cook from the encampment, the woman he'd hired, just because he'd wanted the group of carriers who spoke the most English.

She'd looked unremarkable, he remembered, a dark woman in a dark maid's uniform. Nothing to arrest the eye. Now she looked . . . different. She wore a bright-colored fabric, a bloodred and dark green checkered wrap, tied and cinched around her body in such a way that revealed high breasts, a narrow waist and long legs. Her hair, devoid of the maid's cap, was so short that the contours of her finely shaped, oval head were easily visible and emphasized her large, expressive eyes, her high cheekbones, her sensuous lips.

She'd killed a lion, almost with her bare hands. He looked from her striking fast-breathing beauty to the tawny carcass at least four times her size. She'd killed a lion. His mind could not grasp it.

She stood up and stepped back, away from the

lion's carcass, panting from her recent exertions and staring at Nigel as if *he* were strange and exotic.

"You came seeking death," she said, her strangely musical accent making the words sound merry.

And she looked at him, as if quite unaware of a gentleman's honor and what it might lead him to do. She belonged to some tribe, but Nigel couldn't remember the name. He searched for words, for an excuse, but his tongue could not move. Tribes in Africa were so strange when it came to marital relations. There were those that believed a woman could take several men, a man could take several women.

How could Nigel explain to this woman, raised with who knew what morals, his suspicions and the dark torment of his soul? And if he did, and if she understood him, did he want to malign Emily in such a way? Because he wasn't sure of anything. Still, he couldn't bear to live with it. He couldn't bear knowing that his own wife was in love with Peter Farewell.

He supposed that as the native woman said, he'd sought death. Not so brave as to take his own magic stick and discharge it into his head, not so sanguine as to take his knife and plunge it into his aching heart, but he'd braved the darkness of the night and the unknowns of the jungle alone. Because someone or something would surely kill him there. And then he would be at peace and not have to wonder about who loved him and who hated him, and what he'd done to bring it all about.

The woman was still staring at him. "Why would you do that?" she asked. "Why would you want to die?" She surged up close, looking as if she'd slap an answer from him.

Nigel blinked, as though this would allow him to see the scene more clearly and to better understand what was happening. But it didn't. The woman still stood there, a spatter of lion's blood tracing her cheek on the left side, like barbaric jewels, her demanding gaze turned to him.

"I am...not as I should be," Nigel said. Inadequate words to cross the culture barrier, the personality chasm. "I am not capable of doing the things that are expected of me. I am not the man who should be leading this expedition. I am not the right man to be a good husband to my wife. I am not as brave or as strong or as...knowledgeable as Peter Farewell. I shouldn't be here. I should never have come to Africa."

The woman's eyes widened farther and something like recognition fled through them. It was as though she'd known Nigel long ago, but on meeting him again had forgotten the exact shape of his features and could not identify him for a while. Now such a look of recognition flooded her gaze that Nigel was sure she knew him and he must know her. Even if he couldn't imagine from where.

Then the girl looked away from him, her expression suddenly guarded. "You are wrong," she said. "Even the most ineffective of men would be missed. Have you no family? No parents?"

Nigel lowered his head, feeling the weight of shame. He'd forgotten his mother, waiting in England for Nigel to bring Carew back to her. What would she feel if, instead, Nigel was also found dead? Or disappeared and never returned, as Carew had done? She might not prize Nigel much, but doubtless she cared for the children he could provide to the Oldhall line. Without him, with Carew gone, his parents would be the last of the Oldhalls, rattling around their spacious manor, growing older and older, till at last death overtook them and the line they were so proud of died with them.

He felt himself flush a dark color, and could feel the woman still staring at him intently. "I have parents," he said at last, looking up. "But I'd forgotten all about them for a moment."

He expected her to look disdainful or upset. She did neither, and instead handed Nigel his shoe. "Come with me," she said.

"Where?" he asked, as he pulled some long thorns from his ruined boot, then flinched as he pushed his injured foot into the constricting leather. He felt as if his foot were being wrung within the shoe, leaking warm blood into the toe of the boot. He wondered that he'd not felt the pain before, when he'd left the shoe caught in the thornbush. But he'd been so intent on dying that he'd not thought of pain. His body had been like clothes—like something that belonged to him but didn't have any nerve endings to hurt him.

Now the shock of still being alive made him feel everything with special acuteness—the smell of blood in the air, mixed with the smell of his own sweat and the scent of the woman next to him. His heartbeat seemed too fast, too hurried, dragging air too suddenly out of his chest. He felt his clothes rough against his skin, and the excruciating pain in his confined foot.

The girl looked at Nigel's foot, then up at his face. "Can you walk?" she asked.

Nigel nodded. He would be damned if he was going to have this girl, who'd just rescued him from a lion and certain death, also support him on the way back to camp.

"Good," the girl said, "because we must go." She nodded her head toward the lion. "The smell will attract predators. Come."

She turned her back and set off over the hilly terrain, surefooted and certain, as though she had walked all her life on such land. As perhaps she had.

Watching the way she moved, Nigel's breath caught in his throat. He felt a thrill at her lithe walk, the well-balanced certainty of her body, as graceful, as poised and as attractive as the body of any English lady in a ballroom back home. Then he paused and shook his head. What kind of an idiot was he? He'd always thought that men who went abroad and brought home native wives or acquired strange harems of multicolored concubines were less than honorable. After all, it was not their business to impose themselves on people who, by their circumstances, were unable or unlikely to refuse them. Yet here he was, admiring this native girl.

This woman could very easily refuse him, and probably would. What woman could crave a man whose life she'd had to save? And why would he want this woman to desire him? He was a married man. He loved Emily. He shook his head to clear it of the images that would run through unbidden. The woman stopped and looked over her shoulder. "Are you sure you'll be able to walk?"

"Yes, yes," Nigel said, and biting back the pain, he limped toward her.

She waited till he caught up with her, then set off

at her brisk walk again. Nigel looked away from her, at the terrain around them. He refused to turn and catch a glimpse of her walk, her graceful body, her high breasts. Emily was his wife. He wasn't sure she still loved him, and he wasn't sure that she was faithful. Had she been unfaithful, he had driven her to it with his seeming indifference to her charms. So it fell to him to forgive her, to ignore her transgression, which was born of his own error. It was his duty to take her back and be a loving husband to her.

It was *not* his duty to lust after native girls. What would his mother think? The thought of Lady Oldhall faced with such an unlikely daughter-in-law made laughter bubble up in Nigel's throat and he coughed to hide the strange sound.

The girl turned to look at him, her eyes huge and wondering.

"Er," Nigel said, "what do I call you?"

She gave him a long, considering look. "You may call me Nassira," she said at last. She pressed her lips together and glared at him, full of disapproving dignity. "Nassira, daughter of Nedera of the Masai."

"The Masai," Nigel said. "Aren't we in their territory?"

"Yes."

And on that note, like bad actors showing up right on cue, people—at least Nigel assumed they were people, though in the dark of night it was hard to tell—jumped in front of them. They called something unintelligible but definitely not friendly, in a sort of hoarse croak, and stood, shoulder to shoulder, barring their way.

In the darkness, Nigel could tell that there were

three of them—big and bulky and broad-shouldered, by
the look of the silhouettes, and as tall as Nigel himself—
with what looked like unlikely high coiffures and some
sort of lances.

Natives. He thought of the woman with him.
Nassira had been strong enough to kill a lion by herself. But there were snares on the paths walked by
men at night that no woman could conquer. That
much was true the world over: woman in her peculiar
frailty must be prey to man's predatory instincts. And
Nigel was the man with her. It fell to him to defend
her from these rough strangers.

She'd saved Nigel and now Nigel must save her.

He stepped in front of her, swiftly and—because
he reasoned that such a trick might impress these
savages—he made a pass with his hand and muttered
under his breath the required word. A magelight,
tremulous and shadowy—as it would be when he'd
spent so many years without ever raising it, but only
using the prepackaged ones—glowed in his open
hand.

Before him stood three young black men. At least
their features revealed that they belonged to the
Negro race, but they seemed to have plastered some
sort of reddish ocher all over their exposed skin, which
extended even to their hair. Their features, the race
considered, were almost Roman in their cast and had
a nobility of aspect to them that made them the most
unlikely rogues ever to walk the roadside at night
ambushing strangers. Yet they held vicious-looking
sticks—or spears—in their hands, and they stared at
Nigel and Nassira with less than benevolent expressions.

They sneered at Nigel's hand and the vacillating light upon it. The taller one, who stood in the middle, opened his own hand. Immediately, without the seeming need for any visible passes or any audible words, a light formed upon his palm and glowed stronger and brighter than Nigel's.

Nigel tried to look impassive, but his surprise must have shown in his face.

The three men laughed, roaring and hooting their amusement. Nigel closed his hand and tried to think of a way to gain safe passage for them both.

His father—and Carew, back when he had been alive and traveling—had often told Nigel that all you needed to command the inferior races was a strong voice of command and the certainty that you should be in charge. Natives were like dogs, they'd said. If you acted as the master and didn't let them see your fear, they could do nothing but obey and go in awe of your greater intelligence and civilization.

Nigel doubted it. Even in London, he'd met enough people of other races to think that they would automatically bow to Englishmen as the Englishman's given right. And if they were so willing to obey anyone with a loud voice—or even a working powerstick— then what were all those endless native rebellions that the royal army was forever putting down?

However ... here, in the middle of the night, he wished to believe his father and brother. Pushing his doubts out of his mind, he thought of gallant young Nassira, who'd saved him and who deserved better than to be at the mercy of these creatures. Squaring his shoulders, he yelled, "What are you doing here?

What do you want? Go back to your village and let us through."

The men looked surprised. For a moment it seemed to Nigel as though his father had been right all along, and he had been foolish to doubt parental wisdom. And then the men smiled and elbowed each other. The center one, the tallest man, the one holding the magelight, advanced toward Nigel. He touched Nigel on the chest. "Is this how you command, Water Man? Does your rule depend on bluster?"

Nigel took a step back, startled.

"I see," the native said, "that without your armies, you Water People are not so fearsome. You cannot light a proper magelight, you cannot fight, you cannot even defend yourself." He pushed Nigel on the chest again.

Nigel stepped back again and his injured foot gave under him. A shameful gasp of pain escaped his lips and he felt himself grow paler. By an effort of will, he remained standing, but his weakness had been noted.

"Interesting," the native said. He spoke with an accent resembling Nassira's but stronger. He looked over his shoulder and said something—a long string of incomprehensible syllables—to his companions, who chuckled. He then turned back to Nigel, an unpleasant smile curling his lips. "I tell them Englishmen are like hyenas. Fearsome in a pack, scared when caught alone. We should catch Englishmen one by one, and get rid of them forever."

Nigel stood and clenched his fists. "We're just passing through," he said. "Let us go back to our camp. We have a big camp. Many men, many power-sticks. Our friends will avenge us terribly."

The man frowned. "Your friends? There's more than one of you?" He looked over Nigel's shoulder and seemed to notice Nassira for the first time. A look of recognition widened his eyes and a strange, crooked smile twisted his lips.

"Why," he said, "Nassira, daughter of Nedera, walking with the Water Man. Why am I not surprised?"

Nigel let a sound of despair escape his lips as he jumped back and to the side, trying to shield Nassira. He fell heavily on his injured foot, and felt Nassira's hand on his shoulder as she pushed him aside.

"Don't try to protect me, you fool," she said in a low, even voice. "These are my people." And then she stepped forward, saying words that Nigel could not understand.

THE PAST AND ITS REACH

Of all the people to meet on a dark road at night while she was chaperoning a European, Nassira could have wished for a better person than Mokabi ole Lumbwa.

He was a tall boy—huge—the type who'd always made trouble for his father, his brothers, even his friends. When he was very small and, like other Masai children, had been given the responsibility of looking after his mother's goats and his father's sheep as a preliminary to the cows, he'd often tied things to the animals' tails and forgotten to milk the goats in a way quite unbecoming a future herdsman. To the other children, male and female, he'd been cruel, often throwing rocks at them or stealing their food in the long days in the pasture away from adult companionship.

Nassira knew he was one of the many young men and boys who had complained when Nassira's father had given her his herding stick.

And he was Kume's older half-brother, by Kume's father's right-hand wife. The other two boys, too, were Kume's half-brothers—they had Kume's tall, unencumbered build, his beautiful profile, his proud setting of shoulders. But lacking from their proud, intent gaze was that just slightly hesitant look that had both humanized Kume and made him irresistible to Nassira, who could never turn away the call of one less capable than herself. And Nassira knew there was only one way to deal with this group. She advanced on them, fists closed, pushing aside the Englishmen's ineffectual attempt to protect her. "Go away, Mokabi," she said. "We have no cows for you to raid, no riches for you to take. This is an Englishman who is on an exploratory mission and I'm guiding him."

Mokabi grinned. "You're guiding him, are you? Are you bundling with him? I didn't know you went for Water People. What do you like, the skin like tallow or the way he orders people around? Does he have cows, Nassira? Has he promised you cows?"

The only good response to this would be to thrash Mokabi's dumb body until some light entered his befuddled, self-satisfied brain. Unfortunately, should Nassira do that, it would break every remaining custom of her people that she hadn't challenged before. It would bring shame on her parents.

"If my father heard you, he'd give you the beating you deserve," she said.

He smiled. "But your father hasn't seen you in months, and everyone knows he has disowned you because you left without his permission." He turned aside and spit on the ground. "Weak men who sire only girls and then prize them above all else often cannot control them. If I had you at my command, you'd learn the proper respect and the proper attitude of a well-brought-up girl."

Nassira held fast to her lance, knowing that if the idiot tried anything, she was more than capable of stopping him in his tracks. She'd stopped a lion. She felt the lion's ears and tail in the folds of her wrap, where she'd put them. They weren't cured yet, nor turned into proper fetishes, but they were enough to give her courage. However, his words had found their mark in her heart. Her father had disowned her?

She thought of her father's patient, gentle expression, of his delight at her accomplishments. Had he missed her so much that he could find no other balm for his pain but to disown her? She'd never thought that she would be barred from her native village, from her father's home, from her mother's care.

"Oh, lots of people missed you, Nassira," the man said, his voice harsh, his eyes exploiting the weakness that Nassira had doubtless displayed upon her face. "My brother Kume died of it." He paused. "You did hear of Kume, did you not?"

Nassira took a deep breath. Mokabi was lying—he had to be. Kume could not be dead. Those quick-glancing eyes couldn't be forever closed. His body could not be nothing more than dust. "How...how did he die?" she asked.

Mokabi would tell her some tale of heroism, and then she'd know he was lying. But he just shook his head. "He was so upset over losing you, Nassira, daughter of Nedera, that when you left, he lost his way. In a cattle raid, he got in the way of a flung spear."

"Oh," Nassira said, and her world seemed to collapse around her. Somehow, at the back of her mind, she'd always known she was going back to meet Kume. Inadequate as he was, he would have made her a good husband and she could have kept him from showing his faults. She could have kept him alive. But she had left instead, and Kume had died. Sounds and vision and smell seemed very distant, and there was a noise like rushing water in her ears.

"And you take it so calmly." He looked over her shoulder. "Now that you have your Water Man, Kume does not matter?"

"He's not *my* Water Man," Nassira said. "And I do not *have* him." She looked away from Mokabi, unable to bear the way he resembled Kume and yet was so different from him. "I mourn Kume in my heart and I always will, but his death is not on my head."

"Is it not?" Mokabi stepped forward. "With you near he was strong and accomplished, but he must have loved you too much. For when you left, he couldn't do anything right and eventually died of it. Do you feel no guilt?"

Oh, she felt guilt, but she would never admit it. Not to this proud man with his overbearing tone. She remembered how terrified of him Kume had been. But she could never tell Kume's brother why he'd really died. She could not tell him that Kume needed her for more than his mental well-being. If she did, then she would be betraying Kume in a final way, letting his people know he'd not been a brave, competent warrior, and should not be remembered as such. She could never do that to her erstwhile lover.

"I was doing what I must do for Africa," she said. She could say no more without betraying Hyena Men secrets. "I am working with people from all tribes, from all over the continent, to rid our land of the Water People who steal our land and bring strange foreign diseases down upon our cattle."

Mokabi blinked. "Get rid of them by seducing them?" But his heart was not in it. Nassira's decisive tone had shocked him, her words had surprised him. And something else. He blinked again. "Are you with the Hyena Men?" he asked. "They take women?"

"They accepted me," she said simply.

He frowned. "Yes, but why you, Nassira, daughter of Nedera?"

"Because Africa must be saved."

"Must it? By you? You're just the spoiled daughter of a foolish rich man. If you'd not abandoned your proper place and taken upon yourself more responsibility than could possibly be yours, Kume would be alive, and your father would be happy. And you would be where you belong."

Nassira kept up her front, glaring at Mokabi, but she felt a pang of ache and memory, remembering her mother's hut, the smoky fire, the shuffling and moo- ings of the cows inside the enclosure.

"What do you know of where I belong?" she re- torted instead. "What do you know, Mokabi who stays home and like a cow sees nothing beyond what's immediately in front of his eyes? If they lead you to the slaughter, will you also go? Our cattle have died of foreign diseases, our young men have been killed by powersticks. How long till they come and take you away also?"

But Mokabi wasn't paying attention. He seemed to be listening for sounds in the bush. "Are the other Hyena Men around?" he asked. "Your companions?"

Nassira felt her lower lip attempt to curl in an ex- pression of derision. Oh, she should have known what would scare Mokabi. Like most bullies, he feared only

stronger physical force. And he would fear these unseen men he'd never met, instead of fearing Nassira
and her spear. Which only proved his stupidity, because the only thing keeping Nassira from killing him
was the shape of his eyes, the turn of his chin, those
features he shared with dead Kume.

"They are just around the corner," she said. "If I
call, they will come. Would you like to meet them?"

Mokabi shuffled his feet and adjusted his wrap
around his body. "No," he said. He looked over
Nassira's shoulder again, as though something had
called his attention, then turned to his younger brothers. "Did you hear that? I believe I just heard the roar
of the lion, that way." He looked at Nassira again.
"We're out hunting a lion that's been heard roaring
around the villages for days now. If I were you, I would
hurry to the safety of an encampment, before the lion
finds you."

And, oblivious to the fact that this particular lion
would never roar again, he gestured with his hand to
call his brothers and led them past Nassira and down
the narrow path.

A man stepped out of the shadows in front of them.
Tall and straight, wearing a red wrap, he was clearly a
Masai, and for just a moment Nassira tensed, ready
for another confrontation. Then she saw that the man
looked concerned.

"Nassira?" he asked, his low voice rumbling softly.

"Yes?" she asked, confused. "Do I know you?"

He shrugged and she thought that by the insufficient light of the distant moon she detected a faint
blush on his cheeks. "I am Sayo."

She blinked at the tall man, with his broad shoulders and sculpted features. He had been the one of Kume's companions, but one she'd never thought about. Though he was Kume's age, or perhaps a little older, he'd been small and timid, lurking in the shadows of his more accomplished and stronger companions.

She cleared her throat. "Little Sayo?"

He grinned broadly. "Not anymore."

"Are you with them?" she asked, gesturing with her head toward where the warriors had disappeared.

He made a face of distaste. "No. No more than it takes to follow behind and make sure they don't get in trouble. They are not ... trustworthy. They did not ... bother you, did they?" He looked anxious.

"They told me Kume is dead ..." she said. "Is it true?"

"Unfortunately, yes. He didn't have you to save him, Nassira. Without you to keep him safe ..."

"I know, I shouldn't have gone," she said.

"No. What you shouldn't have done is bind yourself to someone you needed to care for as if for a child. That's not what a lover is supposed to do, Nassira. You're supposed to be equals."

The words cut to the quick of Nassira's brain. It shocked her so much that it took a moment to realize that Sayo, little Sayo hiding in the shadows, had seen the truth of her relationship with Kume. "You ... knew? How it was with us?"

"It didn't take more than eyes to see," he said, and shrugged. Then smiled at her. "Though you never saw me."

"You hid," she said. "You were so small ..."

"Ah, yes. And you were young. And now you are

on a quest I don't understand. Finish your quest, Nassira, and come back home with your eyes open."

And with that, he was gone, back into the shadows. For a moment she remained still, breathless. Sayo. She'd never thought of Sayo as anything but a trailing child. But he'd seen what she'd been about. He'd understood.

With Englishmen to look after and her oath to the Hyena Men, with a magical jewel to find, with Africa to liberate, Nassira found herself wishing she'd never left her native village—wishing she'd been there to notice that Sayo was no longer a child.

Now it was lost beyond retrieval. There was no use thinking about what might have been. Yes, it might have been better if she'd never attached to people who needed her. But there were so many weak people. Strong Nassira must share her strength.

Nassira resumed walking, not turning to see if Nigel Oldhall followed, but half aware of him by the scraping sound of his shoes on the ground, the sound of his labored breathing fighting back the pain. "When we get to the camp," she said, "I'll make you a poultice for that foot."

He took a deep hissing breath. "What did those men want?"

She shook her head and continued walking, minding her footing on the thorny ground.

"Did you know them?" Oldhall persisted.

After a while in silence she said, "The biggest one reminded me of my brother. Not that they look anything alike, but they have the same posture." She turned back to look long and speculatively at the Englishman. He still seemed strange to her. Too pale, too washed out, much more like a transparent worm caught in a rainstorm than like a real human. And yet, in his pale-blue, washed-out eyes, Nassira noticed again the resemblance to Kume. The Englishman's gaze had the same velvety-soft expression, like the eyes of a calf that has strayed into the neighboring kraal and is afraid of being sent away.

Nassira blinked, telling herself it was stupid. What could this Englishman have in common with Kume? And yet... The posture was the same, and the way the Englishman held his head sideways, as though waiting with some trepidation for her answer. As though scared that she would reprove him or make fun of him. In the same way, the gallant effort he made not to show pain when he stepped on his mangled foot held an unmistakable resemblance to her friend.

Suddenly, she realized that Kume would be shocked at her finding such a similarity between him and this creature, and she smiled.

"What?" Nigel asked.

There would be no harm in telling the man something of what was in her thoughts, as long as she didn't describe to him the full contents of the conversation with Mokabi, including the references to the Hyena Men. And it would relieve Nassira's feelings to speak of Kume.

"I had a friend once who you remind me a great deal of," she said. "And that man—" she gestured with her head in the direction in which Mokabi had vanished, "was his elder brother. Well, half-brother, the son of my friend's father's right-hand wife."

"Right hand?" The Englishman sounded truly puzzled.

"The first wife," Nassira explained. "The one a man marries for prestige or cows, for social position." She shrugged, finding no echo of understanding in the pale blue eyes that regarded her with a puzzled expression. "Then he marries the left-hand one for love or for mutual understanding and companionship. My friend Kume's father married his mother because she was a great beauty. She gave him only Kume, and I think Kume was his favorite son. But not the most important." She gestured with her head again. "That one was the most important. That one and his brothers. The heirs, you know, the ones that matter."

Was it her impression, or did the Englishman take a deep, startled breath, the type of breath a man took when a sore area was touched or a wound probed?

He nodded as if he understood her, and she shrugged. "We must get back to camp," she said. "Kitwana will be worried about you."

"Kitwana? Why?"

"He saw you leave and was worried that you'd get lost or caught by a lion," she said. "So he woke me and sent me after you."

The Englishman looked at her with an odd expression, as though his features attempted to set in a rigid pattern but kept melting into a soft haze whose meaning she could not understand. "How kind," he said. "But I should not have to be looked after by natives."

She caught the implication in his voice that they were inferior, somehow, or perhaps childish, and said nothing.

They walked side by side in silence a long time, till they could see, shining between the trees and low brush around the camp, the soft haze of fire. The two men standing guard could be heard, too, talking to each other in a deep, guttural tongue of which Nassira understood not a word.

"I had a brother, too," Nigel said at last. "His name was Carew and he was the important one in my family. The heir. He came to Africa and disappeared. I am, in a way, looking for him. But if I return him, I will be again the unimportant one. Perhaps loved, but unimportant. Do you . . . do you understand?"

She tried to give him a look of annoyance. But she couldn't quite feel it, because she did understand, so she simply nodded. She saw in this man such a resemblance to Kume that she felt much more loyalty to him than she dared express.

He nodded back and exhaled, as though relieved with her approval, as though that mattered. Just as they emerged into the clearing around the camp, she touched his shoulder, "Look, don't go into the brush again, all right? Nothing is so bad as that."

He gave her a look, managing a frozen, opaque expression, but then smiled, as though despite himself. "Oh, things can be just that bad," he said. "But I'll remember I have duties to others."

"Do you want the poultice for your foot?" she asked.

He shook his head, and his smile turned vaguely superior. "We brought medicine," he said. "Magic potions for healing."

Before she had time to react to his show of superiority, the two guards sitting by the fire noticed them— their awareness perhaps slowed by the fact that they were passing a thick, earthenware jug between them. They stood up in a confusion of legs, arms and spears, making sounds that might have been a demand for identification. Then they recognized Nigel and Nassira and exchanged complicit looks and chuckled.

Nassira wasn't sure she liked the tone of those chuckles. She was afraid that, just like Mokabi, these creatures would think she was having an affair with Nigel Oldhall. But she didn't even want to mention the matter, in case she should only lend it credence.

Instead, she told Oldhall, "Well, good night, then," and, parting from him, went back to her uncomfortable leaf bed.

This time, she fell asleep as soon as she lay down.

A BROKEN HEART AND
A PLAN FOR REVENGE

Emily couldn't sleep. The night was too warm, and she kept thinking of how strange this journey was, and how unlikely that she should be here.

She was supposed to be on her honeymoon. She was supposed to be looking around Cairo, taking in the exotic sights at places where other Englishmen wintered every year. She was supposed to be sleeping safely in Nigel's arms.

Instead, here she was, mid-Africa, in the dark of night. She'd seen a dragon, once, and there were rumors of dragons all around. The roar of a lion bedeviled her and she was surrounded by men who looked more than a little wild. Could she trust any of them?

Nigel looked and seemed as lost as she felt. Indeed, he'd let her fall prey to the Hyenna Men, something no man in control of the situation would allow to happen.

With such an example of his lack of foresight and understanding, was it any surprise that Emily didn't feel safe? Instead, she had to trust Peter Farewell, and what did she know of him, other than that he was Nigel's old friend? Nigel's old friend to whom Nigel didn't seem to be speaking. And what did *that* mean? And why would Nigel shun her, also? He couldn't be that intimidated by the lack of privacy in the camp. There were shadows and silent spots aplenty. Surely Nigel knew that. Or maybe he didn't. Emily was not sure she knew Nigel anymore—or ever had. And try as she might, she couldn't fit into her mind that he suspected her—HER—of infidelity. How dared he?

She listened to the sentinels and to much coming and going outside her tent. It was white canvas and through it the diffused light of fire shone. She stared at that light and at the dark shadows of trees outside. She remembered stories her father's friends told, late at night over port, of native revolts only put down by the strong hand of the brave Englishmen. What Englishmen would save her if these natives revolted? Maybe Peter, but he was not her husband, and she could not *count* on him for her protection.

She wished Nigel would come to her and at least share his fears with her. Maybe if he admitted he wasn't in control they could at least share their feeling of being lost in this strange place. If Nigel came to her and loved her, and made her his wife in fact as well as in law, at least Emily would feel as though she belonged to him and was fit to share his perils, by his side.

At that moment, she heard Nigel's voice just outside her tent and her heart sped up in response. She couldn't understand what he was saying, but he spoke softly, and she imagined that he was calling to her, asking her if he could come in.

She sat up.

Nigel spoke again. From his tone of voice, she could tell he was hesitant and tentative.

She stood up quickly and got her dressing gown from where it lay, across her travel trunk. She hurried to the entrance of the tent and pulled back the flap. Outside, the night was moonlit, a soft light that joined with the glaring orange light of the fire. This clear lighting showed the other two tents—dark inside— and the guards by the fire, chatting and passing around the earthenware jug. But she did not see Nigel.

"Nigel?" she called softly.

He did not answer her. Instead, from her left side, where the bush grew high, she heard a woman's voice, as soft and hesitant as Nigel's.

Shocked, Emily stared at the low, thorny bushes, the thick, waist-high grass. Before her unbelieving eyes could adjust to this incongruous reality, Nigel emerged from the bush, his face ghastly pale in the moonlight. For all his paleness, though, he looked calm. Calmer than she'd seen him look in a very long time. Behind him walked the native woman he'd picked to be a cook—though she patently could not cook at all. The woman was tall and had a proud bearing that Emily had only before seen in some duchesses. She wore a colorful wrap that outlined a slim, shapely body taut with pride. She had noble, well-chiseled features that made Emily feel inadequate and small.

The woman touched Nigel's shoulder with a gentle touch and the type of gaze that could only be shared between a man and a woman who'd had a joint inti- mate experience. She might be a virgin herself, but she'd seen her father's renters and friends. There was communication there. A sharing and an understanding that Nigel and Emily had never had.

Emily reeled back, as though she'd been punched. With only a sliver of the tent flap open to admit a strip of firelight, she stared out at Nigel and the woman crossing the encampment together. They spoke to each other in the way that long-married couples did. As though they'd shared so many things, so full of wonder and joy and grief, that no secrets remained between them.

Feelings that couldn't quite assemble themselves into words crossed her mind in tumult. No wonder Nigel had no wish to consummate his marriage—he did have another love. And no wonder Emily's father had found no trail of this love. Such a thing would never have crossed his well-bred mind.

Emily remembered, as from a distance, the image of this woman's face in an English maid's cap. Emily knew then that her first instincts had been correct. She had seen Nassira before. This was the woman who had helped Emily to her hotel.

Emily felt her cheeks flame. She'd asked Nigel's mistress for help.

She could now see it clearly. This woman had been a maid in England, and somehow she'd conquered Nigel's affections. Nigel, being honorable, could not betray his lover with his wife. And here, in Africa—had he truly been sent on a mission, or had he offered to come?—with Nassira and with Emily, Nigel could give free rein to his love and ignore Emily, whom he'd never loved at all.

If Emily thought at all about the fact that Nigel's lover was a native, it was with wonder that Nigel did not, after all, prefer a bland and blond English miss. But then, during their courting, she'd often suspected that Nigel wanted her only for her exotic qualities. And this woman was doubtlessly more exotic than Emily.

And more beautiful, she thought as she looked at Nassira in her barbaric red wrap.

Suddenly Emily felt very tired, as though all her vital strength had leached out in that one sight. Her knees trembled, tears sprang to her eyes. She knew she would cry, but she would not cry here, where someone might look toward her and see it. She backed away into the safe darkness of her tent, letting the flap fall closed. Without noticing the harshness of the mattress, she fell upon her camp bed.

All her life, Emily had trusted those around her. At first, she'd trusted her mother. Her warm, kind mother with the happy laughter and the welcoming arms had been the center of Emily's world. But her mother had died, vanished from her life.

Then she'd trusted her father, even if she had not loved him the way she'd loved her mother. Her father was stolid and always there, a comforting, strong presence, ready to make sure Emily was safe. But then her father had remarried, and more than half of his attention fell to his wife and his new daughters. Now his betrayal of Emily was complete. Still, she'd trusted him. Trusted him to keep her safe, to safeguard her happiness and her honor. And yet her father had allowed—encouraged—Emily to marry Nigel.

Which had led Emily here, to the midst of forsaken Africa, where she was neither a wife, nor a mistress, nor even Nigel Oldhall's equal, and certainly not his love.

Sometime during the night, in the middle of her turmoil, between tears shed on her pillow and rumpled sheets on the camp bed, she decided that from now on she would steer her fate, because she could trust no one else to do it for her. She would lean on Peter, but she wouldn't trust him, either. And she would stop feeling guilty for believing that in this expedition Peter was the only one who could protect her. Here, so many miles away from all the people who'd formed and given boundaries to her life and her beliefs and abandoned or betrayed her, she would tread her own path.

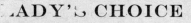

ᴸADY'ᵓ CHOICE

Emily walked with Peter. The day had dawned brisk and humid, but with a promise of great heat beneath its cold-dewed fingertips.

They'd been climbing a great scarp, in a line, with Kitwana ahead—though sometimes the carrier leader dropped behind Nigel and walked beside Emily for a while, casting toward Peter looks that to Emily seemed challenging and defiant.

Nigel walked with Nassira openly and when not staring at Emily talked quietly with the native woman, who seemed to be full of attention and care for both Nigel and his words.

Emily studiously avoided looking at Kitwana. She had not come to Africa to become smitten with a native. She was aware of the differences in their education, in their backgrounds. He was a carrier, someone who made a living by lifting heavy burdens by the strength of his muscular body. No matter how much he behaved like a prince. Perhaps there was even a strangeness to his soul. Some people in England seemed to think Africans were that alien.

And Emily didn't want to know Kitwana closely enough to find out if it might be true. How much could this tall, lean African, used to the boundless forests of his homeland and ignorant of drawing room etiquette and modes of dressing, have in common with an English lady? She found herself watching his broad shoulders, his easy gracefulness, and she told herself it was foolish and also inappropriate.

As for Farewell, he had been quiet. He walked as he usually did in the morning, with a spring in his step, appearing cheerful and happy. Now and then he looked at Emily with a quietly considering look in his green eyes. But he did not talk.

"You look well rested, Mr. Farewell," Emily said.

Having decided she was going to claim Peter for her own, to protect her on her journey through Africa, she was determined to claim his heart. "You must sleep very well indeed," she added with a smile

He looked at her and opened his mouth as though he was laughing, though no sound emerged from between his lips. His eyes seemed to dance with merriment for a moment, then he blinked and looked away. "It comes from a clean conscience," he said.

Was he warning her off her attempt at immorality? She looked forward to where Nigel walked with Nassira. His head was bent slightly, to speak to her, while she in turn looked upward as if she was bathing in the full light of Nigel's regard.

Nigel and Emily had walked like that, along quiet English streets and parks, through their courtship and engagement. A vise of regret clutched Emily's heart. Had Nigel loved her then? Or had it all been make-believe? "I wonder how long Nigel has known the native woman."

Peter looked toward Nigel. "He knew her before he came here?"

"He must have," Emily said. "She was a maid aboard the carpetship that brought us to Africa. And she and Nigel..." Emily's voice failed her and she found a strong need to clear her throat. "They were in the jungle. Alone. I saw them come back to the encampment."

Peter gave Emily a long, calculating look. "Are you sure you're not imagining too much? After all, a man with a young and beautiful wife such as you..."

Emily felt her cheeks flame. This was all the confirmation she needed. Peter thought her beautiful. The wind brought her a faint smell of Nigel's cologne, but all she could see of him was his back, clad in a brown safari suit. She spoke looking at that back, her voice a whisper. "I'm his wife in name only," she said.

For a long while, Peter did not speak. Silence seemed to assume a physical weight between them.

"Well," he said at length. "He is worried. There is so much on his mind—"

"Not enough to keep him from going out with his woman at night," Emily said. "From disappearing with her into the jungle."

Silence nudged between them again, and Emily could feel Peter staring at her. "It's extraordinary." He took a deep breath and was quiet a moment. When he spoke again, it was in an expressionless voice. "One thinks one knows a fellow. I'm sorry, it is a damnable situation, and one you should not be subjected to. I suppose in England you might have returned to your father's home."

He obviously didn't know her father, and Emily

was not about to enlighten him. She made a sound
that he could interpret in any way he wished.

"Nigel is my friend. If I should speak to—"

Emily shook her head. "It would only make things
worse. He'd never forgive me for telling you."

"But . . ." Peter said. He opened his free hand in a
show of helplessness. "But there has to be something I
might do."

In the far distance, a herd of antelopes startled and
hopped away.

"If you think of any way in which I might be of service," Peter said at last, "I am yours to command."

Emily smiled and lowered her head, feeling her
cheeks color. She had thought he was hers, but it was
good to hear him say it nonetheless. Still, Emily knew
now that there were two kinds of marriage—a marriage in law, such as she had with Nigel, which meant
very little at all, and a marriage of minds and hearts,
such as she hoped to establish with Peter. She would
not let the law stand in the way of what was right.
There would always be time to ratify their legal situation later on, should she and he and Nigel survive this
journey.

But for now, she would struggle for the marriage
she wanted. It had better chances of being a success
than her legal union with Nigel.

"Oh, I will ask for your help," she said to Peter,
who smiled at her, "as soon as I think how you might
give it."

THE DRAGON'S LAIR

The way Emily saw it, Peter was now attracted to her, but not so strongly that his reason and loyalty to Nigel could not overcome. However, she knew he desired her. She could feel the heat that smoldered between them. If she allowed him to satisfy his desire, would that not bind him to her?

Peter Farewell was a gentleman. He belonged to an old family. If he gave in to his desire for Emily, he would feel obligated to her. He'd feel forced to shield her from the consequences of her transgression with him, to protect her and to take care of her.

And Emily thought she could take advantage of the moment, while she was the only Englishwoman anywhere near and while Peter felt sympathetic toward her loneliness and her situation.

Looking at Peter's broad shoulders and the easy, effortless elegance of his walk, Emily stopped herself from sighing. Tonight she would be his in fact, which must trump her merely legal connection to Nigel.

Kitwana played into her hands. He'd been peevish and impatient with everyone all day, yelling at lagging carriers and, for inscrutable reasons, shooting annoyed looks at Peter. The sun had barely set when

Kitwana put down the bundle he'd been helping another carrier with. "It would be best to camp here for the night," he said.

Peter left Emily's side and strode forward.

"Here?" he asked Kitwana. "Where we'll be exposed to everyone's sight for miles?"

They stood in a flat promontory amid the uneven, green landscape. It was an unusually flat, denuded space.

"Natives can see us from every side," Peter said. "What's to stop them from attacking us in the night?"

"If they do," Kitwana said, glaring at Peter in a most impudent way, "we'll see them coming."

"I say we go farther on." Peter signaled with his hand to move forward. "Pick up your burdens. Let's walk to that place with the boulders and the large trees, up there." He pointed. "Night won't fall before we've had the time to find a small clearing within it, and then we can camp there. We'll be more protected."

"Or our enemies better hidden," Kitwana said, and stared sharply at Peter, his gaze full of fury. He glared around him, at the carriers. "None of you pick up anything."

The few of them who had lifted their burdens set them down again.

Peter started at Kitwana as though he had spoken in code. What did the carrier mean by *enemies*? Did Kitwana know something about the Hyena Men?

Impatient to carry out her own plan, Emily frowned.

"Look, you hired me to guide you and I'm guiding you. In this terrain, this is the best place to stay,"

Kitwana said. "I am your guide and I tell you we're stopping here."

"Well, I say we go on," Peter Farewell said.

Nigel came forward. The girl, Nassira, came with him, by his side as if she were his wife—his woman—and acknowledgd as such. She whispered urgently to him.

Nigel looked bewildered and stared down at the woman with a puzzled stare. She nodded once—the nod of a woman commanding a man who knows better than to disobey. Nigel's eyebrows came together over his high-bridged nose in a puzzled frown, then parted again. "If you're sure," he said.

It looked to Emily as if he was speaking to Nassira, but he was turning as he spoke and he might very well have been speaking to Kitwana. "If you're sure, of course we'll follow your opinion."

Then he looked around, the bewildered expression back in his eyes. "I say," he told Kitwana, "this does seem like a very strange place to camp."

"There are snakes in the forest ahead," Kitwana said. "They will drop from the trees and they have venom such that one dies in seconds from the bite."

Nigel cast a look toward the forest. "Then I daresay this rocky place is probably the best. No trees, no place for snakes to hide even, like grass or . . . or dead leaves."

"Oh, nonsense," Peter said. "What snakes are these that they infect only this particular forest?"

"They're snakes that prefer this climate," Kitwana replied, impassive.

Peter opened his mouth, closed it, then glared at Kitwana and the carriers, some of whom were sitting on the trunks, others standing but in a sagging position of repose that clearly meant they would go no farther.

"This is the most ridiculous . . ." Peter frowned, his eyebrows low over his eyes. "We're allowing a carrier to order us around. Have you so lost track of who hired whom?"

He brought his hands to his hips and looked around, his body tense, his lips pressed together, his whole expression and posture indicating that he was ready to fight.

Though whom he meant to fight—Kitwana, the carriers or Nigel—Emily did not know. But she knew that if Peter continued arguing with Nigel, then Peter would blurt out something about Nigel's relationship with Nassira and his failed marriage with Emily. It was just the sort of thing men blurted out when they disagreed and tempers got high enough. And Emily could not yet allow it to happen. Not before she had secured Peter. She surged forward and grabbed at Peter's arm. "Peter," she said, and seeing Nigel's eyes widen, amended, "Mr. Farewell. No place to stop for the night can be as dangerous as arguments amid our party."

Peter looked displeased. He started to shake Emily's hand away from his arm. Then he sighed and took his hand to his face, rubbing it like a man trying to remove cobwebs from his eyes. "I see." He looked at Emily, then glowered at the rest of the party. "I see that I cannot stand against everyone else." He shrugged and walked away to the edge of the rocky area. Some bushes grew there, sparse and hesitant. He looked at the sky, then down at the hilly but lower-lying terrain, as if—Emily thought—he were studying an escape route.

Around Emily, tents started going up, Kitwana directing the carriers with no more than a gesture and, now and then, the occasional shouted word. She did not understand the words, but the carriers seemed to understand and obey.

Nigel's lady-love had gathered wood and—lighting the fire with a magic spark—started her daily attempts to burn the water for tea. Nigel, of course, stood behind her, as if her every gesture, her smallest motion, were a marvel to be studied and contemplated.

Peter paced around the area, looking like a caged lion. He removed his coat and patted it down for his cigarettes. He found one, dropped it, picked it up, put it between his lips and patted the coat down for his cigarette lighter, which he then dropped, too. He pushed his lips outward, in peevish annoyance, as he lit his cigarette and put his lighter back in his pocket. Puffing clouds of smoke into the air, he still looked trapped as his green eyes spied this way and that, like a beast looking for a way out amid the approaching hunters.

He stared at Nigel, who stood by Nassira, apparently engrossed in watching her search for tea in the provisions trunk, and frowned. He looked at Kitwana and frowned in an even more menacing way, puffing clouds of smoke into the air. He stomped his foot, looked at Emily and raised his eyebrows, as though attempting to establish a connection, or to send a message with his gaze.

She approached him and he nodded to her.

"Dam—" he said, and puffed smoke. "Awful place to camp. We're out in the open. We're going to be besieged by natives by the end of tonight. We're—"

Emily didn't say anything. She looked away from him. On the one hand, Peter did seem to know what he was doing, to understand Africa. On the other hand, the carriers were supposed to know Africa, too, personally as well as professionally. That was one of the reasons to hire them.

Emily looked toward Kitwana, who stood over the carriers while they put up her tent, stretching the white fabric over the armature. She found him looking at her, his eyes curiously widened, like a man shocked by some revelation. She felt herself blush and didn't know why.

Peter stomped again, as though remembering Emily's not seconding his opinions reawakened his anger. He flicked his cigarette a few steps away and strode forward to step on it. "I have half a mind to just go and spend the night elsewhere by myself, so I can swoop in and save you all before you are massacred."

"I think," Kitwana said, looking away from Emily, as if Peter's words had called him, "you should stay where you are. The last thing we need is your *swooping* in. And leave the massacres be. Because you never know who might be massacred."

Peter looked at Kitwana with wide-eyed shock. Of course, Kitwana had spoken freely, as no servant would dare speak to his employer in England. But Peter Farewell was looking at the carrier leader with a different kind of shock. Again, Emily felt as though Kitwana had spoken in code, a kind of code no one else save Peter Farewell could hope to understand.

Was Emily imagining things? Had her nervous eagerness somehow gotten in her mind and twisted her perceptions around?

"Well," Peter said. "Well, you have a lot—" He blinked at Kitwana myopically, as though the African were something strange, or very far away—a look Emily had seen on people attempting to discern another's aura of magical power. "A lot of magical power. Very strange power, certainly, for someone..." he puffed a cloud of smoke, "in your position."

Kitwana pounded a tent stake into the ground and looked up, his eyes intent and alert. "A lot of us have power we shouldn't have in our positions."

Peter threw the half-smoked cigarette onto the ground and stepped on it. He turned to Emily. "They say if you should go on a trip with friends, be prepared to lose them," he drawled. "Apparently, you can lose employees, too."

"I believe," Kitwana said, "they don't mean by that saying that one should devour them."

Peter narrowed his eyes at him. "You make no sense. Devour? What do you speak of? I believe your lack of knowledge of English betrays you."

Emily nodded. The conversation between Kitwana and Peter seemed like a cipher to her, a mystery language strangely spoken.

She looked toward Peter and offered her arm. "Will you take a turn with me, Mr. Farewell?" she said. "Before the night falls?"

"You've not walked enough for a day?" Peter asked, but smiled and visibly relaxed. He allowed her to support her hand on his arm. "We'll stay well away from those famous trees where the dangerous snakes wait for the once-a-year traveler to walk under them."

Emily smiled, not sure it was the joke Peter thought it was. After all, would not the African know about local wildlife?

She noticed Kitwana's worried look as she left. But Nigel, talking to the native girl, didn't even notice her departure.

A STEP IN THE DARK

Dinner was a strange affair. Since the Europeans and the natives ate apart, Emily and Nigel could not escape some conversation with each other. Their need to speak to one another was made more urgent by Peter's not speaking at all.

Farewell obviously had something on his mind, some weighty subject that stopped him midsentence and made his thoughts revolve upon a soundless round. Emily thought she knew what preyed on his emotions so. From the touches of her hand on his arm, from the sound of his voice when he looked at her, even from Peter's argument with Kitwana, she was sure Peter wanted her. But he was an honorable man, well brought up in the British honor code. He would think that his love for her was impossible, disgraceful. Look how he stole furtive glances at her—glances so full of meaning and longing and frustrated desire. His anger, his silence, his lashing out at everyone—even Kitwana—were all the obvious offspring of what he thought must be his honorable self-denial. And Kitwana, too, rising to Peter's bait. But she wouldn't think about that. She had come to think of the African as an equal. Indeed, in many cases as admirable. Or at least he seemed ever ready to aid and assist her. But she would prefer to throw in her lot with someone who might understand her.

She caught one of Peter's glances and smiled at him while lowering her eyelids in a half-demure, half-tempting expression. He looked confused. It was time she took things into her own hands. She felt confident and strong. A quick, guilty glance at Nigel assured her that her legal husband, too, looked quietly sure of himself. Did his lover and admission of their relationship give him that quiet confidence?

She looked at Peter and their gazes met. His deep, oceanic eyes seemed to draw her in, to pull her toward horizons as yet undiscovered. Somehow—here, in the middle of the jungle, where they hadn't properly bathed in days—Peter Farewell smelled good. It was a strange smell, clean and somehow natural—the smell of a creature living naturally and cleanly. Not the smell of sweaty, tired humans. It marked him as a man apart, somehow superior to them all. Looking at him made her heart race and a pleasant heat spread over her body. She wanted to see him out of his well-tailored clothes. She wanted to run her hands along his golden skin.

She wanted to see if she could shatter Peter Farewell's look of sardonic, well-bred superiority. She had never wanted a man that way, not even when she'd expected Nigel to be her husband forever. The sight of Peter fascinated her in a way she could not fully understand. She imagined that if she touched his skin, it would feel oddly smooth and cold. She was sure he desired her, yet he seemed like a distant, unattainable man, as if he could never fully belong to her or to any other woman. As if he did not even inhabit the same world.

She could barely keep the sensuous smile that twisted her lips from translating to words or to a touch on his arm. And all the while Peter looked at her with that longing, that strange calculating expression, his attraction no longer a secret.

It did not surprise her at all that he chose to retire early, after eating the tough and gristly piece of antelope that Nassira had put on his plate.

Peter set his plate aside and stood with unconscious grace, like a bird spreading its wings. "I will retire now," he said. He stretched his arms over his head, not quite a yawn, but a motion that implied both tiredness and sensuality, like a tiger stretching before springing. "It's been an exhausting day, and who knows what trials expect us in the night."

He smiled at Nigel. "Good night," he said. "And a very good night, Mrs. Oldhall."

Emily smiled at him, showing him she understood his invitation. Or perhaps he meant to come into her tent. But no, she would not stand for that. Never. If he came to her tent, it would make her feel like a kept woman, a helpless creature, at his mercy. She had decided to take her life into her own hands, and she would. She would visit Peter Farewell before he could come to her. As Peter retreated into the tent, she watched his broad shoulders disappear. There was a man—not Nigel's slim tallness, nor the graceful, well-bred aloofness of a properly educated English male.

Oh, Peter was of good breeding, no doubt about it, from as proud an ancestry as any man could hope to have. But his nobility was of a different kind from

Nigel's. It was the nobility of the feudal lord who would be expected to defend his lands and his people by the strength of his arms. The idea of laying with him, of being his, made Emily shiver.

"Listen, Emily," Nigel said.

She turned toward him, surprised that he was still there and hadn't disappeared. "Yes?"

"The other night," he said, "when I went into the jungle. When I . . . When I . . ."

What was he trying to tell her? Was he truly going to confess to her that he wanted another? That he loved another? That their marriage had been a mistake?

Emily didn't want to hear it. She did not know why, since she'd long ago stopped caring for Nigel. She was sure he meant nothing at all to her. And yet the thought of his telling her plainly that he didn't love her and never had made her heart feel like it had been turned into ice—cold and brittle and bound to break at a touch. She did not want to hear how much he loved Nassira, or what qualities had bound him to the regal African girl. Whatever those were, they certainly had nothing to do with Nassira's cooking skills.

"I know," she said.

His eyes widened in surprise, and his lips half parted.

"I know," she spoke quickly, to forestall his words. "I saw you coming back from the jungle that night."

"Oh," Nigel said. He looked startled. "Oh. I didn't . . . know—" He turned very red, a high color suffusing his cheeks. "I—I thought you and Peter—" He shook his head. "It was unmanly of me, Emily. I should never have gone back on my word that way

and forgotten my duty to my parents and all my ancestors. But, you see, Nassira came after me, she
saved me. She was—" He gave the native girl a confused look. "She is like no other woman. She quite re-
minds me of a heroine, out of history. You know, when
the Bible says blessed is he who marries the perfect
woman? It all seemed nonsense to me until now.
Finally I understand how a woman can materially
contribute to make a man happy or fortunate or prosperous or even..." He smiled a pale, fugitive smile.
"To keep him alive."

Emily's heart felt as though it had started crack-
ing, as though it would at any moment fall into shards.
And if it did, it would never be put together again.
Never again. "It's fine, Nigel," she said, quickly.
"Everything is fine. You are forgiven. We all make
mistakes."

She put her hand out to try to silence him, then
stood hastily. "I don't think I was . . . or that we were
ever meant to be..." She didn't finish the sentence,
letting it drop into silence. She didn't know how to finish it, at any rate. To be *together* would do, or to be *in
love,* or perhaps even *to be married.* But to say those
words would sound too stark and defined in her own
ears.

Nigel stood up quickly and reached for her hand.
"Emily," he said. "I'm sure I never deserved you. But
I thank you. I thank you for your forgiveness, your
kindness, your..." He blushed. "Your care. I don't
know what to do about all this, but when we return, I
will find a way to make it right."

Before Emily could quite pull her hand away, he
had hold of it, was kissing it. His lips felt hot, fevered,

like that night on the train when they'd both thought they were going to die. They seemed to burn into her skin like scalding wax.

She pulled her hand away. "Mr. Oldhall. Nigel. Not now. Not now."

"Of course," he said, and bowed a little. "Of course not." He looked around.

He feared that his lover had seen him with his wife! Oh, it would be enough to make Emily laugh, if only she didn't feel so much like crying. She pulled her hand to her, suddenly chilled, and walked away from Nigel. He remained sitting by the fire, doubtless waiting till the encampment was quiet so he could go to his lover. Well, tonight Emily would not cry alone into her pillow. She'd determined to never again let anyone control her that way. Tonight, she'd become mistress of her own fate.

In her tent, where the carriers had put warmed water in a basin, she washed as best she could and put on her nightgown—the good one that she'd packed for her first night of marriage. This would be her first night of marriage now—a true union, despite its not being sanctioned by English law. She shook it out and put it on, relishing the clean, crisp feeling of the cotton upon her skin. She felt hot. Too hot. The cotton was a welcome, familiar relief.

She let her hair down and brushed it, waiting for the noise in the camp to go down, till only two sentinels were left by the fire. Those two were always drinking, or playing some strange game with knucklebones by the fire. They'd never notice her going into Peter's tent. And besides, what did they know of the relationships between the British? Nothing at all.

They probably would not even notice that she was with a man not her husband.

When things quieted outside, she opened her tent flap. The two guards were sitting on the other side of the fire, where they wouldn't be able to see her for the glare.

She walked out of her tent. Just outside, she paused and seemed to hear her father's voice tell her that bestowing her favors on someone besides Nigel would be the betrayal of her soul, the shredding of her reputation. After that, she would be worse than dead. But Emily's father had handed her to Nigel, and Nigel had proven unworthy. Her father had never told her what to do when Nigel refused to be her true husband.

She walked on, to Peter's tent. At the entrance, she considered calling out, but she didn't want to call attention to herself. Instead, she reached for the tent flap. All her senses heightened, she felt the roughness of the canvas cloth against her palm. She heard the incomprehensible words of the guards who talked by the fire, smelled the alien vegetation growing, fecund, around her.

Her heart pounded. Her lips felt dry. Her breathing sounded too loud. The touch of the warm air against her skin, her neck, was almost more than she could bear.

She lifted the tent flap. And stopped.

There was a weird light within—neither magelight nor light from the fire, nor any other kind of illumination that Emily could understand. It was a soft blue glow, alien and unearthly.

Peter stood naked in the middle of his tent. In the strange blue radiance, he looked tall, muscular, golden, softly glowing as if he had been poured of molten metal. He stood without moving and in his standing there was the suggestion of great strength under control, of force, contained and about to spring. His muscles were obvious without being overdone and he had almost no body hair at all. Light glimmered from the even smoothness of his golden skin, making him look like the statue of an ancient idol. Thus had Apollo looked when he appeared to maidens in the olden days. Emily blinked.

Yet something at the back of her mind shied away, horrified. He looked as wonderfully masculine as she'd expected, but something was very wrong. She'd never expected him to be naked. What did he think of her, to act thus? Did he expect her to be so easy, so lost to all civility? Was he so sure of her? Had she so betrayed herself? She wasn't aware of making any sound, but she must have, because he turned half around, and his eyes widened in shocked surprise, as if she were the last person he expected to see there.

"For G—For heaven's sake—" he started, but his eyes widened again, and his face contorted into an expression of unbearable pain. Sweat poured down his forehead and his knees buckled. Reaching for the edge of his camp table, he held it as if it were his only grip on reality.

"Mrs.—" he said, but he could speak no more.

His body twisted, contorted, as though under great pain. He turned away. He coughed.

It was a cough like none other that Emily had ever heard—a body-twisting, nerve-wracking cough, the sounds of a soul coming unmoored from a suffering body.

"Mr. Farewell." He was ill. He was in pain. Emily rushed forward. But he was naked. She stopped, steps away from him. "Peter . . . What is wrong?"

He coughed again, worse than before, a horrible series of spasms. From amid that, his voice came like a high shriek, the scream of a damned soul in the torments of hell. "For God's sake, Mrs. Oldhall—"

"What is it? What do you need? What can I do for you?" She rushed forward and put her hand on his shoulder. A thousand unlikely things went through her head. That Nigel had poisoned Peter. That Peter suffered from some horrible hereditary illness. Was there some disturbing malady he'd come to Africa to hide? "How may I help you?"

Peter wrenched away from her hand, all the while shaking his head no so violently that it looked as though it might break from his neck and roll away. "For God's sake, leave," he said, his voice low, strangled. "Get away from me. Get away *now*."

Emily froze. What had she done? She'd misinterpreted something. Peter Farewell didn't want her. He never had.

She stood very still and felt as if she were freezing from the neck on down. She'd allowed her desire for him to lead her into thinking— The enormity, the horror of her mistake drove all other thought from her mind.

Peter's gaze fixed itself above and past her left shoulder. He started coughing again. As he coughed, it seemed to Emily that his body contorted in a way that didn't look human. It twisted like the shadow of a flame played upon by the wind, his limbs changing shape, extending. His face growing a muzzle, his oceanic eyes—

Emily opened her mouth in shock as she recognized that face, that muzzle, those glimmering teeth.

Someone pushed Emily from behind. A native ran in carrying a lance. Kitwana. He'd lost his English clothing somehow and wore a short, elaborate, leather apron, which made him look more like a prince than ever. His body glimmered, muscular, powerful.

He ran past Emily and leveled his lance at Peter.

At the dragon.

FACING THE DRAGON

It had taken Kitwana a long time to hear from Shenta.
Shenta had weighed the evidence, and—he said—
talked to other members of the organization. Kitwana
wasn't sure there were any other members, but
Shenta had talked to someone.

This Kitwana knew, because all of a sudden Shenta
was full of information. The type of magical pattern
they'd sensed, the creature with the Englishman, was a
dragon. The way the animals avoided Peter Farewell
was the sign of the dragon in human form. Shenta said
there were rumors and stories about him—that he'd
come from Europe with a band of magic-haters before.
That even his own people abandoned him when they
learned he was a dragon.

Shenta had ordered Kitwana to kill Peter Farewell.
It did not matter if the dragon was also an Englishman.
He was a beast.

Yet Kitwana had seen Emily Oldhall look at the
creature. He'd noticed that she preferred Peter
Farewell's company, and spent more time with him
than even with her own husband. For some reason
this hurt him—he couldn't say why. She was, after all,
an Englishwoman. She'd never think twice about

him, much less think of him as an eligible man. But her eyes were the blue of the sky above Zululand, and when she walked, she moved with the gracefulness of a bird in flight.

And there had been something in the last few days—the tilt of her head, the defiant expression in her eyes—that made Kitwana suspect she was infatuated with the were-dragon. She might very well seek the creature's company, perhaps as early as tonight. It could be disastrous.

Kitwana must kill the dragon tonight. He'd gotten clear orders from Shenta. It was essential for the safety of the Hyena Men that this threat be eliminated as soon as possible. Shenta had said clearly that this was the spirit-beast that had killed the other Hyena Men. And now it must be waiting to finish them off.

So after they'd set up the encampment and before dinner, Kitwana had bespelled a lance with the strongest magic he could command. Dragons could not be killed by mundane weapons, but magic could kill them. And Kitwana was trying hard not to think that the dragon was also a man.

He had a splitting headache, and at the back of his mind, his father harangued and preached about human life and hereditary maladies one could not help. Only, Peter Farewell's hereditary illness was potentially lethal for others. Involuntary or not, it must be stopped.

In the dark of night, as he was skirting around the shadows beyond the light of the campfire, Kitwana stopped. He could see Emily Oldhall's shadow within her tent. She was undressing, and Kitwana's thoughts, even his worry about killing a man, fled.

He doubted she knew it, but he could see her body, starkly delineated against the white canvas fabric, as she changed clothes and brushed her hair. Amazing how familiar she looked like that, divested of the voluminous disguise of English clothes. She looked like a maiden of his tribe, strong and without artifice. He could imagine her skin darker, her hair a tight curl— and seeing her like this was like seeing through to her soul and as one like himself. It wasn't that there was anything wrong with her color, either. Her skin shone like burnished bronze and her black hair, with its soft curl, made him wonder if it would feel like lamb's wool upon the palm of his hand.

Kitwana was so confused by the cascading emotions evoked by Emily's image that he stood frozen on the warm, rocky ground. He'd felt attracted to her before, but he knew in his heart that any relationship would be impossible. Yet how impossible could it be? She was a woman. And he was a man.

As Kitwana stood there, Emily opened her tent flap and slipped out, sliding through the night toward Peter Farewell's tent.

His heart leapt into his mouth. She was going to the dragon.

He'd heard before that such creatures held an irresistible appeal to female humans, which explained how they managed to keep reproducing. It also explained all the legends about virgins being sacrificed to strange, eldritch creatures throughout the centuries. But how could Emily Oldhall do that? Kitwana could feel within her a soul he understood and respected more than that of any other female. The way she listened to him, her excitement in adventure, the way she bore the perils of a strange land with neither defiance nor swooning. He had started to feel within her a soul he could love. How could she be so gullible, so foolish, so inexpressibly *English* as to go running into the dragon's lair?

He shot a rancorous look at Nigel Oldhall's tent. It was all *his* fault for not taking care of his wife as a man should. It was all his fault for being bland as milk and weak as water. And then Kitwana heard a sound. A whimper, from the direction in which Emily had disappeared, and it reminded him of what he'd intended to do.

He must go to the dragon, not stand here musing on the shortcomings of the Oldhalls' marriage.

Dragons had uses for beautiful women other than siring their offspring. Dragons ate people as well as animals. Dragons—

Kitwana ran, his bare feet slapping the ground, gripping his bespelled weapon. It would wound the dragon like a thousand normal lances. Though his father disapproved of the weapon—and of all weapons in general—Kitwana knew it was the most efficient form of lance yet invented. It allowed a warrior, in a smooth movement, to get beneath his enemy's shield and pierce his heart.

And Kitwana *would* pierce the dragon's heart.

He dove into the tent of the creature who called himself Peter Farewell, just in time. Emily Oldhall stood before him, a look of sheer terror in her face and seemingly paralyzed by the creature's power, while the were-dragon opened his mouth wide, fangs glistening.

Kitwana jumped between the creature and Mrs. Oldhall, his assegai raised high.

"You creature of evil, you man-eating monster," he yelled, surprised to find himself speaking in English, his own words echoing alien to his ears. "You will die now, and in that way pay for the death of all my friends."

The creature—now fully a dragon, long muzzle and glimmering green eyes slanted long and reptilian—turned toward Kitwana, its expression still somehow holding that civilized irony that was Peter Farewell's trademark. Kitwana even thought that it smiled, its green eyes roiling with cynical amusement. The look disconcerted Kitwana for just a second, but a second was enough. The dragon snapped its jaws playfully in Kitwana's direction, then jumped, tearing the canvas cloth of the tent as though it was old newsprint. The tent's frame splintered and broke, like matchsticks, and the dragon shook itself free of it and then unfolded. Or at least that was how it looked to Kitwana—as if Peter were unfolding in waves of gold and green, of flickering lights and shimmering golden sinew and muscle.

For just a moment, the dragon looked as much a thing of natural beauty as the butterfly that flew shimmering through the dark forests near Kitwana's homeland.

Kitwana gasped, and his grip on his assegai loosened as the dragon spread its wings, blocking out the starry night sky. It roared with outraged pride and looked down at Kitwana, as though asking how he dared think he could face this mightiest of beasts armed only with an assegai. His huge, multifanged mouth opened and let out a burst of flame. Kitwana screamed and ran, grabbing Emily's arm and dragging her with him.

All those years with the Zulus, all the fearful battles in which he'd taken part, and he'd never run. But now he thought only of himself and Emily Oldhall, of saving both of them from the fearsome, strange beast.

Once he had given her the initial impulse, Mrs. Oldhall ran as easily, as forcefully, as a maiden of his own homeland. They ran side by side, and the dragon hopped after them, shaking remaining shreds of tent from its body and wings. Seemingly careful to avoid stepping on the sleeping bundles on the ground, the great beast leapt after them.

The bundles of sleeping people woke with the noise of the dragon's roars and the Earth trembling from its heavy hops. Men rose in shock, eyes rounded, mouths opened, ready to scream. Some reached for lances, some screamed in rage, others just ran in terror as the camp boiled with chaos.

Kitwana stopped running near the pile of weapons and let go of Emily. He found his Zulu shield—a rectangle of leather that protected most of his body. He slipped his arm into the straps at the back and turned to face his foe. Hyena Men rallied around Kitwana, holding their shields and brandishing their spears menacingly. But Kitwana knew better than to wait for their support. He'd learned that lesson from the boys in his village, in the long ago days of his childhood. He was the only one blamed, the only one exiled, the only one sent to live with his mother's family.

He felt his shoulders singe as another burst of flame played, too closely. He jumped in front of Emily Oldhall and raised his shield to deflect the flame. The cowhide would not withstand the fire too long without bursting into flame, but for now, it would work.

The dragon was toying with Kitwana. Toying with him and Emily, like a cat with a mouse. Kitwana would kill the dragon or die trying. Now, as in the dim days of his adolescence, he would protect those he loved.

Keeping his body between the dragon and Emily, Kitwana stood firm and aimed with his assegai, using his shield to deflect a burst of flame. The shield, magically spelled by his mother's brother, repelled the flame as oil repels water. Though assegais were not usually throwing weapons, Kitwana had always made them fly true.

The dragon hopped backward and flapped its immense wings to gain altitude. So it could be frighted. And Kitwana would kill it. A hand closed on his arm at the last second. Turning around, Kitwana looked into a pair of earnest eyes as blue as the sky of Zululand.

Emily Oldhall.

FLIGHT IN THE NIGHT

Nassira turned on her hard bed of rock and branches.
She tugged at the cotton cloth she used for a blanket.
She kicked, trying to find a comfortable position, but
nothing would do.

She thought of her erstwhile lover and of Nigel,
who had been looking particularly exasperated of late.
And what was it to her if he did something stupid
again? If he went into the jungle and disappeared, a
victim of a wild beast or his own stupid folly?

They had the compass stone and the woman who
would operate it. It would function well enough without Nigel. Why should she care what happened?

Nassira could not give a rational answer. She knew
she did not care for Nigel—not as a woman cares for a
man. In fact, if there were any man she cared for that
way, it would be Kitwana. Her attraction for him disturbed her. He was not Masai. And his lack of response disturbed her more. What could be wrong
with him?

He told her his secrets. He confided in her. He
treated her as his right hand, his fighting comrade.
Why didn't he realize they were a perfect couple?
Nassira turned again and, wide awake, stared at the

stars overhead, glowing pinpoints of light in the inky sky.

She threw her cotton blanket aside—much too hot anyway. It was the sort of night when she expected a volcano to erupt. She remembered other nights in Masai land with the smell of gas and ash in the air. Minor eruptions and yet strong enough to cause the cattle to sicken and the men to cough in their sleep. She now had the same sense of foreboding she'd had as a child, before those catastrophic eruptions.

Something was going to happen.

Kitwana screamed. In the still night, she recognized his voice, though she could not discern the string of words that escaped his lips. Fear and rage.

Something like a bugling scream answered him.

Nassira stood. Around her, the camp boiled in chaos. Men ran and screamed, seemingly in all directions. And above—

She held her breath, then exhaled it in a sound half exasperation and half awe.

She'd seen the dragon before, but then it had looked more like a natural creature, made of flesh and blood. Now, between sky and ground, wings spread, it looked like a beast woven of stars and spun from the fears of men. A thing of terrible beauty and cold splendor. Lights ran along its outspread wings, its fangs glimmered like silver in the moonlight and its green eyes shone, bright and hard as emeralds.

Kitwana stood at the foot of the dragon, looking like a toy figure, his arm raised and his lethal assegai held at the end of it. And around him, leaping and reaching like a child seeking an adult's attention, the European girl begged for something. She guessed that it was for the dragon's life, which would be what a fool such as she would beg for, never knowing what was good for her. And around Kitwana, in a circle, the Hyena Men screamed and implored, in many languages, for him to kill the dragon.

Nassira ran toward the weapon pile and grabbed a lance. She ran toward Kitwana and the dragon, and stood beside him, her lance raised.

Kitwana, the Englishwoman danging from his right arm, glanced at Nassira as she came up beside him. He lifted his left arm, the one that carried his body shield, and pushed Nassira out of the way, standing between her and the dragon. Nassira made a sound of inarticulate annoyance. What did he think he was doing? Then she struggled to get past his shield, to fling her lance at the dragon.

Kitwana looked over his shoulder, his face contorted in anger. "Go away, you fool," he said. "Make yourself safe."

"No one will be safe while *that* lives," Nassira shouted back.

"Killing the dragon is my duty," Kitwana said, while pushing Nassira away with his shield. "I'll protect the women." He shook the arm Emily Oldhall held with both hands. "Women do not belong here."

Other Hyena Men were leaping, screaming, throwing their ineffective weapons at the beast—all of them far enough away that it could not reach them with its fiery breath.

Kitwana would allow these men here, Nassira thought, who were too cowardly or too stupid to get closer. And yet he wanted to protect her. He'd called her a woman, lumping her with the hapless Mrs.

Oldhall, who could be frightened in a crowded carpet-port.

For once in her life, Nassira had allowed herself to feel attracted to a man who did not need her help, and he had proven himself a fool, like all the rest of them. To Nassira it was as though years had passed and the people around her were no more than shadowy memories from her misguided past.

Above, the dragon stretched, between sky and earth, a creature of both and of neither, a supernatural creature and yet one fleshed, full of the urges and tempers of its strange body, ready to kill and die to satisfy urges it could no more explain than could any man.

Kitwana stood, his lance raised, protecting the Englishwoman who, of course, was taught to be soft and weak and not very good at protecting herself.

Nassira took a deep breath. For the Hyena Men, this was all about revenge. It wasn't about Africa, nor freeing Africa for Africa's children. It wasn't about bringing Africa up to the level of Europe, nor making anyone's life easier. It was about murdered women and enslaved children; about tongues silenced and tribes destroyed; about hunting lands put to the European plows and warriors left dead, by the power of the strange, alien powersticks. Oh, it was about that, all right. But only as revenge, nothing more.

And to Kitwana, it was—what?—a desire to be a hero? A wish to become one of those demigods forever sung about in legend and myth? Whatever his motive was, Nassira would wager it had nothing to do with anything beyond Kitwana. When she'd been in London, the housekeeper at the club had insisted that she attend the Christian church every Sunday with the other servants. She'd gone along with it, fascinated by the strange ritual, the unfamiliar songs, the interesting and sometimes bewildering tales. On one of those occasions, she'd heard a story of a blind man commanded by the demigod the whites worshiped to wash his eyes in a sacred pool. All of which made much sense to her, for it was exactly what one of the Masai holy men might recommend as a cure for blindness. She remembered the preacher had told how scales had fallen from the man's eyes and he'd seen. The preacher seemed to think this meant more than physical sight.

And, if it were so, Nassira's eyes had now been freed from scales, and she saw clearly for the very first time. She saw the Hyena Men for what they were: people motivated by anger and revenge, who would achieve nothing more for their land than to make it an imitation of the English land, with its all powerful queen, its strong noblemen, its dispossessed peasants and its despoiled countryside.

And she saw Kitwana as he truly was—a proud, heartless man, possessed of a desire for power that would make him the king of all of Africa, as powerful and unique in his magical ability as the legendary ancestor-king of European monarchies. Or the ruler of the whole world. He had ambition and pride enough for that. Cold, shocked, she shook her head. Why had she served this cause? Why had it ever seemed just? She, whom all of the Masai accounted untamable, had allowed herself to believe in an organization and to be tamed by it. An organization that was shadowy and obscure in its reach, and of which she knew no more than a half-dozen people. She, who'd always known her mind to be the equal of any man's, had allowed men to order her around.

It was as though another Nassira, one she loathed, had moved into her body and lived for her these last years. But no more. Nassira would again be as she'd always been: a strong, unbowed woman, the equal of every warrior, the protector of every helpless person. She was through with the Hyena Men, but she had nowhere to go. And before she left, she would save Nigel as she should have saved her Kume. She would not let this one die, a victim to other people's theories and illusions. Her decision made, Nassira scrambled away from dragon and men, and all the commotion, toward the tent in which Nigel slept.

He slept still—a witness either to his despair or to his sound conscience—a straggle of blond hair protruding from the blanket the only visible mark of his presence.

She shook him. No response.

She pulled the blanket away. He wore dark red silk pajamas, and as he sat up, blinking, confused, she noticed his monogram upon the pajamas pocket. *NAO*. Why? Was he afraid his pajamas would get confused with those of the tramping multitudes of Englishmen crossing his path?

The monogram was distorted by a lump in the pocket. He slept with the compass stone. So much the better. She had no intention of leaving it for the fools at the camp or letting Kitwana use it in his grab for glory.

"Wha—" he started.

She shook her head at him. "No time. You must come now."

As she spoke she reached for his wrist and pulled him upright, then dragged him away.

Outside, he noticed the dragon, the commotion. He looked over his shoulder and said something that included the words *Peter* and *Emily*.

"They're fine," Nassira said, and pulled harder, dragging him by the force of her despair. "They'll be fine without you. You must save yourself for once."

He tried to resist, but she waved her lance under his nose. Then she grabbed his hand and started running, forcing him to run, too.

It wasn't until they were well away in the bush, running amid low-growing trees and thornbushes, that she realized she'd spoken to him in Masai. And yet he followed her. She looked over her shoulder and saw his eyes wild and intent.

And realized he thought he'd been kidnapped and dragged into the jungle by a crazy native.

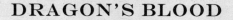

DRAGON'S BLOOD

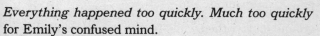

Everything happened too quickly. Much too quickly for Emily's confused mind.

The dragon overhead was savage, dangerous—a creature of fire that thirsted for blood. But the dragon was also Peter, and she loved Peter. At least Emily thought so. And Kitwana, lifting his lance, would kill the dragon. Was he defending her?

She grabbed at Kitwana's arm, her hands clenched on his dark, smooth skin. She felt muscles spring beneath her hands as he lifted her off her feet, yet still the lance flew. Crooked.

"It is a beast," he yelled at her, his words coming with a thick clanging accent she'd never heard before. "It will kill us."

But Emily shook her head and held on to his arm as her gaze followed the path of the lance flying above, till it sank into the scaly dragon's breast, just beneath the neck, where the shoulder joint for the forelimb and wing hinged.

Something wet sprayed down. Blood. The dragon blinked, its mouth opened and trumpeted. A thin wisp of flame flew, parting the throng of carriers. The

dragon keened, then fluttered, listed, struggled to re-
gain altitude.

The dragon above trumpeted again, but its scream
sounded less like a dragon now and more like a human
in mortal pain. It looked down with fearful eyes on
Kitwana, who was leveling yet another lance at its
chest. The enormous teeth gleamed and snapped.

Emily sprang. "No!" she yelled. "It is defenseless.
It would be cowardly."

Through the corner of her eye, she saw the dragon
losing altitude, tilting like an ill-balanced kite and
then falling heavily from the sky. It fell to the dusty
ground and writhed while twenty carriers, full of valor
now that the creature was down, approached with
powersticks and burning embers from the camping
fire. This was why Kitwana had wanted to camp here,
in this open space. So it would be easier to corner the
dragon.

The dragon retained enough strength to snap and
flame at its tormentors—a weak flame. It roared and
grunted and moaned as sticks stabbed it and swords
sliced it.

Emily's mind was a muddle of thoughts, questions
and images she knew weren't real and yet that
seemed more real than the image of the dragon plung-
ing down. In her mind's eye she saw Peter—so handsome, so perfect, with his immense, dark green eyes,
his mouth so disposed to smiling. And he had become
this beast. Was Peter Farewell even within this creature?

Then she noticed Kitwana was not among the
dragon's tormentors. Instead he stood nearby, holding
his lance, a look of fierce concentration on his face.

She ran to him barefoot, her white nightgown billowing in the warm night wind. "You must help Peter," she pleaded. "You must."

Kitwana glowered, and shook Emily away.

The other men ignored her as well. Though they didn't hurt her, they also didn't obey her. She might as well have been invisible. They crowded around the dragon with their lances. Points thudded into flesh, the dragon keened. Fine sprays of blood stained Emily's nightgown.

She heard Kitwana mutter something that sounded like a spell. She looked at his moving lips and realized that he had a power so large and so strange that she'd never fully recognized it as magic before. She now understood Peter Farewell's comments.

So Kitwana was a great magician. But why was he here? Then she realized he was performing magic, setting a killing spell on the lance.

"No!" she yelled.

He ignored her. His lips moved. She couldn't reach his uplifted arm to pull the spear out of his hand. Spreading her arms out to make herself as large a barrier as possible and placing herself between the men the dragon, Emily yelled at the carriers and at Kitwana beyond them. "You cannot kill him without killing me also!"

Kitwana looked shocked, his eyes widened as he stared at her. Some part of her that retained the proper mind and manners of an English gentlewoman protested that she was acting like a madwoman, but she did not care. She danced backward, upon rock and sand, to stand so close to the dragon that she could feel its breath upon her legs—like a deep wind saturated with that slightly spicy smell that Peter always exuded. Was it the smell of a dragon? Should she have known? Or was it Peter's smell, subsisting in this creature, like the trace of a trapped human soul?

Then Kitwana's look changed, anger replacing surprise. He pushed through the crowd toward Emily, his face pulsating with fury.

"Are you insane?" he yelled, and followed with a succession of ever-louder words that Emily could not understand.

His eyes narrowed, his features contorted. He looked for the first time like the savages depicted in the woodcuts that ornamented accounts of African exploration. He raised his hand and screamed at her again—a torrent of incomprehensible sounds that reverberated like drums in her ears.

Then something within Emily snapped—grown from her sense of betrayal by everyone she'd trusted, transmuting her grief into anger. The way her father had treated her, the way her husband had treated her, even the way that Peter and Kitwana had treated her. She was tired of being bullied by men who told her they knew better. She was through with being ordered and lied to and told she was just a frail woman with a childish mind. They were all childish, all of them, to think they could order her around.

"No," she told Kitwana. "I do not care if he is the enemy. He is injured. Do you not have rules of quarter and rules of proper fight? We do not attack injured creatures that cannot defend themselves. Not creatures that can think. Not creatures that are human in any way. At any time."

Her words seemed to mean more to Kitwana than

they meant to her. He frowned, and held his lance half-raised, but he could not command the look of anger he'd shown before. He put his arm down, took a deep breath.

"Lady," he said, sounding like sweet reason itself, "get out of the way. It's a man killer. It *eats* men. Do you understand that? We must kill the killer before it kills again."

Emily heard the words. She even understood them. She could see this beast behind her, this creature of dark beauty and chilling menace, pursuing unfortunates in the underbrush. She was sure this had happened before. But all that could not change the fact that this creature was, in some way, Peter Farewell.

The carriers resumed harrying the beast. Emily felt the rush of warm air as the dragon panted at her back.

Oh, what did it matter what he had done? He could be changed. She was sure of it. There was much good in Peter, such an understanding mind behind his gaze, such kindness in his words. Surely he could be reformed. "Stop. I don't care what he's done! This is a human being."

"There is no human mind in there," Kitwana said. "Weres aren't human once the beast takes over." He gestured with his lance toward the dragon. "That is not your friend. It's not anybody's friend. It does not even remember its human life when the hunger takes it."

Emily took a deep breath. "He's not attacking me."

And, turning, she looked into the huge muzzle of the creature she'd seen from the carpetship. She remembered it then, that vision of beauty and menace gliding silently through the skies above the watery abyss, while its magic made the carpet tremble beneath Emily's feet.

Even then, she'd been scared. Now she stood less than a handsbreadth from the creature and could feel its breath. She could see the light glint from sword-long teeth, whose ivory shone red with the blood of carriers it had wounded defending itself.

She had to touch the dragon. Only that would convince Kitwana of the creature's intentions. But she feared the ferocious glint in its eyes, the half-narrowed, reptilian eyelids. Yet the deep sea-green eyes could have been Peter's.

She stretched out her hand. The space between her hand and that muzzle seemed an endless distance.

The creature didn't move, but the cuscurations of light that ran along its huge, awkwardly-folded wings increased in tempo, the pinpoints of light chasing each other faster to the rhythm of the beast's great unseen heart.

Kitwana's lance remained lodged just above that heart, and blood gushed around the embedded wood, pouring onto the ground. A pellicle, like a milky-white veil, blinked in front of the dragon's eyes once, and then again. It was bleeding too much, too fast. It would die without help. Emily was sure of it, as she was sure that she must help.

She extended her hand, trembling, feeling sweat roll down her forehead and sting her eyes. Her fingers touched the tip of muzzle, warm and pulsing, and the dragon made a low rumble in its throat.

"Leave him alone," Emily yelled at the carriers.

"You can see he is human. He knows me. We have no right to take his life."

Kitwana yelled, too, something rapid and alien. The carriers responded with a rumble of protest.

Kitwana raised his lance. "This is a spelled lance—spelled by me, with my own power—to take the dragon's life." He stood apart from the carriers and his lance threatened them all. "Who opposes me and risks the lance taking his life?"

The carriers backed off, grumbling. The dragon grunted and stood. For a breath, it spread its wings again, then flapped. Once. Twice.

A thin stream of fire shot out at a carrier, engulfing him. The man collapsed, screaming.

The carriers yelled in many languages.

"It is a beast," one of them said, in English. "A foul creature."

The dragon's muzzle touched Emily's hand. She understood it was a plea. She stood her ground, between Kitwana and the dragon.

"I will not continue on this expedition," a carrier yelled in oddly accented French. "Not if that creature will be with us."

"I will not obey a man who lets an elephant eater live and maybe eat us all," another said, and spit at Kitwana's feet.

The dragon stretched its wings again. Emily wished she could be sure these weren't death spasms.

Kitwana looked up at the creature, then down at Emily, and his features hardened. For a moment, Emily thought he was going to kill the dragon. Instead, he lowered his lance.

"This is a human being," Kitwana said. "Whatever

else it is, I will not kill it. Yet. Those who do not abide by my decision can leave."

There was a grumble from the carriers. And then—one by one, and two by two—they turned. It looked to Emily as though the crowd was melting in the warm night air. They dispersed, disappearing into the gloom that surrounded the encampment. Some stooped to pick up lances or bundles of belongings.

Kitwana turned toward her. "They're leaving," he said, as if she were blind or could not interpret what she saw as well as he could. For a breath, she thought Kitwana would tell her that he was leaving, too. Leaving her alone with a wounded dragon in the middle of wild Africa.

Where was Nigel? Looking around, she could not find her husband. But then, Nassira was nowhere around, either.

Kitwana flung his lance down and looked at the dragon, his brow furrowed in worry. "I don't know how to treat dragons," he said. Emily's relief at retaining this one would-be protector was so great that she went weak at the knees and heard herself say, sounding very British and calm, "That's perfectly acceptable, Mr. Kitwana."

Behind her, the dragon collapsed onto the dirt, shaking the ground with its fall. Emily turned around again. Was it dead? But flickers of light ran along the dragon's wings, as it started coughing, writhing and contorting.

"It's changing," Kitwana said, and pulled her clear as the dragon's great head spasmed back on the powerful neck. Peter's well-shaped head, his classically handsome features appeared. Blood gushed from the lance embedded in his shoulder and trickled from the cuts all over his body. He was pale as death and unconscious.

"We must stop the blood," Emily said.

Kitwana said something under his breath, but he stepped up next to her, helped her pull out the lance and found a strip of cloth somewhere to staunch the blood. And Emily, trembling and scared, lost in the middle of Africa with a dragon and a native, unsure of where her husband had gone, thought only in wonder and shock that a man was obeying her.

STRANGERS IN THE DARKNESS

*Nassira ran away from the camp, pulling Nigel be-*hind her. Without thinking, she smelled the night wind, and listened for small sounds in the darkness. She heard the cry of a baby. A cow lowed nearby. Somewhere above, a bird flew.

Nassira was back home. She leapt over the thorny, rocky ground of her homeland, making for the nearest Masai village. She didn't know who they were, and she very much doubted that they would be anyone who knew her, this far from her father's village. But it didn't matter. She was away from dragons, away from proud men of no known parentage, men smitten with British women. Nassira sought the sanity and familiar reassurance of her own people and culture. She ran for a while in silence, pulling Nigel along with her.

She noted that he looked very pale, his odd, almost colorless eyes wide open, his skin a grayish white. His silk pajamas caught on thorns, and the pant legs hung in tatters, showing thorn-scoured skin beneath. The silly man probably still thought that Nassira had kidnapped him.

He didn't even dare speak to her until quite awhile

had passed and the noise from their camp had receded.

"Where—" Nigel started. "Where are we going?"

"Masai," she answered, and lifted her head to listen to the sounds in the night, to get her bearings. Then reaching back, she found Nigel's hand and pulled at his wrist, forcing him to follow as she started running again. She ran until she couldn't run anymore, until her breath tore through her lips in short, helpless gasps. She realized that Nigel was barefoot, and remembered how soft Englishmen's feet were.

Pausing to take a breath, she looked back at him. He was taking deep breaths, too, but he did not complain. She wondered if he was simply that scared of her, or if he had some unexpected reserve of physical courage.

He swallowed and looked at her, and it appeared that he would complain. Instead, he said, "Emily. There was a dragon. I should have stayed. I should have protected Emily."

Nassira raised her brows. Physical courage, then. Enough physical courage, almost, for a Masai brave. His feet were shredded, and he'd probably just run for a longer time than he had since childhood. But he was worried about his wife, about that caramel-colored English lady who had been so interested in sparing the dragon's life.

Emily Oldhall did not deserve her husband.

"Emily will be well," Nassira said.

Nassira didn't feel that she could explain that the dragon was Nigel's good friend Peter Farewell, nor that all of Nigel's handpicked carriers were members of the Hyena Men.

"It will all be fine," she said instead. "We'll go back to the camp in the morning."

"But what if the dragon—" Nigel started.

"The dragon will do nothing," Nassira said, and hoped it was true. "Kitwana, the chief carrier, has a lance bespelled to deal with the creature."

Nigel looked shocked. "How did you know? How did you know a dragon would attack the encampment?"

"We . . . knew there was a dragon. We knew there could be danger. So he had this lance," Nassira said.

Nigel looked puzzled. "But if everything will be fine, why did we run?"

Nassira shook her head. "I can't explain," she said, which was truthful. "But you were in great danger." Which was also true. If there was danger around, Nigel would find a way to be at the center of it.

"Can you walk?" she asked Oldhall, though she had absolutely no idea what she could do if he said he couldn't. "Or do your feet hurt too much?"

Nigel pressed his lips together tightly and nodded once. "I can walk," he said.

He didn't even ask how far they still had to walk. Nor if they must run.

Nassira walked up a rise, and then down it, following neither smell nor sound, nor even an intuition of where to go, but all of these translated by her subconscious into a strong sense that a village of maybe ten families lay this way.

She went up another rise, down yet another, and then she saw it. Or rather, she saw the darker half-globes, shadowy in the night—the profiles of low-slung branch-and-dung Masai buildings. A cow mooed close by, and the pungent smell of cattle and wood cooking fires was warm in Nassira's nostrils.

To her, it smelled like home. She walked down a relatively smooth path, worn down by the feet of countless herd boys and the hooves of their many charges.

She heard Nigel walking behind her and had to admit that the Englishman showed bravery and dignity both. And concern for others, too. Even if he did look like a fat maggot grown in a sunless cave. His feet had to be torn to shreds. Even Nassira's feet, only slightly softened by her time in London, felt sore and prickled by their run.

He didn't complain, but tomorrow, before Nigel undertook any more walking, Nassira must make sure she applied a healing salve to his feet. Coming up very close to the village, she thought that she must somehow wake these good, unsuspecting people and ask for lodging.

Just outside the circle of low, mounded huts, she prepared to call. But before she opened her mouth, a young man came out of the nearest hut. "Nassira, daughter of Nedera?" he asked. Puzzled, Nassira took a step back and nodded. "And this is the European man you're guiding?"

Nassira nodded again. "We need lodging for the night. My employer can stay in the bachelor quarters, and I'd be grateful of a corner of some hut to sleep in." She looked the young man up and down, finding him in every way a stranger. "But how do you know me?" she asked. "How did you know I was coming?"

Were they all Hyena Men, aware of her mission and the route the expedition had been following

through Kitwana's mind-communications? But the
young man smiled. He was a warrior of Nassira's own
age or only a little younger, wearing a high coiffure
covered in ocher that gleamed red in the scant light.
"Your father told us his daughter was nearby, guarding
a Water Man."

"My father?" Nassira asked, her voice catching.

"Here, child," the familiar voice said, close behind
the warrior.

Nassira was so tired. She'd been so intent on the
warrior in front of her that she'd missed her father and
three other people who had come out of the low door
of the hut. Her father stood between two young warriors. In such company, he looked middle-aged and
thick-waisted, yet he still gave an impression of sup-
pressed strength.

Was it Nassira's impression, or did more white hair
glimmer upon his close-cropped hair than before? As
he stepped forward, toward her, she noted that his
face looked creased, as though from many long, sleepless nights. But his solid figure was what she remembered from childhood, when he had stood at the door
to their hut and waited anxiously for her return from
herding. And his dark eyes looked at Nassira with
such longing, such protective love—as if all his sleepless nights had been spent waiting for her and hoping
she'd come home again.

Nassira ran into his arms.

"Father," she said. And when her father put his
arms around her, it was as though she'd never gone
away at all.

LADY'S MERCY

Kitwana would never be quite sure how it came about. One minute he stood ready to kill the dragon, lance drawn and at the ready. And the next he was helping the creature, and trying to think of ways to keep it alive.

The dragon had killed so many of his comrades in the Hyena Men. It had tried to attack him and Nassira. It was even a danger to Emily and Nigel. And, he was sure, to others as well. People who had done nothing to attract the monster's attention except be in the wrong place at the wrong time.

Yet Emily Oldhall had touched it, and it had shown no signs of aggression. Was that better or worse? If the creature retained a shred of humanity within it, shouldn't it be able to control its animal impulses? And shouldn't it be held accountable when it didn't?

Yet now it was a man like Kitwana—if paler—lying upon the ground, writhing in pain. Wounds like pinpricks—the shrunken remainders of lance stabs— clustered on his arms and legs, his back and shoulders.

The wound on his shoulder, however, which Kitwana had inflicted with his spelled lance, bled more profusely than all the others combined, leaking dark blood onto the mud. The Englishman moaned and rolled on the ground, then made a sharp sound, like keening. His dark green eyes looked less human now than they had when he'd been in dragon form. They embodied madness and pain. His eyes were all iris, huge and rolling, the pupils mere pinpoints contracted to the tiniest aperture, keeping light out. Kitwana still held his spear, but he could not use it.

Emily was right. Desperate in his pain and looking maddened by torment, Peter Farewell was, nonetheless, utterly human and completely helpless.

Kitwana knew how easy it was to kill a man. And how irretrievable life was, once lost.

All humans should be allowed to live, unless they proved for a fact that they were incapable of redemption. Because while a man lived, there was hope he would change.

Disturbingly human-looking blood escaped the dragon-man, to mix with the sand and dirt atop the rock and form a rich mud.

Emily had gone very pale, staring at the man, her hands clenched on either side of her blood-splattered gown. "Will he live?" she asked, and looked at Kitwana with such anxious need for reassurance that Kitwana nodded reflexively.

If no one bound his wounds, the dragon would die soon. If Kitwana just pretended to treat him and didn't, then the dragon would die. Kitwana would not need to kill him. It would be nature taking its course.

"Shouldn't we stop his bleeding?" Emily Oldhall asked. Her hair was loose down her back, silky soft, almost begging to be touched. Her eyes shone full of

the same certainty, the same faith in Kitwana's goodness and kindness that Kitwana's father had always
showed. Until their last talk.

Kitwana didn't think he could bear to disappoint
such faith again. He looked around, found a piece of
cotton cloth nearby. It was one of Nassira's ubiquitous
wraps, this one in dark green. It fluttered atop the pile
of sticks and straw that she'd used for a mattress and
was, therefore, not soiled.

He retrieved the cloth, tore a strip off it and
handed it to Emily. "Bind the wound on his shoulder,"
he said.

She stared at him, holding the cloth dangling from
her hand, as though she were quite at a loss to know
how one bound wounds.

"He will die if you don't," Kitwana said. He wondered if he'd found the one woman, from any culture,
who'd never been trained in the care of the sick. But
in the next breath, Emily knelt in the bloody mud, her
hands working deftly as though by long habit, reaching for the dragon, looping the cloth around his chest.

The dragon-man keened again and snapped inef-
fectually at Emily with his human teeth. She pulled
her hand out of harm's way. "Now, Mr. Farewell," she
said.

She said it primly, and it made Kitwana want to
laugh that she could say *Mr. Farewell* to a creature
she'd watched change into a huge, supernatural rep-
tile and then back to human again. To a creature so
confused that he was trying to bite her while she
bound his wound.

It made Kitwana want to cry. He'd felt an odd desire to laugh and cry, both, ever since he'd seen her

standing in front of, her finger raised and wagging. How far out of touch with the world she was that she thought she could save not only the life but the soul of a were-creature and get it to behave like a human being? And how commanding her belief. How like Kitwana's own father, who believed he could reform tyrants and reclaim mass murderers. And who often managed it. Her attitude brought out Kitwana's mixed longing for home and the faint annoyance that his father always made him feel.

He turned his annoyance toward Emily, who was absorbed in tying the strip of fabric around Peter's shoulder. She did it in such way that the flow of blood slowed.

"You know we should kill him." Kitwana said. "More merciful all around."

"Mr. Kitwana," Emily said. Now he was *Mr.*? It was all he could do not to laugh.

She fixed him with her blue eyes, severe and caring, managing somehow to look like his father's eyes when Kitwana vexed him. "Don't talk nonsense," she said. "We don't kill people." She frowned at the person on the ground—naked, covered in minute cuts and mud. "We should get him something to cover himself with," she said. "To make him decent."

The man had turned into a dragon before her and flown flaming into the sky, and she was worried because his genitals were exposed? But then he realized that, in Emily's mind, Farewell's exposure meant humiliation, and she wanted Farewell covered for his sake, not her own.

Now that Kitwana had figured out how much Emily resembled his father in spirit, he thought he knew exactly how her mind must work. And also how unavoidable her demands were, and the futility of arguing with her. She wanted to confer human dignity on this creature and there would be nothing Kitwana could do to dissuade her. Nor did Kitwana *want* to. Instead, he found himself full of strange impulses and thoughts he could hardly control. He wanted to caress her burnished skin, to feel it even and smooth beneath his hands. He wanted to hold her, pliant and solid in his arms, have those blue eyes look at him alone.

He backtracked through the now-dark camp, where the fire had died down or been trampled into the ground. He stumbled on a body, face up on the ground, his chest bitten through by a huge, reptilian mouth. He must have killed these men in the melee. Kitwana stepped over the dead man, not looking at the face, not wanting to remember his name. Emily wanted to help the creature that had murdered this man. Kitwana wanted to believe with Emily. He wanted to think that Farewell could be redeemed. Kitwana wanted to believe again in his father's wisdom, as he had in his childhood. But he knew that the man now half-crazed in pain on the encampment ground was also a creature so terrifying that it could bite through a man's chest.

Kitwana's stomach clenched in revulsion.

And then he remembered the men prodding at the great beast with lances, turning it into a pincushion. How could it not defend itself? And it had no other means but its huge teeth. Why would it not use its natural defenses?

Kitwana stepped over another corpse and went

on. He saw two more bundles on the ground, but for-
bore to go near. He would not think of those men now,
who had been under his command and his responsibility and whom he should have protected better. He'd
let them bait the dragon and the dragon had killed
them. Their deaths fell as much at Kitwana's door as
at the dragon's.

He made his way to the tent of the dragon-man,
and fumbled on the ground to find Peter's pants, his
underwear, his shirt. And then, thinking of those
wounds covered in mud, Kitwana sighed. The creature would never live.

He took the clothes back to Emily. She had bound
the big wound on Peter Farewell's chest. Her forehead was wrinkled in worry, her mouth pursed. "I'm
afraid we're out of disinfectant salve," she said. She
opened both her hands in a show of helplessness.
"The bottle somehow got broken."

Kitwana looked at the dragon. Peter's eyes appeared lusterless, dull. They were the eyes of a mori-
bund animal. He looked up at Emily's anxious face.
This had to be utterly alien for a European woman
who'd probably been cosseted and protected her
whole life. But she wanted to save the dragon.

Kitwana sighed. He handed Emily Peter Farewell's
clothes and said, "Please, hold these." If there was one
thing Kitwana could improvise, from water and sheer,
raw magic, it was a healing salve. His father had provided them for every village around, for every refugee
climbing his mountain. And Kitwana had learned the
trick of it early, had learned to make himself useful and
prevent his father from running his magic—and his
health—into the ground.

Now he found a jar full of water beside what remained of the camping fire. He pulled the jar aside, put his hands over it and wished all his healing magic into the water, so that the water would be an extension of his most potent healing spells.

The water hissed and bubbled. A pale golden light issued from it, making the thick clay jar seem, for the moment, transparent, and lighting the whole encampment like a flash of lightning.

Across the encampment, Emily Oldhall gasped. "What are you doing?" she asked.

"Making a healing salve," Kitwana said. He picked up the jar and brought it to her.

She narrowed her eyes at him, then widened them at the jar. "A salve?" she asked. She pulled back a strand of dark, curly hair that had fallen in front of her eyes. She wrinkled her nose at the water jar he had set at her feet. It still shone, faintly gold, and the dark red clay looked odd.

"Just from water? Don't you need herbs or extracts or something for that?"

Kitwana met her gaze and held it. He did his best to look earnest and honest. He knew there were differences between their magical cultures. For one, no African had ever thought of using his magic in a group with others, or apply it to running a train or flying a magic carpet.

Very few Africans were born totally without magic, but very few had magic to compare to the great European wizards. Kitwana knew his own magic was somewhat smaller than that of European noblemen. Or at least, so he'd assumed.

But if this woman, this English magician, had

never heard of the simple water and magic salve, perhaps Kitwana had underestimated his abilities.

"It's easier with herbs," he said. "And later on, we could make some. But this should do for now."

Emily looked doubtful, but she tore a strip from Nassira's colorful wrap and dipped it into the glowing salve. She looked up. "All the others are gone?"

"Yes," Kitwana said. One way or another. "Some . . . He killed some." He felt bad saying it, as if he were a small child tattling on a playmate.

Emily reacted just as Kitwana's father had once. She compressed her lips, but said only, "Help me move Mr. Farewell to a clean patch of stone. And help me clean his wounds and dress him."

By helping, Kitwana assumed she meant for him to move him. At least he couldn't imagine such a small, frail creature as Emily doing much of the heavy lifting. But she put her hands beneath Peter Farewell's shoulders and managed to raise him about an inch above the ground, which was enough to move him to a relatively clean patch of rock, close by where the fire used to be.

Emily soaked the cloth in the salve and dabbed at Peter's legs, though she hesitated at touching his groin or his back.

Kitwana made a sound of impatience at her prudery, pulled the cloth from her hand and dabbed the few cuts in those areas himself.

Peter Farewell whimpered and made sharp, hissing sounds as the cloth touched his flesh, but he struggled only feebly—too feebly to swat their hands away.

Kitwana redipped the cloth and passed it back to Emily, who dabbed at Farewell's arms and neck, while Kitawana pulled the underwear and pants onto the man, only slightly hindered by Peter's struggles. The pants immediately became tinged with droplets of blood that made them look as though they were decorated with dark red embroidery.

Kitwana tried not to think that the wounded man he was trying to save was the same creature he had tried to kill earlier. But he couldn't avoid feeling Peter Farewell's skin under his hands, all too human and covered in a light beading of sweat from pain and exertion.

Looking at him now, Kitwana would not have believed Farewell was a dragon.

How could two creatures so different share the same bit of physical matter? How could two creatures share a mind and matter and yet no drive, no opinion, no actual fixed purpose?

Or did they?

Kitwana looked at Farewell with narrowed eyes, trying to discern in him the look of a killer. Trying to see the dragon within the man. But he saw only a man in pain, trying desperately to obey Emily's nudges as she made him lift his torso off the ground and slipped his shirt on him.

Kitwana remembered having seen whiskey in Farewell's tent. There was a remedy for Peter Farewell's pain, and, besides, Kitwana needed a respite from the creature's consciousness, from the dragon-man's eyes fixed upon him with such human pain. He needed to be able to speak to Emily about Peter Farewell in the abstract and not while the man was looking at him.

He went back for the whiskey, then knelt beside the man and brandished the bottle.

Peter flinched, and pressed himself against the ground, his face ghastly pale, his lips drawn back from his teeth, his eyes wild.

"Drink," Kitwana said, and he put his hand beneath Farewell's shoulders to prop him up. "It will lessen your pain."

He wondered if the man even understood him, but Farewell pulled himself up on his elbows and opened his mouth to drink a swallow from the bottle, then pressed his lips together and shook his head as Kitwana tried to give him more.

"He needs water," Emily said. "Not alcohol. Please light the fire. We'd all be better for some tea."

Kitwana almost suggested they give Farewell the salve to drink, but he knew what it would do—healing salves when ingested caused a lot of pain. He didn't want to have to explain to this determined woman that he wasn't killing the dragon-man. Not now. Not when he'd just tried that very thing.

He eased Peter Farewell gently back onto the rock and took the bottle away. "You don't want more?" he asked.

Farewell shook his head again. He swallowed once, twice. "I . . ." he said. Then he blinked and swallowed again, noisily. "It lessens . . . control. I don't want . . . to switch."

Kitwana nodded, wondering if the impulse was fear of hurting others or simply fear of being hurt. Did he know that Kitwana could kill him that much more easily if he were not in human form?

Peter Farewell looked at him with seemingly unshattered calm. "You wanted to kill me . . . the dragon."

Kitwana grunted assent.

"Why?" Farewell licked at dry, chapped lips that had turned pale pink. "Helping me? Now?"

Kitwana gestured at Emily, who knelt on his other side. "She won't let me kill you," he said, and thought he saw a glimmer of amusement from deep within Peter's eyes. Farewell turned his head to look at Emily, who nodded and gathered herself, rising slowly. "We're going to make some tea. Would you like some?"

Peter Farewell's pale lips twisted in an approximation of his ironic smile. "Better than dying," he said, his voice just above a whisper but understandable.

Kitwana gritted his teeth and went to the pile of wood, arranging sticks carefully atop the low-burning fire, so as not to smother it. He found another jug of water, mostly full, and poured water from it into the kettle, which needed only a little brushing away of ashes and sand.

He perched the kettle over the fire and looked at Emily. "We're still going to have to kill him," he said.

Emily looked at him, her blue eyes serious. Farewell looked at him, but said nothing.

"He has killed people, you know," Kitwana said. "Eaten them." By repeating the list of Peter's crimes he meant as much to convince Emily as to make himself aware of what the man had done, to push the image of his father from his mind.

Peter Farewell flinched again. Emily looked into his eyes, and he looked away. The kettle boiled. Emily hastened over, got tea from the camp supplies, put it in the kettle.

She poured tea into a cup and brought it to Peter

Farewell. She helped him rise and take a sip. He re-vived visibly after the first sip and took another.

"I might deserve to die for my crimes," he said, looking at Emily, "but the only reason he wants to kill me is because that will leave the hand of the Hyena Men free to mind-enslave you."

GOING HOME

"Father," Nassira said as she looked at her father, still not fully believing he was there. "How did you get here?"

He pulled away from her, gripped his herding stick tighter in his right hand and smiled. "I heard you were back in Masailand and I did a divination to find where I could meet you. Then I set out to find you." He sighed. "Come home, Nassira. Come home and find me a son to look after my cows."

Nassira sighed in turn. She wanted so badly to obey him. She wanted to go home, to see her mother and her stepmother again. She could almost taste the milk of her family's cows. But she knew better. There was Nigel, and he needed her. "I want to come home," she said. "But it's not that simple. There are . . . other considerations."

Nassira's father looked over her shoulder. "The Water Man?" he asked.

"Yes," Nassira said.

"Nassira, I didn't expect— He's not a Masai . . . He's not—"

Nassira realized that her father would have given in to her in this, too, if she should have been strange enough to prefer a Water Person. She almost giggled, but controlled herself. "Father, I do not want him for a husband."

Her father looked utterly baffled. "But then, what do you owe him?"

Nassira looked over her shoulder at Oldhall, saw him cringe. He wouldn't have understood a word of her father's speech, but he would understand the tone of voice quite well.

"I..." Nassira knew exactly why she was doing this, but she had no idea how to explain it.

Her father was proud of her, and they'd always been close. She knew she could confess any misdeeds to him in full safety. However, she'd never told him how guilty she felt over the death of her infant brother all those years ago, or how she'd protected her warrior boyfriend.

She noted that the other people with her father, the local villagers, had now left, returning to their various huts. But they would be listening from behind their walls.

So she spoke in a low tone, designed to keep family problems within the family. "My brother died when I could have saved him. So did Kume. This Water Man will die if I leave him to his own devices. I cannot let it happen."

For a moment, Nassira's father frowned at her. Then he looked baffled. "Nassira. Your brother's death was not your fault."

Nassira shook her head. "I could have saved him. I could have used healing magic, if I hadn't slept so soundly. And Kume..." She felt tears come to her eyes and swallowed.

Her father opened his hands. "Nassira, your young

man seemed like a good man, a credit to his family, but he was... There was something not quite right there, and I very much doubt it was your fault."

Nassira shook her head, afraid that should she speak, her voice would come out tearful and choked.

Her father stared at her for a moment, then glanced at Nigel. "He is a Water Man. What can he be in danger of? That someone will not obey him? Why should you protect the people who brought disease to our people and plagues upon our cows?"

Nassira shook her head. "It's not that simple. There is more at risk. There is danger for everything that's human. There is—"

A swishing sound, like a wind blowing far above in the night sky, a feeling of strong magic from above, made Nassira look up, surprised.

In the dark blue sky, she could dimly see something like fast-growing dots.

Nassira's father turned around at the sound. Looking up, he said, "Flying carpets. Nassira!"

At her father's shout, people emerged from the huts. Soon the clear space amid the huts was crowded. Everyone looked up and pointed.

Nigel came up close behind Nassira, pushed by the bobbing tide of humanity on all sides.

"Those are flying carpets," he said.

Nassira raised a shoulder in a gesture of impatience before she realized that Nigel wouldn't have understood what her father said. "We know."

"Flying carpets are European magic," Nigel said. "At least modern flying carpets are. Who—" Suddenly understanding her father's shock, Nassira looked at Nigel in growing horror.

"Are they coming to rescue us?" Nigel asked.

He couldn't know she belonged to the Hyena Men, nor that if Europeans were indeed rescuing him, it would be from her and her ilk. He didn't mean to threaten her—and yet, if these were Europeans they would threaten her. For why would Europeans be here, unless they'd followed the Hyena Men? And how could Nigel ever trust her if he knew she belonged to the organization that had mind-bound him? Nassira grabbed at Nigel's arm and started pulling him back, away from the main press of people.

In the sky, the carpets grew closer, now revealing themselves to be individual, tiny rugs. A person sat astride each rug, although their features were still indistinguishable in the distance. These rugs were often used by the English army for rapid deployment.

Nassira swallowed. "The English army," she said.

"The English army?" Nigel pulled the other way, toward the approaching rugs.

Nassira let go, but he didn't take more than two steps—hard fought against the press of Masai bodies. He turned around, an alarmed look in his eyes.

The lead rug, now over the village, suddenly shone with a brilliant light—a magelight, invoked by the person sitting on the rug, and it emerged from the person's downturned hand. It was the strongest magelight anyone could command. In its downward beam, Nassira's eyes watered. But there was enough of it reflected around the mage who used it for Nassira to see a powerstick sitting across his knees.

Why would anyone shine a strong light on a crowd, with a powerstick close at hand? To pick a target?

Nassira grabbed Nigel's arm and pulled him. To

her surprise, he didn't resist at all. He gave a strangled cry deep in his throat and ran after her. Perhaps
he, too, had seen the powerstick and drawn the only
conclusion.

Nassira ran into the shadows, trying to keep close
to the huts and trees. The searchlight bobbed and
swayed, trying to find Nassira—or Nigel—again. It
caught Nigel's bright hair for a second and a power
ray flew from the powerstick.

Nigel screamed, but the ray missed him, and he
ran faster into the shadows. But the tree it caught
flamed and burst into fire.

Nassira ran faster, seeking cover. Ahead of her
loomed a thick patch of forest. It would offer them
cover and perhaps allow them to escape this strange
attack. But the forest had always seemed dangerous
to the Masai. The pastoral people of the grasslands
were ill at ease in the close-packed wooded expanse.
There were legends of lost children and of at least one
Moran band who'd gone into the forbidden forest and
never returned. Some people thought they'd become
part of the forest, others that they'd simply vanished.

But now and then, someone saw the Moran band
roaming in the forest, captive of some magic force that
would not allow them to return home.

Nassira had never believed these stories, at least
not fully. But they flashed through her mind while she
ran as fast as she could.

And then the searching magelight found Nigel
Oldhall just behind her. Before it could get a fix—guide
the powersticks on their lethal discharge—Nassira
plunged into the shadows of the forest, with Nigel close
behind her.

DRAGONS AND
HYENA MEN

"A Hyena Man?" Emily asked. She felt as though she could not have heard right. She turned to Kitwana, in whose countenance she'd believed to have found so much good just a few days ago. "You are a Hyena Man? All our carriers... Hyena Men?" Her hand went, as if by reflex, to the place on her sleeve that sheltered the dark mark of the secret brotherhood, the remnant of their attack upon her.

And yet she had expected better. She liked Kitwana, she realized, and had insensibly come to rely on him. Oh, Emily wished her husband would return. But Nigel had left her for the African woman. Was Nassira also a Hyena Man? She didn't dare ask.

She hoped her eyes conveyed her righteous indignation to the man. Her heart felt as though it had clenched in a tight ball. Was she, then, surrounded by treason on all sides?

None of this could be true. The events of this night had to be an insane dream, from which she would presently wake, safe and calm in a room in a hotel in Cairo.

Somewhere, from deep in the jungle, came a roar.

Nigel was gone. And she was left with these two...
creatures, both of whom would cause her harm if they
could.

"I was very young," Kitwana said. He spoke softly,
as a man who speaks of something distant and quite
factual, and not of his own life, his own destiny. "I was
very young and very innocent, having been raised in a
small, insular village. I'd been with my uncle's people
for only a little while. The emissaries of the Hyena
Men told me that if I joined, I could fight to free
Africa, fight to free it from the white oppressor. Was
that not a worthy goal?"

Emily clutched the place on her sleeve that hid the
black mark and swallowed. She wanted to say that
joining an evil organization could never be good, but in
her mind rose images of her own mother talking about
how the British had despoiled India. She heard her
mother speaking of how Emily's uncles were viewed
as inferior creatures, having had the misfortune of being born with brown skin and dark hair. And that in
their own land, where their ancestors had lived from
time immemorial.

Thinking of this, she nodded slowly, then rallied.
"You bound my mind. That is illegal in most countries. It is evil in all. It was not honorable."

Kitwana smiled—an expression that showed no
joy at all. "That is when I started having doubts about
the Hyena Men. I started wondering if people who
were willing to stoop to this sort of behavior should
have power over Africa, or over any continent. If they
treated humans so lightly, why would they treat our
own people better once they had control?"

"But you didn't leave," Emily said.

"I couldn't leave." As he spoke, Kitwana turned away, and Emily wondered what embarrassed him so. "I also didn't want the Europeans to find Heart of Light and finish binding all the magic in the world to them," Kitwana said very evenly, as if he were discussing the weather. "That would only give them yet more power over my people. Surely you can see that."

"And so you decided to stay behind and see that no one found the ruby."

Kitwana shrugged. For some reason, he looked more civilized, more intelligent than ever, in the dark of night and wearing only a loincloth. "I don't believe I had formulated any plans quite so specific as that. I thought only of protecting the expedition from . . . him."

A look at where Peter had been showed her that he had moved. He had crawled on his belly a few feet away, headed for the dark forest. Kitwana put his foot on Farewell's back. Peter groaned, but didn't speak. He looked very pale, his eyes wide and rolling. He'd been pulling himself on his elbows, and now let himself fall on his face, in the dirt.

"You see?" Kitwana said. "He's only trying to distract us, so he can crawl into the jungle and heal, and then come back to devour us."

Peter Farewell groaned again. It sounded as if he felt too exhausted, too hopeless to find words. "You tried to kill me," he said at last, his voice sounding like an echo of itself. "I just want to save myself. I just want . . . I hurt."

Emily thought of the wounded dragon above her, its blood raining down on their upturned faces.

Kitwana looked guilty and combative in equal parts. But he kept his foot on Peter's back.

Emily feared he would say something, do something to bring out the dragon in Peter. She had some sense that the dragon was not in full control of himself. That the dragon—once needled enough, once in enough pain—could take charge of Peter, could commit any crime, violate all decency.

"I was only trying to keep safe those under my protection," Kitwana said. "Dragons eat people."

"And Hyena Men kill them," Peter Farewell said.

Kitwana pushed his foot hard into Peter's back, and Emily felt the barely repressed current of violence between the two men.

"And you never intended harm to me?" she asked Kitwana, as much to distract him as to secure a guarantee that he did not mean to kill her or mind-strip her in the dark.

He looked at her, and his eyes widened a little in wonder, as if he couldn't even believe that she might think that of him. "I would never—" Kitwana said, and stopped, as if the fullness of his feelings couldn't adequately be expressed in words. "I could never hurt you. Hurt any human."

For a moment they stood staring at each other. Emily was conscious of something, not quite a smirk, in Peter's eyes.

Emily would never believe Kitwana fully. After being betrayed by Nigel and deceived by Peter Farewell, she would never believe anyone fully. But she believed Kitwana was indeed telling her the truth, or the truth as he believed it to be. Looking into the man's eyes, she was met again with that open, straightforward expression that had so impressed her before.

"And yet you surely gave the appearance of wishing to harm me," she said softly, her mind only on letting Peter Farewell live. He might be a villain, and perhaps he deserved death, but Emily wasn't ready to see him killed in cold blood. Particularly when his executioner might very well be as guilty as the dragon. Besides, the dragon was something Peter had inherited, a dark evil in his genes. But Kitwana had picked the Hyena Men on his own.

"Perhaps," Emily said, "Mr. Farewell has more good and honor in him than his actions suggest so far. And perhaps you do also, Mr. Kitwana. Let's not judge hastily. Take your foot off his back. And, Mr. Farewell, come near us."

"He'll try to run again," Kitwana said.

Emily looked at Peter Farewell where he lay, pale and shivering, on the ground. He hadn't moved when Kitwana took his foot from his back. She thought that there was a better chance that he would die, alone in the bush. Surely the scion of one of the most prominent British families deserved better. Surely Nigel's childhood friend deserved better.

Peter raised his head from the ground. "You can tie me up," he said, "if it will help you trust me." He made a sound that wasn't quite a groan or a sob. "But please don't kill me."

"If you change into a dragon, you'll break your bonds," Kitwana said.

"Then spell the bonds that tie me, so I can't turn into a dragon. If you can spell a lance to kill me, surely you can bind me."

Kitwana looked discomfited. Emily understood his hesitation. A spelled rope would never stop what was an internal process of Farewell's. And a psychic bind could have other consequences.

"Mr. Farewell," she said. "Give me your word of honor."

Farewell looked puzzled. "You'd trust my word?"

"Yes," she said. "Whatever else you are, I don't think you see yourself as a man without honor."

Groaning, Peter Farewell turned over and slowly sat up. "You have my word, Mrs. Oldhall," he said. He looked toward Kitwana. "And you also, Mr. Kitwana. I will not try to escape. Nor will I harm either of you, now or ever. Not if it is within my control."

Kitwana looked doubtful.

"Please," Peter said. "Would you help me near the fire? I am very cold."

Still looking doubtful, Kitwana half helped, half dragged Farewell to his feet and nearer the fire. Emily wiped her hands on her skirt and turned to Kitwana.

"You say Mr. Oldhall left?" she asked. "With the girl?"

"Amid the melee, I saw Nassira dragging Mr. Oldhall into the bush," Kitwana said. "I believe she was trying to save him."

"Do you have any idea where she would have taken him?"

"I can smell them," Peter said.

They both turned, astounded, to look at him.

Still pale, looking weak and scared, he managed one of his smiles, though in this case it was scarcely more than a trembling of his pale lips.

"Do not look so shocked," he said. "I am a were,

and weres have a better sense of smell than other humans. Oh, I didn't mean I can smell them now. But I can smell them out in the morning and find Nigel."

"I wonder if he wishes to be found," Emily said in turn, and was conscious of both their gazes converging on her.

"What do you mean?" Kitwana asked.

"You don't find it strange," Emily said, feeling wan and tired and afraid of being told exactly what she feared most, "that my husband should leave with another woman and leave me in the middle of a pitched battle?"

Peter shook his head slowly. "You must see that Nigel is often half-awake for an hour or two after rising. I would guess the woman decided to rescue him. She is the type who tries to rescue everyone. She probably tried to rescue him, and Nigel followed, tripping, half-asleep, not even sure of where he was going. I'd be surprised if in the morning he does not look for us before we look for him."

Emily stared at the dark sky above. The morning seemed a lifetime away. And the evening before—the genteel talk around the fire, and her intention of seducing the Peter Farewell, who had been a British gentleman and not a dragon—seemed even further away.

"Are we quite safe here?" she asked Kitwana. "Do you think we'll be in any danger?"

"Danger from what?" Kitwana asked. "I don't think the Hyena Men will return. They were routed by fear of Mr. Farewell's teeth and magic. Besides, I was their leader here away from . . . from Shenta, who leads the organization at large. Without me, it will take them some time and effort to figure out how to contact Shenta, let alone any other member of the organization. I think we're safe from them."

"And I'll vouchsafe for us being safe from beasts," Peter said. He paused and swallowed audibly in the still evening air. "They will not approach me, you see. Not lions and not hyenas, and not even cats or dogs. My father's hunting dogs . . . It was the first symptom of . . ." He paused and shook his head, seemingly overcome by an emotion too unbearable to allow him to continue.

Emily wanted to ask him how and when he'd found out his true nature. Had he always known it? While he went through school, playing childhood games alongside Nigel, had he known that in his heart he was a creature full of rage and destruction?

It seemed impossible, but she could not know without asking. And seeing Peter's expression, close upon itself with pain, she would not dare to ask.

"Let us do some packing tonight," Kitwana said, "before we rest, in case Mr. Oldhall really does seek us out in the morning."

"We can pack no more than two people can carry," Emily said, fearing the arduous way that lay ahead of them through the jungle.

"Three," Peter said. "Dragons heal fast." He spoke in a short, decisive jab, and neither of them dared contradict him.

And yet, Emily decided, they would pack as lightly as the circumstances would allow. She picked up the essentials of the camp spread around the clearing— water jug and other things without which dinner would not be possible. These would be in her keeping now, assuming that Nassira didn't return. And by carrying these, how much room would she have for other things?

As she was thinking, she heard a sound from Kitwana—not dismay, yet something like it. Looking up, she realized Kitwana had thrown open one of her many travel trunks. Within the trunk, carefully packed, lay her dresses, layer upon layer. And Emily realized, with a great shock, how almost impossible it would be to cross Africa with no carriers, no beaters, and still look like a British lady. Her skirts would catch on branches where no one had bothered to cut a path. Her parasol would be a ridiculous affectation that she would have no means of carrying, with her hands full of the cooking implements.

"Leave those behind," she said.

"Are you sure?" Kitwana asked. "For I can imagine how much they—"

Emily shook her head. "I'll wear this dress." She rummaged through her trunk and brought out a garment made of muslin, white and plain. Fitting for the heat. "Just this."

She had no time to worry about what her father would think of her tonight—alone with two males of dubious reputation.

Whether Nigel came back in the morning or not—and why did her heart misgive the idea that Nigel would come back?—she must survive Africa. And she would.

THE FOREST

For a while, creeping and sliding around the trees in the dense forest, Nassira could feel the magic of the flying rugs above them. Now and then, the searchlight shone. Nassira forged forward, without daring to stop and speak to Nigel.

She did not doubt that once their pursuers failed to find them on the rug flight, they would look for them on foot. The farther the two of them went into the forest, the better their chance of escaping.

The forest was dark and noisy—alive with scurries at floor level and sometimes amid the branches overhead. They moved fast, without stopping. After a while, Nassira felt something. It was whisper, the merest flutter of magic. She turned to look at Nigel. In the darkness, his pale eyes were wide open and full of fear. "The compass stone," he whispered. "I thought that's how they were tracking us."

She nodded. So he was not totally stupid. She was sure that was how they'd been tracked. Then she remembered the faces of the men on the rugs and again she was sure she knew them. She was sure they were Hyena Men. But why were Hyena Men pursuing Nigel? Surely they knew that Nigel couldn't disappear or die without alarming the British. If Nigel were killed—and those had been killing powerstick rays—surely the British would come hunting for the Hyena Men.

Having set a bind on the Oldhalls, having gone to great lengths to stay hidden, why would the Hyena Men be so brazen now? Had they only waited till Nigel and Emily were far enough into Africa that they could disappear without a trace and without the Hyena Men being found out? But why would they want to kill Nigel to get the stone? And if they did, why hadn't they told Nassira? Did they fear that Nassira would not condone murder? And why would they try to kill Nigel on the same night that Kitwana received orders to kill the dragon?

Nassira crept through the forest, uneven ground and roots beneath her feet. Nigel walked beside her in silence, except for the occasional hiss of pain from setting his wounded feet down. Overhead, the flights had stopped, which must mean they were now being pursued on foot.

Nassira hurried forward and Nigel followed. Whatever else the Hyena Men might want to do, by targeting Nigel and not the camp, they'd shown they wanted the compass stone.

"It was my brother," Nigel said, in a barely audible whisper. "On that rug."

"What?" Nassira whipped around to face him.

The Englishman's face, always unnaturally white to Nassira's eyes, now looked like chalk.

"My brother, Carew. He came to Africa before I did. On a mission." He looked at Nassira with new alarm, as though an idea had just occurred to him. "You . . . you know that?"

Nassira sighed. "I know what you're searching for. I have been following you from London."

"From London?" Nigel asked. "I suppose this isn't the time to explain. You saved my life twice over. Why would you do that if you . . . But then, my brother—"

He was still afraid to reveal too much.

Nassira nodded at him. "Heart of Light."

Nigel's eyes widened. "Yes. And Carew disappeared in Africa, looking for the Heart of Light. How do you know?"

"It's a long story," Nassira said. "I wanted to make sure the Heart of Light wouldn't be used for bad purposes." Which was true as far as that went.

Nigel tilted his head sideways, not quite satisfied, but went on. "Yet it was Carew on that rug. Operating the magelight."

"Perhaps he's a prisoner, forced to activate the magelight. It could well be."

"But what could those who captured him want with us? With me? And why would they keep him alive? And what could they mean to do with us?" Nigel paused. "Are they the Hyena Men?"

Nassira nodded. "I'm afraid they'll catch up with us unless we get moving again."

She continued between the trees and heard Nigel follow her. Was that a twig snapping ahead of her? Had she just heard a stealthy footstep or a breath forcefully exhaled beyond the row of trees in front of them? She slowed down, but the dark forest appeared undisturbed behind them.

Nigel stopped and exclaimed. Nassira stopped also and turned around. In front of them, a few steps ahead, a group of people stood.

They were all young males, broad shouldered, narrow hipped, their upright, noble bodies and dignified features proclaiming them to be Masai warriors.

Their leader stood a few steps ahead of the others, his hair done up in ocher, a lion skin draped across his shoulders.

Nassira narrowed her eyes and looked at them with magesight. Surrounding him and his companions, a halo of ocher-colored magical light shone so bright that either these were the most powerful magicians ever born, or they were not human at all, but creatures woven entirely of magic.

A FEVERISH DRAGON

Kitwana waited. After they had packed, he told Emily they should rest because they must walk during the day. It would be a long, arduous, heavy walk that would test even Kitwana's stamina.

"Why should we walk?" she asked. "And where? Nigel has the compass stone. Without it, we have no idea where to go. And yet I don't think I can go back. Not without Nigel."

"Perhaps Mr. Oldhall will come back in the morning," Kitwana said. "Reason enough to wait. But if he does not return then, we must go." He gestured with his hand at the wrecked camp. "We can't stay near the corpses. It would be too hard to drag them out to the bush to bury. And they will attract scavengers even with the deterrent presence of the dragon here. By tomorrow, every carrion eater will flock here. Besides . . ." He gestured toward where Peter had sat. The dragon-man had long since slumped sideways and now slept, curled in a tight ball. "He will never survive a march if we leave now."

"But where will we go?" Emily asked, her dark blue eyes turned toward him.

Kitwana shrugged. "I don't know. For now south

and west on the route we were following, as we stand
a better chance of meeting with Mr. Oldhall and
Nassira that way."

This promise finally calmed her down enough that
she agreed to his idea and lay down atop a blanket by
the fire.

"I'll stay awake and keep guard," Kitwana said
"Since I'm the strongest one. Best able to stand the
walk without sleep."

She started to protest, but her eyes closed.

Kitwana waited to make sure that she was indeed
asleep. It had been difficult for him to evoke the
dragon-man's health. It sailed too close to a lie for his
taste. Because the truth was, as soon as Emily fell
asleep, Kitwana meant to interrogate Peter Farewell
and get from him all he could about the man's allegiance and honor, and how trustworthy he might be, in
either form. If he proved treasonous, Kitwana would
rather kill him than allow him to kill or threaten Emily
Oldhall.

But he knew he could never explain this to Emily,
nor convince her of the necessity of it. So he must wait
till she was deeply asleep.

When the regularity of her breath convinced him
that Emily was, he found his bespelled lance and his
personal knife on the ground, near where his bed had
been. Then he crept toward Peter Farewell and,
squatting nearby, shook him by the shoulder.

As Farewell's eyelids fluttered open, Kitwana set
the knife to his throat. Farewell's eyes opened wide,
and he looked questioningly at Kitwana.

Kitwana gestured with his head, indicating the
edge of the camp. Farewell got up at Kitwana's push

and allowed himself to be supported and guided to the edge of the camp where a large boulder obstructed direct view of the fire. Only Farewell's strained breathing gave away how tired he was, how weak. Kitwana rounded the boulder and forced him to sit, his back against the stone.

"I could scream," Farewell said in a half whisper. "Would you dare kill me while the lovely Mrs. Oldhall is awake and watching?"

"Scream and I kill you before the sound is out," Kitwana said, and raised his lance.

Farewell looked at it for a moment. "If you're going to kill me," he said, "could I be allowed a last cigarette?"

Kitwana gestured with his lance. "I don't want to kill you. I want to know why I should let you live."

"Ah." Peter shrugged. "Can't help you there. I myself never understood why I should be allowed to live."

Kitwana raised his eyebrows. "Why are you here? What are your intentions?"

"Same as yours, dear chap. To find the ruby, Heart of Light, that has the power to anchor magic to an individual and his descendants forever."

"To make yourself king of the world?"

"King of the world?" Farewell said. "Forbid the thought. No. I want to find the ruby to destroy it."

"To destroy it?" Kitwana asked, uncomprehending.

"Yes. I have this theory that one ruby having bound the magic to one family line, destroying the other ruby will destroy magic entirely. All humans shall be equal. And free."

Kitwana felt a sudden stab of understanding. "And you'll be a dragon no more."

Peter frowned at him. "I suppose not. But then, I have enough magic that I might also be dead." He shrugged. "It doesn't matter. At least people will be free."

"And without magic," Kitwana said. "Have you ever lived without magic, Mr. Farewell?"

Peter Farewell shrugged without answering. In Kitwana's mind, though, the fact that Farewell was a dragon-man was of the utmost importance. He was now convinced that all of Farewell's beliefs, all of his actions, were a way to free himself of this hereditary burden. The dragon was the key to the man, and the relationship between Peter and the dragon was the hinge upon which Peter Farewell's sanity swung. If he could get Farewell to speak of how he felt being a dragon, he might discover if the man was worth saving.

Without letting go of either knife or lance, Kitwana squatted so his face was on a level with his prisoner's. "When did you learn that you were a dragon?" he asked.

Farewell looked surprised. Then a shadow crossed his gaze. He looked past Kitwana as he spoke. "The first inkling I had came a month after I left school. It was summer, and I intended to go up to Cambridge in the autumn. My father's sheep started disappearing, and all the shepherds said they'd seen a dragon come and take them away. Of course, my parents thought it must be some peasant newly arrived in the district, someone descended from the bastard line of a Welsh nobleman. Dragons were common in Wales at one time." He tightened his hands one upon the other, clasped on his lap, so hard that the knuckles shone white through his tanned skin. "But we'd never heard of someone of a mixed line inheriting the curse. Most people who suffer from it are the result of dragon-on-dragon mating, proud lines who live isolated and feared by all their neighbors.

"Still, my father looked and questioned everyone coming into the district." Peter stopped and his lips trembled. He bit them hard, drawing droplets of blood. "But no one who had come from Wales was found. So my father took me and our steward and a couple of friends. All of us with powersticks, guarding the sheep through the night." He laughed, a strange, uncontrolled sound, like a drunkard's laughter. "Me, guarding the sheep from myself!"

Kitwana started at the laugh and clasped the lance harder, but Farewell didn't move, nor give any signs of changing shape.

"And then I started coughing," he said. "I felt it coming upon me. I knew what would happen, as surely as I'd ever known anything. You see..." He turned earnest, deep green eyes toward Kitwana, although from their unfocused expression, their dazed look, it was doubtful he saw Kitwana at all. "You see, I had always changed in my sleep before and I had no idea why I woke up feeling energized and sated. But now my change came upon me while fully awake and I..."

Farewell took a deep breath, like a drowning man who, for the space of a breath, gets his head above water. "I ran behind some bushes, to hide my change from the others. But my father saw me. He thought I'd discovered our prey and he followed me. He saw me change." Peter's eyes filled with tears and he looked at Kitwana. Then he inhaled forcefully and the tears vanished. Kitwana understood. They were not Peter's tears to cry. They were the tears of a barely grown boy faced with a horror he couldn't comprehend, a horror he could not escape.

"He didn't kill me. Indeed, my father could never bring himself to kill his only son and extinguish his noble line, originating with the great Charlemagne." Peter laughed again hollowly. "And so when I woke in the morning—back in my own bed where blind instinct had led me, after gorging myself with stolen sheep—my father was waiting. He'd called his friends and our steward off somehow, but now he wanted me out of his lands and out of England. He gave me money and said more would come when I told him where I was.

"I'd always meant to make my life in the army," Peter said. "Or in politics. But the army was no place for a man with a dreadful secret. If exposed I would have been burned. And the change happens sometimes when I don't mean it to . . . like in that horrible train to Port Said. The change would come through and interfere with the train-moving spell. I had to go some way afield to hunt an antelope and—" He shrugged. "And politics was right out, too. The same reason. Imagine changing in front of important dignitaries. My father was right. If I wanted to keep my life, let alone any honor, I had to leave, go abroad.

"So I traveled the world, never staying around long enough that the bingeing of the dragon upon livestock and whatever else couldn't be ignored. In Italy I almost managed to control the dragon. Almost. But then I was very low, living on the little my father could spare, often sleeping in the open fields, destitute, per-forming magic tricks for the amusement of low hostelry owners who would, in exchange, allow me a night's sleep or an hour by the fire in the chilly Tuscan winters.

"Living as I did, a member of the nobility at loose ends and often away from the company of all men, I met some people . . . To tell the truth, I fell in with some well-educated Italians, some Frenchmen, some others belonging to the fine flower of intellectual life in Europe. And from them I heard a theory that gave me purpose and reason to live.

"They made me see how unfair it was that Charlemagne, the bastard of a king and a peasant, born with little enough hereditary magic of his own, should steal everyone's magic and use it for himself. They made me see how his imposing upon the people of Europe in that way only made them poorer yet. They made me see that it had to stop, that the noble-men must be killed, that all with great power must be killed, so that it could return to the people who origi-nated it."

"But noblemen were your people. Those with power were doubtlessly your friends," Kitwana said, no longer able to contain himself. "How could you so ruthlessly mean to kill them?"

Peter shrugged. "The individual is nothing. It is justice for the world that counts. As my life could be ruined for the sake of some dragon ancestor I never heard of, why shouldn't others give their lives up for the sake of justice in the world? At least their deaths will mean that the Earth will be a better place."

"And you killed Hyena Men, too," Kitwana said.

Grief and rage rose in him and he realized, in shock, that part of his anger came from Peter Farewell's denying Kitwana's father's lifelong belief that the individual was everything.

Every sense, trained from childhood, told Kitwana that anyone who believed the individual counted for nothing must die. But then, Peter Farewell was an individual also. A misguided one who only wished to rid himself of the were-beast's control, no matter how many lies he told himself about his intentions. And having heard how the dragon's emergence had destroyed Farewell's prospects and best hopes, Kitwana understood him. And understanding, how could he kill this tormented man?

Peter shrugged. "Hyena Men, like the English, mean to do nothing but take the ruby and bind the power to a minority again. They, too, needed to die, lest the atrocities of the oppressors perpetuate themselves."

"The Hyena Men do not mean—" Kitwana started, but stopped, as his thought interrupted his speech. What if they did? A cold finger of dread drew down his spine as he remembered how he'd suspected Shenta back in Cairo. Peter shrugged. He looked too unnaturally hot, as if his skin were only a shell and inside him a fire burned wild, consuming him.

"We—my fellow anarchists and I—captured that old faker Widefield," Peter said. "He was on our list to eliminate. But while we set about it, he offered us the story of the ruby and Nigel's search as a means to escape what he had coming to him. I knew Nigel's name and I offered to meet him in Africa, to gain his confidence—"

"Would you have killed Nigel Oldhall, too?" Kitwana

asked. He didn't know if it would change things, but he had to know. If Farewell said he would have killed his best friend without remorse, Kitwana would have to destroy Farewell now. A beast, a raging lion, had to be destroyed, no matter if it had only acted according to its instincts.

Peter looked at him, puzzled. "I didn't want to kill Nigel," he said. "I loved Nigel like a brother when we were children. But the cause I serve is greater than myself. Greater than any man, or any thing. It is the happiness of the whole of humanity."

"But who are you to say in which manner humanity is to be happy?" Kitwana said, his voice slow and almost a whisper, as if he heard his father's words through his lips. "And what percentage of humanity would be happy? Because I can tell you that you'll never make the whole of humanity happy. So how many would be enough for you? A third? Half? Depending on how you see it, that many are happy now. It all hinges on your definition of happiness. What *is* your definition of happiness?"

Yet Kitwana himself had joined the Hyena Men to save all of Africa, and perhaps to prove his father wrong. To prove that it wasn't just individuals who could be saved.

At that moment they felt magic overhead and heard something zooming past. Looking up, Kitwana saw many little flying rugs. The British army.

He leapt forward and, grabbing Peter, pulled him to standing, pressing the knife against his throat. "You called them," he said. "You used your mind to call the Englishmen down on us. You're going to sell me to save your worthless hide."

Farewell struggled for speech.

Emily bounded from behind the big boulder and grabbed Kitwana's arm. "Stop, Mr. Kitwana. Stop."

He realized in the same instant that Farewell's expression was of sheer bewilderment and his lips shaped "The army?" soundlessly.

Looking up and over his shoulder, Kitwana saw the rugs veer overhead. The night was dark, but not impenetrable, and Kitwana saw well enough to distinguish, on the rug nearest them, a shape and figure that made him think of Shenta.

Farewell's teeth chattered with the shivers of a great fever. "The Hyena Men," he said. "By God, the Hyena Men."

"Are you sure?" Kitwana asked, turning to him and pulling the knife away from his throat.

Farewell didn't seem to notice that the knife had been withdrawn. His state was such that Kitwana was not absolutely sure that he had registered its presence in the first place. But he looked at Kitwana and his gaze focused. "I'm quite sure," he said. "I can smell their power."

"We must leave," Emily said. "Now. And hope we cross with Nigel on the road."

Kitwana looked at her. "You heard everything," he said.

She pressed her lips together in disapproval. "You tried to trick me," she said. "You would have killed him. How could I sleep when I can't trust either of you?"

MORAN IN THE FOREST

"What do you seek in the forest?"

Nassira started. She was sure the leader of the Moran band, the one in the middle of the group, had spoken. The voice and question still echoed in her mind. But when she thought about it, she couldn't remember seeing his lips moving.

"We just want to get through," Nigel spoke from behind her. "We just want to be safe."

And this, too, was a wonder, because Nassira was sure the question she'd heard—if indeed she'd heard it—had been spoken in Maa. But Nigel, who did not speak Nassira's language, was answering it in English.

The Moran leader looked toward Nigel for just a moment, as though evaluating him. "There is no safety," he spoke. Or rather, his words appeared in Nassira's mind as a recollection of having heard them, but there was no sound. The still air was unnaturally quiet. "There is never safety, Water Man. While you're living, you must always die. Not all your knowledge, not all your reading, not even the safe walls of your ancestral home will ever prevent the enemy who comes in the night."

Nigel made a strangled sound and the Moran

turned to Nassira. His eyes were dark and immense, filled with a knowledge that Nassira felt went beyond anything a mere human could accumulate in the short span of a lifetime. "What do you seek, daughter of Nedera?"

Nassira's mind worked. The truth was that like Nigel, she'd plunged into the forest for one reason only—she was being chased. She was being pursued, attacked by the organization to which she'd given her allegiance, the organization that had caused her to go away and allow Kume to die. All she wanted was to get away from them and find out what they were doing and why. But instead her lips were forming an alien word, one she'd heard in London in the church of her employers. "Absolution," she said.

And on saying it, she found that was truly what she wanted. She wanted absolution—forgiveness for all her past sins, assurance that she truly had nothing to do with her brother's death, that she wasn't responsible for Kume's.

Her word echoed in the dark forest, and for a moment nothing happened. The Moran did not move. And Nassira thought that surely there was nothing here—that she was imagining it all. The Moran were just an illusion, spun from her brain, meaning nothing. Or else they were a psychic trap created by the Hyena Men and she and Nigel were already captured, dreaming away their lives while enemies stripped them of their minds and willpower.

Then the Moran smiled, a smile of infinite sweetness and sad irony. "Of what are you guilty, Nassira?" he asked.

And his voice, remembered in her mind, was

Kume's, through the hot summer nights of their innocent love.

Nassira looked back. She wondered how much of this Nigel could hear, how much he could even understand. He looked paler even than normal, a ghostly apparition in the middle of the forest, a man transmuted to ice. But his eyes were intent on her, as if he, too, needed to know, needed to be apprised of her transgressions, her evil deeds.

She shook her head, deciding this was too strange and too dangerous. Why should she confess her transgressions to this creature when she wasn't even sure what it might be? She struck her father's herding stick into the Earth and spoke loudly, as much to scare away her fear as to answer the thing. "I just want to pass through, and I want my enemies detained."

The Moran shrugged. "You came into the sacred forest. You wandered into the glades of power. You will pass, yes, but not before you find the answers you seek."

Nassira felt a dull anger. She'd never been very religious. She was a woman who could understand simple magic and deal in it without fear. Magic lit your fire, with which you could cook your food. Magic healed a sick baby. Magic kept the cows safe at pasture. But magic was clean and concrete—a few gestures, a few ritual words that your ancestors had found influenced the world.

Religion—that was something else.

Having been in London and seen the mighty buildings of the Water Men, having seen the cows in the English countryside, Nassira wasn't sure she could believe the simple dictum that Engai had given all cows to the Masai and the beasts of the field to everyone else. If indeed Engai had done that, he was a foolish God, for he'd allowed the Masai property to wander across the ocean and into the possession of a pale people stranger than any African tribe.

And the whole legend about how death had come amid men by accident, and the legends of sacred mountains and sacred forests, and men who lived in isolation and spoke to God, the whole idea of lost, ghostly Moran living in these places, ready to harangue the unwary. All of it seemed almost silly to Nassira. Why would God play childish games of hide-and-seek with his own creatures? If he existed, why didn't he show himself and speak plain?

So she narrowed her eyes at the Moran in front of her, those solid-seeming young warriors.

"You don't exist," she said. And stepped forward, hurrying toward the dim forest past the Masai apparition. Out of habit, she reached back and grabbed for Nigel's wrist and pulled him forward with her, though she seemed to be dragging him against his will.

"Come, Mr. Oldhall," she told Nigel. "These are nothing. Just illusions. Apparitions."

But as she stepped forward, the Massai did, too. They grabbed at her hands, at her body, and pulled her back to where she had been.

Yet they hadn't moved. She hadn't seen them move. But she'd felt their hands on her, and now she was three steps back, and they still stood in front of her, barring her way.

She struck her herding stick into the ground again, and then, lifting it high above her head as a warning, as a defense, she said, "I do not *believe* in you. I do not believe in sacred forests where one sees one's own soul. I do not believe in Engai, nor that all cows belong to the Masai."

The scary words sliced through the night like a flash of lightning. Without even realizing what she was doing, Nassira had thrown her whole magic into the words. This should dispel the apparition. Whether it came from her own head, or from the Hyena Men's spells, or from the snares of her enemies, these obstacles in her path should vanish.

And none too soon. The Hyena Men would be near at hand.

Nassira brought her herding stick down with a flourish and struck the earth in front of her. As her stick hit the ground, a flare of light sparked, with a sound like tearing fabric.

The light grew blinding. For a moment the whole forest was bathed in white, bright light that shone so absolute, so brilliant that it lit all the trees around.

Nassira felt that beyond seeing, she became the trunks and the low-growing brush, and the creatures scurrying for cover from the magical illumination.

Nigel screamed, and Nassira looked over her shoulder at him. He looked horrified, his mouth wide open, his expression slack with incomprehension.

She looked forward again. And there, in the light— She felt her knees buckle and her throat let out an inarticulate, mindless scream, like Oldhall's. She fell forward, her knees and hands on the ground, her palms pressed hard against the dirt. Tears streamed from her eyes, but she wasn't crying. Then there were hands on her, warm hands. Strong hands.

Hands she knew all too well. They had her by the shoulders and were lifting her up.

She allowed him to lift her, to support her body. She felt his familiar strength as he held her, his arms surrounding her.

"Kume," she said.

"Yes," he said, his voice warm against her ear. "But no. It's not that easy."

Nassira looked forward at where the Moran leader still stood, draped in his lion skin, his band around him. Had Kume been of that band? Were they ghosts?

She looked at her old lover. He didn't feel like a ghost. He felt warm, alive. And his voice was just as she remembered.

But he'd just said he wasn't Kume, had he not?

"Kume?" she said again, and her voice came out trembling, washed in her own grief and the silence she'd kept within her deepest heart since hearing of Kume's death. "You are dead."

"Yes," he said. "And no."

"What do you wish to be forgiven for, daughter of Nedera?" the leader of the Moran asked again, his voice not really in her ears, but in her mind.

They hadn't disappeared. All of Nassira's illusion-dispelling power had not made these illusions disappear. And they wouldn't let her pass until she told them the truth.

Nassira trembled. Her legs felt too weak to hold her up. She must confess now. Confess her misdeeds before Nigel Oldhall, before the Water Man, who would then know that she was one of the Hyena Men. Who would never trust her again. Who would not allow her to save him. Who would die alone in this forest, without her.

Yet she had to do it.

Still, if she was going to do it, she would do it standing proud.

Though her legs still felt weak, though her heart beat within her rib cage, she pushed Kume's specter away. She pushed away the comfort of his touch, the warmth of his body. She held her herding stick tight and leaned on it as a herder would as evening fell and his body grew weary.

She told them of her brother and how, though she'd been jealous, she had not wanted his death. "I could have used a healing charm and kept him alive through the night. I could have saved him."

"And kept him alive all his life after that?" the Moran leader asked. "How would you do that, Nassira?"

"And then my father started paying attention to me again," Nassira said. "Oh, I mourned my brother, but his death brought me my father and mothers' love again. And I rejoiced in that." The sob almost broke through, but she took a deep breath and kept it at bay.

"What child wouldn't rejoice in having her parents love her again? Nassira, you've done nothing wrong. You couldn't be expected to watch through the night and keep your brother alive. You wouldn't have been able to keep him alive through every night of his life."

"And then there was him." Nassira looked toward where Kume's ghost stood, a few steps away, looking solid and substantial and very much as Kume had looked in life, with his soft, warm gaze, his handsome features, his broad shoulders. "Kume was a proud warrior of the Masai, strong and handsome, quick with a poem, ready with conversation. I fell in love with him, helplessly." She looked away from the image of Kume and toward the leader of the Moran. "But I soon realized that he lived as if with a curse."

Again the sob tried to break through and she swallowed it back. She told them of Kume, of his death.

"Again, we find no guilt in you." The Moran leader spoke, but the voice was Kume's. The apparition that looked like Kume came quite close to her. His hand rested on Nassira's shoulder, and he spoke in the well-beloved voice. "Kume was not yours to protect. You could never—even had you married him—spend every minute of every day with him. If he was fated to die young, he would have died, no matter what you did.

"But this greater duty, Nassira," the Moran leader continued. "What was it, and where did it take you?"

"I was bespoken," Nassira said, "by an organization that said it would liberate Africa. It said if it could get enough worthy people to serve it, it would make the Africans the equal of the Europeans. And free us from the yoke of the Water People."

And as the words came out of her mouth, Nassira saw them for the first time. She saw clearly what they meant. To make Africans the equal of the Europeans. To give them a king, who claimed for himself the power of all Africans, leaving the common man stripped of magic, and only a few in power.

Oh, what an idiot she'd been.

"But now I understand that the organization serves only itself," Nassira said. "And that if it does indeed expel the Water Men, it will only be to replace them with the power of one man within the organization, who will make himself our king and our owner."

"And you don't think this is good?" the Moran leader asked. Was that a trace of irony in his tone?

Nassira shook her head, unable to speak.

"You don't think that it would be better to have one power, one man who controls all, and prevents the endless fratricide disputes of the various tribes?" the Moran asked sweetly. "One man who can perform magic such that even the Europeans must cower from it? One man who makes them fear the African races and know us, indeed, for their superiors?"

What did he mean? Was he going to tell her the Hyena Men were right?

Well, Nassira didn't care what he was going to say or what he thought. He might be a spirit. He might be resistant to her magic. He might be able to conjure the form and shape, the feel and sound of her dead lover with no effort at all. But there was something very wrong with the Hyena Men, with their secret structure, their orders that came from nowhere anyone could see. There was something evil about an organization that could tell Kitwana to kill a dragon and, at the same time, seek to eliminate the Oldhalls. Nassira was sure Kitwana had been ordered to kill the dragon, because he would never do it by himself otherwise. He was by nature not very violent.

Nassira realized with blinding clarity what the plan was. Whoever ruled the organization had meant for the dragon to kill them. And if Kitwana died and Nassira with him, and all the carriers or most of them were killed or dispersed, and Emily and Nigel Oldhall found dead near or in the encampment, then anyone coming to look for them or their remains would blame Peter Farewell for their deaths, and the Hyena Men would be free. Free to look for the ruby. Free to claim it. Free to make Africa into another Europe.

"Well, Nassira, daughter of Nedera?" the Moran leader asked.

Nassira looked at him, shook her head. "We do not need a king," she said. "We do not need the Hyena Men and their misguided quest. I don't know what the answer is, but I know they do not have it. Nor do the Europeans. If there is a future for humanity, it is not in a world where one can make decisions for all and make all abide by his rules." She lifted her head defiantly, knowing she would probably be burned to a crisp in the next minute. "When one man has that kind of power, he tends to think others don't matter, and murder and destruction follow. The color of the man's skin makes no difference at all to that. All men's hearts are the same color."

The Moran leader raised his head, then threw it back.

Nassira thought he was about to emit a battle cry, to call down his curse on this blasphemer who'd already told him she did not believe in Engai and now compounded it by saying she didn't believe in Africa. But instead, he let forth a gale of laughter and amusement.

"And I, Nassira," the Moran said. "I believe as you do." He stopped laughing and looked at Nassira with a smile. "But there, you are right. There we find guilt in you. You should have seen through the promises of the Hyena Men. You should have known it wasn't possible. Now you must set right what you did wrong. You must find the ruby of power—Heart of Light— and set it all right."

All of a sudden, things became too confused to follow. She heard a sound—or maybe it wasn't a sound, but a feeling, a scratching on the skin, a rending in the soul, a sensation like she was being turned inside out and upside down.

The Moran, even Kume by her side, seemed to shrink, to be called to a composite giant being before her, a shape—a thing—that grew till it was a young Moran, covered in ocher, draped in a lion skin, but ten times as large as Nassira and Nigel, standing in front of them, with legs as tall as the treetops, arms as thick as tree trunks.

"You may pass through," it said. "Your enemies shall not."

And like that, Nassira and Nigel found themselves on rocky ground. The forest had vanished and Nassira realized they had come through it and were now on the other side.

The sky rumbled overhead, and for a moment she thought that it was the scream of Engai, his rage pouring out on her, the disbeliever. Instead, lightning zigzagged across the sky. And, at first gently, then with increased violence, drops of water came crashing down.

"Rain," Nigel said.

And Nassira, going weak at the knees again, felt herself starting to kneel and held herself upright by the strength of her herding stick. "Rain makes the pastures grow and fattens the cows," she said, her voice small and even. "It is a blessing of Engai."

IN THE DARK

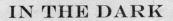

Kitwana spoke in an urgent, scared voice. "I didn't mean to kill him. Honestly, I didn't." He sounded like a little boy, justifying himself to his irate parent. "I just wanted to know more about him, if he was a danger to us."

"And if I were, you were going to kill me," Peter Farewell said, his voice barely more than a whisper. He spoke without resentment, but a trace of his ironic amusement lingered in his words.

"Well . . ." Kitwana said.

Without thinking, Emily felt Peter's forehead with the back of her hand. It was like touching hot coals. Were dragons always hotter than normal humans? Or was Peter Farewell dying of fever?

"No one is going to kill anyone else," she said. She spoke out of annoyance, not sure of what she said, just sure that she didn't want these two misguided males arguing now, when one of them might already be dying, and when all of them were lost in Africa, with enemies hot in their pursuit. "Mr. Farewell, is your temperature different?"

"Different?" Peter asked. He turned his cloudy eyes to her. "Different from what?"

Emily bit her lip. Must he be stupid, as well as feverish? "Different from normal humans?"

"I am a normal human," he said, indignation raising his voice almost to customary levels. "I am just like you or . . . him." He pointed a trembling finger at Kitwana. "When I'm not . . . When I'm not . . ."

"Right," Emily said. She turned to Kitwana. "We can't leave now. We can go nowhere tonight, while he's consumed with fever."

"I'll carry him," Kitwana said.

And Emily wondered what went into making the human male that they could have so little perception of reality. Looking at both men, she could tell they were of about equivalent bulk, the same height and approximately the same weight. Did Kitwana truly think he could carry someone his own weight through the jungle in the dark of night? Fast enough and long enough to evade pursuers on flying rugs?

She just stared at him. "Right," she said. "And you'll . . . fly? You'll carry him so far and so fast that we'll avoid those people on rugs?"

Kitwana looked confused. He opened his hands, palms at the sides of his body, in a show of helplessness. "I don't know what else we can do. We must leave. Now. We must run."

All her life, Emily had been protected and cosseted. Others had made decisions for her, told her when it was safe to stay and safe to go. And look where it had brought her.

She crossed her arms on her chest. "I don't think so, Mr. Kitwana. Even without the hindrance of Mr. Farewell's illness, we could never travel fast enough to get away from flying enemies."

"So," Kitwana said. He looked at her and wrinkled his forehead in confusion. "We are lost?"

Emily shook her head. "We are lost if they're after us. But if they're after us, why haven't they landed? Surely they saw our fire. I think they're after someone else. Granted, they might turn and come after us again, so we should put the fire out. In fact, I think that's just what we should do. Put the fire out and try to get some rest, and get Mr. Farewell better before we leave."

"We can't put the fire out," Kitwana said. "What about animals—"

"Didn't you listen when Mr. Farewell said animals will not come near him?" Emily shot one look at Peter's withered features as he attempted to smile at her. Had she ever been besotted with him? Had she ever thought he would protect her? She could not remember why.

"That salve . . . what you made before. Was it real?" she asked Kitwana.

"The healing salve?" Kitwana asked, and frowned. "You mean, would it really disinfect his wounds? Heal them?"

"Yes."

"Of course."

"Well, forgive me for doubting you, but you did try to kill him."

Kitwana shook his head and looked offended. "Not kill him. Just determine if he was dangerous, if he had to be killed."

"Are you dangerous, Mr. Farewell?" Emily asked.

Peter looked up at her and frowned. "I'm barely alive," he said.

"Which is when beasts become most dangerous," Kitwana said.

"Should you shift your form, would you be dangerous?" Emily asked. "Would you try to eat us? You are in great pain. Would that cause you to attack?"

"You want to kill me, too," Peter said in sudden anger. His tired features set in something like a little boy's scowl. "Everyone hates me. Why don't you set binds on me so I can't change?"

"Because we can't do that," Kitwana said. "You know well that no one can do that, not even yourself."

Emily ignored them both and repeated her question. "If you shift forms, will you attack us? Or do you have any power of self-control?"

Peter looked bewildered. "I have self-control."

"In dragon form?"

"In..." Peter hesitated. "In my other form, I have *some* self-control. I can... Unless someone attacks me." He looked at Kitwana. "Or I'm very hungry. Most of the time I can control myself. But fear or nerves or... hunger..."

"Then you are guilty of murder. You killed strangers. Ate strangers. And you knew what you were doing," Kitwana said.

Again, Emily ignored him. Before Peter's anger could surge, she said, "And aren't you very hungry? Won't you be very hungry if you shift forms?"

Peter shrugged. "I don't know," he said. "When I'm not myself I need more food than as a human. But I don't... I'm not... I'm very ill. I don't know. I always prefer beasts, if I can catch them."

Emily looked at the man in front of her, dressed in his rumpled linen suit, his hair in disarray, too weak to even walk as a man. Would not the dragon suffer the same weakness? "Mr. Kitwana, please douse the fire and bring me the salve. We need to sleep and we need to decide where we shall go."

Kitwana looked as if he'd resist her orders. And why shouldn't he? She was only a woman. As far as Emily could tell, the opinions of women were never very respected. And besides, she was wholly unused to giving orders.

Even now, she would feel more comfortable if one of the men should take charge. But how could they? Peter was half out of his mind and couldn't even give her a straight answer. As for Kitwana, he seemed to be so completely concentrated on the danger Peter Farewell posed that he could think of nothing else that might threaten them.

She watched him douse the fire. What would he know, and how well would he lead? He had fallen for the Hyena Men. And if an organization that bound people's minds wasn't evil, Emily didn't know what would be.

When Kitwana came back, he was carrying something, which he threw over Farewell. His gesture was so aggressive, it took Emily a moment to realize that it was a blanket.

"I thought you might get cold with the fever and with the fire out," he said in a sharp tone. He brought out the jar of water he'd turned into a healing salve and poured some of it into a cup. "Here," he said. "This has no herbs. It's just concentrated healing magic. Drink it."

Farewell took the cup and looked at it dubiously.

"I don't kill men in the dark and by poison," Kitwana said bluntly.

Peter looked at Kitwana, then shrugged and threw the water back in a single gulp, as if it were strong liquor. Then he screamed and folded forward, over his knees, trembling and whimpering.

"You poisoned him," Emily said, looking at Kitwana.

"Shhh," Kitwana said, not so much an order as a request. He put his hand on her shoulder. It felt warm and oddly comforting. After this night of shocks, she had to fight a sudden impulse to lean on him, to be folded into his arms.

If it showed in her face, fortunately Kitwana wasn't looking. He stared at Peter, who was still shaking, then back at Emily. "You know that a concentrated healing magic hurts. The body resists sudden healing as much as it resists sudden wounding.

"I am ... not dying," Peter said as he raised his head. He shivered. "He's speaking the truth. Mrs. Oldhall, please don't distress yourself."

His voice did seem stronger. Presently, his shaking subsided. He snuggled down into his blanket. His eyes closed. Soon, a rhythmic breathing announced that he'd fallen asleep.

Emily watched him in wonder and fear. Had she really thought herself in love with him? She'd never even known him. A were-beast as he was, full of immense magic, and Peter Farewell was like a great British oak with rot at its core—a hollow, soft center that at any moment could cause the whole to collapse.

"I brought you a blanket, too," Kitwana said, from beside her. He'd brought one for himself as well. "I thought it safer if we curled near him, beside the boulder. If someone should come and look for us—"

She nodded and took the blanket from him. Then she curled down on the hard ground—next to a sleeping dragon. She tried to think of Nigel, of how to find him again. But she wasn't sure she wanted to find him. Nigel had courted her and deceived her. But he was as bound as she, whether he loved Nassira or not. Within the tight, rigid structure of English society, could he tell his parents that he was in love with an African woman? Could he hope for their blessing? For a happy life in the Oldhall estate?

She almost laughed. She remembered the expression of Nigel's mother when she'd found out that Emily had an Indian grandmother. In Europe, a darker skin was inevitably, assumed to be inferior. Only Emily's large dowry and her father's name had prevented Mrs. Oldhall from forbidding Nigel's marriage to her. What would she think of a Masai girl who probably understood a dowry to be cows? Emily now wondered if she'd ever been in love with Nigel—and therefore if she'd ever been in love at all. Still, she had a natural reverence for love and a certainty that love came around but rarely. Perhaps it was the novels she had read, but she felt in her heart that if Nigel had found love with his African girl, then he was justified in doing all he could to make their union a reality and to live happily ever after.

What Emily found curious was that it hurt her so little. She mustn't have been very much in love with Nigel after all. And perhaps that was best for everyone.

She wasn't aware of falling asleep, but she woke to

a sound like a growl and sat up, her hand over her speeding heart.

Animals. They were being attacked. They were—

Then she smelled the peculiar odor that she'd identified as Peter Farewell's before. She stretched her hand to where he'd been and found a cold blanket and what was surely the empty leg of his pair of pants.

He'd changed. He'd—

The growl echoed again, followed by sounds of crunching bone and rending flesh.

Emily stood hastily. But there, on the other side of the dragon's abandoned clothing and blankets, Kitwana lay, sleeping—his blanket half thrown off his dark, muscular torso, and an arm thrown up over his head with the abandon of a sleeping child.

Emily looked again to where the dragon—Peter— sat and tore at the flesh of . . . It looked like a horse, its black and white stripes visible by the scant light of a rosy dawn.

A zebra. It—he—was eating a zebra.

As Emily watched, the dragon tore at the flesh and chewed. Its eyes, immense and green and somehow as expressive as they'd been in human form, gazed at her with steady amusement.

Did she dare?

If Peter was a beast and had little control, it would never allow her to approach. If, however, the human lived beyond those huge eyes, that bloodstained muzzle . . .

Trembling, she stood and walked slowly toward the dragon, step by step. It continued eating, looking at her, giving no indication of its intentions. As she got within two steps, it stopped chewing and waited. She extended her hand slowly and lay it upon the dragon's warm muzzle.

For a moment, the creature was still and silent. Then it made a sound like growling, but more like the purring of a giant cat. It blinked the inner eyelids, and then the outer ones.

Emily had a sense—perhaps mistaken—that the great beast was laughing at her. She drew herself up primly. "Well," she said. "Good night, then, Mr. Farewell."

She heard the purring sound again, this time coming in short, staccato bursts. She thought it was laughter for sure, but she withdrew her hand and turned to walk back, pretending she didn't know that Peter Farewell was mocking her.

SEARCHING FOR
DIRECTIONS

*Nassira looked around. This did not look like the bro-*ken terrain and sudden craters of her homeland. In fact, this did not look like any terrain she knew.

She stood with Nigel in the middle of a plain covered in short grass. Looking behind her, she realized without surprise that there was no forest to be seen. She hadn't expected it to be there. She thought the forest she and Nigel had crossed had been more in the mind than in reality. And now they'd come to a place quite different. There was grass and cows. They didn't look like the cows the Masai kept, but more like English cows.

Nassira and Nigel stood just outside an enclosure where some of these cows roamed, where the grass was taller and seeding.

Nigel, his hair on end, his face haggard, tottered on his feet and sat down suddenly. "The angel," he said. "The angel of terrible countenance."

Nassira looked at him, worried. "What angel?" she said very gently.

He frowned at her, his brows descending over his pale eyes and his whole expression one of uncomprehending surprise. "The angel in the forest," he said. "The angel with the sword."

"I saw no angel," Nassira said. "There were only some Moran."

And then her mind reproached her as she realized suddenly that in a forest that was no forest, perhaps the entities found there were also not what they seemed. "You saw an angel?"

"Yes. With a fiery sword and white wings."

"Like the blond angels in English churches?" Nassira asked, amused.

Nigel nodded. He was looking at her in wonder, as if not sure what he could have said that was funny.

"And what did the angel tell you, Mr. Oldhall?" Nassira asked softly.

"That the ruby . . ." He shook his head. "That the queen had no more right to the ruby than the Hyena Men did. That the ruby belonged to all mankind and to the world." He made a little sound that could be a laugh, and then again might be a sob. "That I'd come on a fool's errand."

Nassira didn't know what to say. Coming on a fool's errand might have summed up her own part in this. She should never have left her father's kraal. After a long while, she found the words and spoke them, wondering if the Englishman would understand. "I found myself talking to Moran. They said much what your angel told you. Only, they said I was supposed to go to the ruby, but not take it. That I was supposed to protect it." Softly, she added, "I don't know from what."

She turned around, half expecting to see that the Englishman was not listening, but instead she found his blue, watery eyes staring at her. "To the ruby?" he said. "But we don't have Emily. And she's the one who imprinted the compass stone."

Nassira didn't know any more than he did. She dropped down onto the grass beside him and looked at the distance. There were more pastures and more cows and a few low-growing trees. In the distance, something green shimmered wetly, like an improbably immense jewel lost in the rolling terrain. A river, Nassira thought, because around it the vegetation was lusher and higher. "I wonder," she said, speaking more to herself than to him, "where we are."

He didn't answer, and looking at him again, head to toe, Nassira thought that his friends back at the club would hardly recognize Mr. Nigel Oldhall. His pale hair stood up like dry grass at the end of the season. Smudges, as of old smoke, underlined his too-pale eyes. His face was scratched, and his feet, stretched out in front of him, displayed a mass of cuts and scrapes all over their soles. His sleeping garment had gotten torn, the pants hanging in tatters and mostly missing from the knee down. The side of his face was scratched deeply. The pocket in which the compass stone nestled, making a visible lump, was torn, too—though not quite through.

While she looked at him, she realized that for all she knew, Emily Oldhall and Kitwana were dead now. Which explained why whatever was in the forest had ordered them to go to the ruby and guard it. Guard it against Hyena Men and, presumably, the grasping hands of the British sovereign. Yet if some entity was so powerful as to create a spectral forest and move them out of Masai land, then that entity surely would understand the little problem with compass stones.

Since there was no shimmering ruby here in plain sight, Nassira assumed the entity hadn't just moved her to the ruby. Therefore . . . "Mr. Oldhall?" she said in a demanding voice.

"Yes," he said, startled, turning to her expectantly.

"Are your angels messengers from your god?"

He frowned a little, as if the question didn't have an obvious answer, but nodded and said, "Yes. Generally."

"Is your god a trickster who would command you to do impossible things and demand you obey?"

"N-no. Those who know . . . those who study . . . theology. They say God demands nothing impossible of his faithful."

"And yet, the angel commanded you to go to the ruby."

"Yes."

"Then don't you see?" Nassira asked. "There must be a way for you to find it. Your wife woke the compass stone. No one else seems to have. Do you know how she did it?"

Nigel was looking at her with an expression that would make anyone else think him a half-wit. His eyes were wide open. His mouth sagged, not quite closed. But behind the eyes there was shrewd calculation. "No," he said at last, stretching the syllable. "No. Emily has . . ." He paused and sighed, as though perhaps realizing that his wife might not at this moment have power or life. "She has power that cannot be unlocked. It's great power, but alien. I don't know if it's because her blood conjoins the magical inheritance of Charlemagne and whatever the natural magics of India are. I always assumed so. But whatever her power is, it cannot be used by any European disciplines. The school for ladies she attended tried to make her use it. They tried everything. It never worked. Lord Widefield..." A sudden red flush erupted upward on Nigel's face. "Lord Widefield believed she was holding her own power locked. He said some women did till they were married. And he believed after our marriage her power would be useable."

"And he was wrong?" Nassira said.

Nigel shrugged. He moved his lips as though rehearsing what to answer. "Her power is still locked. Was locked even in Cairo. So she did nothing to activate the compass stone. She just . . . held it."

"Perhaps the stone simply reacted to your wife's power, whatever it was."

"I don't know how to wake it. I never got to the safe house, you see. Or rather, I did, but all the men within were dead. By . . ." His throat worked. "Fire. The whole house had burned."

"Oh," Nassira said. "The dragon got them, too."

"Dragon?"

"There was a . . ." She realized with a start that Nigel Oldhall had not seen Farewell change. He'd been asleep and then she wakened him. "Your friend Peter Farewell is a were-dragon."

"Peter? Impossible!" Nigel said, but even as he said it, she could see connections clicking behind his eyes as his mind linked things half heard and half perceived. "Oh. That explains . . . But—"

"The dragon attacked the Hyena Men, too."

"How do you know?"

"It's a long story, Mr. Oldhall. I will explain in time." Nassira had no intention right now of turning the Englishman against her. "But I do know. So the dragon attacked your English contacts, and you never learned how to activate the compass stone." She thought for a moment. "Aren't there standard formulas?"

"Yes, but usually not for something set this long ago."

"And yet," Nassira said, "it should be the same principle. Are you sure there's nothing you can do?"

The Englishman sighed and put his hand on his forehead, as if trying to stimulate thought from the outside.

With shaking hands, he removed the compass stone from his tattered pocket and held it in his hand, looking at it as if in wonder—as if not quite sure what it was or where it might have come from.

Moving slowly, as if his body hurt—or perhaps as if he were scared of what he was about to do—he knelt and put the stone on the ground in front of him. "You know," he said, "the Hyena Men have marked me. They could trace me with this magic. If they touch me two more times, I'll be their slave and mind-empty." He spoke not so much as though this were a reason not to do it, but slowly and consideringly, enumerating the possible consequences.

Nassira's conscience stung, and she didn't like his taking the risk. Not at all. But the Moran had ordered it. And besides, if they didn't use the compass stone, what could they do but wander forever lost in Africa? She couldn't go home while the Hyena Men still pursued them.

When she said nothing, Nigel nodded, as if she'd

given an answer. He raised his hands. Nassira could feel power and rushing energy, but she couldn't tell what exactly the Englishman was doing.

Would he manage to wake the stone? Or just to attract the Hyena Men?

PURSUED

Kitwana woke with a headache and a feeling of fore-boding. For a moment he didn't know why, though he remembered the fight yesterday, the dragon. Turning his head, he saw Mrs. Oldhall sleeping to one side of him, and then, turning quickly, he saw Peter Farewell on the other side, sprawled. He should feel relieved. He did feel relieved. Mrs. Oldhall had convinced him to spare the creature, but he couldn't say he trusted or believed in the dragon. He might look like a man, but Kitwana knew he was not. So finding the dragon asleep and in human form was reassuring.

And yet, something at the back of Kitwana's mind screamed and jumped and told him that he was in mortal danger. Through his headache, which pounded dully behind his eyes, he felt a threat approaching—unavoidable, immense and lethal. This sense was so strong he had to take deep breaths to keep himself from panic.

But Farewell lay asleep. So what could be threatening them? In the moments just before wakening, he had seen ... he had felt ... His wrist hurt. The place where the Hyena Men's mark had been set.

Kitwana sat up suddenly. He had seen a hyena,

looming spectral and power hungry over him. The dot on his wrist glowed. There were Hyena Men nearby—they were looking for him. Shenta was looking for him. Kitwana hadn't killed the dragon, and Shenta would know that. He looked again to where Peter was sleeping and chewed pensively on the side of his lip. He hadn't killed the dragon, and therefore Shenta would have reason to resent him.

Yet Peter Farewell hadn't killed them or hurt them. And Kitwana had, before this, started having doubts about Shenta's ambition. That he wanted to rule Africa, not to save it. Yet why would Shenta look for him like this? Why not simply tell Kitwana he wanted to find him? They'd mind-contacted before, so why not now?

It all felt wrong. And the back of his mind, that part that was not quite conscious and that sensed magic, was yelling at him loudly. He was in danger; he needed to defend himself or get out now.

Because he had to move and obey his instincts, or sit there and let panic envelop him, Kitwana got up. Almost without thinking, he cast a spell over his tingling wrist, to stop the Hyena mind finding him. The spell wouldn't last and it wasn't very strong—just a magic barrier between those searching for him and the magical dot. Deliberately, he got up and folded his blanket and went to collect his assegai. He followed the throbbing on his wrist as though it was a signal, as if it were the beating of drums in the night, growing louder as he approached. His wrist throbbed more intensely when he walked in a certain direction, and the pain receded as he backed up or walked in other directions. Thus he followed the signal of the pain, down from the promontory they'd occupied and back along the path they'd meant to follow, before Kitwana had hatched his plan to kill the dragon. He walked amid the trees, trying to be as stealthy as he had learned to be in his uncle's war band.

After a few minutes of walking in the green light-shadow of approaching dawn, Kitwana felt as if a dot of fire had alighted upon his wrist, burning into it with a steady flame, and his spell was barely holding, barely keeping those searching for Kitwana from finding him. He transferred his lance to that hand and with his other hand clasped the painful wrist, thinking even as he did that it was useless.

A few steps after that he heard voices—one above all ringing very clear and recognizable. Shenta. The recognition ran through Kitwana like a lightning bolt splitting the night. It truly was Shenta. And yet Shenta hadn't contacted him. Why not?

Kitwana dropped to his hands and knees. The terrain amid the trees had been covered with vegetation, but there was still enough of the thorny growth that flourished in this part of the world that crawling was impossible. Kitwana would now and then find his hand or his knee planted upon a sharp thorn, a sudden painfully sharp lip of lave. But he had been trained in the arts of war and ambush. Oh, not by his father. He allowed his lip to curl in amusement at that. Wamungunda would have told his only son that there was no need to learn such arts, because all of the world and its races of men were destined to live in peace. It never occurred to him that destiny counted for nothing or less than nothing when war and strife raged all around. Instead he stuck to his pure way and trusted in his faith in humanity to deliver him where the gods would have feared to.

But Kitwana had gone to his mother's people, and amid them learned the virtues of a man and that to which a man must hew if he intended to defend tribe and family. There he'd learned to take hurt and not to show it, and not to flinch from pain, nor cry out from surprise. This training now served him, as he crept closer, his wrist burning, his hand clenching tight on the assegai.

He no longer needed the aching of his wrist to tell him where the Hyena Men were. He could hear their voices clearly. Shenta's, and a younger man's, and then what appeared to be Nigel Oldhall's voice, only deeper and more assured.

For a moment, Kitwana stopped, while his thoughts ran riot. Nigel Oldhall here? What was he doing? Was that why he'd disappeared? Had he always been working for the Hyena Men? Was that why he and Nassira had been close? Was that why they'd vanished together?

But then the voice that sounded like Nigel's, with its well-bred British accent, said, "Well, there is nothing for it. Nigel and the woman disappeared."

Kitwana's moment of confusion broke, and he crept closer, attentive to his footfall and the placement of his body, until he was just behind a curtain of heavy-growing trees whose green tendrils hid him from sight of the camp ahead.

As Kitwana closed in, Shenta said, "If they have some magic we don't know, perhaps the dragon has taught them. And then we'll have no luck at all with the Englishwoman and the traitor."

The traitor? Kitwana blinked and indignation swelled in his heart and mind. He wanted to say that he was no traitor, that he had hurt no one and never left behind any of the ideals that Shenta so clearly was betraying. But if they thought him a traitor, he had to keep quiet.

So it was in silence, his heart beating at a deafening pace in his chest, that he approached the encampment and saw tents. Many tents, white and billowing in the early-morning breeze.

The strategist in Kitwana, who had been part of war parties before, noted that the encampment housed no less than twelve men—probably more; he couldn't count any that might be in the tents; and that they seemed so well provided with powersticks and lances that they littered the ground like so many leaves dropped from the trees.

"But," Shenta said as Kitwana approached, speaking to someone who was hidden behind a tent flap, "if we can't find the ones who have the compass stone, what good is it to—"

"Oh, I didn't say we couldn't find the compass stone," the well-educated English voice spoke, in measured tones. "Only that Nigel and the woman with him seem to have disappeared. But if I know my brother"—he came fully out of the tent to reveal himself as a ruddy-faced, broad-shouldered man, with blond hair tinged with red where it stood in stiff, rumpled curls—"he would not leave part of his party behind. Softhearted to a fault, Nigel is."

Kitwana didn't need the heavy sarcasm of those words to feel the man's personality. He had strength and poise and the ability to command. Here stood the

sort of man who would attract many to him. The inse-
cure, the lost, the confused. But the sarcasm in his
voice gave the whole a different cast. There was no
comfort in this man—only stiff-backed pride and self-
seeking.

And he was Nigel Oldhall's brother? And what was
he to Shenta? He spoke to Shenta as he must speak to
all other men, of whatever color, as a man addressing
an inferior, a being hardly worth troubling with.

It might not mean anything. He might not know of
the Hyena Men. Shenta might, in fact, be doing in
this group much what Kitwana had done with Nigel
Oldhall.

But if that was true, why wouldn't Shenta have
told Kitwana that he intended to go into the jungle
also, with his own party? And why wasn't he talking to
Kitwana now, instead of sending a spirit-beast to look
for him?

"Get one of those rugs aloft," the Englishman said.
"And if you can't find my brother, then find his lovely
bride, or the dragon, or the gentleman you so insufficiently bound to our group."

"Kitwana is sufficiently bound," Shenta said. "But
his power is so odd . . ."

The Englishman raised masterful eyebrows. "Odd?"

"It is not like other magical power. I never know
what he can do with it and what he can't," Shenta
said, a hint of impatience in his voice. At the edge of
the clearing, a lance that was lying on the ground
trembled, like a bird seeking flight. "I'd bet you it's his
incompetence more than anything that's stopping us
from finding him. Kitwana is undisciplined. But he's

smart and he came through the organization very fast."

"Ah, but Shenta, don't you know better than letting someone like that come through the organization very fast?" the mocking British voice asked.

The lance lifted from the ground. Shenta's levitation and telekinesis powers always increased when he was agitated.

"No, Shenta, drop the lance," the Englishman said. And like that, the lance dropped. "And get one of those flying carpets aloft, can you? If we can't scout the surroundings and find the missing parties by magic, we must instead find them by looking. If the traitor is so good or so undisciplined that he can't be found, surely he must have left physical tracks, and those we can see from the air."

It hit Kitwana starkly that if they took rugs up, they would see his group.

He thought of Mrs. Oldhall and Peter, asleep, unknowing, upon the starkly exposed ground of the clearing, and found himself running, half bent, avoiding trees and shrubs and obstacles by instinct. He must get back to the clearing. He must get back and warn Mrs. Oldhall. And Peter Farewell.

ATTACKED

Emily woke to the sound of running feet. Sitting up, she saw Kitwana come sliding into the camp. "Get up, get up, get up!"

"What?" Emily said.

"They're coming," Kitwana said. "They're after us."

"Who is coming?" Emily asked, making sure she was decent and getting up.

"The Hyena Men." Peter's voice sounded from beside her, in a very matter-of-fact tone. He grabbed Emily's arm with unwonted familiarity.

"Behind the rocks," Kitwana said.

"Is there some way to stop them seeing us?" Emily asked, as she was forcefully pulled behind some of the tall standing rocks.

Kitwana and Peter were kneeling. Somehow— though she didn't remember either of them going near the weapons cache—they'd gotten all of the power-sticks in a pile between them.

Kitwana shook his head at her question. "Not from above. This is the best we can do. Not enough magic to cover sight of us from the air. They'll know we're here."

Here was a narrow space between giant boulders. Not so much a circle of boulders as a space barely large enough for the three of them to stand between the huge rocks that would hide them, mostly, from sight. Hearing a sound above, Emily looked up. Above her were two small flying rugs. She could see the dark men sitting on them, and hear the excited voices in which they talked to each other. One of them aimed a powerstick down.

Emily started to jump up and found Farewell's hand holding her wrist. "Stay," he said. "They can't hit you here. I'm shielding."

"You are?" Kitwana said, sounding surprised.

"I am," said Peter with a casual look.

Kitwana shrugged and said, "No need for double protection, then." And Emily felt as if a layer of something had been removed between her and the sun and sky. Allowing her to see the carpet rugs all the more clearly—as if through a suddenly clean window—and the powerstick aimed at her.

She didn't want to run, but still she jumped and would have dived out of the way if Peter hadn't kept a casual hold on her wrist. The powerstick above discharged, the white power flying in a ray straight at her heart. But the power hit an invisible dome above, and spent itself harmlessly in a flash. Emily dropped to her knees and heard herself whimper.

"Don't worry, Mrs. Oldhall," Kitwana said. "We might not be able to make ourselves invisible, but we won't let them capture us."

Emily wondered again at the reasoning of men as she heard a noisy party make its way toward them, running. The ones on flying rugs had alerted these

Hyena Men, doubtless via mind-talk, and they would be hastening to capture their prey. And Kitwana, Emily and Peter were here in this narrow space between rock and rock. No food. No water. What could Peter mean he wouldn't let the Hyena Men capture them? How could they not?

She opened her mouth to tell them just that, but a ray of white power flew straight between the rocks and spent itself on the barrier. Her words changed, before being pronounced into, "How long can you keep the shield over us, Mr. Farewell?"

Peter glanced over his shoulder—a quick glance, almost furtive. "Usually five hours or so."

"I should be able to gain us another five hours," Kitwana said without turning, watching between the boulders, holding a powerstick in his hands.

"And what is your plan for us getting out of here," Emily said, "before the ten hours run out?"

She thought the two men looked at each other as though it had never occurred to them that they would need a plan. Then Kitwana shrugged. "We have powersticks. We can grind them down and tire them out."

Emily sighed. She picked up one of the powersticks from the pile. She knew how to fire it, though her father had disapproved of letting her do so, even in pursuit of foxes or hares.

Peter knelt beside her. He bent to look through an opening between the two boulders at the back. Almost as soon as he looked, power burst in that space, spending itself harmlessly against the barrier. Halfheartedly, Peter reached for a powerstick. Cautiously, he pushed the tip through the barrier, aimed at the two natives firing at them, and moved his finger over the trigger point to release a shot of magic.

The magic flew white hot and true. And met a barrier with a harmless flare. Peter cursed.

Emily sighed. The Hyena Men had a barrier, too. Only there were so many more of them. They'd have magic for a much longer time than Emily and Kitwana and Peter.

They were safe for now, but their shelter was also a prison.

COMPASS AND SACRILEGE

Nigel knelt on the grass with the compass stone in front of him and felt as if he'd broken in two. Deep inside, there was the Nigel he'd always known—filled with terror and doubt and convinced none of this would work. But surrounding that was something else. Something that had been born of the woods and the terrible moment facing the angel with the sword. Something that had seen itself reflected in an inner mirror, and both had been appalled and risen to the occasion.

He was still Nigel, the Oldhall's youngest, sickly son. He still knew his limitations and his flaws. But part of him, stronger than that, had decided he couldn't be sickly or weak. That he must be stronger than his origins. Stronger than himself.

That part was now telling him he must wake the compass stone. And it was no use at all for the other Nigel to whine and moan and speak of its being impossible. Nigel would try. He *was* trying.

The problem was that all the spells he'd been given to awaken this ancient spell had never met with anything this ancient or powerful. It was said the great Charlemagne himself had set his spell on this stone.

Withdrawing into his mind, Nigel could sense the spell like a coiled creature. In his mind, it was a cat, sleeping in the tall grass. Not a domestic cat, either, but a creature both tame and wild, a thing of jungle and a familiar of men.

Nigel approached it as he had approached such animals in his youth. Warily. Carefully. With bated breath and extended hand, promising love and protection, he extended his magic toward the creature.

He imagined one eye opening and surveying him. He sensed that it was green-golden and full of cunning, not easily bent to man.

"In the name of Charlemagne who set you," he whispered. "In the name of my ancestor who created you. By your nature and for what you were made, I adjure you to show me the way to the heart of the world and the jewel it guards."

The big green-golden eye closed. The spell was asleep again. Nigel's heart contracted.

The spell didn't feel like something made by man. Its very shape, as something animal and wild, seemed to transcend humanity and its history and its beliefs.

What if—the very thought felt like heresy— Charlemagne had not spelled the compass stone but only found it? Spelled by an ancient force, long before the beginning of kings or civilization?

That was as heretical as the thought that the queen of England shouldn't get the ruby after all. And yet . . . The angel had told Nigel.

Not that he believed in angels. Most of his life, his belief in God had been a thing of duty and obedience, learned from books and ministers and kept in its place, with church services and pious utterances, but not truly felt and certainly not with him every minute of his life.

But the spirit in the forest had been so overwhelmingly real that it could not be doubted. It would be like doubting one's hand or one's foot. Or that the sun came up in the morning. And that creature of light and strength had told Nigel that the queen of England was not entitled to the ruby. And, in fact, that the ruby should not be used in magic of any sort. On pain of some catastrophe that Nigel felt hadn't been named—not to spare him, but because its magnitude was such that the words of humanity were insufficient to contain it.

If a sacrilege such as the angel had spoken could be true, then why couldn't this spell, quiescent within the compass stone, be something old and passing all of Nigel's understanding?

The compass stone chose who it wanted. It was a union of the mind and the soul, and not a mechanical process. And the stone chose one human at a time.

Discouraged, confused, Nigel started to retract his magic probes.

Suddenly, he felt as though something dark and immense had dropped on him.

He saw the spirit hyena before him, just before his arm flared in pain and a familiar voice spoke in his mind, saying, "Found you!"

Darkness closed.

INTERNAL COMPASS

Nigel woke with Nassira bending over him. He felt pain on his arm and a fog in his mind, and he remembered the spirit hyena.

He put his hand to his wrist and looked at Nassira. She appeared tired and resigned.

"The Hyena Men," he said.

She nodded. Unlike any woman Nigel had ever known, she seemed completely able to adapt to any situation suddenly, with no transition. Her eyes were clear and her look completely calm. "They didn't capture you. I managed to deflect it. But I am afraid they've touched the mind-bind again."

Nigel lifted his arm and looked at the stain, which seemed to pulse and writhe with a light of its own. "The second time," he said. In his mind, Peter's words echoed. They'd found him long enough to touch his soul, to reinforce the bind on his power. If they touched Nigel three times, his mind would be empty and he'd be enslaved to them forever. He frowned slightly.

He lay on soft grass and above him the sky was blue. He didn't know where Emily was. Nor Peter. For some reason all that seemed very distant and unimportant, compared to the present danger of the Hyena Men.

"They might feel for me again," he said.

Nassira shook her head slowly, as though clearing her mind. When she spoke, it was softly and in the sort of gentle voice one might use for a confused child. "I think they already know where we are."

He sat up suddenly, in a panic. "They know where we are." His hand closed on something—hard, round, cold. "The compass stone," he said. "Did it show a direction? Where?"

She shook her head, looking grim. "It is truly bound to your wife," she said slowly. "But perhaps we should go the way it showed last? The Moran and your angel seemed to think we'd know what to do. If your God truly isn't a trickster, what else can they mean us to do?"

"We continue like this, on faith?" he asked.

Nassira nodded, her limpid eyes full of confidence. "When our gods took the trouble to speak to us, how can we not have faith?" She smiled suddenly. "We can at least try. We should go south-southwest and cross that lake."

"A lake?" He looked at where she was pointing and saw only a narrow strip of water, and for a moment was tempted to correct her, to tell her that it was a river and not a lake, that her knowledge of English must be at fault.

And then a memory of a map of Africa and of some travel journals he'd read asserted itself, and he remembered a lake, narrow as a river and deep green—the color of the water that shone in the distance. It might well be Lake Tanganyika. Only twenty to forty miles wide, yet it was one hundred and fifty miles long, and more like a river than a lake.

"I have no money," he said, sitting up. "To pay our passage."

She stood up and extended a hand to him. "We'll think of something."

But Nigel thought there was nothing to do. He not only had no money, he didn't even have clothes. He wore no more than the tattered remnants of his pajamas. And he was lost with a native woman in a land that wasn't his, and that he did not understand in the slightest.

She'd killed a lion. She'd defended Nigel from hostile natives. His self-image and the stories he'd heard of what white men did in Africa were upended. He was supposed to be protecting her. He was supposed to be more competent than any female and certainly more than a benighted female born to a backward tribe in a country with no knowledge of civilization or advanced magic.

Nassira was smiling at him—an indulgent smile that made her copper-skinned face seem very attractive indeed. "Come, Mr. Oldhall," she said. "We'll find a way."

He took her hand and stood.

He could have performed magic. Done some service for the natives. But as the pain in his arm reminded him, if he did so, he would end up no more than a mindless thrall to the Hyena Men.

He walked beside Nassira, his feet bare on the soft grass, still smarting from pain inflicted by torn trees and rocks in another land, long ago, before they'd entered the magical forest.

"It's not supposed to be like this," he said, his frustration tainting his voice.

"What is not?" she said, turning to look at him.

"This," he said in frustration. Then, at her puzzled look, "When I was very young, I used to dream of going abroad. Of seeing exotic lands."

He wondered if any of it made sense to a woman of her background, but she only nodded. It was as though she was a friend, someone he'd grown up with and with whom he'd shared his longing to leave behind the close and confined society in which he'd been brought up. Not an Englishwoman, who would only have asked him why he wished to penetrate uncivilized regions. "I used to want to go abroad and to . . . oh, see everything different and new. But in the books and adventures I read, it was never like this."

She was silent awhile, and he thought she would be upset. There was the hint of a frown to her expression—vertical wrinkles above the chiseled nose and between her wide-set eyes. And her mouth was set in a firm line. But then the edges of it twitched, and Nigel realized the frown was only an effort not to laugh. "You mean that you did not expect to be chased by Hyena Men? That you did not think that you would find yourself transported through some mystical agency across a space of land that wasn't there, into another place? That you did not expect to see yourself, barefoot, ill dressed and with no means of support in Africa?" The twitching smile became a broad grin. "You astonish me."

He opened his mouth, ready to ask if she was mocking him and to take offense at it. But her face suddenly collapsed into an expression of dispirited discouragement. "Neither did I," she said. "Expect it to be like this."

"You said," Nigel added as they walked along, the now-tall grass whipping at his legs and what remained of his pajamas, "something about knowing the Hyena Men."

Nassira took a deep breath. "I was one of them," she said in a hollow voice. "Kitwana and I and the others joined your group so that we could follow you."

He should have felt painful shock, but since he'd been in Africa, so many things had gone wrong that he felt dulled to all but the greatest of dangers and the more immediate problems. Instead, he heard himself laugh and saw Nassira look at him with near alarm. "The group," Nigel said. "The group I hired because you were clean and spoke English. The group of carriers that Peter didn't want me to hire." His laughter dried up suddenly. "And Peter is a dragon." He heard a cackle escape his throat, without his being aware of any amusement. "I was surrounded..." He shook his head. That Nassira could have been one of his enemies seemed impossible. She had gone so far to try to rescue him, to attempt to keep him safe. "You said that you were one of the Hyena Men?"

"I was young," she said. "And I believed Africa..." She took a deep breath and seemed to hesitate about what she could tell him and what he would accept. "You must know that most Africans feel like they are being crushed by Europeans. Oh, I know," she said, and he knew it cost her in saying it, but she had seen enough of London and Cairo to admit it. "You brought us some technology and some innovation. You brought us some improvements, but . . . Thousands have died or been enslaved, and I was . . . Back then, I thought that surely Africa would be better off if it could free itself of Europe. The only way to do that, the Hyena Men said, was for us to become more like Europe."

She told him of a plan to steal the other ruby, the Soul of Fire. Of how she'd intercepted his correspondence at the club. And he should have been angry, but he wasn't. Had someone asked him, he would have said that he'd gone past anger. But it was more that the vision in the forest had robbed him of his purpose and Nassira of hers, and all of a sudden Nigel wasn't even sure which purpose had been the most egregious. His in wanting the ruby for the queen, or hers in wanting it for Africa. So he shook his head and asked only what puzzled him most. "But why did you need to follow us if you had the brand on Emily and me?"

Nassira shook her head. "Kitwana didn't want to use the brand to follow you. He said its being illegal didn't matter, but that it was immoral. That he felt tainted by it."

Nigel looked at her a long while. "He did?" His first thought was that this was a very fine feeling coming from an African. And then he immediately felt ashamed of himself. He had no reason to think that Kitwana was anything other than moral. He realized he'd been thinking of the man as inferior because of his skin color alone—something he'd never even have questioned back in England, but that now seemed churlish while he was traveling with a Masai woman who had saved his life twice.

"He did," Nassira said. "Kitwana is . . . odd. I don't

know who his people are, but he has very strict ideas of right and wrong."

They had come, by degrees, to a hut that stood a ways apart from the others, and stopped talking at the same time, as the thin, disconsolate cry of a baby echoed through the flimsy wooden wall of the house. And from within came a feeling of need.

It was a feeling very familiar to Nigel. When he'd helped manage his father's estate, it fell to him to look after the tenants. One of those—which should have fallen to his mother, but that his mother didn't feel equal to since Carew's disappearance—was to take care of any minor illnesses and look after the health of all the inhabitants of the estate. As such, he'd gotten used to feeling need in the peasant cottages.

The need calling to him from within that hut was the same. Without thinking, barely noticing what he was doing, he veered to the low entrance of the hut, then inside. The inside didn't look much different from some of the meaner cottages of his father's estate. There was a smell of fire and soot, and a smell of illness. There was a large central fire, or the remnants of it, and around the edges, pallets of sorts to sleep upon.

And on one of the pallets lay a child. A woman knelt at the foot of the pallet. And bending over it, his back turned, was a man. He turned as he heard Nigel's footsteps.

"May I help?" Nigel said. "Your baby is sick?"

A confusion of words left the man's mouth, and it took Nigel a few moments to realize they were actually very badly spoken German.

"I'm sorry," Nigel said. "I don't speak—"

Another confusion of syllables, these unmistakably another language. Nigel spoke slowly and clearly. "May I help? Can I help?" He used all the courtesy, all the clearness of voice and expression he would have used with a peer. The man might be naked save for neat rolls of copper wire around his middle, but in his grief, looking at the small, pale child upon a soiled mattress, he was every father in the world who'd ever been on the verge of losing a child. He was Nigel's own father, grieving over Carew's disappearance.

"He says the baby has had diarrhea," Nassira said from the entrance. "He hasn't been able to feed or keep any sustenance within him for four days, and they fear he'll die of dryness."

"Oh, you speak his language," Nigel said in relief, turning to Nassira.

She shrugged. "It's a trade language. Many tribes speak it and it's spoken in the group I was with."

The Hyena Men. Remembering them reminded Nigel that if he helped the little boy, he would be risking the Hyena Men's vengeance. He would risk being . . . worse than killed. He would risk being destroyed and eliminated, while his body still would walk the land, a slave to whoever commanded it.

But he looked at the boy's face, eyes half-closed, the dark skin gone grayish, the eyes full of childish incomprehension when a catastrophe that could barely be understood threatened. And the father looked at Nigel, too, with an intent expression, his eyes narrowed in suspicion, or at least vigilant against unwarranted hope. He spoke hesitantly.

"He asks if you can heal his baby," Nassira said.

"He said he'd be grateful to you and do whatever you want."

Nigel nodded. He knelt by the filthy mattress and extended his hands toward the child.

"Mr. Oldhall," Nassira said, managing to sound exactly like Nigel's first tutor, "they touched you when you tried to rescue Mrs. Oldhall, and once when you tried to activate the compass stone. If you do this, you will be risking—in fact, you will almost surely be consigning yourself to mind-vacant slavery."

Nigel wasn't sure what to do or what to say, but he found a part of him knew very well, and that part of him spoke with an unwaveringly firm voice. "If I don't do it, then the child will die."

"But—" Nassira started.

"Please tell him I'm going to heal his son and that he should not be alarmed. If I . . . If the Hyena Men get me, please ensure that no harm comes to these people."

"Mr. Oldhall!"

"No, please. Children shouldn't die of stupid illnesses when there is someone who can heal them."

He heard Nassira speak, the same words the man had used, but sounding more liquid and assured in her voice. The man emitted a muffled sob and expressed his gratitude with words that needed no translation.

But Nigel was already entering a trance, his mind looking for the invaders in the small body, to stave off their work, to heal the ravaged child.

And he suddenly felt the spectral hyena form in his mind and smelled its horrible stench.

BETWEEN ROCKS

Emily could feel the power in the shields faltering. It was worse than that. She could feel the power faltering and she was thirsty. Ten hours between the two rocks, much of it under the unforgiving sun of this region, had drained her of moisture and seemingly of life.

She'd had no more than two swallows from the only beverage available—Peter Farewell's brandy flask. Worse, she could see, amid the enemy who surrounded them, jars that she knew contained water from their encampment.

She held on to the powerstick, ready to shoot everyone she could when the shields failed.

"They will get us once the shield goes," Farewell said. He and Kitwana also clutched powersticks, and they sat with their backs to the cool rock, turned toward Emily. "They will come at us then."

His voice shook slightly as he spoke, and Emily knew he was tired from his effort at keeping the shield going. Now it was Kitwana's turn, and from his half-closed eyes, his look of high concentration, it was easy to tell that he, too, would falter soon. Even if she didn't feel the shield above them, thinning with each breath.

"There are sixteen of them," Kitwana said. He swallowed, as though attempting to get more moisture to his parched throat. "Sixteen of them and two shooters among the three of us. We have enough powersticks. If only we could...If I hold them, Mr. Farewell, can you get Mrs. Oldhall to safety?"

"How can I get her to safety past all of them?"

Kitwana looked up at the reddened sky, past his failing shields. "It will be night soon and their shields are going, too. I can feel it. Their power for magic shields has to be smaller than ours, since none of them are a...one like you. When their power goes, if I can just keep them busy," he said, "perhaps you can change? While I hold their fire?"

Peter cackled, and Emily couldn't decide whether it was a sound of amusement or just a lament. Emily thought suddenly and with unwavering clarity of the beast trapped in Peter Farewell's mind. His eyes were narrowed and looked like a stormy sea as he said, "You know, I haven't had anything to eat in...twelve hours at least. I haven't had anything to drink but alcohol in ten. I couldn't guarantee..." He looked over at Emily and touched his parched lips with the tip of his tongue. "I couldn't guarantee Mrs. Oldhall's safety, Kitwana."

Kitwana took a deep a breath and he, too, shook his head. "Something we must do," he said. "When darkness falls and the shield goes. Two of us. Can we each get eight of them? Wound them so they can't rise again?"

"Three of us," Emily said, shocked as she heard

her voice. "Three of us. I might not be a man but, by heaven, I can shoot."

The two looked at her for a moment, then Kitwana said, "Are you any good? We can't stand to waste power."

Emily took a powerstick. She knew that she could not hit the enemies, who were all gathered in a knot, behind some trees a ways back. If she squinted at them, she could see light glinting off their shield, like the sun shimmering on water.

But Emily could hit objects. "Pick your target," she told him. "Not the enemy, of course. Some small target, difficult to hit. I will only use one charge."

Kitwana nodded once, then said, "The hanging branch in that tree," and pointed near the enemy. "That will be about as far as we'll have to shoot." He looked very matter-of-fact. Farewell was looking intent.

Emily gathered her dress under her knees and knelt down, rising just above the top half of the rock to look at the parched landscape bathed in red by the sunset. As she appeared—still protected by the shield—a few men in the group behind the trees moved. She couldn't tell what they were doing, and though it seemed to her that a white man had risen behind the trees, dressed in khakis with the light glinting red off his pale hair, she knew it must be an illusion.

Instead of looking at them, she concentrated on the branch Kitwana had chosen, pointed her powerstick at it and, her tongue protruding between her teeth for concentration, let the power fly. The branch exploded in myriad pieces.

"By God," Peter said, sounding very amused. "By God, she can indeed shoot."

"Yes," Kitwana said. "Perhaps Mrs. Oldhall would care to dispatch them while you and I make our get-away."

Emily, who had never before thought Kitwana had a sense of humor—and who, at any rate, did not know if his culture had any tradition of protecting females—turned around in shock. To meet with unholy glee dancing in his tired eyes.

She was trying to think of a suitable reply when a voice called from behind them, in the direction of the enemy, "Mrs. Oldhall?"

It sounded like Nigel's voice, but much deeper. Emily scrabbled again, to look between the rocks.

Just in front of the trees stood a tall Englishman. One would say he looked like Nigel, only he truly didn't. The features might have some similarity, but where Nigel was long and elegant and pale, this man was hearty and broad of shoulder and chest and looked like he'd lived his life on the playing fields. His face was tanned, the color fair people acquire from long exposure to the sun. And his hair was darker than Nigel's—a dark gold-red, with a curl that made it stand in waves on its own.

He was smiling confidently, a grin on his handsome face. "Or should I call you Emily? Since I can claim you as my sister?"

FOR THE SAKE OF A CHILD

Nassira didn't know whether to laugh or cry: in her many years of playing protector to the helpless, she'd never had one of them turn around and try to help the yet more helpless. And if anyone had told her just days ago that the fussy, mannered Englishman would try to save a child's life at the risk of his own she would have said that person was crazy. Yet here Nigel knelt, pale and battered-looking in the remains of his silk pajamas with their careful monogram on the pocket.

He was risking his life—no, almost surely giving up his life—for the sake of a skinny, hapless urchin, whose family, from its unremitting poverty, must be of low enough status even among their own people.

She could see him opening his hands, lifted above the child, and she could see the blue light of European magic forming between his fingers and spiraling toward the child, to envelop him. She had seen this in England, when doctors came to look after the sick, and she knew that Nigel Oldhall's power was not as strong as that. But this illness would also be as nothing to British healers, who had conquered most childhood illnesses and a lot of adult ones.

Waiting, braced as she was for the Hyena Men's attack, it still surprised her when it came. She felt it hit—the spectral hyena's impact mostly on Nigel, but making the sign on her arm flare as though someone had pierced a dagger through her flesh. She gave a whimper of despair and went to her knees, her eyes closing in momentary pain. When she opened them, she expected to see Nigel Oldhall on the floor, utterly consumed. Instead, he knelt, upright, with blue light pouring out of his hands onto the child, whose complexion had changed to a more healthy hue and whose sunken eyes now seemed normal, fluttering on the edge of wakening.

The spirit hyena was there, struggling, it seemed, against that same blue light that now encased all of Nigel's body, glimmering in a faint shimmer all over his pale hair, his unnaturally white skin.

Nassira wanted to scream and shake him and ask him how he was holding the spirit attack at bay. She had never heard of anyone surviving it. And the black mark on his arm was writhing and coiling, and whatever it was doing caused his skin to crackle and split. Blood dripped in a steady rivulet from his arm, and yet Nigel didn't seem to notice, all his being leaning forward toward the child, whom he bathed in blue light.

The little boy sighed and turned, taking a deep breath and opening his eyes.

The man beside Nassira said, "My son lives," in the trade language, his hand reaching out to clutch at

Nassira's upper arm. The woman gave a shout that was almost a song and reached for her child, lifting him.

In the turmoil, all Nassira saw was the blue light around Nigel flare, and then somehow the spirit hyena vanished.

"Please, can you help me?" Nigel said, in a shaking voice, standing up.

Nassira thought the spirit hyena must have gone within to mingle with Nigel, and prepared to do battle, though she knew she could not do much. She was so sure of this, it took her a moment to realize that Nigel was holding, in one shaking hand, a strip torn from his pajamas, while holding out his other arm. The mark of the Hyena had disappeared, to be replaced by raw flesh and dripping blood.

"I cannot tie the bind on my arm myself," Nigel said, his voice shaking a little, from mingled tiredness and pain, "not having another two hands."

It was a weak joke, but Nassira giggled all the same—relief and shock combined as she bound his arm. "How?" she said. *"How?"*

He shook his head, frowning. "I don't know," he said. "I've never heard of anyone fighting off an attack once they'd been bound. But I felt I needed to save the child." He glanced aside to where the child was being rocked in his jubilant mother's arms. "And I could not give up on him. My purpose . . ." He grinned weakly, his face paler than normal. "No one ever told me that intensity and resolution could fight off a powerful magic."

"But," Nassira said, saying the words as she thought them, "it's not so surprising, since most magic is intent and one's power is a reflection of one's intensity of desire. So it's logical that intent could fight it."

Nigel shook his head. He flinched a little as she tied the final knot in place on his blood-soaked arm. "But I never heard of it."

"Perhaps no one had single-minded purpose enough to fight one off before," she said. And then, in a fading voice, "And you did it for a stranger."

"A child," Nigel said. "And he needed me. Besides, you, too, have risked your life for a stranger, with the lion, and—"

She nodded, but she was not too sure she could have resisted such an attack for Nigel's sake. She could not be sure. And she had no time to think, because the poor man in the hut was pressing gifts upon them. A wrap that looked to Nassira a lot like the patterns of her people, and a pair of crude sandals, all straps.

"For him," he said to Nassira.

"He wishes to give you those," Nassira said.

"Me?" Nigel said in wonder. "Why?"

Nassira couldn't help smiling. "Because you saved his son."

"No, no, I mean ... why clothes?"

"Mr. Oldhall!" she said. "Your pajamas won't hold much longer."

He looked down at the expanse of tatters. "I suppose not," he said ruefully, and looking down at his bare feet added, "And sandals would be a blessing, but ... He doesn't look like he can afford much."

Nassira sighed. "And will you shame him by showing him so?"

Nigel started, then bowed to the man and thanked

him effusively. His words were so obvious from his expression that Nassira didn't think it worth translating. Instead, she stood by while Nigel ducked outside and behind the hut. When he returned, he'd wrapped himself in the bright green wrap, which covered him from chest to ankle. She had to help him secure it, but he seemed quite able to figure out the tying of the sandals.

His discarded pajamas were taken up by their host, who held on to the monogrammed pocket as if it were some sort of magic.

"I suppose I look completely ridiculous," Nigel said, straightening.

And of course, he did, and yet... "Probably no more than I did in an English maid's uniform," Nassira said with a smile. "Not that you'll ever pass for a native."

He grinned, his nose crinkling. "No, never that."

The woman of the house was proffering to Nigel a spear made from a sturdy wooden shaft and a crude stone tip. He took it with a smile, as if it were a gift fit for a king. And Nassira thought it was given in that same spirit.

Turning, she asked the man, who was now holding his son, "I don't suppose you can help us across the lake?"

The man's face split in a wide smile. "Of course I can. I am a fisherman."

Weak with relief, Nassira turned to look at Nigel diffidently holding a spear, wearing an African wrap, and staring at her with obvious craving for her approval. He was very pale, and still looked very much like he had crawled out from under a rock. Nassira could not imagine, ever, being attracted to him as a male. But as a man, she realized, he was just...human. He'd risked his life to save one of Africa's children. More than many Africans would have done. He was not a Masai; but then, not everyone could be perfect.

"You'll do," she told him curtly. And as he smiled, she realized she had bestowed her approval upon him in the idiom of his own kind.

TEMPTATION

"Come, Emily," the British voice said, speaking with all the precision of its accent, all the certainly of a man who knows his position and his rights. "Your husband isn't here, and I am your closest male relative present. You know you can trust in me. And even if you couldn't, it would still be your duty to obey me. Come from behind that rock. Nothing will happen to you. You can see we're not your enemies and all is safe."

Kitwana leaned forward. He was so thirsty and tired he felt nauseous, and holding the shield over them was taking his whole strength. But he thought he knew enough of Englishmen and their women, and he knew this one could not resist such an appeal. Beautiful as she was in her way, and as strong as Kitwana's own father, she was still a woman. An Englishwoman. Through his parched throat he asked Emily, "Is he really your husband's brother?"

She swallowed and nodded, then said, "I've never met him, but he looks like the pictures in the house. His mother..." A sigh. "His mother had a whole sitting room adorned with pictures of Carew, and it looks like him. More scarred and sunburned, but—"

"It is Carew," Peter Farewell said, his voice sounding oddly dead. It was, Kitwana thought, like the voice of one who's long departed and sounds still in the place of his demise, more memory than sound. "I know Carew."

Emily nodded, then turned away from them to look between the rocks. "But, Mr. Oldhall," she said, raising her voice. "How can you guarantee my safety when you're amid those who've spirit-bound me?"

A hearty laughter answered her. "Oh, that's a mistake. My associates got overanxious. Come on out, and I'll help you to the ruby—and we will find Nigel, too, and then we can go home and have the happy family reunion, yes? Mama and Papa will be so delighted."

Emily half rose. From Peter's lips, a faint, long whisper came. "No. Not Carew. He was supposed to be dead."

Emily looked over her shoulder at Peter, and Kitwana knew she was wondering, the same way Kitwana himself was—if Peter had assumed Carew to be dead because of his disappearance of if Peter had greater reason to make such an assumption. But she didn't say anything. Instead, she picked up Peter's brandy flask, which he'd dropped on the ground with the powersticks. She took a small sip, then spoke, louder than before. "But, Mr. Oldhall, you had a compass stone yourself. You lost it and it was found by Widefield's men and that's how it ended up back in England. But you had it and you were supposed to have found the ruby. Why do you need us now? And why do you keep such strange company?"

Carew looked over his broad shoulder at the people with him, one of whom was the square-built African that Kitwana had seen talking to Carew before. Then he looked at Emily and grinned, and Kitwana thought that Carew Oldhall was used to employing that grin instead of discussion. That he believed his grin should be enough to make all fall at his feet in adoration. "Come, come, that's too long a story to explain. Surely as a woman you have better things to concern yourself with? We have a trunk of your dresses here. Perhaps you would like to change. And we can give you water."

Knowing how thirsty he himself was, Kitwana looked at the beautiful Englishwoman and expected her to give in, to step out. And in a way, he wasn't even sure it would be wrong.

"You could accept," he said, consideringly. "He'd probably keep you safe. I don't know why they're besieging us; it must be because of him." He gestured with his chin toward Peter. "Of course, they might kill me, too, because I'm protecting the dragon. I've heard them call me traitor before and that must be why. Still, if I can talk to him for only a few moments, I'm sure I can explain to Shenta why it happened. And maybe we can all get safe conduct out of here and I can go home."

He had only the time to be embarrassed by how resonant his longing was on that last word before Farewell roared. His eyes looked mad—not fully human, but swirling with something of the dragon's pain when he'd been struck through with the magic lance. He reached for the flask, took a swig and said in a voice that was like the tattered remnant of his nonchalant tone, "A last drink before death."

"Death?" Emily said. "Surely not. Oh, I know English law, but we are not in England now, and besides, Carew is not a Royal Were-Hunter. Surely he can't wish to extinguish your line, any more than your father did."

"Oh, no," Peter said, taking a swig of the brandy and making a face. Kitwana knew well the sensation he must be enduring, as the wetness was countered by the alcohol's desiccating properties. "Not extinguish my life, Mrs. Oldhall. Carew just wants to kill me. Mind you, with reason. I did leave him for dead. But he won't just kill me. He'll torture me a long time until I die." He grinned at her expression of bewilderment. "Carew has always wanted to torture Nigel and me. Succeeded, too, through most of our school career. That bluff and ready look you see, the mythical English sports-field hero, has served him well. Inside, he just craves the pain of those weaker than himself. He's more beast than I am."

Kitwana cleared his throat. "But—"

"Come, *Mr.* Kitwana!" Peter said. "Doesn't it strike you as odd that your African organization would be headed by a white man? My kind attacked Carew's expedition when he first came to Africa. We left him for dead. He should have some extensive scarring under those clothes. Then I sent the compass stone back to England, because none of us could impress it. We hoped they'd send someone who could. And they have. Now the Hyena Men want the stone. The Hyena Men who only appeared after Carew was lost in Africa. After he'd been robbed of the compass stone and was adrift. What do you think that means, Mr. Kitwana?"

"Your kind?" Kitwana said. "Weres?"

Peter smiled, a very odd smile. "Anarchists. Those who believe in the equality of man."

In Kitwana's mind, everything was swirling. He'd always thought that someone was the head of the Hyena Men. He'd thought Shenta was. And he'd been afraid that Shenta meant to take over Africa. And now he found there was a white man over Shenta, because Shenta obviously deferred to this man. "He is that loyal to his queen?" he asked, his voice hollow. "He wants to take her the ruby that much?"

Peter Farewell cackled bitterly. "Carew Oldhall is loyal only to Carew Oldhall."

Emily stood and spoke. "We accept your offer of safe conduct. As proof of your good intentions, you will remove your brand from my arm, and you will withdraw with your men to a safe distance. And you will not disturb me as I seek out the ruby." She spoke with the assurance of a man, Kitwana thought. A man who rises to speak in the councils of his elders.

In that moment, Kitwana—who'd never have thought to find a woman he could take home to his father's village—realized that he'd found her. And yet she was European and would never look twice at him. Which might be just as well, since he was exiled and not sure he could ever go home.

Carew Oldhall was silent a moment, then his voice roared in outrage. "Why, you impudent chit. I order you to—"

They never knew what he ordered Emily, because at that moment Peter Farewell glowed with an inner light, as his body twisted and writhed in the grip of change.

Kitwana—although knowing it would be insufficient to defend them—grabbed a powerstick and prepared for a desperate fight against the dragon.

LION IN THE GRASS

"A lion," Nassira's voice sounded, high and suddenly, startling Nigel.

He widened his eyes at a flash of something tawny and airborne.

They'd been walking through the tall grass most of the day, talking calmly. The fisherman had brought them safely across the lake, then left them with his profuse thanks. They'd walked on, south and west on faith, hoping that indeed God wasn't a trickster.

All of a sudden, it was as though everything around him moved unnaturally slowly and became terribly clear. He could smell the tall grass, verdant and full of sap, and the green, refreshing aroma of water somewhere nearby. And he could smell the lion, its musk hot and pervasive. He could see it so clearly that he would have been able to count the hairs on its body. It seemed to him, too, in that stretched-time moment, that he would have the time to.

But the inner Nigel, the one not affected by his fear or surprise, informed him that Nassira was somewhere behind him, unarmed and unable to defend herself. That ahead of them was a half-eaten carcass of some animal that the lion had been eating. They'd come on the lion suddenly, startling him at his feast.

And then Nigel remembered Nassira's actions when she'd killed the lion, and he repeated them, with sudden, balancing grace that he had never displayed on the playing field.

He thrust Nassira away, as she had once thrust him away from danger, and stepped neatly in front of the airborne lion, lifting his lance aloft, knowing rationally that it didn't have a chance of piercing the lion's hide with the force Nigel could put behind it.

But he'd seen Nassira's crude lance kill a lion before, and now he ran forward, so that the lion's body was directly above him, and held the lance firm. And saw—still in that unnaturally slowed time—it pierce the tawny hide, and felt the shower of blood. He felt the lance give under his hand as the wood splintered, just as Nassira grabbed Nigel's arm and pulled him aside forcefully.

They fell in the tall grass, Nigel still dripping blood, and Nassira yelling at him, "Why were you standing there? It could crush you as it falls."

There was a loud roar, and Nigel turned to the lion, sure that the creature would be ready to ravage them. But the beast was writhing in its death throes.

Nigel sat up, rubbing his hand on his face and bringing it away blood-tinged. And Nassira was looking at him, wide-eyed, shocked. "Mr. Oldhall!" she said.

"Call me Nigel," he snapped, suddenly impatient with formality, impatient of all but this reality—blood on his fingers, grass under him, and ahead of him the corpse of a lion he'd just killed—on his own and with no help from anyone. The lion that surely not even Carew could have killed.

There was a sound like strangled laughter in Nassira's throat, and had she not been a Masai—had she been a properly brought-up British woman—Nigel would have known she was about to be hysterical.

He turned sharply to her and heard his voice say, snappishly and full of English propriety, "Don't go missish on me. It's not like that. But we are comrades-in-arms. We've both killed lions."

And Nassira threw her head back and laughed—a full-throated, roaring laughter that Nigel had never imagined could come from a feminine body. "Oh, I wouldn't know how to be missish. Nigel, don't you understand?"

He looked at her in puzzlement, wondering if she had gone crazy or if this was a form of hysteria peculiar to African women, and wishing vaguely that he had on hand the ubiquitous bottle of salts his mother carried everywhere.

But Nassira shook her head. "When you said it was not . . . what you expected . . ." A gurgle of laughter. "The greatest of honors, the highest courage is attributed to the young man who kills a lion. He's respected lifelong for it. And here you are, a Water— an Englishman whom we must now consider a brave warrior of the Masai."

Nigel looked at her curiously. This added to the vague exhilaration he felt at being competent enough to save himself and her, his feeling that even Carew could never have done this. But he disciplined his face to show nothing, and said nothing beyond "Really?"

She nodded at him desperately, a frantic expression beneath her shining eyes and smiling mouth.

"But now we've both killed lions, Nigel! A woman and a Water Man. Oh, Mokabi would die if he knew. Comrades-in-arms indeed. We *must* make you a headdress and a fetish from it. I know how to do it by magic. And you must have it."

Sitting on the ground, with lion's blood on his face and suddenly wondering how long it would be before he could wash, Nigel nodded absently.

FIRE AND BLOOD

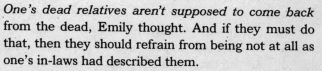

One's dead relatives aren't supposed to come back from the dead, Emily thought. And if they must do that, then they should refrain from being not at all as one's in-laws had described them.

She'd just gathered enough from the conversation with Peter to know that Carew was not at all like the selfless man his mother talked about the brave, reserved creature of his father's fantasy; or even Nigel's more subdued but still conventional portrait of the son and heir. Nor did she need Peter's words, having quite a good brain to think with, and having managed to realize that no man who was truly good and kind and loyal and brave would come in search of his sister-in-law with an armed party and then proceed to besiege her for hours before speaking.

So Emily, despite Kitwana's seeming reasonable analysis of the situation, had never intended on surrendering, never considered for a moment that she might want to walk out into the open and deliver herself to the men who'd been preventing them from leaving. She merely wanted to know why and what was at the back of Carew's plan. And why Carew had disappeared.

And then Peter explained, seemingly without realizing. He, and others like him, had ambushed Carew's party and stolen the compass stone. Left for dead, Carew had refused to be defeated and leave Africa. He'd formed or taken over the despicable organization that had branded Emily.

Seething, she paused for a moment and then realized from the eerie light and the contortions that Peter was changing shape.

She was startled by a thought that Peter was not as well made as Kitwana, whose legs were longer and turned in exquisite perfection between slimness and muscle. She wanted to laugh at herself. Since when had this African become the paragon of masculinity in her mind? And since when was masculine beauty the most important thing when you're about to be trapped in a small space with a dragon? Perhaps she'd had too much brandy.

Seeing Kitwana lift a powerstick aimed at Peter's heart, she didn't even turn from the horrible yet beautiful spectacle of the dragon changing. "Don't be ridiculous, Mr. Kitwana," she said. "Put that down."

And Peter—a changing Peter, his mouth filled with suddenly sharp teeth, his tongue seemingly too long to pronounce words properly—hissed out, "She is right, *Mr.* Kitwana. I mean you no harm."

Then Peter's body writhed a final time. Kitwana, startled, let go of the shield for just a moment, but it was enough. Peter—the dragon—sprang.

It had to spring, Emily thought. There was no possible way the narrow space between the rocks would contain the immense body that jumped and unfolded overhead, wings spread to the sky.

For a moment, Emily could not breathe. Then she heard the screams of the Hyena Men and then their shouts.

"Lay into him. Use the spelled powerstick," someone yelled.

"No! The lance for the dragon," another shouted. Carew's voice. "The one with the silver tips. Grab them. I brought enough for all."

Emily turned away from the voices and was aware that the shield had been lifted and that the Hyena Men could now fire upon them. But no power surged between their insufficiently sheltering rocks to singe her. There was nothing save flashes of light, as if from a fire, that reflected in on them. And she seemed unable to turn, unable to see the dragon—such a beautiful creature she'd once felt her heart go out to, she'd once saved—lay waste to human flesh.

Instead she looked at Kitwana, who was looking over her shoulder and between the opening in the rocks. His face had gone ashen, his lips almost gray. And looking into those horror-stricken eyes, she could well imagine the chasing dragon, the fire blasting from its jaws, searing human flesh.

The odor of burning flesh and wood reached her. And the screams were now loud, incoherent. And not a powerstick had been fired. Not one.

"Tell me, Mr. Kitwana," she said, making her voice loud to be heard over the din, so that he could understand her in whatever state he'd abstracted himself into. "Are the lances they brought effective against him?"

"It...They seem to be," he spoke, his eyes still wide, his voice sounding as if it came from a very distant place—a chill place full of cold and dark recrimination.

"He's bleeding more than he did when—" A forceful swallow. "But he's still attacking. He's..." He swallowed again, hard. "Mrs. Oldhall, he's sacrificing himself for us."

And on those words there was a sound like that of a giant tree falling. A trembling on the ground, like that of a giant animal spasming underfoot. A high keening that could not come from a natural throat.

And then nothing, save the crackle of fire and—slowly, faintly, at first almost imperceptibly—the steady patter of a soft rain.

WRONG AGAIN

*Kitwana had been wrong again. Not that he was sur-*prised anymore. There had been so many mistakes, so many faults.

He was still not certain that he'd been guilty of that first crime, the one that had gotten him expelled from his village to live with his mother's brother in Zululand. Yes, he had killed someone, but...

At the time he'd been convinced the man—a particularly pustulent-souled and nasty specimen to whom the ever-kind Wamungunda had given refuge—had meant to kill Wamungunda and his family and take over the village. He'd heard enough to be sure of it before he'd put his plan in action. He was still sure of it. And part of him still smarted at his father's reaction, at Wamungunda's evicting his only son from his ancestral village because Kitwana had tried to save that village and his family, too.

But the other part... the part that had been wrong about the Hyena Men and about Peter Farewell... Kitwana feared to look deep within at that first incident and find out he'd been wrong there, too.

Watching Peter Farewell fall to the ground like a dead thing—after setting all the Hyena Men to flight—Kitwana could only think how wrong he'd been since he'd left the village. All his years in Zululand, all his learning of the arts of war, everything he'd done had been in vain—or worse than in vain; against his best interest. Worse, against the best interest of mankind.

He felt such anger at himself that he didn't move for a long time.

He was aware that the dragon's body was shifting and changing, and he remembered hearing in his youth that shape-shifters always changed in death back to their human form as the magic left them, and only the human stayed behind. The rain started to fall, yet he knelt there between the rocks, looking out at the Englishman now laying on the ground, gravely injured. It was a soft rain, gentle on parched skin.

Emily lifted her face toward it, opening her mouth a little, and ran her hands backward through her hair, as though to rub the rain in. "I don't hear any Hyena Men, Mr. Kitwana. We should help him."

"I think," Kitwana said, his voice still coming from so deep within that he sounded not at all like himself, "I fear that he's past all the help we can give him."

She looked at Kitwana as if he were crazy, shook herself slightly and stood up. "Oh, for heaven's sake," she said. "You can't mean to stay there and just . . . assume he is dead."

With sudden determination, she leapt over the rocks and up to where the dragon-man lay in his human form, naked and looking pathetically inoffensive. She leaned over him and called out, "Mr. Kitwana, please come quickly. Help me bind his wounds."

Kitwana got up, trembling, sure he must dispel her illusion and show her the task was futile. But when he approached, Peter Farewell's eyes fluttered open, and there was a trace of the man's old mockery in the way he looked at Kitwana.

Emily had gotten fabric from the trunks remaining from their encampment. Silk and lace were ruthlessly torn into strips and wrapped around the man's bleeding limbs and his torn middle. As soon as the pale silk touched his skin, it became red.

Farewell swallowed, and opened his mouth to the gentle rain, but it wasn't enough, and he whispered, "Water."

Kitwana mechanically found one of the sealed water jars and brought it back, tipped it to Peter's mouth. Peter drank as though he never meant to stop, draft after draft of the water that had been sitting under the sun all day. But at last he pulled away and looked at Kitwana, completely ignoring Mrs. Oldhall, who was binding his wounds.

"Mr. Kitwana," he said hesitantly, his voice faint though his eyes still shone with amusement. "I think I'm done for. Can you and Mrs. Oldhall take it and imprint it, and continue your journey without me?"

Emily drew a loud breath, but when she spoke it was in a light tone, as if she were calmly discussing something with a friend. "Oh, don't be foolish, Mr. Farewell. We wouldn't continue the journey without you."

"I'm afraid you must," Farewell said raspily. "You must continue without me. And after you kill me . . . take one of my eyes."

Emily looked at him in shock, repeating, "One of your *eyes*?"

He smiled and said, "I'll have no more use for it. And you must know a dragon's eyes, properly spelled, make a fine divination instrument. With them you can find anything. I'd wager with my eye—once I'm no longer using it—you can find the ruby."

A CHOICE OF SINS

"Why?" Emily asked. "Why should we want to kill you?" She held both ends of a bandage with which she had been binding Peter Farewell's largest wound—a palm-long gash on his thigh. She knew she needed more than that. She needed the strong healing magic of a surgeon. But such magic as she had was locked within her and useless.

The tourniquets and bandages she wrapped around Peter were ineffective and served primarily to soak up the blood.

"To spare me suffering?" Peter Farewell said, speaking as though each word cost him too much effort.

"But . . ." Kitwana said. He knelt by Peter's head, holding a jar of water. "Are you dying?"

Peter took a deep breath, as though needing the energy to animate his words. "Yes, I am dying. Only it will be slow. I've lost too much blood. And I'm too weak to move. If I stay here, Carew will eventually come back. I got most of his people, but not him. He ran and hid behind them. He will come back, and he will—"

"We could carry you," Kitwana said.

Peter shook his head slowly. "That will only slow you. Then Carew will find you, too."

"Why are you so afraid of him?" Emily asked. "He is an English gentleman after all. I realize there is something wrong there, but what can you fear from him you that think death preferable?"

But Peter only shook his head and said, "Mrs. Oldhall, the wounds were made by silver. Spelled silver. They will take weeks to close. Till then, I'll be alive, but barely." He turned, not to Emily but to Kitwana, with a beseeching gaze. "Kitwana, please kill me now. More merciful by far than leaving me to fall into Carew's hands, or to be eaten alive by jungle beasts."

Emily expected to see Kitwana reach for one of the bespelled lances still on the ground, not five steps away, and fulfill Peter Farewell's request. But instead of getting up, Kitwana only let the water jar go and grabbed at his own hair, his hands clenched in it.

"What, man?" Farewell said, clearly taken aback by this reaction. "You've wanted to kill me since we met."

His voice, though barely more than a gasp, managed to be full of gentle teasing.

"I can't," Kitwana said.

"Surely you can. The lance is there." Peter looked at the instrument. "One thrust through the heart will do it. None of the others had decent aim."

Kitwana shook his head. "My father . . . My father believed all human life is sacred."

Peter's laughter resolved into coughing. A froth of blood covered his lips. "I'm not human."

"Human enough," Kitwana said, and turned to

Emily. "I'll make the healing potion out of the water again. We'll clean his wounds with it. We'll get every trace of silver out. Then they'll stop bleeding."

Emily nodded and waited while the African bespelled the water, till the whole container sparkled and popped with golden magic. She untied one of her laboriously wrapped bandages, and dipped the cloth in the magical water to touch to the wound.

Peter hissed and arched as the water touched his thigh. His eyes were dumb with suffering, but his voice came out still tinged with irony. "You're only prolonging my agony, both of you. Surely you can understand I'll never be able to walk? Stay behind with me and keep me alive a few more days, and we all die. Or take my eye and go, on your own, toward the ruby. But give me mercy first."

Kitwana did not reply, and Peter looked at Emily. "Mrs. Oldhall? Can't you see I don't deserve to suffer a slow death? For all the horrible things I've done, I did try to rescue you from Carew."

He had tried to rescue her. Yet as much as she saw the wisdom of his words, Emily couldn't imagine killing him.

As she shook her head, she heard Kitwana say, as though from very far away, "Elephant country isn't that far, and there are some around here even. Shamans can call them and tame them to their will with magic. It takes a great deal of magic, of course. As much as you have, Mrs. Oldhall."

Emily looked at him, stunned. Her lips moved but she couldn't find the way to words for a long time. When she spoke, it was only to say, "I can't. My power is locked."

"You can," Kitwana said, "if you let me merge my mind with yours. I can access your power. I know the way of it. I can unlock it. Together we can call an elephant. We can then travel on its back, and Mr. Farewell won't be a hindrance."

"But," Emily said as she sat back on her heels in shock. "To merge minds . . . is . . ." She'd heard of it, of course. It was said to happen spontaneously at the most hallowed of marriages, those preordained by fate or gods. And it happened, it was said, between married couples, sometimes, in moments of complete ecstasy.

She looked at Kitwana's face in front of her. A stranger from another race, another continent, another civilization. Did he understand what he was asking? "But if we merge minds," she said, half outraged, "you'll know all there is to know about me. And you'll know me more intimately than a husband. You—"

A soft laugh escaped Peter Farewell. It wasn't exactly mocking. Or if it was, it would be mocking himself as well as her. "A choice of sins is before you, Mrs. Oldhall. You can take my life, or you can violate the sanctity of your virgin mind. Or you can leave me here to die slowly. To my mind, the last is the worst sin of all." He paused, then said with his voice more feeble than ever, "But perhaps not to yours."

BEASTS AND MEN

Kitwana looked at Mrs. Oldhall and heard Peter Farewell laugh softly. He knew immediately why he was laughing.

Farewell didn't believe Mrs. Oldhall would consent to it. He didn't think someone like her, a woman from her background, would allow someone like Kitwana into her mind. And the fact that Kitwana wanted to merge with her, mind and body—the fact that she was the only woman he felt he could ever love—made it all the more difficult for him to ask her.

Kitwana understood that a mind-merge was a very intimate thing. How else could it be, when, for the duration of it, you'd know everything about the other? How could he be daring enough to merge with this woman of golden-brown skin and blue-sky eyes, this woman who managed to be by turns an innocent child and a world-striding goddess—and with all of that, still the most human person he knew?

But then . . . how could he not do it? Let him merge with her for a moment, even if the result would be for him to suffer the grief of separation forever more.

In most tribes—even among the Zulu—such a merge was a marriage, as good as if it had been performed by contract and bride price and firmed by both families. Boys and girls with any magical power at all were told not to allow their power to lead them to mind-merge, even in societies such as the Zulu, where mere sex was seen as the pleasure of the crossroads and meant nothing unless it led to a child.

He understood all that, and he felt a great sorrow for the scruples he could read in Mrs. Oldhall's shocked gaze, but really there was nothing he could do for her in this. She had her choice and he had his.

He would take this almost-marriage, this few minutes of union. He knew that neither his family nor his people could ever approve of her, and that her family would shun him just as violently. But this almost-marriage would not just save a man who'd gotten his wounds saving all their lives, it would also give him his heart's desire for a too-short instant.

And in his mind and heart, forever he'd call her his. His Emily.

But he would not speak nor push his choice on her. He looked at Emily and saw a blush climb, dusky beneath the gold of her cheeks. She ran her hand back, as though to fix her hair, though it had long since slipped the demure bun in which she normally kept it, and twisted wild and dark over her shoulders to her waist. Then she nodded, once. An answer to an unasked question.

She put her hands forward, palms up, offering the physical contact necessary for the mind-merge. Because Peter was between them, her hands were held above his chest. And reaching down to meet them, Kitwana met Peter's eyes, to read in them great shock and surprise, as though this could not be happening at all.

"It might not work, Mr. Kitwana," she said in a

piping voice that seemed to come from someone much younger. "Others have tried to open my power before, and it could not be done. It might be defective."

He frowned, a quick, impatient frown. "It is not defective," he said, the idea offending him in a way he could never explain. "There is nothing wrong with your power. I don't know what keys attempted to open it, but I can do it."

Her hands felt small and moist, beaded with sweat, shaking with nervousness. He closed his hands on hers, and willed his power to touch hers. He knew he had a large magical power. It had been inherited from his mother, he'd always thought, though now he wondered if Wamungunda hadn't simply kept his own power hidden. After so many mistakes, Kitwana was no longer sure he had ever known anything. Certainly other people treated his father as though he had great power. And besides, to have great power, you usually had to inherit it from both parents. Emily Oldhall had great power, too, and he could feel his power touching hers, gently coaxing it into allowing him the freedom of her mind.

For a moment nothing happened. It stretched, silent and impossible—a moment of silence and desolation. He was kept outside of her magic, and she outside his. Their powers only touched, and he could tell hers was at least as large as his—warm and fluttering and beautiful, like a winged creature unsteadily held in the shell of his hand—but he could have known that before he touched it.

And then . . .

And then there was a feeling like the sound of shattering glass, and in the next moment he was a small girl, in a country he could not identify. India, a female voice told him. Mrs. Oldhall's voice. No, not Mrs. Oldhall. Emily.

And Emily was with him, and in him, as he was with her and in her, their minds mingling and their memories—a boy herding goats on a verdant slope, and a girl in lacy dresses watched by her ayah, a young man killing to preserve his people, a young girl mourning for her mother, the stranger in Zululand and the stranger in England. All, all shared, all the same. The knowledge of each other's body as their own, the touch, the melding, the being one.

Hands on hands and mouth on mouth and the vague feeling of the rain falling on them, very far away, in a forgotten world. While their joined hearts beat as though in a single breast and they drew their breaths—combined, in his mind—Emily stood and twirled, laughing, and she wore the wrap the girls of his tribe wore, her hair free. And her glorious eyes—like living pieces of the summer sky—looked into his full of laughter and rejoicing and said, "I never knew it could be like this. I never knew."

Emily held her power like a golden ball in her hands and extended it to him. "Here, here, here. I wish you to open and use it."

Kitwana tried to tell her he wasn't worthy. He tried to tell her of his crime. That he'd killed a man and disobeyed his father. But she looked at him and shook her head slightly. In her eyes was the full knowledge of what he was—and perfect acceptance. Acceptance beyond guilt and forgiveness. Instead there was caring and admiration and . . . joy in what he was.

Kitwana had never thought he'd see such an expression in any woman's eyes, much less in the eyes of this woman from so far across the seas.

"I want you to have my power," she said, enveloping him in the sweetness of her mind, in her admiration. In her love? "You see, I wish you to take whatever you want from me. For now, we're one. And there will never again be a barrier between our souls."

And Kitwana's mind reached for it, and it cracked in his hands, like an egg, birthing light and love and all goodness—a cascade of warmth and pure joy that fell over them both, like water washing him clean after a long day in the field.

They stayed like that, bathed in her magic a long time, his magic resounding and echoing through hers, like a child delighted to discover a companion, a playmate, after years and years of loneliness. Then from somewhere came a distant voice, one that he remembered as Peter Farewell, the dragon-man, and the voice was amused and cool and distant but also gasping, out of breath and wounded. "Well!" it said, in tones of great surprise, and then mildly, "You might as well call the elephant."

And they did.

SURPRISED

"Water," Nassira said.

To Nigel, the word echoed as though she had shouted, "Behold the promised land!"

He had been walking for almost a day now, sweaty and tired, and still splashed in lion blood. Oh, he was grateful for the sandals that kept his feet from being cut or stabbed, but he could still feel blisters form above them. And just recently thirst had joined the other torments, and they had all contributed to his discomfort.

They'd walked through the whole day and into the night, because if they stopped they knew they would both fall asleep and they could not afford it. They'd walked, weary of the sounds in the bush, keeping an eye out for predators. All night, there had been no sign of human habitation. And now, with the sunrise, they had been facing the prospect of walking all day again, without relief, until Nassira had said, "I think I hear water." They'd followed that suspicion of a sound till it became clear. Now Nassira pointed to a glimmer amid thick vegetation ahead.

There was only one path amid the shrubs and trees and grass that grew wild at the riverside. A narrow path, beaten down by animal or human feet, Nigel couldn't tell. But the water ahead looked limpid and sparkled. "Do you think it will be clean enough to bathe in?" he asked Nassira.

"Oh, yes," she answered, laughing. "And to drink, too."

She skipped ahead and he ran after her, longing for the feel of water on his abraded, tired feet.

Suddenly, he saw someone spring out of the bush and grab at Nassira, but he didn't even have the time to scream before something heavy hit the back of his head. And then there was darkness.

THE FAVORED SON

Nigel woke. His head hurt as though something had been driven into it at the back—a blade that had splintered his thoughts and shattered his memory.

He was lying down on dirt and rocks. And his hands and feet were bound with something that felt like some sort of natural rope or vine. Opening his eyes hurt. The light was too bright and sharp, like a blade, and he groaned.

"So you are awake, Nigel," a voice said with a great deal of amusement.

Nigel blinked. The ghost of Carew was sitting before him, looking much as Carew usually did—cool, self-possessed and more satisfied with himself than anyone truly had the right to be. Scars marred his skin, which had acquired the reddish tan of a fair person in Africa. The right side of his face was a crisscross of scars, like a network of fine spiderwebbing. But it was Carew, right enough. He smoked a cigarette whose aroma tickled Nigel's memory—Turkish cigarettes. Peter's.

He frowned slightly and his brother's ghost smiled brilliantly. "Gone native, have you, Nigel?" he said, grinning mockingly.

And Nigel was suddenly very conscious of wearing only a wrap and a lion headdress and a belt. The lion fetish—which Nassira had fashioned for him out of the tail and ears, promising Nigel it would have great power under all circumstances and greatly increase his magic—was threaded through the belt. Nassira had told Nigel that with them, Nigel could force someone to tell the truth. Nigel felt ridiculous, but the thought of Nassira distracted him, and he tried to rise and look around. He saw her lying beside him, still unconscious.

"Nassira," he said.

"Oh, your lady friend is fine," Carew said, taking a deep puff on his cigarette. "She will not suffer anything worse than a headache." A deep and devious grin twisted his proud features. "And very pleased our mother will be, I am sure, to meet her future daughter-in-law. Do you plan to get married wearing lion bits?"

"It's not like that," Nigel said, speaking thickly through a headache that seemed to stop his thoughts between one word and the next. "She's not . . . Comrades in arms, we are. I am already married."

"Oh, really? Well, when last I saw the lovely Mrs. Oldhall she was consorting with a tribesman and a dragon, so doubtless you will be able to have your marriage annulled. As for your friend, I really don't care what you call her, but I want you to know this . . ." Suddenly Carew's voice changed. He'd been using his company voice, the voice he used when playing the young man about town: urbane, cultured and controlled. Now his voice changed in tone to one that only those who had been on the wrong end of Carew's cruelty would recognize.

Nigel had heard him sound like this long ago, in the lost days of his boarding school life. Away from teachers and parents, Carew had allowed his voice to sound this slitheringly cruel, like . . . like a serpent crawling, poisonous and bright, from the undergrowth.

"Whether she wakes at all is your choice, my dear brother. I have picked up your compass stone, but it won't talk to me. It seems you have bound it to yourself—or at least I assume so, since my associates in the Hyena Men got a fix on you when you were so foolish as to use magic to activate it—and now it won't talk to me." He set the compass stone on Nigel's stomach. "Ask it to show you the direction to the ruby, Nigel. Do it now, and your lady friend and you will be released."

But in Nigel's mind, things were moving and shifting, and several conclusions were forming. The first was that Carew wouldn't let Nigel go once the compass stone showed the direction. Of course not. He wouldn't let Nigel go until they reached the ruby. And then . . .

Carew had talked of his associates in the Hyena Men. That meant he had admitted to a criminal bond to a native organization wishing to overthrow England's queen. Or at least to rob her of her African domains. This was a crime, and there was no reason at all for Carew to admit to a crime to Nigel. Unless Carew intended to kill him.

"Why do you need me and my compass stone, Carew?" he asked very mildly. "Didn't you have it first? Do you mean you never imprinted it, brother?"

Carew flinched and Nigel knew he had hit a sore spot. "Never mind that. Only use the compass stone for me, show me where the ruby is and I will let you and your lady friend go."

"Why do you want the ruby, Carew? For the queen?" Nigel's vision was now clearing and he saw that he lay in a sort of clearing, on rocky ground, and that there were several natives around as well as Carew. The one standing behind Carew—an ugly-looking, bulldog-like customer—frowned at Carew when Nigel said that.

And Carew shifted again, becoming once more the daylight Carew, the polite society Carew—engaging, fervent and seemingly all goodness, the delight of drawing rooms and the hope of marriaging mamas. "No. I have seen so much injustice in Africa, Nigel, that it seems to me that the ruby should be used for Africans and their good. We have no business here. Let them have their own power. I shall find the ruby for the peoples of Africa."

The African man behind Carew nodded approvingly and Nigel thought that he, too, would have been convinced by so gallant a speech. He would have been convinced if he hadn't known Carew all along and been all too intimately acquainted with his self-serving, self-centered, utterly ruthless mind and heart.

As it was, he heard a small gurgle of laughter escape his lips before he could stop it. "Carew, I don't believe you," he said softly. "I've known you too well."

If he hoped to shatter Carew's calm, he failed. Carew took a deep pull on his cigarette and said, "The sad thing for you, Nigel, is that—whether you believe me or not—you are my last hope. Yesterday, I lost track of your wife's power. I don't know if she died, or simply changed. However, I do know I can't find her.

So, dear brother, you are confronted with two choices. You can activate the stone for me, and you and your lady friend will not be harmed . . . at least not yet. Or I can torture her slowly to see if you'll give in. And if you don't . . . well, then we kill you to rinse the stone clean of its attachment, after which I can hope to attach it to myself or to my friend Shenta here. Mind you, the sacrifice might not work. And if it doesn't, one or both of you will have died in vain. However it's a risk I have to take if you won't cooperate."

"Don't do it," Nassira's voice said from beside Nigel. "He'll still kill us if you help him."

Turning around, Nigel saw Nassira's eyes open and fixed on him, and was so relieved to have his reasoning confirmed that he only said, "Don't worry. I won't."

"How touching," Carew said mockingly. "Well. I did say if one way didn't work, the other would." He got up and stood, revealing behind him one large stone that some of his helpers had just set up, as though for a ritual. "Now, which way is it going to go? Are you going to do what I wish? Or do I play with the girl?" His blue eyes sparkled in amusement. "I've known you to be many things in our lives, but none of them is stupidly brave, Nigel. So . . . let's see."

He spoke rapidly to the men behind him. Two of them came and grabbed Nassira, despite her desperate attempts to free herself from their grasp by writhing and twisting. They carried her to the stone. Another one approached and gave Carew an old stone knife, which sparkled with power.

Carew took one final pull of his cigarette and threw it on the ground, stepping on it with a foot still attired in glimmering shoes. How had he kept his shoes polished in Africa? And although he limped a little, he looked as if Africa hadn't changed him at all.

"I hate to do this, truly, I do, Nigel. Such a waste. But since you won't help, you leave me no choice." He grinned at Nigel. "Are you sure you won't change your mind?"

Nigel's heart beat very fast at his throat, so loud it seemed amazing he could hear anything else. And his headache pounded, just behind his eyes. But he had to think. He could not do what Carew wanted, but neither could he let him kill Nassira. He had to stop Carew now.

That this thought was overreaching pride, considering he was bound and laying on the ground utterly helpless, did no more than add desperation to his thought. If only he could get Carew's followers to see him for what he was!

And then, out of his confusion and desperation, the same sort of instinct that had allowed him to kill the lion found voice. "Carew," he said, uttering the words he'd never dared speak when his brother tormented him in childhood. "You're too much of a coward to sacrifice me. You want me to use the compass stone? I'll fight you for it."

Carew's look of utter surprise and disdain showed Nigel that Carew was not afraid and that Nigel had, possibly, just made the greatest mistake in a lifetime of them.

WEDDING NIGHT

They'd used the elephant—a suddenly tame creature— to get away from their campsite. Not anywhere in particular as much as far away from where the Hyena Men might find them.

Emily found it odd to sit atop the beast with these two strange men, surveying the countryside. It all looked different that way. But then, everything looked different anyway.

Having shared Kitwana's mind had not been a temporary or momentary thing. She hadn't expected it to be. She'd read enough novels to know how special such a joining could be, and how permanent. In most such novels, it stood if not in place of a marriage, in surety of it, for no two people with magical power could share so much of themselves and not be united forever.

Other things she knew—or thought she knew—from her novels. If they didn't lie, then this joining between a man and a woman, no matter how unacquainted before, only happened if the two of them were predestined to be one.

She knew all this and kept it to herself. Because she felt Kitwana was a part of her, as vitally linked to her as her own soul, she *could not* impose her feelings on him. Perhaps it wasn't the same among his people. And she could imagine what opposition he'd face from his people if he brought her back as his bride.

She amused herself with a fantasy of taking him back to meet her father—of introducing this African son-in-law to him. She could well imagine that his family would feel the same about her. Only perhaps more so.

From his mind, from the memories, some of which weren't clear as to place and time, but all of which were clear as to feelings, she'd realized he was a cherished son—and a well-loved one. She'd also acquired the feeling that his family was important, his status high.

It probably would be as disastrous a marriage for him as for her. And while she was willing to risk her status for him, she couldn't demand the same of him. No. She loved him enough to leave him free. Even if a portion of her would always keep the image and memory of him.

And then there was the other result of their merge. Her power had been released. She'd have to learn to use it, but she could feel it—all of it—within her, vital and alive, and no longer closed in or unusable.

She now had more power than just about anyone else she'd ever met. And with this power, which she'd learn to use, she would look after herself. She didn't need anyone to protect her.

With such lofty thoughts she rode through the day. They traveled almost in silence, Farewell being too wounded and Kitwana too seemingly absorbed in his own thoughts to make more than casual conversation.

They camped for the night in a cave accessible only through a narrow passage between rocks, and that passage was guarded by the elephant that would obey their mind commands. In the cave, Kitwana built a fire from wood he'd found. Then he'd disappeared for some minutes, to return with fish impaled in his spear.

"They rise to a magelight," he said, as though that explained everything.

Emily had taken over then, gutting and cleaning and roasting the fish over the fire, while Kitwana made tea. Peter ate more than Emily expected—but she supposed that was good, because it meant that he was less likely to feel famished in the night and go in search of prey.

After eating, Kitwana sat silently for a moment, then stood up and bowed slightly. "I'll sleep now," he said. And, taking one of the blankets they'd managed to salvage, he retreated with it to the other side of the fire.

Emily could imagine him there, lying on the stony floor. She imagined him stretching, arranging himself for sleep. And she realized, startled, that the mind-merge had given her a knowledge of how his body moved and felt from the inside. He'd be too big and too heavy to sleep comfortably in this cave. And he wouldn't complain, because no good would come of it.

"Go to him," Farewell whispered.

"I beg your pardon?" Emily said, looking up, her voice louder than she meant it to be.

Farewell put his finger in front of his lips. "Go to him," he whispered. "I've been seeing you look at each other for all these days now. I've seen what the merge did to each of you. Go to him!"

Emily tried to pull her nonexistent dignity about herself. "Mr. Farewell," she said. "How can you suggest that? I am a lady of quality and I—"

But the impish eyes only smiled at her, the green in them glinting by the firelight. "You came to me once. And I wish I could have deserved you, but I didn't. I could have loved you—indeed, I had dreams of it—but I could never be worthy of you. He is worthy of you. Go to him."

"But he . . . I can't force . . ."

"Let him decide. Mrs. Oldhall, you should never decide for a man what his heart contains."

"How absurd," she said, "that you call me Mrs. Oldhall in these circumstances."

He smiled at her and said, "You are right, Emily. But you are wrong if you don't follow your heart now."

"How do you know so much about the human heart?" Emily asked lightly. Only when he flinched did she realize how he would take it.

But his answer was soft, pensive. "Because I know another kind of heart. And I know the difference."

It took her a moment, sitting on the ground, thinking. If she went to Kitwana, she would be shunned by all of English society. If she ever went back to English society. But who really cared? At this moment, here, in the depths of Africa, English society might as well be a chimera or a children's story. And then . . . and then perhaps Farewell was right. Perhaps she should go to Kitwana. Perhaps she should not make up his mind for him.

Doing all that was expected of her hadn't worked

so far. Perhaps she should do what she must do for herself now.

Her body decided for her. She found herself by the trunk, looking through the contents for what to wear. Her sprig-embroidered nightgown, meant for her wedding night, had gotten torn in that dreadful night in the encampment. Yet she felt she should not go to the one who was her husband in everything but English law without proper raiment.

As she turned over cloth, she found her grandmother's shawl, embroidered with its vivid flowers. She grabbed it and ducked into the shadows, away from Peter's gaze. In the shadows she undressed quickly and, wrapped in the floral shawl, walked around the fire to where Kitwana lay.

She had a moment of blindness, from the fire, and then, as her eyes recovered, she saw him, laying on the ground. She'd thought he'd be asleep, but he wasn't. He was awake, his gaze turned to her.

She had imagined this moment many times, and she'd imagined what the man she married would say, what she'd answer.

Kitwana didn't say anything. He merely looked at her, his eyes widening. Then his lips curved slightly in a smile. And, sitting up, he opened his arms.

She stumbled into them as if it were the most natural thing in the world. And, indeed, clasped in his arms, she felt whole—as though she'd been away from home for a very long time and had now found her way back. As though she'd been lost in the desert and stumbled headlong into an oasis.

His muscular arms closed around her. She could

feel their strength, their protection, and feel herself strong and safe within them.

He kissed her jaw and neck, and everywhere he could reach, and then their lips met.

Outside, a bird called and the elephant shuffled uneasily. Inside, the fire burned down, and presently they could hear Peter Farewell snoring softly from the other side of the embers.

But it didn't matter. For all that was concerned, they might have been alone in the whole world. Kitwana explored her body slowly and, in doing so, showed her the glories of his own. At the moment he entered her, she expected pain, but there was none. Instead, their minds merged, effortlessly, as they had before. His heartbeat was hers. She felt her pleasure and his. Her soft skin, his rougher one. Caught between physical pleasure and the magical sharing of it, she felt him within her and shared his sensation of being enveloped and embraced by her flesh. Surrounded by Kitwana's arms, united to his body and soul, Emily found the one place she belonged. Not India and not England, but with this one man.

EYE

Emily woke. There was light in the cave—gray and fil-
tered through the small opening. Kitwana had his arm
and leg over her—as though unwilling to let her go.

A sound from the other side of the cave called her
attention and she turned sleepily to look. Peter
Farewell was awake, standing. She checked that the
blanket was over her and Kitwana, then looked back
at Farewell. He was looking through the trunks and
she momentarily wondered why.

When he picked up the knife, she half sat up. But
he did not cross the cave with the knife in hand—and
indeed why should he, after almost dying saving
them?

He must mean to go hunting, she thought, then
closed her eyes and went back to sleep.

A cry woke her again, and she sat up. Peter
Farewell had his back to her. He dropped the knife.
She heard him whisper some incantation and said,
"Mr. Farewell?"

He turned around. In his hand was an egg-size
green globe, glowing. And one of his eyes was gone,
tearing just a dark cavern, from which blood flowed
down his cheek.

He didn't seem to notice the blood. Instead, as it dripped from his face, he extended the green globe to her, on his palm, and said steadily, "It worked, you see. I believe the eye of the dragon will help us find the ruby."

FIGHTING FOR TRUTH

"Do you really mean to fight me?" Carew asked, grinning in amusement. "Do you truly think, Nigel, that I would need to prove myself equal to . . . you?"

Nigel managed to grin, though inside he was cold with fear. "Oh, yes. If you don't fight me, I'll have to assume you're afraid of it." He looked slyly behind Carew, at the men assembling on the clearing. "They'll know you're afraid. They'll remember that you weren't man enough to fight your brother—whom you outweigh considerably—and instead preferred to torture an African woman."

Nigel could see his meaning hit Carew as his eyes lost their unconcerned look to become focused and suspicious. He slowly looked behind at his followers, then turned back to his brother and arched his eyebrows. "Oh, well played, Nigel, well played. Who would know you are truly my brother?" He stood and muttered something to the two men who had carried Nassira, then grinned at Nigel. "Very well, brother, how about this? I shall fight you. You can even have a knife to meet me on equal ground. And if I win, you will use the compass stone for me, until I have no use for it. It really is for the best, you know."

Nigel nodded. He wasn't such a fool that he didn't know that Carew would give him a dull knife and not fight fairly. But Nigel's purpose was not to win. Even if he won, what would it mean? He couldn't activate the compass stone, and Carew would kill him. His purpose was to get Carew to confess to his intent about the ruby. If he got that out in the open, then at least the Africans would turn against him.

While Carew's lackeys cut through his bonds, Nigel thought that Carew, after all, had entirely too good an opinion of himself, and that the best way to get him to confess would be to taunt him.

He received the knife from the hands of the natives with a grin and said, "So, I assume this is not a fight to the death, since a fight to the death would mean you couldn't use my services with the compass stone afterward."

Carew rounded, half-crouching, in the pose of the expert knife-fighter. "Oh, brother. I would not fight you to the death. It would be unfair."

Nigel sprang, and managed to almost get his knife at Carew's throat before Carew threw him. But Nigel managed to get up quickly and come back at him.

He must argue. He must get Carew to defend himself.

"So you're going to all this trouble for Africa, are you?" Nigel asked, short of breath, as he came at Carew. He was aware that Carew had already knifed him, and that blood was trickling, warm and sticky, beneath his clothes.

"Why wouldn't I?" Carew asked, loudly, theatrically. "Why wouldn't I, when I saw the needs of these people and how badly they had been treated by our kind?"

Strangely, Nigel had heard the same from Peter. When Peter spoke of the people of Africa and of their being oppressed, Nigel felt that he spoke the truth, or the truth as he saw it. When Carew spoke of it, it held the same feeling as when Carew spoke of loving his mother. Or of protecting his little brother.

Nigel met Nassira's gaze. Her eyes, fixed on him, seemed to be trying very hard to tell him something.

Between parrying Carew's thrusts Nigel noticed she was looking at the lion tail and ears fetish on his belt, and he got her meaning. He allowed Carew to throw him yet again, and as he was getting up, he got the fetish out of his belt and held it with his knife. As he came back at Carew hotly, ducking under his arm and ignoring the knife at his throat, he pressed the lion fetish to the bare skin of Carew's arm. "Carew? Why do you really want the ruby?" he asked.

"The power, Nigel, the power," Carew said. His voice was still hearty and bluff, but he looked surprised at hearing it, as though he wasn't sure at all what he might be saying. "Think of the power in that. Charlemagne made himself king of Europe forever. I could be king of the world."

At that moment, Carew felt the lion tail upon his arm and shook, realizing what he'd done. He roared, from deep in his chest, and threw Nigel across the clearing, then ran at him with hot rage, knife drawn. "Traitor to your family, your race, your breed!"

Nigel closed his eyes as Carew raised his hand to slam his dagger through Nigel's heart. And then he heard a puzzling sound. The looked up to see a lance halfway through Carew's shoulder.

The man with the face like a bulldog was at the back, blinking—too far away to have thrown it. "Sometimes," he said, sheepishly, "I throw things with my mind, when I'm mad. I can't help it."

Nigel noticed his brother was still breathing, but it couldn't be for long. Time would take care of it. And though he hadn't intended for the man to kill him by accident, he had hoped for exactly this result.

He got up and dusted himself, and went to untie Nassira.

"Nigel, he said he couldn't find your wife's power, that she's either dead or somehow vanished."

"Yes, I heard," Nigel said, worried. "But there's not much I can do about it." He felt too tired even to feel grief.

"No," Nassira clutched at his wrist. "If your brother couldn't find it, perhaps the compass stone can't, either? Perhaps now you can bind to it? Isn't it worth a try?"

GOING HOME

"Are you sure the eye shows that mountain?" Kitwana asked Emily.

The three of them—Emily, Kitwana, and a fast-recovering Peter Farewell—stood near the magic-tamed elephant: an impressive beast with a mean countenance that, after Kitwana's and Emily's magical taming of it, had proven itself gentle and kind. It even let Peter ride it, though it never seemed to take to him.

They huddled around the glowing green globe, while the elephant—which Emily insisted on calling Samson—stood nearby, tearing up and eating large tufts of grass. And the globe showed a nearby mountain—an odd mountain, steep and rocky, and surmounted by an almost flat top so large that several crops and an entire herd of cattle could be kept on it. Enough to feed the a modest village.

"Certainly," Emily said, frowning slightly. "Or at least, we're close enough that, surely, if it meant for us to go around, it could point slightly away and then correct."

"But the mountain is such a small area," Kitwana said, his heart contracting as he looked for a way to evade the inevitable. "If we must climb that mountain, then the ruby must be on it."

"Or in it," Peter Farewell said, lighting a cigarette with shaking hands. He'd lost his cigarette case in the confusion of the camp, but he'd found several packs of his cigarettes and he retained his lighter. The vaguely minty tobacco smoke wreathed around him as he exhaled it, blue and gray into the morning air.

"But it can't be," Kitwana said, exasperated.

"It can't be?" Emily asked. "Why not?"

"I know this mountain," Kitwana said, hearing his own voice too hollow and remote.

The others waited for him to explain, and after a long while Peter clicked his tongue against his teeth and said, "I wonder what you mean by that."

At the same time, Emily said, "Do you mean there's no path up it? It looks very steep."

"Oh, there's a path. It's narrow, and it winds between scrapy rocks. It's only broad enough to take a boy and a herd at a time, and it can be wholly blocked by rolling a large rock across it, something that sentinels will do if the party approaching is at all suspicious."

Peter's lips elongated in a slow smile, and he looked away from Kitwana, as though he had already glimpsed something indecent.

Emily simply blinked and looked at Kitwana, uncomprehending. "How do you—"

"That," Kitwana said, "is the place I grew up. My home village."

"Oh," Emily said, and then, suddenly brightening. "Oh. But that means you'll be welcome."

Kitwana's bitter bark of laughter was echoed by

Farewell's amused chuckle. For a moment—for just a moment—man and dragon-man looked at each other in perfect understanding. Yet Farewell could not know. "Why do you laugh, Peter?" he asked. Ever since the mind-merge and through the day after, when Kitwana had used their magic, jointly, to heal Peter's wounds and since Peter had removed his eye to lead them here, they'd called each other by their first names.

Kitwana was not too sure what each of them knew about the other. While healing Farewell from his eye injury he'd gotten enough—a feeling, a remnant of sensation—to realize that Peter was one vast hurt, barely covered over with the scabs of pride and self-possession.

He felt a certain compassion for the man, though he disdained the pretty lies with which Peter covered his desire to get revenge on the world at large. He understood the anger and the desire to lash out at magic and those who held it. But he thought it unworthy of the intelligent and urbane man to lie to himself about it and say he wished to do it for others.

Now Peter smiled at him. "I think we are kin, you and I," he said, and before Kitwana could bridle at the idea, he added, "You and I were thrown out of the places where we were raised, out of the destiny we thought should be ours."

Kitwana bit his lip, but looking at Emily's intent gaze, could only sigh. "He's right, in a way. That mountain," he gestured with his hand, "is where I grew up, but I don't know if I'll be allowed up the path and to the village itself. They might roll the stone across the path."

"Why?" Emily asked.

He couldn't have told it to anyone, but she'd been in his mind and he in hers. Between them there was a bond stronger than anything that he'd ever shared with anyone. So he spoke simply, confident it would not change her opinion of him—because that could not change, any more than his feeling for who he was could change. "Because I killed a man."

She started just a little, then said again, "Why?"

"Wamungunda, my father, is a strange man," Kitwana said slowly. "Though now that I've been in the world and seen how things are, I've come to believe perhaps it is the world that is strange and not my father." He paused and sighed. "Africa has been a land of carnage for his whole life. And my father will allow refugees into our village, no matter who they are—the despot or his victim. All are allowed to come and live with us, provided they will harm none while they're there. One of those men..." Kitwana shrugged and felt his cheeks warm. A month ago he'd have told this story more assuredly, more certain that he had done the right thing. "One of them was a chieftain from the Congo who sold his entire people into slavery to the white invaders and retired on the profits. He still bragged about it, and it seemed to me that he intended to do the same again, in my village. I didn't... I can't say I intended to kill him, as such. I was thirteen and I was very upset. I confronted him and told him I wanted him out of our village. He taunted me. He said not only would he not leave, but eventually he would be the chief of the village, after my father and I died. Since he was my father's age, and so much older than I..." He let that sink in, and sighed. "I threw a rock. It hit him on the head and he died. And my father . . ." He paused again to collect himself. "My father sent me away to live with my mother's brother, among the Zulu. He said I might be happier in the rest of world."

"And were you?" Peter asked casually.

Kitwana shook his head slowly. Right now, it seemed to him the most foolish thing he had done. He longed to greet his father, to hug him, to confess his misdeeds and to be absolved. To be at peace again, in a place of peace.

"The problem is," he said, shaking himself. "If the ruby is in the village, wouldn't I know it?"

Peter took a deep pull of his cigarette. "Who knows?" he said. "Perhaps it's hidden in the ashes of your grandmother's cooking fire. It's been done. I say we get on Samson, go up and find out."

"Assuming they let us up," Kitwana said.

THE GUARDIAN
OF THE PATH

*Sitting astride Samson, they climbed up the path, be-*tween boulders, as Samson set his feet daintily, like a well-trained ballerina. At the top of the path, where it narrowed, Emily could catch glimpses of a field filled with some green crop. She could also hear the lowing of the cattle, and a woman's voice singing something high and sweet that sounded like a lullaby.

Kitwana sat astride Samson's neck, with Emily behind him, leaning into him, and Peter behind her, somehow holding on to the elephant while managing to smoke.

For a long time they climbed, higher and higher on a gentle spiral, till at the top a youth stepped onto the path and looked curiously, but without alarm, at the elephant. And Emily remembered Kitwana had told her that in his youth, men on horses had come up here, along with entire scouting detachments, on foot, fully armed.

Now the boy stood. He was dressed in what could have passed for a short toga, dyed in vivid red, and his features, like Kitwana's, were an amalgamation of all

Africa with nothing predominant. He was darker than
Kitwana, and his nose was straighter.

Emily remembered Kitwana saying his people
were an amalgam of a thousand different migrations
and of refugees. Isolated, atop their mountain, they
spoke a language that time had forgotten, and they accepted all who came in peace.

She wondered if that would mean they, too, would
be accepted, and sighed as she felt Kitwana's shoulders tense under her hands.

The boy asked something in a defiant tone, rapidly
followed by something in a different language, and
finally in English—with a look at Peter and Emily—
"Who comes here?"

Kitwana answered in his own language, his shoulders more tense than ever. The boy looked confused
and turned to shout something at someone hidden
from them by the turn of the path. There was a sound
of surprise, and then the sound of sandaled feet running.

"What did you tell him?" Emily asked.

"That I am Kitwana, son of Wamungunda, and
that I come in peace and to speak to my father," he
said, and took a deep breath as though steealing himself for an ordeal. "If there's a jewel here, anywhere,
my father will know. He and all my male ancestors,
back before anyone can remember, were priest-kings
of this village."

"Priests of what god?" Emily asked curiously.

"Oh, it's not that clear," he said resignedly. "They
worship him who created all and they protect his creation. At least that's what my father said. This some-

times involves fighting demons. Particularly demons that control sorcerers and deposed despots," he said.

She nodded, though she knew he couldn't see her. They were so quiet that, behind her, she could hear Peter drawing deeply on his cigarette.

Then the path in front of them exploded with noises and voices. Excited voices. Emily felt Kitwana tense again, and tensed with him—until two people appeared on the path, a middle-aged man and woman. The man was shorter than Kitwana, and stockier, but the woman was a tall graceful beauty who, except for her gender and the strands of white in her hair could have been Kitwana's sister. As it was, Emily could only assume these were his parents.

There was parental anxiety in the eyes turned up to him, and a smile that only parents can give a long-lost child, and they were both talking at once, anxiously.

She felt Kitwana relax, and suddenly found him speaking English. "And these are my friends," he said. "Emily Oldhall and Mr. Peter Farewell."

"Ah, you bring us a bride," his mother said, her English heavily accented and oddly intoned. "You fulfilled your quest, then."

Kitwana sighed. "My . . . quest? No, we come . . . Father, we must talk to you."

His father said something that they couldn't understand, in a liquid language. Kitwana frowned. "He says he knew I would be coming, and we do indeed need to talk."

With such cryptic words, Kitwana's father turned and led them, Samson walking sedately, up the path. Suddenly it became a level road, which then became a vast expanse of fields and houses. The houses were stone, Emily noted. Stone houses, thatched, almost Mediterranean. And amid the fields and the houses were the most beautiful people Emily had ever seen. They didn't all look the same, but they all looked happy and well fed and ... contented. The word came to her like a revelation.

When she was little, her religion book had a picture of the Garden of Eden. It had very little to do with this, being just a mannered garden, with rosebushes and, among them, a blond Adam and a blonder Eve. Yet that picture and this scene had the same feeling. Here, on this cloud-wreathed peak in Africa, there was a feeling of a place where one could belong. A place away from the cares of the world and the sometimes confused loyalties of life in a time of empires and wars.

War would never come here. Something told her this place had stood for millennia, and would still stand.

Wamungunda led them to a handsome stone house, only slightly larger than the others. At the door, they dismounted, and two smiling boys took Samson off to a field.

Wamungunda said something and Kitwana translated. "He says Samson can wait for us there. He wants us to come in."

Inside, it was clean, with fresh breezes blowing through the door and one window. He had a table and two simple benches. "Sit, sit," he told them all, his words almost clicks, his smile showing how proud he was of that one English word. His wife busied herself setting in front of them a drink made from fermented cow milk and something that looked like chunks of orange fruit pulp roasted in a mass, but that, on tasting, was a lot like bland and sweet cakes.

Kitwana ate one and then three in quick succession. He begged Emily's and Peter's pardon, then spoke rapidly in what he said was his native language and easier for Wamungunda to understand. When he was done, he was silent a moment, then turned to Emily. "I told him everything," he said, "since I joined the Hyena Men. And I asked about the jewel. I'll now translate what he says."

Wamungunda nodded slowly in confirmation and spoke. And Kitwana echoed him in English, clearly translating his words verbatim. "Before you came," he said, "I got a message from...the spirit of the shrine. It told me you would be coming, and that the avatar of the mother of worlds had chosen you as her protectors.

"You see," he said, speaking simply, "when the first jewel was stolen from the eye of the goddess, the white king seemed to believe all the power he could get from it was free, and that it meant nothing how he used it. He was wrong. Those jewels were spelled, in the beginning of time, to anchor the possibilities of the world together.

"Every time there is an event where there could be two outcomes, the world can split and create another world, identical yet different, like pages in a book. Once there were enough people in the world, this ability became dangerous. Our ancestors knew this and, being wise, bound it all with magic and put it in the rubies. And mounted them, in turn, into the eyes of the great avatar, the first statue sculpted by mankind."

Kitwana ate a small cake pensively and went on, translating his father's liquid words. "But when the other eye was gone, the anchor was gone, and some splinting occurred. The world started separating from itself, like an onion being peeled layer by layer. If the second eye goes..." He shrugged. "Reality will splinter. All life will become impossible, because there won't be a single part of the world in accord with itself. Each part will be different, and in a different reality from all others."

"How do we know you're telling the truth?" Peter Farewell asked.

Kitwana translated and Wamungunda gave Peter a long look, then smiled and spoke. And Kitwana translated. "You don't. But you will. The avatar has chosen you to be its protectors. It says the jewel won't be safe here, because too many people will know where it is. And since the statue has only one eye, it lacks the power to hide itself from the world as it did in ages past. The two of you are to guard it and to restore its other eye to it."

"How are we supposed to do that?" Emily asked. "Of all the jewels in the world... The Soul of Fire vanished years ago. It is possible it's been cut into smaller pieces or destroyed."

"The avatar says it exists still. And it can be found and reconsecrated," Wamungunda said through Kitwana's translation. "It says that Kitwana and you, my dear," he smiled at Emily, "will be—"

At that moment a young man came to the door, shouting. Wamungunda rose quickly, and Kitwana himself half rose before turning back to speak to Emily. "He says people have arrived by flying rugs. Several people.

Two of them are a blond Englishman and a woman of the Masai. They are coming to look for an ancient jewel."

"Nigel?" Emily asked.

The young man at the door looked at her. "Nigel Oldhall," he said in a horrendous accent. "And Nassira of the Masai."

Emily looked at Kitwana and found him staring at her. It had been a beautiful dream while it lasted. Since their mind-merge, Emily had felt she knew Kitwana better than she had ever known anyone else. She had felt that Kitwana was . . . oh, not so much the man for her as another half of her that had gotten separated somehow, and thrown to the other end of the globe.

As much as it would shock her friends and relatives back in London, Emily Oldhall would have been happy, contented, to be allowed to live here, in Africa, with the man of her choice, and never again hear of society or the ton or even of the British Isles.

But as easy as it would have made everything, she had never really wished Nigel dead.

GIVING IT ALL UP

Nigel should have been more upset when he saw Emily and Kitwana together. Not that they were doing anything improper. Merely standing side by side, him regal in his leather apron and she small and bedraggled in her much-stained and torn dress.

She looked tired. Her hair was a mass of tangles. The sun of Africa had deepened the color of her skin beyond all fashionable bounds. She had never looked more beautiful.

Yet there was a certain expression in Kitwana's eyes when he looked at her, and in Emily's eyes when she looked at him. Nigel, just debarked from a one-person flying rug, which had brought them the rest of the way that the angel had told him to take, found the ground lurching under his feet.

He'd expected many things. To see Emily in love with Peter, perhaps, or Peter so wholly ensconced in her heart that the only honorable way out was to divorce her and let Peter marry her. But he hadn't thought to find her in love with an African, or an African in love with her. And immediately he decided that he was being churlish and dishonorable. After all, he'd been saved by and saved an African

woman, and she was, in truth, his comrade-in-arms.
He turned to where Nassira and Shenta were talking. Who was he to resent Emily's happiness, whatever form it took?

He'd divorce her, or else tell everyone that she'd
disappeared in Africa. Let them think what they
would, but let her be happy. Nigel realized now that
as much as he loved Emily, his love for her had been
that of a man for a younger sister. He'd never really
known her well. He knew there must be a woman
out there for him—but who she was and where Nigel
would find her was a mystery. Instead, he said softly,
"Hello, Emily. Sorry to run off on you like that.
Nassira was trying to protect me from the dragon's
wrath." Then looking quickly at Peter, as he smoked,
"Hello, Peter. I understand you are a dragon?" He
would have asked what happened to his eye—as
Peter's left eye seemed to be missing—but the question seemed unimportant. They'd all lost something.
Or gained something. Or perhaps both.

"Oh, now and then," Peter said, and smiled a little, though his eye showed shock at Nigel's lack of
horror.

"And now, children," Wamungunda said. Kitwana
translated it neutrally, but Wamungunda's voice
sounded as though they were, indeed, all in the earli-
est of infant classes. "We must go down to the avatar
and find its will for you and for the ruby."

He led them all determinedly back to his home,
where he pulled up a stone in the floor. Below it was a
spiral staircase. Nigel heard Kitwana gasp.

Kitwana went first. Peter followed him, then

Emily and Nigel and Nassira. There the priest stopped the others from entering and Kitwana translated the words echoing down the stony vault. "No. These five have a mission and deserve to know what it is. They were chosen. The rest of us must wait."

THE WORLD AND
EVERYTHING IN IT

Down there were caves, immense and endless. Peter wanted to smoke, but it would be like smoking in a cathedral. In fact, this had much the feeling of a cathedral—one carved out of living rock.

They passed two large chambers with oval arched ceilings that seemed to await millions of worshippers, then past them into a narrow hallway. Somehow, Peter had gotten ahead of Kitwana, and he walked unsteadily, leaning on the walls.

He'd had time to recover while on the back of the elephant, but not enough to be up to endless underground treks in caves of eerie beauty, where the pale, creamy walls glowed with a light that came from everywhere at once and nowhere.

He held on to the walls as he walked, but nothing prepared him for the cave the hallway led to. There, the glow was stronger, and it was coming from a spinning globe suspended in midair. The globe showed the world—its oceans and continents and the white glitter of its ice caps.

Peter stared for a moment, wide-eyed. The odd thing was that he could feel that this was, in some way, the real world. If he squinted at it, he could see the cities of men covering it, and the men like ants upon it. And anything that happened to this globe happened to the world out there.

Falling to his knees, unable to stand any longer, Peter crawled to the globe. "The thing is the image; the image is the thing," he heard himself say, his voice intent and small. "I could crush all the oppressors in here, and the world would be free."

He heard a tongue click behind him, so full of intent and derision that he turned to look. Nigel was behind him, shaking his head. "Leave off, Peter. If you kill tyrants, others will only rise up to take their place. There are always humans who want to have power over others. And some, perforce, will be intelligent enough to acquire it. You can't kill them all." He paused and frowned. "Or you can, but then you'd be awfully lonely."

Peter stared. "I could kill all the ones with magic."

"They'll find some other tomfool way to make others' lives miserable. And their own."

Peter heard a bark of laughter climb through his throat, and looked up at Nigel. "How you've changed."

"Well . . ." Nigel said. "Killing lions while walking in Africa leaves you a long time to think." He offered his hand and arm to Peter, to pull him up.

They skirted around the globe and walked on.

ACCEPTING THE CALL

They came tumbling in a confused group into a large chamber that glowed and sparkled as if each of the walls were diamond encrusted. Facing them was a statue of the most beautiful woman that Kitwana had ever seen. She was sculpted so that she could be every woman of every race on Earth. Turning one way made her look white, and another African. And yet another other, she had different faces. Every woman that Kitwana had ever seen was there, in that one statue, which stood giving an impression of utter serenity.

One of its eyes was empty. From the other, a red ruby glowed—the Heart of Light.

A feeling of awe like the belief and magic of centuries gathered around it. In the air, golden motes of power flew. As soon as they approached, the glow increased, till it filled the whole chamber in warm, reddish light.

"Kitwana," a voice said. It was a woman's voice, but it was not a sound. Rather, it echoed deeply within the head.

He looked up, wondering if everyone else was

hearing it, but since everyone's head lifted at the same time, he assumed they had.

"Kitwana, I am glad you are come home, with a bride, to inherit your father's work, in the fullness of time."

"But . . . I didn't bring a bride," he said. "Mrs. Oldhall is Mr. Nigel Oldhall's wife."

"Is this true?" the voice resounded.

"No," Nigel said, almost barely a whisper. "My wife by contract, but not in truth. I would be a horrible husband to her. Emily, you are free to be happy."

"But," Emily said, "my father gave me to you."

"Ah," the avatar said. "But did you give yourself?"

"I—" Emily blushed. She looked at Nigel. "No."

"Then you are free to bestow yourself, in any way you wish. I command it, I who am older than any of the gods of mankind."

Emily blushed, but when Kitwana extended his hands, she put hers tentatively in his.

"You will stay here and tend these sacred caves," the avatar said. "And learn the way to keep things as they have been throughout the millennia. And you," a look at Nassira, "and you, daughter of the Masai, you have served me well. You may now go and help the men on their mission."

"But my father!" Nassira said. "Our cows."

The statue—without moving—gave the impression of smiling.

"It is your choice, Nassira. Of all here, you have the most to lose by going on with your mission. I know that among your people, girls marry young and that you are your father's only daughter."

"I can chose?" she asked.

"Yes. You may go on with the mission or go home to your father, where you'll find a husband with whom you'll stand as equals. A worthy son-in-law for your father, your husband will never try to crush you and will always understand that you are worthy of all respect. Engai will give you cows. But if your sense of duty leads you on this adventure ..."

"No," Nassira said in a shout that seemed to surprise her. "No. I have served enough. Now I will live." She hesitated. "Sayo?"

"He will be waiting. Peter Farewell."

Peter had been standing at the back, slouching slightly as he still felt weak from his wounds. He walked forward slowly, his stride a shadow of his normal confident step. "Yes?"

"You were hurt and you hurt in turn. But I think you've learned the world is not yours to make over, and the injustice done to you, though great, is not the end of all. Your becoming a dragon is a gift, however the rest of the world views it. That gift will allow you to find the Soul of Fire for me. To find it and recover it and bring it back to me. Will you do that for me, Peter Farewell?"

"There are other men, lady," Peter said in a low voice. "Real men, not dragons, of resource and ability. Men who've never killed in pursuit of a misguided scheme. Men who never fooled themselves into believing they can save the world."

"Ah, but Peter, those men don't know the evil of which they're capable yet, so they cannot be trusted to know the limits of their own good. You have hit bottom, Peter Farewell, and you have skimmed the heart of darkness. Come into the light now and be my champion. Soul of Fire, too, was touched by the depths of evil. Let it, like you, come back into my light."

There was a long silence, while the rosy glow of the ruby bathed them all. Kitwana felt as if the light were warm water pouring on abraded flesh. So was the light to the spirit and soul.

They all must have felt the same, because Emily gave a little sob beside Kitwana, and her eyes were full of tears—though she didn't look unhappy. And from behind, Peter, too, sobbed, and answered, shakily, "Yes, I will do that. Or I will try. But I am an odd champion for any holy cause."

"I trust you, Peter Farewell. I, who has seen the millennia and men pass, have faith in you. You will make me proud. Nigel Oldhall?"

"Yes?" Nigel asked, almost surprised.

"You will take the Heart of Light. You will take it with you and keep it safe, till both jewels can be returned to me in safety. As you kept Nassira safe on your journey, you will keep this part of me safe—until both the rubies are returned to me and kept here, where I can then keep them safe."

But," Nigel said. "But if I do that, won't the world splinter?"

"No, because the jewel will not be out of my control. You are my champion and working for me, carrying my jewel. You can remove it because through you I'll still be holding it."

"But I'm not strong. Or resourceful."

"You defeated the Hyena Men's spirit-bind. You

saved a child. You have killed a lion. And you brought Nassira here safely. I choose you, Nigel Oldhall."

At the last words, the ruby dropped and floated as if on unseen currents of air to land in Nigel's hand.

THE ATTACK

As they emerged, dazed, into the light outside, Kitwana heard his father call. "Come quickly, the soldiers are here."

Unaware of what soldiers his father might be speaking, Kitwana rushed forward. Outside the hut he stopped.

There were little red rugs in the air, everywhere, and on the rugs were Red Coats holding powersticks. Kitwana felt the other ones come up behind him. The rugs were landing on fields and among surprised-looking cows.

"Here," Nigel said, extending the ruby to Kitwana. "You know how, in its light, you feel the truth? Perhaps . . ."

Kitwana understood. Taking the ruby he held it high above his head, its light bathing the mountain and painting the hazy clouds that wreathed the peak a rosy red. But nothing changed and the rugs kept on floating ever nearer, till it was clear how many people were on them.

"Hundreds." Kitwana heard his own voice. "Hundreds of them." The hand with which he held the ruby trembled. From the corner of his eye, he saw Nassira grab a lance. Peter held tight a powerstick, found who knew where.

And atop the rug landing nearest them, with a soft thud on the field at Samson's feet, sat none other than Carew Oldhall, with a bloodred bandage around his torso.

Kitwana started to put the ruby away, and behind him Nigel exclaimed. Nassira, too, said, in a tone of dismay, "He can't be alive." Peter Farewell drew a sharp breath as though something pained him.

"An invulnerability spell, I'm sure," Peter said. "They eat at your soul, but they will keep you alive. And Carew has no soul." Peter lifted his powerstick to Carew's face.

But Wamungunda stepped forward, standing in front of Carew, effectively protecting him from attack.

"What do you wish, sir?" he asked.

Carew glared at him. He pointed at Kitwana. "I want the queen of England's ruby, which was stolen by these savages." He looked at the men behind him. "Seize it."

Kitwana felt a sudden need to reach for a powerstick himself, but how could he kill hundreds of Red Coats with one powerstick? "You can't have the ruby," he said tiredly. "If you take the ruby, reality will dissolve. It's not—"

"Now," Carew said, pointing his powerstick at Kitwana. "Give it to me now, or I shall fire."

"Just shoot me," Nigel said, stepping from behind Kitwana. "You know it's me you wish to shoot."

But Kitwana's father just looked serenely at Carew aiming his powerstick, then back at Kitwana, and said in his atrocious accent, "Kitwana, the man needs the ruby. Give it him?"

Kitwana blinked. This was the same father who had warned him that the world would splinter and reality stop to exist should the ruby fall into the wrong hands. He looked at Wamungunda blankly. "Just... give it?"

"Yes. Give it. You have it. He wants it. Give it."

There were many things that Kitwana could say to his father, the most important of them being that Wamungunda didn't understand the world. If he gave the ruby to Carew, he'd only be ensuring that Carew killed him immediately after. Which meant Kitwana would die just ahead of the rest of the universe. And all of this would have been in vain. He couldn't let Emily die. He couldn't let the one he loved most disappear.

But all of this, all of the arguments he could make, sounded much like the arguments he'd given his father as to why a certain despot needed killing, years ago. They sounded like the arguments he'd advanced to himself about why Peter Farewell must die.

Kitwana knew two things. His father didn't want the universe to end, and his father had lived with the ruby for far longer than Kitwana could imagine. And presumably had heard the experience of those before him.

That meant that he must know something Kitwana didn't.

Those three steps toward Carew, who closed the distance between them in an impatient stride, were the longest of Kitwana's life, punctuated with questions and visceral fears.

What if Wamungunda in fact knew nothing and was only going on the reflexes of a lifetime? What if it all went wrong? What if these were the last seconds of the universe?

Just short of Carew, he looked over his shoulder at Emily and smiled at her, not sure if the smile wasn't their farewell.

And then he extended the ruby, which Carew snatched, midair.

The glow seemed to envelop Carew and the entire mountain, fiercer than ever, making every blade of grass clear in the unnatural light.

Carew smiled, a slow smile, and Kitwana closed his eyes, knowing the world was lost.

And then the light flared and flashed. Where Carew had been there was only a pile of ashes on the ground. And a mass of Red Coats were staring and slowly turning away.

THE BEGINNING

Samson stepped gingerly down the mountain pass, walking with the awkward gait of an elephant trying not to slide down the mountain. Atop it, Peter and Nigel sat, rocking with the motion.

"I wonder if Wamungunda knew what would happen when Carew touched the ruby," Nigel said pensively, sitting astride the elephant's neck.

The sound of a flint lighter came from behind him, followed by the sound of Peter inhaling smoke, then exhaling. "Had to, didn't he? His family lived with it for generations."

"Yes, but . . . Charlemagne had it, didn't he?" Nigel said, troubled. "And he performed a spell with it."

"Probably without ever touching it," Peter said. "I don't think the emissary touching it was the same thing. Wamungunda said the effect of destruction was triggered by sheer ambition and will to power. The emissary would not have that. Only a wish to serve his king."

"Yes, yes, you're right," Nigel said, and sighed. "As I had a wish to serve my queen."

Peter made a sound from behind that was not quite a chuckle. "We've all been . . . redirected." And then, "If you want to wave good-bye for the last time, we're about to go around the curve in the path."

Nigel turned back. Kitwana and Emily stood side by side, his arm over her shoulders. She had never looked as beautiful as she did in a native wrap, her long, dark hair windblown.

"They look very happy," Nigel said, and sighed heavily.

"Does it hurt to lose her?" Peter asked.

"Oh, no. It was never right. Somewhere out there, there's a woman for me. It's just that they're home, and I have to roam the world and keep this ruby safe all the while, until you find me and bring me the other jewel. And I have no idea how to do any of that."

Peter chuckled softly. A thread of tobacco smoke floated forward to tickle Nigel's nostrils with tobacco and mint. "You did very well, Nigel, going all official on the regiment and sending them away, back the way they'd come."

"Well, they were only boys from a nearby garrison. Carew had gotten them all talked up to defend the queen's jewel. You know what Carew was like." He paused, remembering the moment when his brother had been incinerated. "The fact that he'd just become a pile of ash in front of their eyes probably didn't hurt. You know, this will become one of those stories they tell in drawing rooms forever after, and no one believes."

"Yes, but all the same, you talked them down very nicely. I'm the worst off. I'm just a man with an unwanted tendency to turn into a dragon. Will you tell me where to find the Soul of Fire? And how I'm going to discover it? It's been lost for, what, five hundred years?"

Nigel smiled despite himself. "Well, Wamungunda said it was somewhere in India. And we have a certain dragon's eye. Doesn't mean the dragon himself can't use it to locate it."

"Yes. And that makes things so much easier," Peter said, exhaling forcefully.

They'd come around a turn on the mountain path, and they could see plains and hills crowned with green-blue vegetation, rolling with herds of wild beasts.

Nigel took a deep breath, savoring the sheer strangeness of the landscape and how odd his life had suddenly become.

Behind him, Peter chuckled softly. "Come on. Let's go save the world."

ABOUT THE AUTHOR

Sarah A. Hoyt was born in Portugal more years ago than she's comfortable admitting. She currently lives in Colorado with her husband, teen sons and a clowder of various-size cats. She hasn't been to Africa in twenty-some years, but she would like to visit again. Around four dozen—at last count—of her short stories have been published in magazines such as *Weird Tales, Analog, Asimov's* and *Amazing,* as well as various anthologies. *Ill Met by Moonlight,* the first book of her Shakespearean fantasy trilogy, was a finalist for the Mythopoeic Award. Sarah is also working on a contemporary fantasy series starting with *Draw One in the Dark,* and—as Sarah D'Almeida—is in the midst of a Musketeers' Mystery series starting with *Death of a Musketeer.* Her website is http://saraha hoyt.com/.

If you enjoyed *Heart of Light,*

the saga continues with Peter's story in

SOUL
of
FIRE
by
Sarah A. Hoyt

Coming in August 2008

Here's a special preview:

SOUL OF FIRE

Coming in August 2008

"Mama, don't make me marry him," Miss Sofie Warington said.

Seventeen years old, clad in a white dressing gown and clutching a blue muslin dress to her ample bosom—with her hair quite untamed and her expression wild—Miss Warington should not have looked ravishing. But the way her dark hair fell in tumultuous waves to the bottom of her spine; the way tears trembled at the end of the long eyelashes surrounding her blue-violet eyes; and the way her lips opened to let through her impetuous words would have brought strong men to their knees.

They had less effect on her mother, Lavinia Warington. "Don't be foolish, girl," she said, her voice severe. "What are you doing out of your room? And why are you not dressed?" As she spoke, she skillfully shepherded her daughter up the spacious stairs, carpeted in expensive red velvet that showed wear in discolored, threadbare patches.

Sofie resisted, but it was useless. She felt out of step and like a stranger in this house. She'd been born into it seventeen years ago, and she'd spent her first ten years in its vast, resounding, sun-washed rooms, attended by a native ayah and adored and indulged by her parents' various servants. But at ten, she'd been put aboard a carpetship to London, where for seven years she'd been a pupil in Lady Lodkin's Academy for Young Lady Magic Users.

The summons to return home two months ago had overjoyed her. London had never felt like home to her. Too dark, too dank, and people were too ready to sneer at her honey-colored skin—the result of an affair between her great-great-grandmother and an English officer. She'd felt like a wayfarer in London. And yet, now home proved to be no home at all.

Instead, she'd found her mother and father to be far from the mythical, godlike figures who had watched over her childhood with pride and care. Her mother had grown bitter and her father . . . Her father didn't bear thinking about. She knew nothing of magical maladies, but she knew enough to guess when someone had been using dark magic, and using it far too extensively. And she knew it was an illness that could hardly be cured.

And then there was the reason they'd summoned her back home a year before her education was completed. It wasn't a longing for her company, as she'd hoped. And it wasn't even that they'd missed her. "Lalita told me that the man visiting tonight was a rich native prince from a distant kingdom," she accused her mother. "That he offered for me several months ago, and you . . . you accepted! Before I even returned."

"And how would she know this, since she has been in London as your attendant till just three months ago?"

"She says the kitchen servants talked about it. They said that's why you sent for me."

Sofie's mother's lips closed tightly, until they seemed to be but a single red line. "Lalita talks too much."

Sofie turned around fully, still clutching her dress, anxious fingers digging deeply into the folds of the material. "But is it true, Mama? Did she tell me the truth? How can you agree to give me away to a man I haven't even met? A man who..." Oh, if it was true, she had to run—somewhere, somehow—and find or make her own fortune.

"Child, you're being foolish beyond permission. We are not giving you away to anyone. We found you a most advantageous marriage, one that most women in your position would give their eyeteeth for. The Prince Ajith is a powerful man, the ruler of a vast native kingdom, and he's agreed to make you his only wife. You will live covered in jewels and surrounded by servants. Trust me, Sofie, your lot could be worse."

As she spoke, Madam Warington propelled her daughter up the steep staircase, till, at the top landing, she could put her arm around the girl's small shoulders and shepherd her gently into the open door of her room.

The room, if not her parents, exactly matched Sofie's memories of childhood. It was, by far, vaster than anything she'd seen in England—almost as large as the dormitory that, at the academy, she'd shared with twenty other girls. The walls were whitewashed, since to wallpaper walls in India's hot and humid climate was quite futile. Even magically applied wallpaper started mildewing within days of being put up, and peeled altogether from the humidity and heat within months. But the whitewash was fresh, and if the occasional lizard wandered in through the open balcony door and climbed the walls, it looked like a planned ornament.

The bed was piled high with lace and silk pillows,

and was covered in an intricate, colorful bedspread. A tightly woven lace netting draped over the bed lent it an air of romance, although its main function was to keep out the noxious flying insects that flourished in this climate. And all the silk and lace might give the impression of riches if one didn't know how cheap it was in these climes. Why, even the servants wore silken saris and gaudy gold jewels on ears and nostrils.

Still clutching her dress, Sofie allowed herself to be pushed all the way to the vanity in the far corner. The mirror—showing dark spots in its silver backing—gave her back her own image, with high color on both cheeks and moisture in her eyes, and she wondered how her mother could distress her so and not care.

Meanwhile, her mother had removed the dress from Sofie's clutching fingers and clucked at the wrinkles marring the fine blue fabric. "Why, you absurd creature, you nearly ruined this. Lalita!"

Sofie's maid and the constant companion of her adolescence emerged from the balcony, where, doubtless, she'd run at their approach, trying to evade Mrs. Warington's wrath. But Mrs. Warington was visibly more preoccupied with her daughter's attire right now than with punishing her garrulous maid.

Lalita, whose name meant playful and who looked it, wore a bright sky-blue sari, and large golden hoop earrings through her ears. Her hair was pulled into a heavy braid at her back. Not for the first time, Sofie found herself envying her maid's vitality, her beauty, and, most of all, her unrepentant certainty of who she was. Lalita didn't wonder whether she was more Indian than English. Lalita—the daughter of people born and raised in Calcutta for generations uncountable—might have gone to London with Sofie, but she never had any reason to consider herself anything but Indian.

She walked into the room with an expression of repentance that was no more believable than an expression of humility upon a cat's face. Bobbing a hasty curtsy, she took the dress and fairly ran with it out the door, presumably to do whatever it was one did to a dress to remove wrinkles. Sofie, who didn't know or care what that might be, allowed her mother to fuss over her hair. "I can't believe you'd go out there like this, Sofie," Mrs. Warington said. "What if anyone had seen you?"

"Lalita said *he* was with Papa on the veranda off the parlor, and she said he is quite gross. And, Mama, she was right." She shuddered at the memory of the enormous native grandee, his shapeless form covered in bright silks that would have done better service as sofa or bed coverings. But it was not his gross physique that had disgusted her. No. What made her tremble and swallow hard in fear were his features. She'd never seen anyone who looked like him. His face was broad and oddly arranged, with a very low nose and cruel lips. Between the scars crisscrossing his features, and the intricate tattoos marking his forehead and cheeks, he looked . . . not quite human.

And then there were his eyes, slitlike and quite yellow. The pupils were yellow-gold, but the sclera, too, had a yellowish tint, like aged porcelain or the teeth of a heavy smoker. Sofie shuddered at the memory.

"Mama, I—"

"Hush, girl," Mrs. Warington said, pulling hard on the heavy tresses she was plaiting into a braid on either side of her daughter's face. "Don't make this into a melodrama. No one is going to force you to marry anyone you don't wish to. All I ask is that you look at

Prince Ajith and think whether you could stand to marry him."

"I've looked at him," Sofie said, as she remembered the man's smile, and the large sharp fanglike teeth that protruded from his thin lips. "There is nothing that could prevail upon me to consider marriage to—"

With a clatter, Mrs. Warington set Sofie's silver-handled brush upon the polished mahogany dressing table. "Sofie, listen. You are old enough to know the truth. And the truth is, the chances of us finding you a respectable marriage with an Englishman in either England or India are next to none."

"I know you're going to say this is because I have Indian blood, but... Mother! Plenty of girls with more Indian blood than I have married exceedingly well. And besides—"

"Yes, doubtless," Mrs. Warington said. "Your father's grandmother married very well, but she brought with her an immense dowry accumulated by her Nabob father. Enough for no one to say anything about her blood, or about the fact that her parents never married and her mother was nothing but her father's native bibi. Yes, Sofie, money covers a multitude of sins, but that's where we fail, for we have none."

"No money?" Sofie asked, somewhat shocked.

A shadow crossed her mother's features. For a moment, the greenish eyes meeting hers in the mirror looked away.

"But you sent me to England!" Sofie protested. After all, only a small minority of girls got sent to England for their education, and certainly not those born to the very impecunious. Officers' brats, as a rule, stayed in India. As did almost any girl with any Indian blood. "And Papa inherited his mother's money, and—"

"We spent all our money sending you to England," her mother said, looking down, seemingly wholly absorbed in arranging Sofie's hair, and therefore not looking at Sofie in the mirror. Sofie wished she would look up and meet her eyes. Then she might judge the truth of her mother's words. Unnatural or not, she didn't feel as though she could trust her. "There is none left for your dowry, but surely you must understand what you owe me and your father. We ruined ourselves for your education. The least you can do is consider the marriage we arranged for you."

Sofie was stunned into silence by this consideration— a silence that subsisted till she was mostly dressed and her mother left to allow Lalita to drape a shawl artistically around Sofie.

As soon as the door closed behind Mrs. Warington, Lalita looked at her mistress and said, with remarkable understatement, "You don't like him?"

"Like him?" Sofie said. "How could I? Lalita, he's the most despicable—" She didn't notice her own voice rising until Lalita put her finger to her lips.

"The other servants say he's not . . . Not what he seems," she said, in an urgent murmur. "His kingdom is very distant, but there are rumors . . ." She made a gesture, midair, as of someone averting a curse. "They call it the kingdom of the tigers, and it is said all English who go there disappear."

"But . . . what could he want with me?" Sofie asked, bewildered. It all came down to that one question. Granted, this man was a local ruler of some distant domain, but why would he want her? What could he possibly see in an English miss freshly returned from Britain that would justify a promise to make her his only wife? "I don't think he's ever even glimpsed me."

Lalita looked grave, an expression ill-suited to her normally smiling countenance. "He told your father he saw your face and heard your name in a seeing. That you were the only one for him."

"He told my father . . ." Sofie repeated, as she absentmindedly arranged the folds of the shawl. "But you don't think it's true?"

"I . . . don't know. I think . . . I mean, I know he was very interested in your dowry."

"My dowry?" Sofie asked, shocked. "I have a dowry? But my mother said . . ."

"The ruby," Lalita said.

Sofie stared, astonished. "The ruby?" It wasn't that she didn't know what Lalita was talking about. She knew well enough. The jewel was all that remained of her father's half-breed grandmother's dowry. The money had been spent, and the other jewels had been sold. All except the ruby.

The only reason it had been preserved was that though it was deep bloodred and of exceptional size, it was also flawed. A dark crack at its center marred not only its aesthetics but its magical properties as well. You could feel power flowing off the jewel, but it was erratic—now starting, now stopping, as unpredictable as the lightning that crossed the sky at monsoon season. And as likely to be harnessed for anything useful. Why, then, would the Raj want that? Surely he was neither crazy nor stupid?

It had to be an excuse, and the excuse had to mean that he wanted *her*. But why?

"I don't understand it, either, miss," Lalita said, and shrugged. "Only, all the talk in the servants' hall is that he insisted on the ruby for your dowry."

Sofie shook her head. In the middle of her room,

she could see her reflection in the mirror without turning her head fully. Half glimpsed through the corner of her eye, she looked to herself like a comely woman, shapely enough to command love where her dowry could not demand respect.

She didn't think much of her dark locks, or her honey-colored skin. But she had to admit she looked well enough.

Desperately, she thought of her days in London, and the carefully chaperoned balls she'd attended. There had been several men who had tried to fix their favor with her—though she supposed that her mother would say they did it in the belief that her father had made his fortune in India. Perhaps they did. Sofie had always been a little suspicious of those men who declared they'd fallen in love with her after one look, or that one glance from her was enough to sustain them for days. She was doubtful of the ones who sent her roses and other flowers and danced attendance on her night and day, with no encouragement and very little sustenance.

But one man hadn't been like that. In her mind rose the image of Captain William Blacklock—slim, dark-haired, and ravishing in his red regimentals. He had told her he would marry her if he could, but he didn't want her parents to think him a disgraceful fortune hunter. Well, they couldn't think that now.

Her mind brought her, unbidden, the image of the man her parents had chosen for her. Beside Captain Blacklock, he didn't even seem to be the same species. And Sofie had no doubt whom she preferred.

Captain Blacklock had shipped to India three months before she did. He'd told her he was being sent to Meerut with his regiment, to put down some disturbance related to weres. Sofie had never heard of weres in India, except in her nursemaid's stories, so she wasn't sure she'd heard Captain Blacklock right.

But she remembered Meerut. She had no idea where it was, but she knew it was somewhere in India. Surely she could make it there? She must run away from home anyway. She had decided that as soon as she'd looked at the cruel, inhuman face of the unknown prince.

In his last words to her, William Blacklock had said he would gladly marry her if their circumstances permitted. Surely if she could make it to his side, he would not refuse her now?

Without a fortune, surely she was not beyond his reach.

Peter Farewell stumbled down the streets of Calcutta, looking like a drunken man but feeling all too starkly sober.

A tall Englishman with dark curls, his classical features—whose symmetry could have shamed the marbled perfection of ancient statues—were marred only by a black leather eye patch over his left eye. The right one, as though to compensate, shone brightly, and often sparkled with irony.

Many a woman had gazed into that eye and been captivated by the verdant depths that seemed to hide all promises and sparkle with possible romance. Peter Farewell knew his gaze's power and had consciously avoided capturing any hearts when he could not offer his own in return. For the last ten years, he'd known he wouldn't make a good husband. Once, he'd dreamed of a world where he could live like anyone else—a world where he loved and could be loved. Now he did not know what dreams he had, if any. All he had was a mission. One at which he was failing miserably.

He walked blindly through Calcutta. He'd arrived here six months ago, and was staying in one of the palatial mansions of Garden Reach—that place inhabited by East India Company employees and their families. The vast houses would make most noble families in England blush with envy, and it put Peter's own inherited estate, the rambling Summercourt, to shame.

Summercourt . . . As his mind dwelt on his ancestral house, his hand plunged into the pocket of his exquisitely tailored suit to feel a bundle of papers. He did not need to take it from his pocket to see its text floating before his gaze as vividly as if he were reading. The top line read: *To Peter Farewell, Lord Saint Maur.*

He hadn't needed to read the next lines—though he had—nor the twelve pages following to know what his estate manager was telling him. That Peter's father was dead. That Peter was now the only heir to that ancient and noble family name descended from Charlemagne.

The manager's faithful account of Peter's inheritance made Peter groan. He'd received the letter by bearer just before dinner, and how he'd got through the meal, he'd never know. He'd left immediately after. He'd come, without quite knowing how, all the way to Esplanade Row, where he now stared at the impressive facade of Government House. Like his estate manager's letter, it resonated with the power of the expected and the prearranged. The manager never said it, but it was clear in his every word that he expected Peter—who, for the last ten years, had been abroad and sown his wild oats, such as they were—to return and shoulder the name of Farewell, the title of Saint Maur, and the responsibilities and needs of his house and retainers.

Not that there was much. At least, there hadn't been when Peter had last seen it. The estate consisted of a large, rambling farm, and an assortment of smaller farms let to various tenant families. It supported a shabby gentility akin to the life of a wealthy farmer, with pretensions that would make the Royal Family's seem small.

But compared to the way he had been living, it would be paradise. He couldn't think of his north-country domains without longing for the smells of the fields around his house. He craved the twang of local speech; the Sunday afternoons in semi-deserted streets; the parks visited by serene families, the children named for kings and queens; the museums; the lending libraries; the places that had sheltered his childhood when he was, in fact, still full of illusions. When he still thought that he might grow up to be Peter Farewell, Earl of Saint Maur, scion of a noble family.

Only it couldn't be. Oh, England had shape-shifters aplenty among its noble families. Despite the law's command that they all be killed upon discovery, it was an open secret that several noble families threw out weres now and then.

But all known noble weres were foxes, or dogs, or—at worst—wolves.

There was even a charming story of a Scottish nobleman who turned into a seal at the waxing of the moon. But Peter didn't have that innocuous a form. His other shape was a dragon. An eater of humans. A killer.

It was beyond the pale to even think of such a dangerous beast being tolerated. Witness the story of Richard Lionheart, trudging his weary way home from the Crusades, only to be put to death because more of him was a lion than just his heart. The laws that had allowed John Lackland to execute his older brother and lawful sovereign were still extant. And still enforced.

Early tomorrow morning, he'd pen a letter for his manager, apprising him of his intent to never return. The man would be disappointed. He would possibly be heartbroken, destroyed by such a complete break with the past and by his internal certainty that Peter did not care about house or family. Let him think it. If that kept Peter's secret—and if it kept Peter safe—it was enough.

Peter would stay in India and try to fulfill his mission here. He'd find Soul of Fire, the ruby once used to bind all the magic of Europe to Charlemagne. Six months ago, on the highlands near Darjeeling, he'd separated from Nigel, who might be his last friend in the world, and he'd promised Nigel that he'd find the ruby. And then he'd reunite with Nigel—who held the ruby's twin, Heart of Light, which would attract Soul of Fire like a beacon—so Nigel could return both stones to the oldest temple of mankind, at the heart of Africa.

Neither man knew what would happen once the jewels were returned to the temple. They'd been convinced that such an act was necessary to prevent horrible catastrophe. But Peter didn't think it would in any way improve his life or his material circumstances. He presumed he would still be circumscribed by his curse, still separated from normal men and limited in how close he could live to them. Yet, since his visit to the temple six months ago, the curse had been so slight and so easily controlled that he'd dared to dream. Perhaps once the rubies were returned, he would be free....

But now, after six months of following a long-dead trail for the ruby that Charlemagne had used to bind magical power to himself and his descendants, Peter had grown to believe the jewel had been cut up or destroyed, and no longer existed. His scrying instruments and all his attempts at divination had led him here, to Calcutta, and then the trail had vanished.

Meaning he'd live out his days in India, futilely trying to find an artifact that couldn't be found.

He'd already broken his father's heart through no design of his own, on that cold morning so many years ago, when his father had discovered Peter's secret. He had packed his son up and told him to get out—and stay out. Money would find him, but Peter must not—he must never—make his way to Summercourt again. He remembered his father's dour face and the instruction to "seek some form of employment that will not disgrace you. And strive not to commit more sins than needed."

Did his father know, then, that it would be the last time they'd see each other? He had to, didn't he? He'd told Peter to stay away and never let their paths cross again.

Something caught at the back of Peter's throat, something that might have been laughter or tears; he wasn't sure which. He looked up, trying to find something to fix his eyes upon, something that would take his mind off his own misery and the final renunciation of his inheritance, his birthplace—his own being—that he must do in the morning.

And he saw the girl creeping along the outside of a veranda's railing. "Good God," he said to himself. "What can she be doing?"

Then his body contorted in cough, as fear for the stranger's circumstances disturbed the balance of his mind, and allowed the beast within to take control....